WHILE RUNNING AWAY

Hayri Zafer

Hayri Zafer

He holds a degree in Radio-TV Journalism from Istanbul Journalism and PR Higher School (later converted to Marmara University, Faculty of Communication) and a Hons BA degree in Accounting from Guildhall University (later merged into London Metropolitan University).

He was Editor-in-Chief of two weekly papers, **"Awakening"** and **"Socialist"** in Turkey.

He left Turkey in 1989, after the Court of Cassation upheld his conviction by the Istanbul Military Court, resulting in an eight-year sentence.

In addition to his political writings, he adapted Nikolay G. Chernyshevsky's novel *"What Is to Be Done"* for the stage in Turkish and was performed by The London Street Theatre. Furthermore, his one-act play, *"Golden Shot"*, was also staged by the same theatre group.

He recently translated and edited his semi-autobiographical novel ***"While Running Away"*** *(which you are about to read)* from Turkish into English -the original Turkish version was published in 2019-. He has also recently completed his two-act play, **"Three Women and Their Knickers."**

He is a member of the English PEN.

ACKNOWLEDGEMENTS

My daughter, Dicle, with whom I shared some experiences from time to time, had persistently urged me for quite a while, saying, 'Write about them, Dad!'

Some of my old-time friends from my youth in Turkey also provided continuous encouragement throughout my writing endeavours.

As you can imagine, I am quite fuelled.

Thank you all for your persistent encouragement.

While Running Away

Rien n'est jamais acquis à l'homme
Ni sa force
Ni sa faiblesse ni son coeur
Et quand il croit
Ouvrir ses bras son ombre est celle d'une croix
Et quand il croit serrer son bonheur il le broie
Sa vie est un étrange et douloureux divorce
Il n'y a pas d'amour heureux.
Louis Aragon
from "There Is No Happy Love"

Fear... Emin was aware that this was the emotion he was experiencing, though he did not utter the word. Running away was a way out of an eight-year prison sentence, but it came with a price: uncertainties. Uncertainties about the future brought fears that troubled him.

Fear... The emotion that disgraces people if they cannot overcome it, the emotion that Emin struggled with like every human being...

He found what he sought in a sentence he remembered from an article. He clung to that sentence, recalled from an article by Uğur Mumcu. As fear crept in, he repeated that sentence and would often repeat it afterwards.

Mumcu quoted a foreign proverb: "Only the brave has the right to live!"

He had been trying to instil courage in himself with this sentence since he decided to run away. However, years later, Emin would say, "Everyone has the right to live, whether fearful or brave!"

It was one of February's chilly but honey-sunny days when he set off from Istanbul. After passing through Silivri[1],

---

[1] Silivri is a town near Istanbul and is nowadays famous for its jail where political prisoners have been held captive.

his eyes darted to the empty fields adorned in post-harvest yellow along the road.

When he boarded the bus, all the seats were filled up. The bus conductor directed him to the rightmost seat in the back row. In a Yugoslavian bus, which might be exhibited as an antique today and which could be considered a clunker even for that time, that seat was usually reserved for the bus conductor in those years. However, this was the seat assigned to him, and he had no way to object. Once seated, he surveyed his surroundings.

"So, it seemed they were quite well-acquainted," he concluded from the constant chatter of the other four people beside him. His observation would be confirmed later. Beyond the doorway, Emin couldn't see the person seated by the window in the front row. On the aisle side, an older man, who appeared to be a middle or high school teacher in terms of age, was quite noticeable. His thick, Stalinist-style moustache completely covered his upper lip and almost concealed his mouth, unlike Emin's carefully trimmed moustache. He couldn't refrain from using a concept he had pondered for a while. "Most probably," he thought, "the man is a leftist, and, like me, he is on the run too!" However, based on his appearance, Emin was not overtly revealing his "leftism."

The bus conductor, conversing with the passengers there, prevented him from seeing the passengers on the left side. The bus conductor? A man posing as a bus conductor is the one who manages the smuggling operation on this bus. He would later remark, 'Everyone is running away. You're all running away.' However, that time had not come, and he had not used these yet.

Emin carried his interest in the surroundings out of the window. He was now adding strands of thought to each other.

The road prompts contemplation. As one travels, thoughts emerge, and concentration follows. It's as if it's not the road but the thoughts themselves that flow.

As the Earth begins to turn its back on the sun...

Since childhood, if he was alone or when he was his own, the disquiet that began with the equinox and ended with the arrival of the night had now started knocking at the door once again. The uncertainty about the future and the inability to predict what would happen intensified this feeling.

He looked away from the yellowed sunflower fields and at the sun, slowly turning red. Murmured himself: "The sun was setting!"

Whenever he watched the sunset, he would first feel sadness. As the sun travelled towards the darkness, the sadness would evolve into a disquiet with an increasing intensity. Although he could not give any reason with certainty, there were days when, as a child, under the influence of a mixture of disquiet and fear, he would ask his mother to perform the evening prayer in his room. He was then in the fifth grade of primary school. In those years, which are long gone now, the moments when his fear would be exacerbated would coincide with his father's arrival home. The father meant violence against the mother. Over time, the disquiet had continued, but the fear, which he didn't fully understand how it disappeared, was likely due to his growing self-confidence to challenge his father.

"No..." he argued with himself, "the setting of the sun did not always cause disquiet. There were also beautiful moments. In one of them, on the back of the island ferry, Nazli was by my side, and the sun had just touched the sea.

While watching it together, I described that moment to her: 'The sun starts to blush as it nears the sea. It's because of its shyness.' As a matter of fact, I was trying to express my own feelings to Nazli—my hesitations and fears about touching her. I felt that if I touched her, she would vanish like vapour. Even the tip of my finger felt like an elephant in a glassware shop in that relationship. This was the fear Nazli instilled in me."

That's how he described his feelings, describes them, and will continue to do so whenever he talks about it.

Whenever they argued about their relationship, a fear constantly grew inside him. If Emin were to touch her, she might not speak, perhaps wouldn't even look at his face again. Without raising his voice in the slightest, he could pour his anger into bullet-like words, transferring his resentment from one day to the next, and then to the next, and to the next, but he couldn't touch. It was the boundary of sin between them, and it should not be crossed. This was the unwritten, unspoken prohibition.

* * *

Three weeks later, after their unprecedented and somewhat surprising meeting on 2 July 1983, when they sat down for lunch as they had previously agreed, Emin was taken aback by Nazli's comments on their past relationship.

"Do you know, if we had gotten married, I would have beaten you up!"

It wasn't something minor; it was a shock-like daze that one could snap out of with a slap or maybe even a couple of slaps. Not a word of defence or objection would escape Emin's lips. Nazli was narrating and interpreting the events from her own perspective. Over seven years ago, in the summer of 1976, following their exit from the last exam, he had, at the very least, voiced his objection to Nazli's words that put a cross on their shared experiences: 'I think differently; what we went through has different meanings for me.' But seven years later, he was left speechless. His mind was paralysed by adding Nazli's comments to the shock of finally sharing the long-awaited moment with her. What surprised him even more was the realisation that Nazli's biased judgment, her one-sided perspective, stemmed from her failure to truly understand him.

Without dwelling on how closely her perception aligned with the reality, he had distilled two sentences from what Nazli had said, separating them from the excess of words:

"You didn't stop loving me because I didn't sleep with you."

"You've not only ruined the lives of just the two of us but also four other people's lives!"

Nazli took another jab regarding their private lives, but Emin didn't take it seriously.

"And you didn't keep your promise. You didn't name your daughter after me, but look, MeHeBe did. His daughter's name is Nazliyel."

[Flashforward - 2017:

Forty years later, Emin would discover a side of Elsa that was unknown to him until he read Ahmet Altan's[2] essay "Restless Souls," and only then did he give a new meaning to Nazligül's reproach, accompanied by a question that stuck in his mind: "Elsa and Nazligül..." The last person who sent me Aragon's "There Is No Happy Love" poem when I was in Bursa Prison in 1977!

---

[2] Ahmet Altan is a distinctive journalist and author in Turkey, having been arrested and imprisoned several times.

And Aragon's Elsa, who wrote in her diary: "I want everyone to love me, all men to admire me"]

"MeHeBe, who married their classmate, did not name her daughter Nazligül but 'Nazli-yel'! Maybe you don't know, but in my home town, something else is called 'yel'! He's got the wind, the southernly wind! You may get confused, so let me put it another way: Southernly gas!" Emin wasn't going to say that. He wouldn't say it, even if it crossed his mind. He didn't want to utter that word that might hurt her; he couldn't say it.

In the flow of their conversation, attempting to convey something and respond to Nazli's questions, Emin, despite his efforts, couldn't utter a single word to counter these blows. He harboured only a destructive desire to reach out to Nazli's hands, but once again, the old fear—the fear that she would vanish upon his touch—clipped his wings. He neither touched her comments nor her hands, although the immunity she seemed to possess had nothing to do with reality; it was merely his illusion.

After Nazli dropped the line, "Because I didn't sleep with you," coupled with another one of her remarks, he intuitively understood the implied invitation for a one-night stand but ignored it. He would return to work despite informing his line manager that he "might not return in the afternoon" when the meal was over.

Nazli, on the other hand, went to Serap, to whom she had displeasingly and contemptuously said to Emin, "Are you still friends with her?" It was not a question but an expression of her dislike and disapproval. Emin wasn't surprised by Nazli's reaction as he was aware of the cold shoulder between these two women, the roots of which went back to their university years. However, Nazli had visited Serap in her

While Running Away

office and said whatever she had said... And whatever she had told Serap confirmed Emin's intuition during lunch. Serap couldn't be making it up because she would have heard from Nazli that she had lunch with Emin. What Nazli told Serap apparently went beyond that; otherwise, Serap could not have known the details of the conversation at lunch between Nazli and Emin. She wouldn't have drawn a conclusion out of nowhere: "Actually, Nazli had the idea of sleeping with you, but you had run away!" Emin had already been surprised by Nazli's visit to Serap but was even more surprised by the nature of their conversation. He repeatedly asked, "What exactly did she tell you?" However, Serap was adamant not to share details with Emin: "It was a conversation between two women, and it stays that way." Emin wondered what could have led Nazli to confide in Serap, whom she still despised. Nevertheless, he couldn't uncover the hidden secret within the bond of female solidarity.

While conversing with another mutual friend, Nevin, who shared connections with both Serap and Nazli from their university years, Emin linked his scattered narratives to a question:

"But didn't Nazli herself pave the path of my evasion?"

With a smile that combined sympathy and sarcasm, Nevin commented:

"I really like this side of you, but let's set aside the flowery language for a moment. While you were dwelling in our past, she managed to overcome all that and find a solution to your problem. What she had in mind was to rescue you from your love for her."

"But she knows my stance on this matter. You know, the night when Yakup somehow got involved in the argument. When she unilaterally said, 'We can sleep together to overcome our problem if you want,' I replied with a short 'No!' and refused her one-sided proposal of 'if you want.' If you remember, I told you about that conversation. She had said to me, 'Cevat and his girlfriend were right. I told them I was going to suggest this to you.' They said, 'Emin, the guy you profiled to us won't accept your suggestion,' and continued to say with a smile, 'They were right.' I was astonished – how could she not understand me when the other people, to whom she herself had profiled me, did? How could she not figure out what others had realised?"

"Yes, you told me this."

"That's how she constructed the walls. In reality, she built them herself. She placed words in my mouth to excuse her own retreat. She herself handed me the bricks. As I stacked them, the wall grew higher and higher between us. Take a look at the picture. Since I seemed to be the one who placed the bricks on each other, consequently, who would be seen as a builder of the wall: Me... However, she was the one who actually placed the bricks in my hand. In the end, she burdened me with the guilt of 'ruining not only our lives but also the lives of four other people.' By 'four other people,' she meant her daughter, my daughter, my wife, and her husband. 'The lives of four other people!' Those were her words during our lunch. She held me responsible for what transpired."

"We women are masters at this. Mentally, you men are not as well equipped. We play chess; you play backgammon. We make our current move by calculating forty moves ahead. I understand what Nazli is doing. More than just understanding, I know. I know because she and I have shared our problems. But I have a hard time understanding you. Your agility turns into a 'once upon a time' story and disappears when it comes to Nazli. Of course, she would say, 'I'd beat you up!"

"There was a wall, but there was also a bond between us that neither she nor I would dare to give up. I was terrified this bond would break."

"What happened then? My poor boy," Nevin said as she began giving him advice. "Look, you don't understand women. That's why you're failing. Actually, it's not just you; none of you men understand. In your relationships with the women you fall in love with, you create a world in your imagination. In other words, you live in a fantasy world; it is a sort of illusion. On the other hand, we women are much more realistic in our relationships. The words you quoted from Uğur Mumcu's article are also applicable here. Didn't he say, 'Only the brave has the right to live!' You were scared, and, of course, your hands got tied up. What could a woman do with a man whose arms are not lengthy enough to reach her? You didn't move for fear of destroying a glassware shop. What happened when you didn't move? Simple. What you feared happening happened. You'll take a step, and if you get a negative response from the other one, OK, withdraw in your corner. If it was bound to break, let it break like this. The hand you don't use to reach out will remain empty for years."

"You say so, but watching the waters embrace the sun behind the island ferry, watching her hair wave alongside the foam of the sea, sharing those moments with her... it is hard to describe how it felt."

"Go buy a bottle of wine. Pick a secluded spot. And then weep."

Emin responded to Nevin's reference with a slightly sarcastic, self-mocking smile. And he had done it on 2 July 1983! And that day, he had seen Nazli on the island he had

9

travelled to without knowing that he would see her or even that she was in Turkey.

* * *

Remembering his conversation with Nevin brought a momentary breeze that temporarily dissipated his disquiet. However, upon his return to the present moment, his unease resurfaced and settled deep within him. The setting sun was intertwined with the uncertainty he was experiencing.

What if he were to be caught at passport control? This fear intensified his disquiet. If he were apprehended, it was uncertain how much time might be added to his prison sentence, but what was not in question was the torture he would undoubtedly endure. 'They don't call the state 'father' for nothing.'"

State as a father! Not a mother, but a father! Power! In society, it's the state; in the family, it's the father!

And, 'Allah, the father!'

We are expected to fear all of them; we are asked to have fear of them.

He repeated Uğur Mumcu's words to himself once more. He continued: "You cannot be brave if you are not afraid. Be afraid, but don't be a coward, and challenge your fear. Being brave is not 'not to be afraid' but challenging whatever fear you experience. Everything exists with its opposite. Like the setting of the sun. As every night has its morning. The point is to be able to read things from their opposites."

As he contemplated 'the opposites,' a new thought emerged. "If the sun is shining at the other end of the world, how correct is it to say 'the sun is setting'? The world is the same world; the sun is the same sun."

While Running Away

He sought refuge from his disquiet by delving into contemplative thoughts.
And that's when...

* * *

Just then... Nolina opened her eyes as the first rays of sunlight hit her face. Eban's right arm was draped over her shoulder. His wrist was resting on her right breast, and his fingertips were shyly touching the nipple of her left breast. He had slipped quietly into the bed where he had nestled after work in the early morning, trying not to wake Nolina. He had fallen asleep tiredly as he laid his head on the pillow.

Unlike the nights they slept naked when they came to bed together once a week, Eban was wearing shorts, but Nolina felt the swell of his manhood on his bare thighs. Overwhelmed by the need to urinate, Nolina gently slipped out of Eban's arm and off the bed. She went under the water in the bathroom. The initial chill from the cold water faded as the warmth of pee going through her legs gradually replaced it, and she felt a sense of relaxation. She liked it like this. Unlike sitting on the toilet during the day, she is used to starting the day by standing under the shower.

He did not wake up when he felt the emptiness on his arm, a space left by his woman on the bed, but instinctively, his hand went to the pillow that still carried the warmth of Nolina's head. The void awakened Eban, connecting it to the sound of water from the bathroom. The thought that Nolina was in the shower disturbed his sleep. He got out of bed, obeying the silent call of Nolina's nakedness in the bathroom. In the bathroom, where he tiptoed, he gazed at the beauty of Nolina's hips, which spiralled as she walked for a few seconds. Nolina was bent over with her back turned, soaping her legs. She felt Eban's presence even though she didn't see him. When she turned her head towards the door, their smiles connected in each other's eyes. During their first dating, Nolina had to ask, 'Why are you avoiding eye contact?' as he had been 'hesitant to look.' However, Eban's unease has long since faded.

Eban made Nolina wait for a moment. Nolina bit her lower lip with her upper teeth to seal her invitation in the dark moss-green eyes surrounding her glossy black pupils. His eyes shifted from Nolina's swan neck to the rebellious nipples of her perky breasts, to the petite navel piercing made of crystal in the shape of a cross in her belly button, to the water flowing through the curly hair between her legs. When his gaze travelled down to her heels, he again stripped Nolina's body of its picturesque figure. Noticing Eban's ritual, Nolina entered their cryptic dialogue with a contented, soft voice: 'You are baptising me again with your eyes!"

Nolina, whose smooth dark brown skin aroused his manhood every time he touched it with his fingertips, was just two steps away. He couldn't wait any longer and didn't keep her waiting. Nolina's body wrapped around him, warming up the refreshing chill he felt when he went under the cold water.

As they carried their discoveries, uncovering each other's innermost secrets on the journey from the bathroom to the bed, the heat of their bodies, meeting the sun's warmth that began to envelop Honolulu, scorched them until they turned to embers. 'You are my sun,' Eban said as they collapsed in each other's arms with sweet exhaustion, trying to catch their breath on the bed drenched by the water particles they brought from the bathroom and by their sweat, blended with the wetness of their satisfaction. Eban completed his words on Nolina's lips.

When Eban fell back to sleep under the cover of his lover's hair, Nolina got up. She tightly closed the curtain from which daylight seeped through the edges to shade the sun rays that had risen high in the smooth sky. With a tender smile on her lips, Nolina whispered to herself:"

"Love is also to protect the sleep of my man from sunlight, lost in my most intimate darkness! Or it is a disappearance of my man, whose sleep I protect from sunlight, in my most intimate darkness!"

At the same time, in the same place, the time could be a day for some, like Nolina, while for others, like Eban, it could be the night of sleep.

And in another place a hundred and eighty degrees beyond the meridian? In the opposite geography inhabited by those who would not be different from Eban in having the same shyness for looking at their beloved but are scared to live their love!

* * *

If the sun is shining on the other side of the world, how accurate is it to say 'the sun is setting'? The world is the same world, the sun is the same sun," Emin remarked, unaware of Nolina and Eban or what they were doing in Honolulu. He knew the people experiencing the 'sunrise' right then, even though he didn't know who they were, their names, and what they were doing. Nolina and Eban were just two of them. Like their experience of love, their portrayal of their relationship with the sun at that moment was the complete opposite of what Emin experienced.

"Isn't the way we define events and phenomena according to where we stand, rather than as they are, a typical example of our folly of seeing them from the centre where we are? The sun stands where it stands, while the Earth, in its dance around itself, changes its point of view of the sun from one point to another. The Earth turns away from the sun, embracing it at one point, and a hundred eighty degrees in the opposite direction at the other end... It is, in fact, the world that is in motion. The sun neither sets nor rises. When we try to explain events by centring both the world and our place in the world, we keep repeating a very absurd definition of the truth. And everyone... Old, young... People of all nations, languages, sexes, religions, and so on!"

His internal dialogue had effectively dispelled the disquiet that came with the solstice. A conclusion he had previously reached on other matters was also enlightening for Emin this time. One more drop would fall into the glass, even if it didn't fill it.

The sun was neither rising nor setting. It was the 'world-centred point of view,' which he had never questioned before, that he had now hung on the 'question hook.' Was it not he himself who once said, 'If we can question the centre from which we look at events, perhaps we can shatter the circle we have constructed around that centre'? Unaware that it was with this approach that he had sown the seeds of differing thoughts and departures from the paradigm that he would later explore. As he gazed at the road passing by, he fell asleep.

As the bus slowed down, he woke up to the voice of the bus conductor. Although the conductor had previously announced, "We will not stop anywhere until customs," this time, he said, "Ladies and gentlemen, we will take a fifteen-

While Running Away

minute break soon. Attend to your needs and do your shopping where we will stop. After passing through Bulgarian customs, there will be no stops until we reach Yugoslavia. We won't even be able to stop for the call of nature; that's what the Bulgarians require. So, please take note."

They were in Edirne[3] and Edirne was in lights. As the day turned into night, the discomfort he was experiencing would always dissipate in the glow of the lights. It was like that again... "A little bit due to the effects of sleep, too," he thought. When he got off the bus, he thoroughly woke up with the cold hitting his face. He glanced at his watch; it was nine twenty-five. He had slept for about three hours. "I'll wait until nine thirty-five, then I'll go to the restroom," he had decided, delaying it to extend his comfort later. They wouldn't be making any stops in Bulgaria. That's what he was thinking at that moment.

While drawing a cigarette hesitatingly from his pocket, he ended the hesitancy by placing the pack back where it belonged. He had changed his mind and decided to shop first and then smoke. The reason was the same as the thought of going to the toilet at the last minute.

He rushed to start shopping, and outside the shop, fruits were displayed at its front. "I should share some with the people sitting next to me," he thought, so he bought about two kilos of tangerines and placed them in a bag. Explicitly choosing the ones with greenish skin, he enjoyed the tartness of both tangerines and oranges. Moving into the shop, he grabbed two packets of biscuits from the shelf, and the tempting smell of freshly baked pastries beckoned him. He couldn't resist and bought one of the pastries on the

---

[3] Edirne is a province in East Thrace that shares international borders with Bulgaria and Greece.

15

counter. The young man at the counter, doing the math and putting the packages in a net carry bag, bore a striking resemblance to Salman—short, stocky, chubby, with a slightly angular face. Or was it Emin himself imagining the resemblance? The cold of Edirne and the young man, so much like Salman, were about to take him back to years ago. After taking his change, he went outside and indulged in a freshly baked pastry. Hungry, he then took out a cigarette from the pack. As he lit it, he inhaled the smoke alongside the cold and the fresh air, triggering the repertoire of his memories.

* * *

Emin had promised Salman that he would visit him during his leave from military service, and he had kept his word. At the end of the infantry training, in the selection by lot, he had been assigned to the military unit in Hasdal.[4], while Salman had been assigned to a unit on the Bulgarian border.

Salman was the only non-leftist among the ten trainees in their army infantry training team. The other eight were "leftists" of one tendency or another. Five or six of them, he couldn't remember exactly, were teachers. Still, all the other eight had narrow-minded and stubborn personalities. As for himself? No, that wasn't the point, although he was leftist too. They were the "What I know is the sole truth!" types... He put the chain of questions about his knowledge and practices on the "question hooks".

In that environment, he had no choice but to tolerate the nonsensical behaviour of the 'leftist' teacher in front of him during the morning gathering, even though the teacher, like Emin, was the child of an officer and constantly caused

---

[4] Hasdal is another area near to Istanbul.

While Running Away

trouble. Yet there was also the selfishness he shared with his other seven teammates...

Here is an ordinary person within this environment with no interest in or connection to leftism. He had studied at a university-level Vocational School in Karabuk.[5] This type of person was often described as "neither a right-wing player nor a left-wing player but a football player," which is a popular expression with rhymes in Turkish for an "apolitical" person: "Ne sağcı ne solcu, futbolcu." Is that so?

According to Emin, Salman was an organic leftist with his stance in life; however, others did not regard him as a "leftist." This spontaneous friendship resulted from a shared attitude Emin would later describe as guided by his intuition. Emin would often wonder, "We were leftists, but what kind of leftists were we?" He would eventually conclude: "In fact, the true leftists were the ordinary people who willingly shared their bread. They are even more leftist than our leftists. The culture of communal solidarity exists in these lands like an ember under the ashes. When the right time and place come, especially when the conditions impose themselves, particularly when a wind blows and scatters the ashes, we see how it begins to catch fire. We failed to blow the ashes. The problem was we did not know how to be the wind, and we were not very aware of that ember of the fire covered with ashes."

There was an arrangement for taking turns distributing food at the team's table in the infantry training camp. During his turn, the army officer's son, the teacher, would claim the best part of the meal for himself and place the remaining good portions on his close friend's plate. In contrast, Salman and Emin would do the opposite—reserve the best part of the meal for others and keep the rest for themselves.

---

[5] Karabuk is a city in the Black Sea region of Turkey

One night, Salman, who slept on the top bunk, woke Emin up with the sound of his teeth grinding in his sleep. In response, Emin woke him up. However, when Salman went back to sleep, the teeth grinding persisted. In the morning, they talked and joked about it, solidifying a friendship that began from there.

One day, when it was his turn to distribute the seagull-scented chickens served every Friday at lunch, Emin said, "Today, there are chicken drumsticks for those who missed out on the good part of the seagulls," jokingly referring to two chickens on the table, and he distributed four pieces to those who had not received their share the previous week. Yet, once again, neither Emin nor Salman had chicken drumsticks on their plates. The following week, although it wasn't his turn, they asked Emin to distribute the chicken. This time, the other four who had missed out on chicken drumsticks the week before received their share, and this continued until they completed the infantry training. For some reason, everyone was to believe that this dish was the only one without alum. Whether it was due to training in the summer heat without the opportunity to seek shelter under a single tree, whether it was because there was, in fact, alum in the food, or perhaps a combination of these factors, the trainees lacked sexual desire during the week. However, it was a different story on the weekends when they had a break from the training centre. Upon their return, they would joke, "Guys, my bird sprouted wings this weekend!"

When the lots were drawn at the end of the training period, it became clear who would be assigned where. Salman and Emin made a promise to visit each other during their military service leaves. Emin kept his word, first going to Edirne and then to Salman's unit. On guard duty at the border post and with a good rapport with his lieutenant,

While Running Away

Salman asked the lieutenant to bring Emin there. The lieutenant and Emin set off in a jeep from the Second World War. Fifteen to twenty minutes later, while descending a slope, the lieutenant's efforts to respond to the driver's cry of 'Sir, the brakes are not working!'—who was expressing his helplessness due to the brake pedal that he was constantly pumping deep down to the bottom—by tugging on the handbrake, did not work either. After about five hundred meters, the slope was to end with a wooden bridge that could only be crossed by a single vehicle. At the end of the bridge, there was a sharp left turn to take the road.

As soon as the lieutenant shouted, 'Turn left!' the driver swerved toward a pile of construction sand left over from a house under repair. The front wheels of the jeep hit the sand pile with all their speed, causing the vehicle to lift into the air. The jeep landed with its front wheels inside the garden and the back wheels outside, hanging on the garden wall, which was less than half a meter high. With a shout, the lieutenant turned back and hugged his seat, miraculously escaping injury. The driver, tightly gripping the steering wheel and contracting his whole body, also emerged unscathed. It was different for Emin, who, due to the tremors, couldn't avoid hitting his head against the iron bar on top, causing his right eyebrow to split and bleed. He tried to reduce the bleeding by pressing it with a handkerchief. The villagers running from the neighbourhood rescued the jeep from the wall. The driver attempted it and found that the jeep's engine was still running. The lieutenant asked, "Can you take us back to the unit by driving in first gear?" The response was brief: "God willing, sir." And indeed, he did.

After the nurse cleaned the wound on Emin's eyebrow and gave him two stitches at the nearby health centre, they returned to the lieutenant's unit. His intention was to go back to Istanbul.

Going back?

* * *

Going back!

When he remembered this, he returned from the memories of the past moment to the present moment.

"Yes, I could turn back now. I don't know what will happen to me at the customs. Is it that easy to get through with a fake passport? In addition to losing my chance of living as a fugitive, a few years, for sure, will be added to the eight-year sentence because of this fake passport. I wonder how many years is the penalty for using a forged passport?" He didn't know! "But it must be at least two years," he thought. "Don't be ridiculous!" He forced himself to clear his mind of these counterproductive thoughts. "Remember, "Only the brave has the right..."

* * *

He, once again, went back to his military service days. Yes, he was planning to return to Istanbul after the accident. Yet, Salman, whom they had informed about the situation by phone, was insistent. In fact, he wanted to "see his friend while he was here," but he could not bring himself to say, "Take me to the border unit," to the lieutenant.

"I've already arranged for two big bottles of raki.[6] No 'seagulls'—referring to their joke about the chicken in infantry training—but we'll make 'menemen'[7] with lots of

---

[6] Raki is an anise-flavoured strong alcoholic drink (45%) made of twice-distilled grapes, similar to Greek Uzo.

While Running Away

eggs. It'll be fine if you request from my lieutenant to bring you here."

When he conveyed Salman's words to the lieutenant, he said, "You have come this far; you cannot not go. Besides, military service means *'pacta sunt servanda*,'" and ordered the driver to take the other jeep out.

When they reached the bridge at the end of the slope where they had the accident earlier, the lieutenant, with joy, said, "It was a close run. We couldn't have entered this bridge at that speed. They would have collected us from the stream."

Upon their arrival at Salman's unit, everything was almost ready. The table was laid with plenty of watermelon and cheese, and a big tray with green peppers and tomatoes was on the stove, waiting for the eggs to be cracked.

The lieutenant, who stated, "It's getting dark, your friend has been handed over to you, the mission has been accomplished, so I'm leaving," was persuaded to have "at least one glass." The first large bottle of raki was opened. While consuming "a double," the lieutenant delivered a lecture on "military service and loyalty" and then left. Following his departure, the two friends began their conversation, reminiscing about their memories at the Infantry Training School.

The weather grew colder and colder. With blankets on their backs, they talked about their personal lives, subjects they had never discussed before, as they progressed from the first bottle to the second, all while under the watchful eye of the Bulgarian sentry in the opposite tower.

In reality, Salman had little to share. He was single, and when he departed, his family would arrange a marriage for him. Most of the questions came from Salman:

---

[7] Menemen is scrambled eggs with tomatoes and green long peppers

"If there's a child, why are you breaking up?"

"I don't know how much it makes sense to you. It wasn't love. Yes, we indeed liked each other in some way. But it was more of a rapprochement brought about by the fact that we were working in the same political organisations. In a way, our relationship was based on this foundation. When that foundation disappeared, the union also collapsed. Actually, my story is a bit complicated. To cut a long story short, I loved someone while we were both studying at the Uni. It was, in a way, a platonic relationship. I always looked for that person, or rather, I looked for what I found in that person. As you can see, that relationship and that person lived with me while I lived with someone else."

An unexpected reference came from Salman at that moment:

"I mean, you're saying, 'I have an 'I' within me, deeper than myself,' as Yunus Emre[8] put it. You're pretty romantic. Let's drink to romance," Salman said and raised his glass. While clinking glasses, he added: "Long live romance!"

Then silence fell for a while... Not knowing what Salman was thinking, Emin warned himself, "Enough chatter. No need for details." In fact, he had briefly discussed his story with Salman, a tale he passionately narrated in great detail when conversing with close friends from that era. Noticing that Emin was getting quiet and lost in thought, his friend wanted to clear the air.

"Never mind, don't worry about it... We make a living by what we get. Even if it's not always what we want. Raise your glass... We'll drink to romance again, but this time differently... Down with romance."

---

[8] Yunus Emre (born c. 1238, Turkey—died c. 1320, Turkey) was a poet and mystic who influenced Turkish literature.

While Running Away

They laughed. When they finished two big bottles, they entered the military station, rubbing their hands that were cold in the frost.

When Emin got up in the morning, although he drank more than his friend and consumed the highest amount of alcohol in his life, he did not have a headache, probably because of the fresh air blowing on the Bulgarian border.

* * *

[Flashforward - 2017-18:
It was like that in Armenia, too, after adding the years that the poet equalled to half of a lifetime[9] to the day that he and Salman had met and drunk. This time, there was the spring coolness not of the Balkan Mountains but of Mount Ararat, whose very name was even a matter of dispute between Armenians and Turks and whose snow had not melted on its top yet.

The day before, he had participated in a visit to the Genocide Museum, under the guidance of Sarkis Hatspanian, that added depth to the sad remembrance of the suffering of the "Great Disaster"[10], which took place more than a hundred years ago, even more meaningful. Actually, he went to the 24 April commemorations alone. A series of coincidences unfolded, leading Emin to encounter a group of people who are originally from Turkey but living in Germany and are members of the Association of Genocide Opponents in Germany.[11]

---

[9] It is a reference to the Turkish poet Cahit Sitki Taranci, who wrote:
"*35 years! Means half of the way*
We are in the middle of life, like Dante."
[10] Reference to the term "*Meds Yeghern*" in Armenian
[11] Verein der Völkermordgegner e.V. (in German)

On his first visit to the Genocide Museum, he realised the shallowness of his knowledge about genocide, which had been limited to only the events in 1915. He returned to his room at the Azoyan Guesthouse where he was staying, sat down at the computer and did a search. Armenians saw the genocide as a process that started in the 1890s, as they described what happened in 1915 as the "Great Disaster". During his search, he came across a speech Sarkis gave at a panel. The points Sarkis made about confronting the past caught Emin's attention. His approach was similar to what Emin himself had been saying. With the murder of Hrant Dink, Emin had started to look at the genocide in 1915, which until then had been limited to what could be called surface information for him. A video he watched on the internet about the Armenians of Marash led him to look at his personal side of the issue. He had previously expressed his thoughts mostly in friendly conversations with Zafer and sometimes in writing on social media.

"When we went to the grocery shops in Marash, we couldn't say, 'Give me a kilo of grapes.' There were all and many kinds of grapes. I think it's still like that. You have to say the name of the variety. For example, you would say, 'Can you weigh a kilo of bubbles? My maternal grandfather had a huge vineyard. He was a civil servant. He had come to Turkey during the population exchange between Greece and Turkey. He was not there during the genocide, but those vineyards were given to him by the state in return for his property in Macedonia. From whom did he inherit those vineyards?"

Emin had no concrete documents, but he was trying

to reason based on known practices, trying to hold the mirror to himself.

"If confronting the genocide and apologising for it is not going to remain in words, if it is not going to be a shallow confession, we also have a part to play as individuals. The basis of nationalism in Turkey is deed nationalism. This nationalism of title deeds lies at the root of what is happening in Turkey today. In all political strands from the far left to the far right, a ferment, or at least an influential force of nationalism, exists in varying tones and degrees. All types of Turkish nationalism have a basis in material interests, the root of which lies in the looting of the properties and capitals of non-Muslim peoples. The rulers recruit their militants from this source. This must be recognised. Those who consider what the Armenians went through only as a matter of conscience, which of course has a conscientious dimension, look at what has happened and say, 'We are haunted by the fate of the Armenians'. This is not a coherent approach that stands on its own feet, Zafer."

In his arguments with Zafer -he will explain them better when he "writes"- Emin also had an internal reckoning. He continued:

"If what was inflicted on the Armenians is haunting us today, this cannot be explained simply in metaphysical terms such as 'bad karma-good karma', nor is it a phenomenon that can be expressed as 'what goes around comes around'.

"Maybe you reaping what you sow is a better expression. You know... It corresponds to some extent. But only to a certain extent. It is not an expression that covers all aspects. Besides those who themselves or their ancestor actively participated in the genocides on the ground, the nationalistic attitude of the 'immigrants' in Turkey, particularly those who came from the Balkans, was rooted in something. There is an issue of plundering Armenian properties, even if it is indirectly. This is the point where the rubber meets the road... This is precisely where individual responsibility comes into play. In addition to what should be demanded from the state, I mean the Turkish State, we should also ask ourselves, "Did anything fall to me from this plunder?" If so, we should be concerned about 'how can we return it' to its original owners. We should be trying to do whatever is necessary. Otherwise, even if it contributes to sobering society, it turns into a show-off to prove how democratic, conscientious, etc., we are. Moreover, for some... Remember Hayko Baghdad's response to a government clown: 'You've turned our pain into an appetiser! Can we have a say about this cry? If we don't follow through with our reckoning and act accordingly, we'll also inevitably receive this plea!!"

When the similarities in Sarkis Hatspanian's words caught his attention, he searched the internet for how to reach him. Sarkis had been imprisoned not only in Turkey but also in Armenia for challenging the government. He tried to reach him on Facebook.

He responded to Sarkis' reply of "I am in Yerevan" with the message "I would like to have a coffee if you have time, but tomorrow is my last day", and after the phone call, the next day he met Sarkis and the people from Germany. They were the people whose conversation had caught his ear the day before when he had walked past them, and he couldn't help joining in, saying, "What's Roman ice cream compared to Marash ice cream!'". He had inserted himself into the conversation in Turkish.

On his second visit with them to the Genocide Museum, Sarkis clarified what he had learnt on his first visit:

"We call 1915 the 'Great Disaster'. Genocide is a process that started in the 1890s."

Then they went to the History Museum and ended up with a dinner at the restaurant of an Armenian family, who had fled Syria when the war broke out, to taste the familiar flavours. From stuffed meatballs to raw meatballs, from "lahmacun"[12] to stuffed leaves; Emin lifted the dietary limit he had placed on all the flavours he missed and the raki that accompanied them. As the toasts were being made, he remembered but didn't mention the conversation with the director of the Genocide Museum in Ece Temelkuran's book 'The Depth of Ağrı' but kept it to himself, as he was not sure if it was appropriate in terms of political correctness regarding women. Even though he had overdrunk, he did not have a headache when he got on the plane the following morning. He said to himself: "Maybe because of the fresh and clean air of Ararat, which, like the Balkan Mountains, both have been the cradle of revolts!"]

* * *

He had a headache at the end of another farewell night in Turkey. They had drunk too much, "Who knows if we will meet again? Even if we do, it's the last time we'll see each

---

[12] Lahmacun is a thin layer of dough topped with minced meat and various vegetables, sometimes described as "Armenian pizza" or "Turkish pizza".

other until we do," he said as they spent the night in conversation and poetry. He had slept very little. "It must have been the lack of sleep. I'll take an aspirin when I get on the bus," he said and went to the toilet.

"Come on, brother, we almost left without picking you up," the bus conductor whined to Emin, who inaudibly said, "OK, thanks". The bus had already started cruising through the city while he sat.

When they arrived at Kapikule[13], the bus conductor looked at the queue and shared his expectations with the passengers, ending with his instructions:

"Ladies and gentlemen, we will wait for our turn for about an hour, maybe a little longer. Stay in your seats and do not even think about getting off the bus. Let's keep things trouble-free!"

Until then, Emin had initially regarded the person in the seat in front of him as just another fugitive on the bus. However, the bus conductor's tone quickly snapped him out of his misassumption. Perhaps it wasn't just the two of them on the run. He remembered the warning given to him. The bus conductor was the man of the network, and if there was a problem, he would deal with it. Now, that guy who had spoken to him imperiously when he was getting onto the bus a little while ago was addressing everyone with the same tone. Emin thought about how the bus conductor had addressed the passengers before. It was different. Could the difference be related to the place? Most probably! For people hurrying to run away, the bus conductor would play a vital role at the customs gate, and they were obliged to submit to him. 'Here is a small power for a small period in a small space!' Emin was to place the problem in the context

---

[13] Kapıkule is the Turkish border crossing point in Edirne Province on the border of Turkey and Bulgaria.

of power and authority.

As the car in front proceeded to the customs control point, the bus conductor announced, "Get your passports ready; I'll collect them." Emin reached for his passport in his pocket, flipping through its pages to refresh his memory. He rehearsed the story he and his friend had concocted earlier about the reason for his travel.

When it was their turn, the bus conductor descended from the bus and placed all the passports on the customs officer's desk in the control booth. The officer meticulously examined each passport, leafing through page after page of lists, cross-referencing them with the passports, separating some passports to one side and others to another. Emin drew an inevitable conclusion:

"So, some passports are problematic!"

Emin made a guess only after one of the groups was handed to the bus conductor. He speculated that the problematic ones were the ones placed in the corner, and these were the passports that the police officer looked at mainly towards the end. A considerable portion of the first ones they examined were the ones given to the bus conductor. Once again, Emin contemplated the possibilities:

"The bus conductor took mine last and put it on top. My passport must have been among the first ones checked. Since the last ones, most of which were problematic, were left in the cabin, there is a high probability that mine was among the unproblematic ones."

He was wrong.

The bus conductor came with passports in his hand. "Passport holders whose names I am going to read, come down," he said and then started reading the names. The first name he read out was the name of the passport holder seated near the front door of the bus. When he reached out his hand to take his passport, the bus conductor scolded him with his imperious style: "Go down and wait. I will keep your passport."

He began counting those called. Two, three, four... and finally twenty-four, nearly half of the people on the bus. Emin's name was the last to be called. He disembarked from the bus. The bus they had gathered on its right side stood between them and the booth. Neither could they see the booth, nor could the people in the booth see them... Moving a bit further away from the bus, the bus conductor called out to those who had disembarked:

"Come this way, gather round me!" With a touch of sarcasm in his imperious tone, he summoned the passport holders with issues to his side. Not a single woman was among them. In fact, there were very few women on the bus.

"Gentlemen, it is impossible to pass this point with these passports. One way or another, there is a problem with each of them." The last words of the bus conductor were lost in the noise of "What shall we do?", "What will happen?", "Shall we go back?" and so on.

Emin turned around and gazed in the direction they had come from. Going back without getting into trouble was not an option; they were all inside the passport control area. "Now, stop grappling with the dilemma of whether to go back," he scolded himself again. He returned to the crowd and reality from which he had detached for a moment with these thoughts. He tried to clear his head. "Well, if the customs officers were not going to let us pass, they would not have left the job to the bus conductor; they would have said "get down" and arrested us. Moreover, if they had realised that his passport was fake, they would have called him down and arrested him instead of handing his passport to the bus conductor. No..." He was correcting the legal terms that he used before. "They wouldn't arrest us; they would detain us." This detail was absurd in that situation, but it came to his mind then. As he was thinking, "Actually, something else is going on here," the words of the bus conductor confirmed this thought:

"Wait, don't panic. Wait a minute."

The noise died down at these words. The bus conductor was grinning, pleased that all the attention was on him. He continued:

"Now listen... Your passports are problematic. I don't know which one has what problem. Everyone's running away. All of you are running away. But I know how to handle these things. We'll give a few hundred Deutsche Marks and get away with it. Come on, give me five or ten Deutsche Marks each."

Emin pondered for a moment. "Now, if someone offers a small amount, and the bus conductor says, 'This is not enough,' it could become complicated. It's best to take the initiative." With this in mind, he decided to act.

"OK, if everyone contributes ten Marks, will that be enough?" Emin asked while simultaneously taking out ten Marks from his wallet. This time, he turned his back to the bus to avoid making it obvious to the passengers looking at them through the windows. This act, which he found somewhat amusing when he reflected on it later, was a reflex. It was as though the people on the bus wouldn't understand, or the holders of the 'problematic passports' wouldn't mention anything to others upon their return.

The bus conductor immediately totalled the bill himself: "That's two hundred and forty Marks. I'll add another ten Marks to top up two hundred and fifty Marks. I'll convince the officer."

When he finished collecting the money, he said, "Let's board the bus orderly. No pushing and shoving!" and walked towards the customs booth.

"It's probably collusion. Why would the bus conductor also put ten Marks by himself? Probably forty would go in his pocket and two hundred Marks for the police. He'll probably get even more for himself. Didn't he say five or ten Marks?" Emin resented not the money he had given but that he had been taken for a fool. "But what can I say!" he consoled himself. After taking one last puff from the cigarette that he had hastily lit, he threw it on the ground, not even half-smoked, and boarded the bus as the last passenger. Now, he had embarked on a task contrary to his impetuosity: Waiting.

No more than five minutes had passed when the bus conductor came round with all the passports in his arms and, reading out the names of the holders, went up to those who said "Mine!" or "Here I am!" or the ones who raised their hands and he handed everyone their passports.

"Who hasn't got their passport?"

When no one made a sound, the bus conductor went to his seat next to the driver, and then the bus started moving.

Emin was relieved. He was crossing the border with a fake passport, and a new phase of his life was beginning.

That's what he thought. Halfway to the Bulgarian customs, the bus stopped once more. A police car was waiting in the middle of the road.

When one of the two policemen who entered the bus through the opened door said, "Everyone takes out their passports," Emin felt a momentary panic. Still, the voice inside him spoke once more:

"Only the brave has the right to live! What will be will be. It is no longer in your power to change it... You left the possibility of going back behind when you got on the bus at the stop. Wait and be calm."

While one policeman was chatting with the driver, the other checked the passports one by one, looking at the picture and the person before handing them back. Although the policeman did this most of the time, every once in a while, he would ask some passengers short questions. After getting the answer, he would check another passenger's passport. Emin paid close attention when it was the passenger's turn with a Stalin moustache. Nothing happened. Without asking any questions, the policeman looked at the picture and the man, then returned the passport. The fact that the four people next to him were talking to each other during these checks must have caught the policeman's attention, too. When he was checking the passport of the second among them, he asked the first passenger for his passport again, having previously only looked at the picture and the person.

"Are you related?" he asked, without clarifying which one he was addressing. The two of them answered in unison:

"Yes."

He gave them back their passports. He took the third one's passport. He looked at it. The answer to the question "Are you from the same village?" was short:

"We're relatives."

While checking the passport of the fourth person sitting next to him and handing it back, the policeman said, "It seems that you are also a relative!" When he received the answer "Yes," he asked without looking at the passport Emin handed him:

"Are you a relative too?"

"No, I don't know them."

The policeman, who listened to the answer without

looking up from the passport, finished his check and handed the passport back. Emin sighed a heavy "Oh!" subtly, relieved that no further questions were asked.

The policeman was half-turning to leave when he paused as if something had occurred to him, then turned to the quartet and asked:

"What are you going to Yugoslavia for?"

"We are going to our relative's wedding," they replied in a polyphonic chorus.

Emin, who thought the police officer saying, "Well, congratulations," would leave, was now faced with the same question:

"Why are you going to Yugoslavia?"

He was prepared for this question, but since he had assumed that the police were only interested in the people next to him because they had attracted attention due to their constant chatter, Emin did not think it would be his turn. He paused for a very short moment.

"I am going there for a holiday to see my relatives. My parents are Yugoslav immigrants."

"Where are your relatives?"

"In Novi Pazar."

"Is that its name? Half Turkish!"

"That's what they say there too. Some words are Turkish because there are many Turks."

In a way, the information he gave was correct. Because he had asked Eşref Abi[14], who had relatives there, and received the answer, "I think so," along with the suggestion that his relatives might be able to help Emin.

The police pressed on:

"Where is this Novi Pazar?"

---

[14] "Abi" means elder brother. Not only is this word used for family members, but also the way to call close friends, especially the respected ones.

While Running Away

He reiterated the information he was given:
"About five hours from Belgrade."

In fact, this information wasn't accurate, but Emin did not know that. The police officer didn't know either, so he didn't ask further questions. When the policeman got off, they set off again. The bus conductor came to the centre of the aisle again and said, "No more checks. The Bulgarians are next. But they will check one by one in person. We will be there soon, so get your passports ready." A wave of joy passed through Emin. Taking advantage of the fact that the back seats on the bus were a little higher than the others, he fixed his eyes on the windscreen. He was trying to see the sign for Bulgaria.

There was only darkness until he saw the sign. The road wasn't illuminated. The bus proceeded after the sign was lit by the bus headlights, gradually advancing under increasing lights. It then stopped in front of one of the control booths. There was no queue. When the bus conductor got off, a Bulgarian customs officer was waiting by the bus's front exit door. They spoke briefly, and the conductor returned to the bus.

"Everyone, come down with their passports and line up in front of the booth on the left!" the bus conductor shouted. No matter what, it was a command, an order to be obeyed!

And all the passengers started moving. Unlike the practice at the Turkish customs, the bus conductor opened the back door, and Emin was the first to disembark. He joined the others, who were queuing up disorderly. When everyone had disembarked, the bus moved and stopped on the other side of the booth. Two officers in the booth were checking passports through the half-oval slit in the window. The Bulgarian officers were quick. Emin had taken place in the middle of the queue. By the time it was his turn,

35

everyone who had been checked, except for two people, had retrieved their passports and returned to the bus. The remaining two people went to the bus conductor, who was smoking a cigarette about three meters away from the booth and talked to him.

A razor-sharp frost had blanketed the Balkan night with cold. The sky, devoid of clouds, was crowded with stars, and the half-moon completed the picture. On the other side of the borderline, the same sky stretched. Those unable to share the Earth were still sharing the sky without claiming ownership of it... This was the magic word, or rather the word that broke the magic: Claiming ownership... Claiming meant picking a fight.

When it was his turn, Emin handed over his passport. One of the officers, a big man with a red face —whether from the cold or alcohol, who knows— took the passport. He first examined Emin's photo on the passport and then scrutinised Emin himself. Returning his gaze to the passport, he inspected the pages one by one before focusing once more on the page with the photo. Emin sensed something was amiss, but he had no doubts about his picture on the passport. It had been taken about two weeks before he received his passport, and he had even trimmed his moustache the day before to match the one in the photo.

In response to the officer's question, "Where are you going, neighbour?"[15] Emin reiterated the same answer he had given the Turkish police: "To visit my relatives in Yugoslavia." However, his emphasis on 'To my relatives' did not deter further questioning.

"Where are your relatives, neighbour?"

Emin became uneasy when he realised that the answer

---

[15] Neighbour" is the word the Bulgarians use when they address the people from Turkey.

While Running Away

"in Novi Pazar" did not erase the question mark in the officer's eyes.

The officer looked at the page with the photo again. Emin, with a surge of anxiety, began to wait for the next question. But the officer did not ask a question; he expressed his conclusion as if he was pouring a bucket of hot water over Emin's head in the cold of the night:

"Neighbour, this passport is not yours!"

"No, the passport is mine, neighbour!" he said, trying to sound confident. "Neighbour," he had repeated the officer's word, thinking it might lighten the mood.

Pushing a white sheet of paper about a quarter of the size of a notebook and a pen through a gap in the glass, the officer cut it short and sharp:

"Sign it, neighbour!"

This time, he felt uncomfortable with the word "neighbour", which he had just used himself. "F… your neighbour and the signature…" he said inwardly. He was in trouble with this signature.

***

"Cheer up, your passport has arrived," jubilantly said Hasan, who entered the room with his bag in his hand without even saying "Hello". As soon as he took off his coat, he opened his bag, took out the passport and threw it on the table with the joy and firmness of a player who wins a card game and throws the last card.

"Oh, thank you very much," he said as he took the passport. Excited and curious, he opened the page with the photo and concentrated on the cold stamp. The part of the stamp outside the photograph and the part in the picture showed continuity in a way that left no room for doubt. His name was Sunullah Devir.

"How's that? Good, isn't it?"

"Well, it looks good. Thanks a lot. When do I leave?"

"Not tomorrow, the day after tomorrow. Probably, you'll be gone in a week. We depend on the men who organise the trip. Whenever they say!"

Hasan's answer overshadowed for a moment the joy of getting the passport. Without uttering any name, Emin asked, "Will they determine the time?" What Emin was referring to by this question was a group from the same political tradition but following a different path, a group that was not organised legally. Even though Emin was not on good terms with the ones in their foreign wing, but knew the leader of the group in Turkey. He was an honest and daring person. It was part of why he had agreed to Hasan's suggestion when they discussed how Emin could leave the country. Although he had no trust in that group in general, he trusted the leader of the group in the country, who said, "Of course, we will do it for Emin," as much as Hasan did.

"No, it's out of their hands now. It's a network that they're transferring the work to. They're not in the loop. They won't know what happens from now on!"

When Emin said, "This is good!" he referred to the issue discussed initially. He wanted not to get involved with any political movement and not to have the problem of dealing with their demands after he went "abroad". This was a condition, which he defined as "Not to be tied to someone's apron strings". And it was also a step that only a few people should know about. The few friends who had helped him to live as a fugitive for nearly six months, the starting point when he learnt that the verdict against him had been upheld by the Court of Cassation, and his mother was aware that he was going to leave the country. Before that stage, he had

While Running Away

only spoken to Hasan about what could be done.

"We'll have two glasses of raki in honour of this step. Let me prepare it, and in the meantime, you work on the signature," Hasan said, heading for the kitchen.

It hadn't occurred to Emin until that moment. He looked at the signature on the passport. It was a short signature, but he could not find where it started. The letter "S" was readably visible, the scribbles turned backwards, and a semi-circle passing over the letter "S" merged with this letter. It was unclear whether the line at the end was the beginning of the letter "S" or the line ending there. Maybe the signature started with the scribbles after the letter "S" and ended with the letter "S" drawn inside the semi-circle drawn in the return. He couldn't figure it out. He tried twice. It wasn't working. He couldn't concentrate on what he was doing. His mind was stuck on who to inform, who not to, and who to say goodbye to. Partly because of this, he could not pay attention to what he was doing. He stopped trying. He would work on the signature later!

Saying goodbye to someone meant telling them he was running away!

* * *

Emin had not even told his brother he was planning to run away. Although he and his brother, whom he had drawn into politics, had worked in two different factions for a short time, their paths had eventually merged in the same Party; even their departure from the Party had happened at almost the same time and for the same reason, with a short time difference. He had resigned without consulting anyone, including his brother. As usual, his brother and Turan had written a long letter of resignation together without consulting him. Emin had not seen this letter until his brother gave him a copy. It was Turan's idea, who years later would passionately chant the nationalist tune for *"Turan,"* [16] to elaborate on the reasons for his resignation. He had never experienced direct conflicts with this person in internal party discussions or in private. However, he had not been able to establish a close relationship with him either.

"With some people, you may have arguments, even fights, but there is still a human warmth. There is a human connection. He was one of the people with whom I could not have that feeling among the Party members," he had told Aydın about his relationship with Turan and never got involved in any factional activities within the Party.

Despite all this, they had taken similar attitudes during the last period in the Party. Çelik, who had tried to lead the Party from prison as an ideological leader, had, as a result of a dispute with the Party Presidium, suggested to Emin that the Presidium should be suspended and that Emin and his brother and Turan should replace them. Referring to Emin's criticism of the work of the Central Committee, the "leader" said to Emin, "Instead of beating the donkey, you beat the donkey saddle. The real problem is not the commissions of the Central Committee but the Presidium. Take their places, and I will give all the theoretical and practical support." Emin had rejected this proposal without a second thought during the prison visit to which the "leader" had specially invited him. Çelik also asked Emin to tell his brother and Turan to pay him a visit. When he had conveyed

---

[16] The writer uses a double entendre. 'Turan' is a name for boys, just like the person mentioned. However, it's also the name of the Turkish 'Megali Idea,' which aims to create a greater Turkish empire. This empire would encompass not only Turkey but also extensive regions of southern Russia and eastern Siberia, along with portions of Greece and other areas in the Balkans, Central Asia, China's Xinjiang province, Mongolia, and Iran.

the "leader's" request to them, explained the reason and also his refusal to Çelik's suggestion. Since the proposal Emin had rejected from the beginning had already fallen through, they had no option but to take the same stance as him. Although they had become so close politically, Emin still could not feel closeness personally to this person. There was a feeling of distrust. He sensed a pretence, some careerist elements in Turan's behaviour. The fact that Turan sometimes spoke with an air of authority triggered this intuition. This distrust increased after they departed from the Party when he heard rumours that Turan continued to have relations with the members of the Presidium despite his resignation protesting them.

At a time when, with a few exceptions, Emin had severed political ties with almost everyone, including his brother, whose proximity to Turan played a significant role in this, he had refrained from engaging in political discussions with anyone. He had spoken to his brother and explained the reasons for his behaviour. When he learnt that his brother had conveyed these reasons to Turan, he had also stopped talking about politics with his brother.

What Emin had heard about Turan's relationship with the Presidium would later be essentially confirmed by Turan himself. While the case was being heard at the Court of Cassation, they followed the developments through the person who acted as the lawyer for all three of them. When Emin heard that his brother had accepted Turan's suggestion to give a power of attorney to his lawyer, even though he was not consulted, Emin said, "Since you accepted Turan's suggestion, and this lawyer has already analysed the details, let him handle our case." The lawyer of the three was not actually the lawyer of all three! Due to his brother's negligence, a power of attorney for both brothers would only reach the lawyer three days before the first hearing at the Court of Cassation. The lawyer used this delay as an excuse to refuse to represent his brother and Emin at the hearing. However, Turan and his brother only informed Emin of this when the case was about to be finalised at the Court of Cassation. Emin didn't know who had played what role in this, but the reality was stark: He was left defenceless during the appeals process. Later on, despite all of this, he accepted Turan's request that came through his brother: "We are nearing the end; let me come to Istanbul, and we can assess the situation together."

During the meeting, Emin had summarised his suspicions and thoughts on the recent events in the Party. In parallel with Emin's suspicion of the Presidium's activities, Turan had provided some information by recounting the events that had taken place when a member of the Presidium was the Ankara Provincial Chairman. Turan's account had increased Emin's distrust of him. Later, Emin would say, "Maybe Turan hoped for the opposite; he thought he would establish a rapprochement." However, the opposite had happened, resulting in new questions hanging on the hook of questions in Emin's mind. Why was he telling all this now? Why didn't he tell all these before? He had asked this question to Turan. The answer was evasive:

"I didn't consider those events important... At least not at that time."

Regarding the question, "So, what are you planning to do?" Emin chose to beat around the bush:

"Well, I haven't made a decision. Let's wait until the end."

Turan was fishing:

"We've come to the end, actually. There's not much to do except to go abroad."

"How will that work? First of all, my stance is unwavering.

While Running Away

I will not ask for help from any political movement. No to any apron string, and I don't want to deal with anyone's demands abroad! In any case, I will remain independent. I will not compromise on this point!"

Turan had spilt the beans on this.

"Don't worry about it. Some people would help and not ask for anything in return. I've made contact."

Emin was sceptical again. How did Turan know that he had such an attitude towards those abroad? Without knowing what Emin's conditions were, how had he discussed these "conditions" with them? Emin had never mentioned these to his brother either. The friends he had spoken to had not only kept the matter a secret but were also not people who had any connection with Turan. The questions about Turan overlapped and multiplied in Emin's mind.

Yes, Emin had already made up his mind, and Hasan was busy with making the arrangements. But he was determined not to tell his brother and Turan anything. Yet, Emin didn't overcome his curiosity. He asked a further question to evaluate Turan's intention:

"Are those who would help, Ergin and others?"

Turan answered Emin's pluralised question by singularising it:

"Yes, Ergin!"

Emin was adamant:

"I have nothing to do with them. Not even a hello from me. If I were to take such a path... I mean... leaving the country, which I have not decided yet, these despicable names would never be in the picture in any way. Do you remember what was said at the last Central Committee meeting before my resignation? I addressed my words to the Presidium, especially Ferman. I said, 'With this action of yours, you have violated the Party's Constitution and the motion of the last Party congress. Your party membership has been voided because you have been involved in organisations and activities outside the Party organs.'

"Ferman responded, 'Are you going to hand us over to the police? There is no other meaning and consequence of our membership being dropped with such a decision.' Ferman resorted to demagogy. We didn't hand them over to the police; instead, they exposed us to the police, fully aware that they were leaving the documents behind. Even if I decide to leave the country, I won't give them the chance to absolve themselves of responsibility for what they did or to ease their consciences."

In fact, after discussing the situation with Hasan, Emin had already made up his mind to leave the country. While there was some truth in what he had conveyed to Turan, his trust in those who remained in the Party after his departure, particularly those responsible for the *"infamous incident"* and the surrender of party documents to the police, had significantly eroded. Yet, there was no sense in disclosing this to Turan, whom he didn't trust at all. "For the time being," he thought, "it's wiser to create the impression that I have no intention of running away. Let everyone believe that I have no plans to leave the country." Hasan had already concurred with him on this tactic.

Turan was persistent:

"What's the harm in making preparations in advance? If things go well, we won't use the passports that they would provide."

"My decision not to seek such help from these people is final. Running away may be on the agenda in the future. But it is still early. Let's wait; there may be other developments," he said.

Turan was curious, and when he asked, "Like what?" Emin dodged this question with an evasive answer:

"I don't know the details either. I don't want to say anything right now because I don't know whether or not it will happen. I will let you know if there is any development."

Creating an impression of secrecy, Emin successfully diverted Turan's inquiries. Turan didn't press the issue any longer and concluded the discussion with, "Alright, let's reconvene later and assess things based on the developments."

Yes, there was a new development, although it was debatable how much of a "development" it could have been called. Although Emin's maternal uncle had passed away long ago, his wife had expressed a wish to help Emin. She consistently sent messages saying, 'Emin should take some time off work and come to Ankara. Let's meet with the Vice President of the Constitutional Court, who used to be a friend of his uncle and might be able to help."

Despite his mother's insistence, who was asking him, 'When would you go?' every now and then, he kept dragging his feet, partially under the influence of his father's words: "I don't think so, the Court of Cassation is one thing, the Constitutional Court is another."

He didn't know the real reason why his father was pretty sure about the outcome. He would learn about it many years later. His father, a retired colonel, was told by the President of the Istanbul Second Martial Law Courts, who was also his father's friend, "Commander, there is an order from above. We wanted to save at least one of your children, but since there was an order from above to convict both of them, there was nothing we could do." Yet, the final verdict at the appeal was different. But why?

"His brother and Turan, who always acted together in the

Party's internal decisions, had submitted a lengthy resignation letter written in very sharp language and signed together when they left the Party. In contrast, Emin, who had written and spoken at length on many subjects to the point of boredom for some people, stated, "I resign from the Party." He had condensed his resignation into five words."

For some reason, when the verdict came out, the decision concerning his brother, who had not been represented by a lawyer like Emin in the hearings at the Court of Cassation, would be overturned. The case would be returned to the Martial Law Court requesting a new trial. Turan, who had met Kenan Evren, the head of the military junta, on behalf of the association he worked for and appeared comfortably at this invitation, which was also broadcast on television, was among those whose court decision was overturned. "Because my brother always acted with him, because what he wrote and didn't write were the same, so he was rescued by those who wanted to save Turan 'by necessity,' perhaps," he would think years later, making connections between certain events."

When the decision of the Martial Law Court against Emin was upheld by the Court of Cassation, another lawyer friend of his friend Serap, who was also a lawyer, examined the file and started initiatives for getting the verdict revised; Emin also travelled to Ankara and visited his maternal uncle's friend in his office together with his uncle's wife. But nothing hopeful had happened. It was too late, according to the Vice President of the Constitutional Court. "Why didn't you come to me earlier? Then maybe I could have done something. And why haven't you run away yet?" he was going to say. He and his maternal uncle's wife at least drank the soda of the Constitutional Court -he referred to it later jokingly- and left!

While Running Away

When they came out, he tried to find words to console his maternal uncle's wife, whose sorrow was evident.

"Don't worry, Aunty, everything will work out in the end! Life goes on!"

These words didn't carry a hidden fatalism. While containing some excess, Emin was trying to be cautious by not revealing to her that he was planning to escape.

"Oh, my brave-hearted son, what would have happened if you hadn't constantly gotten into trouble? Running away might be the best option!"

Like the Vice President of the Constitutional Court, she was also advising him to "Run away!"

Even years later, when he reflected on these moments, tears would fill his eyes as he remembered her, who offered motherly love without expecting anything in return. There were other people in his life like her, whom he would recall similarly later.

Hasan interrupted his journey through memories with a question as he entered the room with a tray in hand:

"How did it go? Did you succeed in replicating the signature on the passport?"

"No, I have no talent, but I'll work on it later!"

* * *

He would quickly get tired while scribbling pages and pages, attempting to replicate the signature he would need at the Bulgarian customs.

On the other hand, when he sat down to write, pages flowed effortlessly one after another, and he would become so engrossed that he lost track of time. It had happened like that once again.

It was getting dark, and the lights in the house where

Emin was remained off until his friend Aydin arrived. His friend's home was one of Emin's hideouts. They didn't want to draw attention to themselves and potentially encourage a nosy neighbour to become a "respected informer citizen." Although he could barely see in the twilight, he continued to write, getting carried away once again.

The desk he was writing on was close to the outer door, separated by a narrow hallway. Despite this short distance, Emin didn't hear the key being inserted into the outer door's lock and turned. He was startled when the outer door opened. Aydin had noticed Emin's reaction and whispered, 'Did I scare you?'

'No, I wasn't scared. I was so engrossed in writing, so I didn't realise you were coming. I was startled for a moment. As you know, when it's sudden when you're engrossed...' Emin felt the need to explain. He was afraid of the word 'fear' and of being misunderstood.

"What are you writing?"

"A letter!"

He didn't answer Aydin's question "To whom?" immediately and just paused initially...

"Well, you know, it's my way of pouring out my heart when I feel down. A letter that wouldn't be posted. No address!"

"Roger! Nazligül again!"

The reference that Aydın, dressed in the pragmatism overalls of mechanical engineering, made by saying "again" was to Emin's letters, written from Bursa Prison, all of which Emin had taken back and burnt. These were letters written on lined notebook paper, each exceeding twenty pages, each sent in four or five envelopes.

"Why do you write if you're not going to send it?"

Was there an answer to Aydın's question? Emin fell silent

to write the last words that would end his sentence. Emin felt the need to answer his host. Emin's scribbled lines were a draft forming the basis of the novel he intended to write eventually. Not knowing what the uncertain future would bring, Emin preferred to state his other reason while collecting the A5-size notebook pages scattered on the table:

"I want to write down my experiences, the emotions I felt while living them, much like I did in Bursa Prison; in a way, trying to pour out my inner thoughts, and it somehow comforts me!"

"I'll complete the rest! Nazligül is the only person you can pour your heart out easily... what did you say before... 'emphatically, without a burr'... No one else but writing to Nazligül is a must!"

Aydin paused.

"You can't get this woman out of your head... even though she got up and married an insidious jerk like Yakup!"

"No, Yakup is good. He's a good man. And he knew what happened between Nazligül and me... And he also knew what didn't happen, so he was the best choice that Nazligül could have made."

Now, Emin had wanted to close the subject with these words he had also said to Yakup before, but he did not know that he had opened Pandora's box while trying to enclose it.

"You always defended Yakup. Especially after his affair with Nazligül started. Actually, you know what? You defended yourself. You tried not to create an impression on people to think that you were bad-mouthing him only because he was with Nazligül. It is understandable, but you were wrong! You made excuses for him!"

"Don't exaggerate! What makes you think that?"

Emin's objection made Aydın furious. Even though Emin

realised this, he ignored it. Their relationship with Aydın was like this. They would push each other's buttons and have quarrels. However, it would not harm their friendship. They were similar in this respect. No lies and deceit had ever come between them in their friendship.

[Flashforward:
Years later, during Emin's visit to Turkey, after a tense discussion following Emin's statement, "This country has a 'Turkish problem', not a Kurdish one, which makes all the peoples live a life of hell," a coldness set in between them. Sometime later, when they reconnected on Facebook, in response to Aydın's remonstrance for "not taking time to meet him" during his visits to Istanbul, Emin wrote: "Every visit is a rush, I wasn't able to stay for a long time anyway. On the other hand, you are a bit far away too," referring to the fact that Aydın was working outside Istanbul. Although Emin concluded his words by writing: "I will let you know the next time I come," he would not have the opportunity to fulfil this promise. Three months after this correspondence, Aydın would post a three-minute "burial" scene from the film "Rembetiko" on his Facebook page with the note "You can go like this!". Another three months later, a photograph of Aydın would appear on Emin's page with a note in English: "A friend left behind memories without lies or pretence."]

But he was years away from writing these words.

Aydın added angrily, "Look here, we used to go hang up posters, despite the risk of an armed attack or the police catching us at any moment, while Yakup would just curl up and go to sleep, saying, 'I'll go to the printing house tomorrow morning.' You used to take his side, claiming, 'Friends, if something happened and Yakup got caught, the weekly newspaper's work would be left unfinished.' You actually were defending Yakup."

"So what? I was right and stating the fact. That's why I say you're exaggerating."

"It's not like that at all. When has Yakup ever undertaken a risky mission? He always had an excuse."

At the Culture Commission meeting of the Central Committee, when Yakup used the same reasoning to avoid taking the position of Editor-in-Chief of the newspaper, which carried the risk of prosecution and imprisonment due to the Press Law, Emin assumed the role. Despite Emin's recollection of this incident, he continued to argue with Aydın:

"What you referred to as 'excuses' were actually valid reasons. The issue you mentioned also occurred when I was in a relationship with Nazligül. Yakup was not involved with Nazligül then. So, my defence of Yakup wasn't related to that."

"You reckon?!"

"There's nothing to think about. Since there was no such relationship, there is no such issue for me to defend Yakup for that reason, as a matter of course."

"I didn't mean him when I said, 'You reckon'."

"What did you mean, then?"

"They were working together at the printing house with Nazligül. Who knows whether he didn't make an effort for that back then or didn't pave the way for a relationship?"

"Now you're talking nonsense. There's no such thing. If you were talking about Fırat or Ali Atmaca, I'd understand. They made such efforts. Nazli told me about it. But Yakup didn't do anything like that. Besides, I'm sure because

Yakup proposed to Arzu a week before Nazligül proposed to him."

"Are you serious? How do you know?"

"It's a long story, never mind. But Bahri told me. So, there's no need to doubt its veracity."

"Arzu's brother Bahri?"

"Yes."

"Interesting. But you should admit that you have always defended Yakup, and you still do, even though he handed you over to the police."

"You are exaggerating again. It's Ferman's and Ergin's mess. They fled abroad and didn't care about the rest. Look, Ferman named his son Tufan (Deluge), which was a kind of declaration: **'Après moi, le déluge,'**[17] After me, the deluge! – like Louis XIV."

"You're obsessed with them too, but they left Yakup and Bakir in charge of the warehouse where the party documents and Central Committee Resolutions Book were kept together with the publications. They were appointed to take care of it."

This was the first time Emin had heard this, and despite being shaken, he remained obstinate:

"Even so, it is a question of political responsibility. Without the decision of those who fled before, Yakup, whom you call 'insidious jerk', and Bakir, whom I call 'meathead', cannot make such a decision on their own."

"OK, let's say it's so. Couldn't these guys have informed someone before they left and told them to take care of the warehouse?"

"They may not have trusted anyone because they hid

---

[17] **"Après moi, le déluge,"** a French phrase, conveys the sentiment of "After me, the deluge!" It is generally regarded as a nihilistic expression of indifference to whatever happens after one is gone.

their escape," Emin replied, but he had started to consider that Aydın might be right. He recalled an incident mentioned during his meeting with Turan and his brother. Turan had stated that he and Ünal, a former pilot, had offered thirty thousand Turkish Liras to buy all the warehouse contents. However, their offer had been refused. Regardless of their intention, if such a transaction had occurred, it could have saved hundreds of books and the Party documents and perhaps even avoided a trial. This incident was adding weight to Aydın's argument. When Emin met with his brother and Turan on that day, he had once again considered this issue a "political irresponsibility" of the Presidium. It hadn't crossed his mind to inquire about the individuals handling it on the ground, a typical habit of the days of illegality.

He agreed with Aydın, "Maybe you are right. At least they could have telephoned someone after they went abroad and informed them and asked for the rent to be paid," he said when he remembered these things.

Aydın laughed sarcastically: "Your brain finally started functioning," and went on: "What happened? When the landlord couldn't get his rent, he opened the warehouse, and when he saw all that stuff, he called the police. At the end, the party members, who were left behind in the country, faced the music."

There, actually, were other events that were justifying Aydın.

In the early months of 1981, a group of Party members and sympathisers were detained in Ankara. Yet, on the grounds of insufficient evidence, the Ankara Martial Law Prosecutor's Office decided not to pursue charges and ultimately released the detainees.

And then what?

In addition to the incident that the Party's membership

slips hidden by a friend working there inside the seats of a large hotel, which had been discovered when the seat covers were being changed, various documents such as the Central Committee decision book and writings presented at party organisation meetings had been seized in the mentioned warehouse. As a result, in 1984, the Istanbul Martial Law Command began arresting some party members as they could find them.

After all that had happened, he once again thought that he had been right not to trust Turan, who had suggested running away from Turkey through the people responsible for all this. According to Emin, "the pieces were falling into place".

"Never mind. Let's do what we need to do. I am hungry, what about you? Aren't you hungry," Emin changed the subject and removed the papers he had collected from the table.

* * *

On the first day the passport arrived, after two attempts, he thought he couldn't concentrate on the efforts to replicate the signature because memories and thoughts about the past were hindering him. Later, he continued his attempts to replicate the signature, yet couldn't manage it. "Well, this guy who tried to sign an artistic signature, who knows, might have just finished elementary school. What's the point of you trying to be an artist!" he first found fault with the man. Curious about the man's profession, Emin looked at the passport. It said, "Salesman-Marketing." Good thing he had checked. During his travel, for a moment, he would forget this and barely recover from the mistake he made concerning it.

Then, he had started blaming himself: "The man was a salesman, and maybe he wanted to sign a signature that could hardly be forged. Who knows what kind of deals he signs; he possibly didn't want someone else to be able to forge it easily! You have no talent for drawing. Aren't you the one who failed only the drawing lesson in the last year of secondary school?"

One way or another, there was a fact. And now the Bulgarian customs officer, having looked at the signature on the paper and the signature on the passport, repeated his previous sentence, "Neighbour, this passport is not yours!" with a slightly mocking smile on his face, as if to say that he had been caught. Even though Emin was aware of the dissimilarity, he had no choice but to persist:

"This passport is my passport."

The Bulgarian officer handed him another piece of paper without saying anything. However, Emin's signature was even worse this time. "Go there, neighbour!" the officer said, gesturing toward where the other two men and the bus conductor were standing. He was in trouble, but it would be better for him to go "there" than to be held somewhere else. Now, he could talk to the bus conductor. What had he been told? "The bus conductor is the man of the network and will help if there's a problem."

When he reached them, they were all smoking cigarettes, and the other two passengers had their eyes on the bus conductor. "We'll wait; there's nothing else to do," the bus conductor concluded, taking a deep puff from his cigarette. Apparently, he had reached the end of the conversation. Emin waited a little longer; maybe the others would say something, but everyone remained silent. He approached the bus conductor by circling around the person next to him, said in a low voice, "Can I talk to you for a moment?" and stepped away from the group. When the bus conductor caught up to him, Emin said, "There is a problem regarding my passport. How much will it cost?" based on what he had heard long before.

His maternal aunt, who travelled back and forth by car from Germany, had said, "I will never come through Bulgaria again. The Bulgarian policemen block the road at every turn and demand bribes." This aunt, the subject of family jokes due to her exaggerations and lies, might not have been taken too seriously if it weren't for his other aunt's husband, a Bulgarian immigrant, confirming it. He used to be a socialist and had significantly influenced Emin; his word was one of the most trusted by Emin. This man had travelled to Bulgaria a few years before the campaign to Bulgarianise the "Turkish" minority started, to visit some of his relatives still living there and to observe socialist practices on the ground, yet he had been very disappointed. His conclusion of what he witnessed was very negative: "They have failed to create the socialist human type; bribery is rampant everywhere. Instead of a workers' state, they have created a bribery state!" Although Emin would later question this approach as to what it meant to "create a socialist human type," the phrase "They have created a bribery state instead of a workers' state!" was engraved in the back of his mind.

Now, ironically, Emin was hoping for help from this bribery mechanism. He hoped, but he was wrong. The bus conductor, who had previously spoken in imperative tones, partly because he could not fulfil his function of "solving problems when they arise" and partly out of caution, would say in a lower voice, in a more subdued tone, "Brother, this is not possible. Bribery does not work in Bulgarian customs."

Emin was surprised. He pressed on:

"Maybe you didn't offer enough money. Maybe the

While Running Away

customs officers wanted more. Give it a try!"

"There's no way. I can't even suggest it. We'll get in trouble!"

"So, what's going to happen now? They told me you'd sort it out if there was a problem. Guaranteed transport to Yugoslavia. Is this what we paid so much for?"

Emin's demanding behaviour seemed to irritate the bus conductor. He suddenly reverted to his old style:

"Don't you get it? There's nothing to do. You, yourself, should take care of it if you can! We'll wait an hour. If you can't fix it, we'll leave."

"What do you mean?" Emin expressed his disbelief.

"It's not like we'll wait till morning! We'll wait an hour. That's it! It's written on your ticket; read it!"

Emin didn't really know that; he hadn't read his ticket!

"Open and look at it!" the bus conductor repeated, and Emin took out and opened his ticket. At the same time, the bus conductor pointed with his finger to the last article of the conditions written in small letters at the bottom of the ticket. "In case of problems at customs, your bus may wait for one hour. If you do not return to your bus within one hour, it will continue on its journey."

From that moment on, he started looking at his passport often. It was as if time had stopped. About fifteen minutes later, the queue of people waiting for passport control was over. The customs officer, who gave the last passenger his passport and sent him to the bus, came out of the booth, approached him, and called Emin, "Come here, neighbour."

When he arrived, a paper and pen, similar to the previous ones, were waiting for him. His signature this time, as he nervously signed the paper, was no better than his previous ones. The other Bulgarian officer stood next to the checker, observing him. The first officer hadn't even bothered to look

57

at the signature on the passport, and the other one took the paper and placed it next to the signature on the passport. Meanwhile, Emin was saying, "It's cold, and my fingers are numb," while blowing on his hands and rubbing them together. The two officers exchanged a few words in Bulgarian, and the first one said, "Go and sit on the bus, neighbour!" and put his passport on the side of the counter.

"My passport?"

The question that would remain unanswered just came out of his mouth, but the answer was obvious. Emin did not repeat it and walked to the bus.

His hands were, indeed, cold. Nevertheless, he knew this was not the main reason for his clumsiness. He took his seat on the bus. He was not quite sure what it meant that he had been sent to the bus, but Emin thought that it was not a very promising event since he had not been given his passport. "But why not?" he said to himself, "Maybe they would send the passport with the bus conductor!" This was the human being's endeavour to create hope for himself even at the most inopportune time, even as small as a pinhole. Could one hold on to life without this endeavour?

* * *

[Flashforward - 1996:

Years later, Zafer opened a parenthetical pause while Emin was recounting his story:

"This was a reflection of that popular saying within you."

"Which saying?"

Emin did not grasp the reference as he was immersed in the memories, attempting to extract them from the haze of the past.

"As the saying goes, 'hope is the bread of the poor!' Yours was something similar!"

"You could say that... at least momentarily. Actually, I find a great irony in this saying. On the one hand, it encourages us to cling to life through hope; on the other hand, it suggests that a physical need cannot be fulfilled by waiting beyond the bounds of physics."

Zafer responded to Emin with his customary exuberance.

"Wow, you're going too far again!"

"Wait, it's not over. How can hope fill your belly? How can it be the bread for the poor? Or can it? Hope won't fill your belly; nevertheless, it is bread! Is it?"

"I'm confused. Bread that doesn't fill you up!"

"Hope can be just despair in disguise. Hope can be a tool of self-deception. It consumes you! The presence of hope, coupled with the resilience it fosters, has the potential to pave the way for survival. That's true, but it can't last forever. Hope must have a defined objective to open the door, leading you to find sustenance."

"Realistic hopes! Or hopes must be realistic!"

"You could say that. Hope must be rooted in reality. Otherwise, 'hope' that is expected to descend from the sky takes the one to the paradise promised in the so-called afterlife."

"I thought you said, 'Those who cannot dream cannot even pickle.' Doesn't hope to correspond to dreaming? Aren't you contradicting yourself?"

"You're at it again! You're on the hunt for contradictions! Your hunts wouldn't kill my appetite, but, on the contrary, it provokes me! Come on, get up and bring another cup of tea. It's your turn while I go to the loo?"

"You're stuck and trying to buy time."

"Oh yeah! I am not on the run, so I'm going to the toilet, where I get my best ideas!"

When Emin returned, he lit a cigarette from the packet Zafer handed him and took a sip of his tea before asking his question.

"What pickles do you like?"

"Mixed, but the peppers must be hot. I know where you are about to go with this."

Emin took no notice; he was going to repeat what he had written somewhere before:

"If you don't dream of eating pickles, you won't try to make pickles."

He paused for a moment and then continued:

When you try to make pickles, the first thing you do is put the ingredients together. OK, get the pepper from Urfa![18] Cabbage, cucumber, carrot, aubergine... Whatever you need, buy them from wherever you can find them! You can realise your dreams and hopes when you roll up your sleeves. When all those vegetables are pickled, their colour and hardness change more or less, but the main thing that changes is their taste. There is a fermentation, and this is the result of that. Change is such a process in both individual and social life. Marx describes this in the 'Preface' to A Contribution to the Critique of Political Economy and what Doctor Hikmet Kivilcimli describes in his "History Thesis." The issue is a matter of bringing those materials together. And those materials do not just fall from the sky. They are to be sown, reaped, and so on. Where? In where they exist. In their natural environment! You also need to know how to make

---

[18] Urfa is a Kurdish province in southeastern Turkey famous for its chilli peppers.

pickles, and this is a knowledge passed down from the past. Without that knowledge, you would waste a lot of ingredients until you succeed in making pickles."

"Are you aware that you are digressing?"

"Well, how else can I explain it? It's all connected. Anyway... In short, as long as our hopes and dreams are not based on our own endeavours, they are nothing more than a temporary deception. Self-deception. Even if it helps us to hold on to life for a moment, in the end, we find ourselves in a void. This is what I was doing while waiting on the bus. An attempt to hold on to life. An endeavour to hold on to hopes, even if they are empty, even if these are sometimes far from reality. This contradiction is a trait shared by all humans. This is the way of looking at life through the window of 'tecâhül-i ârif'[19]."

* * *

Emin was trying to hold on to life while waiting on the bus, even though this effort was not rational. Within ten minutes, first one, then the other, and the two other passengers, who had been kept waiting, had arrived and taken their seats. The bus conductor was still nowhere in sight. A tap on the window where he was sitting brought him out of his thoughts. The Bulgarian officer was signalling "come, come" with the palm of his right hand in the air, opening and closing his four fingers.

He got off the bus. The officer had nothing in his hand. Apparently, his passport was in the booth. "Come on, neighbour," said the officer, and they went to the booth

---

[19] Tecâhül-i ârif: One of the rhetorical devices in Turkish literature. To convey a well-known fact as if one does not know it to create subtlety of meaning.

again. While he was taking his place in front of the booth, the officer who had entered inside of the booth asked:

"How are you, neighbour? Have you warmed up enough?"

"Thank you, I'm fine, yes, I have," he said, but when the "enemy paper" was handed to him, he whispered unnoticedly, "Oh, shit!" Nothing else he could do but sign it, and he did so.

He couldn't get it right. The officer took the paper, placed it beside the signature on the passport, and he and his colleague examined it. After exchanging words in Bulgarian with the other officer, who shook his head disapprovingly, he turned to Emin:

"This passport is not yours, neighbour. Tell us the truth!"

There was no point in denying it any longer. He would be at the mercy of the Bulgarian police.

"Yes, this passport is not mine. It's someone else's passport," Emin said and continued in an absurd defence at which he later would laugh:

"But it's my photo."

He wanted to close the subject with a shortcut explanation and pave the way back to the bus as soon as possible.

"I was sentenced to eight years in prison by a military court because I was a communist. In Turkey, I was a member of the Party's Central Committee and the Editor-in-Chief of the Party's newspaper. Since my appeal was denied, I am running away from Turkey and will go to Yugoslavia."

He wouldn't go to Greece or Romania on the bus travelling to Yugoslavia! But in his haste to save the situation, he couldn't stop himself from talking rubbish again. He went on:

While Running Away

"The bus is waiting and won't wait more than an hour. I have told the truth; give me my passport, and I'll go."

"Don't rush, neighbour," said the officer, turning to the other officer and saying something in Bulgarian.

"Come with me, neighbour!" he said softly but firmly.

They started walking towards the bus together. Amin was trying to guess what was going to happen? If they would allow him to leave, why hadn't they given him his passport yet? Moreover, the other two passengers had come to the bus alone, and no one had accompanied them.

"Why would this officer accompany me if they let me go?" With this question, he's started paying more attention to adverse probabilities.

When they arrived next to the bus, the customs officer said the bus conductor, who met them, "Put his suitcase down." They waited for him to take his suitcase out of the trunk near the front door. After Emin's suitcase was unloaded, the customs officer asked:

"Have you got anything on the bus?"

Realising he wouldn't be released, Emin replied wanly, a trace of disappointment in his voice.

"Yes, I do."

"Go and get it, get it!"

"Why didn't I get on the bus from the rear door?" he scolded himself as he walked down the aisle with its half-extinguished interior lights, without looking at anyone, as if he were guilty of something. He picked up the net bag he had placed on the seat, then changed his mind and only took out two packets of biscuits. He gave the net bag with the tangerines inside to the man seated by him.

"It's for all of you, enjoy them."

He received the man's blessing:

"Thank you, my friend. May Allah bless you and Godspeed!"

"So, he understood," Emin thought anxiously but still appreciated this expression of good wishes. In fact, he felt that "doing good things will bring good things to you" deep inside him, and receiving good wishes from someone had brought him a peculiar sense of serenity at that moment.

When Emin got off the bus, he said to the bus conductor waiting at the door, "You'll wait, won't you? Maybe I'll catch up," not really believing what he was saying.

"I told you before. An hour, tops. If you're not here in an hour, we won't wait any longer, and we'll leave."

Emin had realised that whatever he said to the bus conductor would be futile. Glancing at his watch, he noted that it was five past midnight. He grabbed his suitcase, and Emin heard the officer say, "Come on, neighbour." Together, they began walking from the pale-yellow light of the streetlamp near the bus into the darkness on the wide asphalt road where eight vehicles could easily pass. On the opposite side of the road, aligned with the bus and running parallel to the road, there was an empty shack, nearly four times longer than the booth where his passport had been checked earlier. They entered it.

The lights were on in the shack. Immediately after the entrance, the benches are placed lengthwise side by side, at a distance of half a metre from each other, similar to those in picnic places, with long tables in the middle. Of the five windows, spaced one metre apart, the second one on the door's side had no glass. The officer who closed the door sat on the bench immediately before him. He pointed Emin to the opposite side:

"Sit down, neighbour."

While Running Away

He sat down. Attached to the wall, about one and a half metres behind him, two radiators of domestic size with peeling paint caught his eye. "I hope they are on," he thought. Fortunately, they were on, and he would realise this when he felt the heat reaching his back a few minutes after he sat down.

As soon as he sat down, the officer started counting:

"Now, neighbour, you will tell me everything slowly, so I will write it down. You will tell me the truth about everything. You tried to enter Bulgaria illegally with a false passport. The penalty for this offence is at least six years. So, no lying. Otherwise, you might get punished even more. I don't know what will happen. You may go to jail here; we may send you back to Turkey. We may let you go. It's up to you. It's better for you if you tell the truth. Is that clear?"

"The police are the police everywhere, and their narratives are very similar; I have heard them from the Turkish police, too, and even from the army captain who interrogated me in Selimiye Prison[20] and was probably working for the 'intelligence service'. There is no harm in telling the Bulgarian police what the Turkish police know!" was the final conclusion of his thoughts, which lasted for an unknown fraction of a second. He gave the officer a short and clear answer:

"Understood."

"First, tell me who you are, your real name, surname, date of birth, place of birth, the names and ages of your father, mother, siblings, if any."

He listed his answers.

"Do you know the man whose name is on the passport?"

---

[20] Selimiye Prison is a military prison located within the Selimiye (Military) Barrack on the Asian side of Istanbul, near the Bosphorus. It is the main base of 1. Army in Istanbul. During the Crimean War (1854–56), the barracks were allocated to the British Army.

"No."
"How did you get this passport?"
"From a network that smuggles people out of Turkey."
"What are the names of the people in the network?"
"I met one of them; I did everything through him."
"What's his name?"
"Osman."

He had made it up, but he had deliberately chosen the name: "Osman". Osman was the first name that came to his mind after Hasan, and it was also the name of their friend in London, for whom they had waited in vain for months for a forged passport. He could easily remember it if asked again. It was out of the question for him to give Hasan's name. Even if it was a Bulgarian official, "Just in case, the earth has ears". Especially if he was sent back to Turkey. Here, too, he would read out the script he had prepared for the testimony he would give in the country of asylum. Names were the crucial elements of this scenario. Although he did not realise that he would have to use them at this stage, it worked for him.

"What's his surname?"
"I don't know. I didn't ask. I wouldn't be told, even if I asked."
"Is his name real?"
"That's the name I was told."

He hardly refrained from saying, "What a stupid question?" The officer possibly realised his question did not make sense regarding the illegal nature of the conduct, and the officer didn't insist on asking the same question.

"How did you find this guy?"
"When I was serving time in the military prison, one of the other political prisoners had given me the information."

While Running Away

"Did you buy it with money... Did you get the passport made?"

"Yes."

"How much did you pay?"

"Three hundred and fifty Deutsche Marks."

"Oh, you gave a lot."

"Yeah, but they organise everything."

"Did they organise your bus ticket too?"

"Yes, but I paid another hundred marks when I bought the ticket?"

"Too much! How much money do you have on you now?"

"About five hundred Deutsche Marks."

The officer paused for a moment as if he did not know how to ask and then continued expressing the scepticism in his gaze:

"You said you were a communist."

"The party I was a member of was a Marxist-Leninist party."

"OK. Now you will tell me about your life, starting from your childhood. When did you get involved in political movements? What was the organisation you worked for? What were your duties in the organisation? Tell me everything you have experienced until today."

"Fine, but it'll take too long. I've told you before, and you've also heard what the bus conductor told me. The bus doesn't wait more than an hour," he looked at his watch and finished his sentence, "It's 00.30. Half an hour left."

The officer's words, "Forget the bus!" completely destroyed his hope. Indeed, he was at the mercy of the Bulgarian police. "Is it possible that the words, "mercy" and "police" could come together, even if it is the police in a country that claims to be 'socialist'? Even if it is socialist, it is the police in a bureaucratic, centralised and militaristic mechanism", he thought, as he slowly narrated his life in main headings.

The necessity of speaking slowly to match the officer's writing speed provided Emin the chance to carefully consider what to disclose and what to withhold. He was narrating the account he had premeditated for a probable asylum application in the future. There was no objection to recounting the incidents and activities that fell within the bounds of the law. The idea of "What difference would it make if the police of another State knew what the Turkish police already knew?!" defined the scope of his narrative.

The problem was that he had to recount his personal history to the Bulgarians. Three issues worried Emin, which he contemplated.

The most important of these was the fact that he had taken part in a movement following Dr Kivilcimli's line. On the one hand, when he considered the treatment of Dr Kivilcimli[21] by the Bulgarians in 1971, he thought, "What importance can I have next to Kivilcimli?" But on the other hand, he pondered, "The hostile attitude shown towards Kivilcimli could also be shown towards his followers."

In his mind, he was adding a second reason to this hostile attitude, which could add an even more hostile dimension: The "Bulgarianisation" policy, which was then in full swing. But even if he was not an "authentic Turk", in the eyes of the Bulgarians, he was a Turk. Moreover, he was a member of the Doctorist movement. You reap what you sow. Many, many, many years later, he would remember his state of mind in February 1989 and all of these when Sirri

---

[21] Hikmet Kivilcimli (1902, Pristina, Kosovo Vilayet, Ottoman Empire – 1971, Belgrade) was a Turkish communist leader, theoretician, writer, publicist, and translator. He founded the Vatan Partisi (VP) [Homeland Party].

Süreyya Önder would jokingly say, "I am Turkish too. May God not bring any other sorrow!"

The third reason was directly related to himself. Emin had been a hardline anti-TKP throughout his political life from the beginning. In various periods of the movement, he had always been the most ardent opponent of the proposals to join the TKP expressed on different platforms. While he had narrated this in his writings, especially when discussions on the subject came to the agenda within the legal Party, he had also severely opposed the idea of joining the TKP, in conjunction with the thesis that the Soviet Union could not be considered "socialist." Of course, he was not going to tell the Bulgarians this. The article about the USSR that he had presented during the "[Extraordinary General] Organization Meetings," alongside some of his other articles, had gone missing. It was not among those seized by the police in the warehouse where the Party publications were kept.

* * *

[Flashforward - 2005:

"Emin was going to tell Zafer before making him read an article he had written on the internet.

"In contrast to the ordinary members, there was a significant tendency among those who had considered themselves leaders within the Party to be enthusiastic about joining the TKP. After reading a kind of summary history about the Turkish left on the webpage of Anarşist Bakış,[22] I wrote down comments on the page. By the way, at the time, I did not understand Selamettin Oksuz's games at all. What he was doing wasn't making

---

[22] A website published by a group of Anarchists in Turkey named "Anarchist View".

sense sometimes, at least for me, until what I was told in Sweden in the autumn of 1989. Although Faik Feryat's staunch commitment to TKP had been exposed at the "[Extraordinary General] Organisation Meetings," I was unaware that the roots of this tendency went back much further. What Faik's wife told me in Sweden clarified the matter, at least in my mind.

"Leyla Feryat herself said, 'It was a decision taken by Faik Feryat, Selamettin Oksuz and Alp Oktem, who was probably representing TKP at that meeting, to join the TKP. She wouldn't make it up, after all. Even though she invented a nonsense story about Faik Feryat's disappearance afterwards as a product of her paranoia, this is an entirely different matter.

"Anyway... In short, that's what Leyla had said on a cold Swedish night when we were digging into the past; all of these had been discussed within the framework of the paradigm that I had still been stuck in at that time... Thus, it was like getting an icy cold shower because I was still looking at the issue from the conventional old perspective.

"The efforts of Selamettin Oksuz, who was more skilled at pushing away people than organising them, ended in a complete fiasco. Faik Feryat's endeavours, which was his final attempt, had failed at the start. If you remember, I had mentioned these in connection with the past when I was telling my experiences on the run. And then, another person: Çelik Dolunay. When I exposed Faik Feryat's hidden support for the TKP during the "[Extraordinary General] Organisation Meetings" and when I presented an article discussing the 'socialism' of the TKP and the USSR by interpreting Kivilcimli's letter to Brezhnev from a different perspective, I suddenly noticed that Çelik had disappeared from the scene!"

"Wasn't Çelik already in prison? What do you mean "disappeared?""

"Metaphorically, I mean. Yes, Çelik was in prison, but by sending a letter in which he claimed that I was already actively addressing the issues on the current agenda while he was working on matters at a more significant scale, he chose to step out of the debate."

"Well, he supported you!"

"It may seem that way from the outside, but I didn't perceive it that way, and neither did any of our friends. It was more like, 'I'm not interested in these discussions. These are small matters,' which is what he meant. In fact, he was avoiding discussing the subject. It was reminiscent of Faik Feryat's withdrawal from the Party. After his unsuccessful attempt to persuade us to join the TKP, he returned to Sweden and made some flimsy excuses for not coming back to Turkey. What I heard from Leyla Feryat during my visit to Sweden in 1989 made me realise why Selamettin Oksuz had left the Party. Thus, the pieces fell into place. All three 'leaders' had run away when it came to the issue of their stance concerning the TKP. Çelik, unlike the others, stayed in touch and continued his efforts to lead the Party from prison."

"He didn't run away then!"

"Maybe in this sense, but because the issue of the TKP fell off the agenda, his position was consequently swept under the carpet, or more precisely, it was not brought up. In 'Anarşist Bakış,' the history of the Party was summarised, omitting all of these."

"What attitude did the Party Chairman take?"

"Clark Mahmut?"

"Clark?"

"Mahmut Suzer! I nicknamed him after Clark Gable."

"Why is that?"

"It's another matter. I'll tell you about it sometime later, never mind for now. According to Ferman's story, they first made him the Party Chairman because he had completed his military service. Therefore, he wouldn't be called up for military service, ensuring there would be no interruption in his role as Chairman; and secondly, because 'he would come across as charismatic due to his physical appearance.' As you know, it is quite common in this country; people often mistake cunning for intelligence. This also appears to be an attempt at cunning in its own way. We don't know what kind of internal conflicts were taking place at the top in the past... When Çelik mentioned in one of his articles that he didn't 'warmly welcome' the idea of joining the Vatan Party or the TSİP,[23] Clark Mahmut made a side-slit criticism with comments like 'Not 'warmly welcoming' is not a political stance; explain your stance."

"Well, he's right; that's not how you establish a political position."

"That's where the cunning lies. Clark Mahmut actually knows the reason. It's once again related to the issue of the TKP, but he doesn't openly discuss it. Why not? What they discussed at that time is unknown, especially among Party members. Most likely, Clark Mahmut took a similar stance or abstained, which is highly possible. Otherwise, he would have attacked Çelik directly, saying, 'I was against the TKP at the time,

---

[23] TSİP: Socialist Workers' Party of Turkey.

but you were in favour of it, which is why you didn't 'warmly welcome' the idea of joining the TSİP.' Clark Mahmut doesn't use Çelik's position regarding TKP against him, or more precisely, he couldn't do that. Anyway, we digress. But there was something else interesting in Anarşist Bakış. It was written that the basis for Clark Mahmut's Socialist Homeland Party splitting from us was their support for armed struggle. There is no truth in that claim. Such discussions over this issue never took place. Besides, the debates were happening during legal party congresses in the presence of the police. It was a ridiculous claim. I noticed that no one objected to what was written on the internet."

"They might not have seen it!"

"OK, let's assume they didn't see it. I then brought all the issues to the 'Socialist Discussion Forum,' where Çelik occasionally wrote, but he didn't respond. Later, a young individual shared the writings with the 'Kivilcim e-mail Group.' It's not a matter of not seeing. Anarşist Bakış probably obtained information about the reason for the departure of the individuals who founded the Socialist Homeland Party from them. Later on, Clark Mahmut, with his two articles in a newspaper, initiated another provocation."

"What did he write?"

"It's a separate matter. Now is not the time. Let's not get sidetracked. You know what's interesting? Supposedly, Çelik also favoured an 'armed struggle against fascism!' Check it out! Everyone claims to have a favour for armed struggle. Of course, that was never the case! Contrary to what he was saying now and then, there's no question of him breaking away from the

Party. He always remained in the Party but tried to create the impression that he had nothing to do with the Party's actions. He washes his hands of it. Yes, he became a Trotskyist, and the Party didn't fully embrace this line. Anyway, during our disagreements with the Presidium, Çelik sent a message asking me to visit him in prison. During that visit, he suggested that I, along with my brother and Turan, take over the Presidium, and he would provide us with all sorts of theoretical and practical support. I promptly and firmly refused him with no hesitation. Later, my brother and Turan declined this offer when visiting Çelik. Years passed, and perhaps Çelik thought nobody remembered all of this. On 8 April 2003, Çelik wrote a response to what I had written under the name 'Communalist' on 4 April 2003, stating that he had 'coincidentally come across what I had written' and that none of my claims were true. He asserted that his views were articulated in the articles he had been publishing and that 'a serious researcher would recognise that the allegations put forward have no basis in truth.' After stating these points, he continued by saying, 'It's not the accused who must prove his innocence, but the accuser who must prove his allegations,' accusing the writer, the 'Communalist' —by the way, not knowing it was me— of acting with the logic of inquisition law. He didn't forget to advise the 'Communalist' to have 'some responsibility and seriousness.' It had a familiar patronising tone. Then, I replied on 9 April."

"What did you say?"

"What's more important than what I said is this: When I replied, I didn't write under the signature 'Communalist.' I used my own name. I pointed to events directly related to him, stating that I was a witness and interlocutor of those events and that there were other witnesses. Finally, I asked, 'Which of the allegations weren't true?' He couldn't have missed this response, yet he remained silent."

Zafer got curious: "I'm going to read all these all through."

"Let me find it. While you read, I'll go buy bread from the corner shop."

Emin located the file on his computer where he had saved his writings. He also noticed another article he had placed at the top but had not mentioned.

"Oh, at one point, I poked fun at another article by Çelik and referred to this correspondence. You'll see it at the beginning of the article. However, once again, there was no response from Çelik."

"It is in your nature; you will surely delve deeper!"

"I'll tell you about how I delved deeper later. You go ahead and read. Everything is here. The writings are in chronological order. The letter characters in Çelik's writing are different, probably because he wrote them from Germany. It seems Çelik typed them in haste, without converting them to Turkish characters, and I didn't make corrections. I left my own writing errors as they are. Anyway, read through, and after you've finished, I'll tell you more when I return."

Zafer, who was still reading the articles when Emin returned, went to the kitchen when he finished.

"Is there anything I can do to help?"

"No, it's a one-person job. If you want, sit there. So, in the meantime, we'll chat. Have you read everything I wrote?"

"Yes, I read it. The part about Çelik is interesting. You said you were going to tell me about how you delved deeper. What did you do?" Zafer asked while trying to keep his balance on the stool squeezed into the tiny kitchen.

"When he came here last Newroz,[24] we met at the Halkevi[25] in London. They had invited him as a speaker on the subject of the 'Democratic Republic.' I agreed when the Halkevi management asked if I would also participate as a speaker. They know me as a 'Doctorist.' I had also told them that Kivilcimli's Homeland Party program envisioned a 'democratic republic' at one discussion before. Anyway, I went there a bit early on the meeting. I had thought that if the opportunity arose, I would have a chance to have a word with Çelik Dolunay. Upon my arrival, the person who had previously asked me to be the next speaker said, in a hollow-sounding voice, 'We won't be able to have you as a speaker; only Çelik Dolunay will be speaking. Sorry about the change.' I wasn't expecting this, but I wasn't surprised either."

"Why did they do that?"

"Don't you know me? Do you think I'd ask? But the real question is, 'Who excluded me' or 'had me shut out'? I didn't ask that either, of course! I cut it off by saying, 'I'll take the floor and say what I have to say' to them."

"Do you think it was Çelik Dolunay?"

---

[24] Newroz is the Kurdish New Year. In Kurdish legend, the holiday celebrates the deliverance of the Kurds from the Assyrian tyrant Dehak in 612 BC. It is seen as an essential expression of Kurdish identity and solidarity and a celebration of victory for the people over their oppressors.
[25] Halkevi in London is an association of Kurdish and Turkish-speaking communities in London.

"Probably Çelik, but there was a newcomer in that organisation who's a bit of a strutting youngster, so it could be him. Could there be room for me on the stage where this youngster doesn't appear? Anyway, it doesn't matter. By the way, I saw Çelik in a corner. He didn't come to us. I went up to him. After some 'Hello, how are you?' I interjected, 'There's something I've been willing to ask you for years. Let me recount the dialogue between us to the best of my memory."

"Çelik, there's something I've wanted to ask you for years. Something I don't understand. Why did you go full circle and act together with the Ferman and Ergin group?"

"There is no such thing; where are you getting this from?"

"You took a stand in favour of them in the discussions in the Party in the later stages. We went through these together. It was said that you were with them when you migrated to Europe."

"When I first went Europe, naturally, I met with them but did not act with them."

Zafer was also surprised; he interrupted Emin's narration.

"Did he really say that?"

"Exactly. I was already aware that conflicts arose later, leading to their separation. I think Çelik was trying to make the first episode of his relationship with them in Europe evaporate. This is also his habit. The answer he gave me, remember, not me actually, it was Communalist, in the correspondence on the internet, was a product of the same behaviour. But wait, there is more. When Çelik denied his relationship with the others, I thought it was the right time to place the stone on the spot."

Emin returned to the dialogues between him and Çelik.

"Çelik, I don't understand you. You are the most productive person in the socialist movement in Turkey after Kivilcimli. You are one of the living socialists in Turkey today with a broad knowledge. All friends who know you agree on this. No one can deny your high level of intelligence. That's why I don't understand, I really don't understand, why you need these lies. You also exhibited this behaviour in the Socialist Discussion Forum. That's why I felt the need to use my own name instead of the name Communalist when replying to you there."

"Was it you who wrote under the signature 'Communalist'?"

"Yes, it was me."

Growing more curious, Zafer interrupted Emin's story again.

"What did he say when you told him that?"

"Nothing. Çelik said something like, 'It's time for the meeting; let me make my final preparations.'"

"He had to be very upset."

"I don't know about that. The important thing was to send Çelik a message that his stance on TKP and his position in the Homeland Party cannot be hidden behind the inability to talk about the period of illegality and turn it into a tale of 'once upon a time' by saying 'what I wrote is obvious and public' or something like that. As far as I'm concerned, the purpose was fulfilled."]

* * *

It had been said that the documents related to the period of illegality were in the hands of the Bulgarian authorities. Yet, since Emin used a pseudonym in the discussions of that time, he thought, "It won't be a problem." What puzzled him was whether the Bulgarian authorities had his writings from the legal party period. He had written everything with his own signature. He evaluated the possibilities while the Bulgarian officer was writing down Emin's statement.

"If the Bulgarians have these writings, will they come to light? Would they undertake a long investigation? If so, how long will it take? How long will they keep me here?"

He was tired of thinking.

"Time will tell how this ball of uncertainties will be unravelled and whether or not it will make me jump out of the frying pan into the fire from the unravelled threads. There is only one thing I have to do: Answer the questions without giving anything away. Whatever is going to happen will happen! Once the arrow is out of the bow, there is no going back... You'll see whether the Bulgarians send you back or not!"

He was thinking about these things as he again paused for the officer to complete what he had written, and the bus had already left.

When Emin concluded by saying, "Finally, here I am, as you know," the officer asked two more questions one after the other, the most difficult of which came last:

"Where will you go if we let you go? Do you want to seek asylum here?"

"First, I will go to Yugoslavia and then, with the help of my friends in England, continue on to England," he began.

Now it was time to improvise for Emin! He faced a situation that had not been in his script before and had not been considered. What he would say next did not reflect reality or his true thoughts.

"According to the decision taken by my Party, I will contribute to the Party's activities together with my friend in London. That is why I have to go to England. It is an honour to live in a socialist country. I would like to live in Bulgaria, but of course..."

He paused. He did not know how to summarise his sentence. He took refuge in the communist tradition:

"But you know I have to obey the party decision."

He was thinking of the rumours about the leader of one of the left-wing movements and his relations with the Bulgarians. If these rumours were true, Emin would never be in such a position. No matter what the cost. He had tried to stick with the principle of not being a tool of any political organisation or institution. Especially if it was a state, even if it was labelled 'socialist'! So, should continue to do so.

The officer asked when he finished writing:

"Do you have anything else to add?"

"No, that's all. What now?"

"You'll wait. Our superior isn't here but in Sofia. You'll wait for him."

"When will he be back?"

"I don't know. Maybe tomorrow."

He didn't say what he asked himself:

"Could it be that the head of customs doesn't live in customs or somewhere in the neighbourhood? It's not credible. Let's say he does; what is this 'maybe'?" However, the hypothesis that came to his mind wouldn't be easily disregarded: "The one coming from Sofia will most probably be a member of the Bulgarian secret service."

"You're here tonight," the officer said as he got up.

"Do I stay in this building?"

"Yes."

"Where's the loo?"

"There's no toilet here."

"What am I supposed to do?"

"Outside?"

"Where is it?" he queried as he walked after the officer who was on his way out.

The officer pointed with his hand to the land, starting right behind the shack, and said, "You can do it somewhere there. Just don't get up to mischief. Go out when you need to, but return when you're done."

"Well... Can I go now?"

"Go."

Emin walked in the direction the officer pointed. After going about ten or fifteen steps ahead, he turned back and said to the officer, "This is..." There was no need to finish his sentence. The officer walked towards the booths where he had done the passport control. Behind that booth, a bit further inland, was a two-storey building that looked almost new or at least freshly painted. "Since no cars are coming and going, he must be going to that building, not to the booth," Emin thought. The officer didn't even look where Emin was going. He was very sure that Emin would not and could not run away. If he ran away, where could he go to Bulgaria?

"Emin finished his business and went back to the shack. He touched the radiator behind the bench they had just sat on. It was hot. He went and touched the radiator behind the second bench. It was also hot. Moreover, it was further away from the broken window and more sheltered. Leaning against the radiator, he tried to warm up while examining the inside of the shack; at the end of the two benches, placed side by side and about half a metre apart, another small booth, 2x2 metres, made of wood on all sides. The door of this inner booth faced Emin's side, similar to the shack's windows facing the road. The gap between them was almost one metre. When he looked through the open door of the booth, he saw papers and extinguished cigarette butts on the floor. Butts were scattered everywhere. So, he could smoke here. He took one out of the packet and lit it, smiling as he thought about the last part of his statement: "It is an honour to live in a socialist country!" However, he was not angry with himself for this lie."

"Well, my dear mother, if you had heard these... look, it turned out that I can do politics too!"

His mother used to say, "Politics is not for you, son. You're not a diplomatic man. You don't know how to keep your mouth shut; you say whatever's on your mind."

But now...

While referencing Bulgaria as a "socialist country" and hiding his true thoughts, she also spoke of the "honour" of living there.

As he said these things, he had a "valid, understandable" reason, but he had lied, not stating his true beliefs. He would again come face to face with the truth that justification and correctness don't always align.

Being forced into the "honour of living in a socialist country" was the third shitty option. Still, he could put up with it instead of counting days in Bulgarian or Turkish prisons, of course, as long as the state would not put a bill on his table that he is unwilling and unprepared to pay. However, this was the unpredictable part.

"Will they send him back to Turkey? Shouldn't they take into account the negative impression that handing over a 'socialist' to the Turkish police would create? An ordinary customs official at the gate may not think about this;

nevertheless, if, as I suspected, a secret service member is coming from Sofia, he might consider such a possibility!"

He sought a thread of hope to grasp onto, but within seconds, he recognised the naivety of his approach. "What about what happened to Dr Kivilcimli? Why should those who showed no concern for their treatment of him spare me?" With the intensity of his questions, he pulled out a second cigarette, adding it to the one nearing its end without needing a match. "Who knows how long I'll be stuck here; let's conserve matches!" he remarked, attempting to find another glimmer of hope in the thinness of a matchstick. "Perhaps," he mused to himself, "They can guide me on a way to slip into Turkey without handing me over to the Turkish police. That's the best-case scenario if they deny my entry to Yugoslavia. I might consider Nevin's suggestion unless I contemplate another escape!"

After going through all the possibilities in his mind, he took refuge in the warmth of the memories of the night he said goodbye to Nevin.

All possibilities?! "That was all" was his thought. Was it all?

* * *

"Punctual as always," Nevin greeted, rising from her seat.

They shook hands. As Nevin kissed Emin on the cheeks, she continued:

"A real kiss, not the one that flies through the air. The kind that leaves lipstick on your cheeks!"

Even though she had veered toward a completely different political path pursued by another leftist organisation, Nevin had always made him feel the warmth of the friendship established in their early university years.

Their friendship had also been tested by painful experiences, which prevented him from leaving without saying goodbye to her. However, Nevin was not yet aware of his decision.

"Have you been here long?"

"About half an hour. I left early, just in case. You never know what might happen with Istanbul traffic."

The waiter had run out on them, by the way.

Emin looked at Nevin's glass. There was feta cheese, cold cuts of cucumber and tomato, and a winter melon on the table. "A double raki for me," he said to the waiter.

"Abi, would you like anything else as an appetiser?"

"Do you have fried aubergine in tomato sauce?"

"Abi, there is nothing we don't have. We can create it, even if we don't have it, just say it!" The waiter was exaggerating by uttering the word 'create' instead of 'make'.

His behaviour seemed sly to Emin. He had encountered such behaviour from some male waiters before when they noticed a man and a woman having drinks one-on-one. He had often encountered this attitude when having night outs with his second wife. However, he wasn't in that mood at all this time. He decided to nip it in the bud, hoping to avoid the waiter coming around frequently and asking questions like, "How are you? Are you satisfied? Do you have any requests or wishes?" and so on!

"If you have it, bring it; if not, it doesn't matter; you don't need to 'create' it!"

His intonation was slightly harsh. Nevin realised that there was something off but waited. When the waiter left the table, she lowered her voice and asked:

"What is it? You're a bit tense."

"No... Maybe... But I wanted him to stay away, so he wouldn't come round and get cheesy..."

While Running Away

The unfinished sentences were actually a sign of his edginess. Nevin sympathetically said:

"You'll relax after two glasses!"

"It's only two glasses anyway. Otherwise, it'll be too much."

Nevin understood what he meant because she knew what it meant to live on the run.

"So, what's up? Serap's friend's efforts didn't work either. What are you going to do?"

"That's why I wanted to meet you."

He paused. Nevin was curiously waiting for Emin to follow his sentence.

"Actually, it's kind of..."

Seeing the approaching waiter, he paused for a moment.

"I'll tell you in a minute. My raki is coming; let me have a sip."

Nevin realised from these words that the waiter was coming towards their table, even though her back was turned, and joined the silence.

This time, Nevin answered the waiter's question, "Do you have another order?" as he put the plates and glasses on the table:

"Thank you, no. If it happens, we'll call you."

By putting Emin's behaviour into words, she was warning the waiter. The implication was clear: "Don't bother us unless we call you," that will have worked in the following minutes.

When the waiter left, she put her hand to her mouth, hiding her smile, and said, "God knows, the boy thought we were lovers with problems."

"No, he can't find me suitable for you!" said Emin, taking a big sip of his raki. He soothed the heat in his throat with a drink of water.

"Oh, I see you've learned to compliment women. Being a fugitive has paid off."

"Yes, I've been reading romance novels!"

"Seriously?"

"We couldn't save the country; maybe we can save love!"

Nevin couldn't tell whether Emin was being sarcastic or not. She had sometimes seen him make fun of people, even himself, all while succeeding in maintaining a poker-faced appearance. He also had a side that didn't shy away from self-criticism. She phrased her question differently:

"So, what are you reading these days?"

Seeing Nevin was taking his words seriously, Emin stopped his playful tone.

"I'm just having a laugh; don't take it seriously! Yeah, what was I saying? Oh, well, this is a somewhat farewell meeting."

Her curiosity led Nevin to another question:

"What's up, where are you going?"

"To abroad."

"Where to?"

Nevin's question, posed in astonishment, was a bit of time-buying inquiry. The unexpected answer, "To abroad," had struck her. She remembered Emin's prior stance, "Going abroad can only be on the agenda when all remedies are exhausted." It wasn't merely a political stance but, in the meantime, was a reaction to a significant event.

When Emin served as the editor-in-chief of the Association's newspaper before taking the same role at the Party's newspaper, he had spoken to Ferman about the lawsuits filed against him and discussed arranging a passport. Ferman had cut him off with his condescending reply:

"It's not feasible for every person in trouble to go abroad. We should take Kivilcimli as an example. He didn't go abroad until the last time he was ill. Despite facing numerous troubles and enduring suffering in jail, Kivilcimli persisted."

Even later, when more risky lawsuits were filed during his tenure as Editor-in-Chief of the Parti newspaper, Emin would not raise this issue again.

As Nevin fell silent, Emin felt the need to remind her of an old story regarding the passport issue:

"After my release from Bursa prison, the same man would commend me, saying, 'You are petite, but you stood up to the police during torture. Well done, I can't do it at my age,' patting me on the head like a child. Peculiarly, we have only a five- or six-year age difference. He had conveniently forgotten how he treated me like a coward when I spoke to him about obtaining a passport."

Nevin was surprised as she recalled this incident and Emin's reaction. The question she had posed to Emin during their conversation that day resurfaced in her mind. She had said:

"I think your desire to go abroad is partly motivated by the desire to be with Nazli."

His reply had shown no hypocrisy at that time. They have always been sincere with each other. Because of this, their friendship has not lost its warmth despite all the political differences. Nevin was about to ask the same question again, this time with a slight twist:

"Did the hope of seeing Nazli play a role in this decision?"

Nazli! Actually, her full first name was Nazligül. Despite this, her family and former friends always called her Gül, except Emin. When she entered their circle, others called her Nazligül, but Nevin, like Emin, preferred to call her Nazli.

Nazli had been living as an au pair with a family in Paris when Emin had expressed his wish to obtain a passport for him. She saw this as a solution to stay away from Emin besides improving her French. Then she came back. When the junta years came, this time with her husband and child, she would be on her way to Paris again.

"Do you remember you once asked me the same question years ago?"

"That's why I asked, to be frank, because I remembered it!"

"Is everything the same now? I've divorced my wife while she's still married. That's one aspect. Moreover, she's in Paris, whereas I'm not heading to France!"

"And where will you go? Germany?"

Continental Europe, especially Germany, was the destination for most who fled Turkey. In addition to the ease of transport, the thought of reaching a large mass of workers, having an acquaintance or relative, and the chance of moving easefully between countries were the reasons for this preference. Naturally, Germany was the first country that generally would come to mind, but Emin had a different destination in mind.

"To England."

"That's not so important; travelling from one country to another shouldn't be that difficult once you're in Europe. And the marriage is an excuse? You know, as well as I do, their marriage is hanging by a thread. You even told me about it."

"Yes, I told you, but haven't you forgotten something?"

"Like what?"

"Lopukhov,[26] would you remember?"

---

[26] Lopukhov: One of the protagonists in Nikolai Chernyshevsky's novel "What is to be done?"

"That's in novels. Novels may be taken from life, but life cannot be copied from novels."

"That novel, 'What is to be done', for me, existed as a style of relationship beyond being a novel. That's why, at the time, I said it was the first novel I read while underlining some parts, but it was also a novel that underlined my life."

"I do remember, but I think you're exaggerating."

* * *

[Flashforward - February 1995:
After locking his bicycle, he was slowly climbing the stairs, repeating the words "You'll climb these stairs slowly as if there's shit up there," inspired by Ahmet Haşim's poem. When he entered the upstairs room of 666 Players, Uğur put down the book in his hand.

"Oh, here you are, you're honoured. Belkis, look who's here?"

Belkis, who looked up from the glasses she was washing, had already asked her question before she turned her head towards the door:

"Who?

"I haven't met her yet," Emin had answered the question before her.

Belkis confirmed Emin's words, while asking with exaggerated politeness in tone of her voice:

"Yes, I don't know him either, but welcome. Would you like tea or coffee?"

After placing the coffee cups on the counter next to the sink, Belkis rubbed her wet hands on the sides of her trousers several times.

"No, I won't drink anything; the bitter test on my mouth is like poison. I think the number of coffees I drank from nine o'clock last night until the morning is more than the number of coffees I've drunk in my entire life in England," he said, placing himself on the chair at the opposite end of the table where Uğur was sitting and placing the book bag in his hand on the table.

While Uğur took the books out of the bag that Emin brought, Belkis placed the coffee cups on the table and asked:

"Are you sure you don't want anything?"

"He's sure, Emin... Emin! Like his name. You really don't know Emin Hodja?"[27] Uğur had intervened, playing with the word "emin," which means "sure" in Turkish but is also a name for men.

"No, it's the first time I've seen him," Belkis replied.

"Ignore this 'hodja' bit. Don't follow Uğur's footsteps."

Emin maintained a formal demeanour as he shook Belkis's hand.

Uğur intervened again.

"Belkis has just joined us. She's very young but very talented. What have you been doing? Are the exams over?"

"It's over, it's over. I took the last one this morning. Now I can fulfil my promise to you."

"Actually, if you'd been in the play, I had offered you in the first place, but you missed. It would have been the perfect role for you."

"That's in the past now. I had already explained my situation. Let's move forward from here. What did you do with your accounts? Did you get them sorted out?"

---

[27] In the meaning of " scholar ", the leftists commonly add Hodja to the person's name when they address the person on their horizon, in the meaning of "scholar".

"Oh, no. It's good that you came. I will apply for funding for a new play, but the funders want me to prepare a budget and send financial reports. You can give me a hand with this."

"OK, no problem. But I can't do anything today. I'm too tired. I didn't sleep at all last night in preparation for today's exam. On my way back from the bookstore, I thought, 'It's on my way,' so I stopped by. I'll come back tomorrow."

"Where did you get the books?"

"From the bookshop of the Halkevi. The four-year self-prohibition ended today. I didn't read books in Turkish all this time, and now I'm going to make up for it."

One of the books Uğur leafed through caught his attention.

"There's also the novel of Chernyshevsky, 'What Is to Be Done!'"

"Yeah, yeah. I've read it twice before. First, twenty years ago, and almost ten years ago at the latest. But I want to reread it."

"Why?"

"I believe I will have read it with a different perspective this time, especially after all the accumulated experiences. I also believe it has gained more meaning after all that has happened, especially after the collapse of the socialist system."

"In what sense?"

"It is a complicated subject, but let me try to explain it through the book's title. The publishers translated the book's title as 'How to Do It?' in Turkey so as not to confuse it with Lenin's 'What is to be done?' In my opinion, the title of the Turkish translation is actually good, although not accurate. It really tells 'How to do it.' The contents naturally tell us how not to do it! From this point of view, an answer can be drawn to the demoralisation after the collapse of socialism by saying, 'Wait a minute, look at how we should do it. The alternative is actually in this book. Hikmet Kivilcimli obliviously provided the same answer. It is also somehow in the thought of Marx. From these, I could say that both explained the reasons for the collapse of the socialist system, and they consequently pointed out the alternative. Of course, it is my interpretation."

"I'm not interested in these socialist theories any more. Engaging with theatre is enough for me."

"This is your choice, no matter what anyone says! Actually, if you were a filmmaker and not a theatre director, I would suggest, 'Come and adapt this novel for the cinema.' This is something I've dreamed of from the very beginning. I've always said, 'Someone should adapt it for the cinema to reach a wider audience. It seems even more important to me now, but no one seems willing to do it."

"Can't it be a theatre play?"

"It won't have the same effect... but it might be adapted. Do it, Uğur, adapt it to the stage!"

"I've got my hands full. I work my arse off to keep this place afloat. You should adapt it for the stage if you care so much!"

"Me?"

"Yeah. Instead of babbling, sit down and write a play. You're a man with writing skills. Then I'll stage it!"

"Well, I... My writings have so far been about politics."

"It's no big deal. You're interested in theatre; you've read plays."

"Writing is something else."

Uğur turned to Belkis this time:

"These old leftists are like that. They talk a lot and do little."

Ugur had deliberately pushed Emin's buttons.

"Don't be ridiculous, Uğur. It's a field I don't know, a job I haven't done before."

"Sit down and work on it, and we'll see if it's all right."

Emin was in a dilemma about whether he could do it or not. Even though he wasn't entirely convinced, he had begun to circle around the question, "Should I try?" while Uğur was leafing through the pages of "How to Do It?"

Emin broke the silence:

"Well, let's do it this way. I'll write a few scenes. We'll sit down and look at them together. If you say, 'It works,' I'll continue. We'll go through and evaluate a few scenes as I complete them. I will consider your criticisms and suggestions and make the necessary amendments."

"There you go, get in line like this!"

"But I have one more condition: You won't tell anyone about it until it's over. It stays between us."

"OK, but you cannot wait for it to the end. We need to make a very extensive advertisement. When we say, 'OK, this is happening,' we announce it. No need to wait for you to finish. You got me excited, too!"

"Will I get a part?"

Belkis asked with the flirtatious behaviour that Emin would observe frequently later on.

Uğur winked at his new favourite with his answer:

"It'll come off. Maybe the lead role!"

"All right, then. I'll come back tomorrow and start tidying up your accounts. While doing that, I'll read and finish the book, then after start writing."

"Why do you need to read fully? Read a few chapters, then write the scenes."

"No, let me read it first. While reading it, I'll think of how those parts can be staged, but I shouldn't start writing before reading the whole novel."

"It's up to you, but don't give up once you've read it."

"Would I do such a thing? If I said I would try, it means I would try. I told you, it was the first novel I read by underlining some parts. The novel also underlined my life at times. It is also important for me in this respect."

He did not tell what experiences caused him to say these. The memories that would surface with "How to Do It?" would open a breach through which Nazli and the memories with her would seep through in the wall of "Finished" that he thought he had built and done!"]

* * *

Emin, disturbed by Nevin's words, "I think you are exaggerating", tried to explain the reasons for his statement, which he would repeat about six years later, "This novel underlined my life":

"No, I don't think I am exaggerating. I am inspired by that novel in my continuous inquiries into the past, including our own, and the ongoing search for answers. There are important clues about how social life should be organised. The issue of women, for example. Forget others, we... On the one hand, it discusses 'giving priority to women first' in the Party program; on the other hand, it contradicts this commitment in practice... Moreover..."

He paused for a moment. Nevin was curious: "And what?"

"Let me start with myself! While I became a Party professional, Hüsniye had a job and looked after me. Naturally, I, who had more opportunities to read and write, improved myself in theory. The opportunity to devote more time to the Party work created the opportunity to improve myself in practice as well. Hüsniye, on the other hand, worked and earned money to look after me. How was she going to improve herself? Or did she have the opportunity to improve herself as much as I did? No! The result? I progressed more... Put a big exclamation mark next to this word... even put it in quotation marks... yes, as a more "progressed(!)" member, I took part in the Party management, which was in accord with the Party constitution, but Hüsniye remained at a lower stage. Was this a phenomenon peculiar to me? With one or two exceptions, this was the general situation in the Party. Apart from the kind of careerism this led to, it was also against the principle of "putting women first". But we justified ourselves by calling it "objective conditions". Inevitably, it was "male culture" that dominated the whole left, not only our Party, as the other leftist organisations were no more different than us. Honestly, it's more accurate to say that we were no different from the others despite our claims to the contrary. The policies produced by such organisations would also be in accord with the character of those organisations. What was left to you, the women, was to accept the practice of patriarchy. Even if they took high positions in the Party! Look at some of the women who have climbed to the top. For example, Rüya."

"I told you last time, I don't know her."

"I know, but I've mentioned her name before concerning an incident. The broader point is that women like her have also become 'more manly than men'. We have seen it firsthand. Even when the issue of women's liberation was directly on the agenda. Haven't our Serap for years demonstrated an example of submission to male domination, even though she was aware of the reactionary nature of patriarchy, even though she was aware of the importance of challenging it?"

"It's precisely because of what you've said; it seems wrong for you to go abroad."

"I won't give up these ideas when I go abroad! Am I?"

"I didn't mean that. You are an inquisitorial person; you are questioning all of these, including your own actions. Another one is Hasan. I believe that the two of you can put your heads together and bring a new approach. I have met people from many different circles. Still, I have never come across anyone other than the two of you who questions by trying to get to the bottom of things, who does not try to make excuses, who does not avoid questioning even if the subject is himself or the movement he is in."

"I think that's a misconception. Why don't you question it all, not just as a woman but also as a socialist? Besides, this should be an advantage. Besides, I honestly don't know what we can do when we put our heads together. Hasan is questioning different aspects."

"I know, but it is important that he, as a Kurd, takes a questioning attitude about the PKK while you have been staying away from questioning."

"It's complicated."

"What do you mean?"

"Even though there is Kurdishness on one side of my family—on my father's side, connected to someone who was even a minister in Demirel's cabinet, someone who was Kurdish even though he denied it—in the end, I am known as a Turk. Beyond the issue of Kurdishness and Turkishness, we don't live in Kurdistan. Taking this into consideration, after reading Kivilcimli's work, I will, of course, say to myself, 'Know your place!'. Since Hasan is Haso[28] Kurdish, he is a bit more immune in that regard as opposed to the fact that my hands are more tidied. And to tell you the truth, I am confused about Hasan's approach to the Kurdish question."

"What? "What is there to be confused about? Shouldn't the PKK's behaviour towards other movements be condemned?"

"These are aspects where my knowledge is insufficient. I need to understand the subject before I can say whether it's right or wrong. It would be best if you talked to Hasan about these things; he knows much better. I contemplate the issue in terms of principle. There are Party decisions under which I have my signature. For example, we state that 'Kurdistan is a colony'; a decision was made in the Central Committee that we should stop organising in Kurdistan. We stated that 'the people in Kurdistan should set up their own independent organisations.' So, are we now going to stand up and say, 'We don't like that party, we want this party, we don't like that method of struggle, and they should apply this method'? Wouldn't it contradict the principle of accepting and recognising the independence of the Kurdish organisation and the struggle of the people of Kurdistan? I participated in the decisions taken by the Party at that time, agreeing with

---

[28] The writer, again, uses a double entendre. Haso is short of Hasan as a name but also means purely. [i.e., Purely Kurdish]

and believing in them. Today, I still think those decisions were right. After all, the people of Kurdistan are in a state of self-defence."

"Didn't Hasan support those decisions?"

"He and his faction weren't in the Party then. Their group had left before those decisions. In short, they were not part of those discussions. But that's not the point. When I say, 'we are questioning different things,' what I am trying to explain is different. There is no such thing as taking up certain issues, examining them together, reaching mutual conclusions, and coming up with shared theses. Therefore, there is no such duality as you think. Moreover, there are other serious differences of opinion between us. I have been clearly stating since 1978 that the Soviet Union was not a 'socialist' country. My view, presented in writing during the "[Extraordinary General] Organization Meetings," was not discussed properly. You know, this article did not even appear in court as evidence. Other peoples' writings were there, but most of mine were not, including this one, which, as far as I am concerned, is the most important one. I don't know if the Party Presidium destroyed it. Because they thought it was dangerous or if they destroyed it because someone's career was threatened by it. In the end, it was thrown out of the archive. What would have happened if it had been preserved? That article didn't resonate among our friends, so why should it resonate among those outside our circle? If someone were to come out and say, 'It is a wrong opinion,' the discussion would deepen, but there is no response. Hasan's attitude is no different. He thinks that it should not be brought up. 'It is a socialist country after all,' he cuts it off; he does not discuss it. As you can see, we also have important differences."

"Does that prevent you from working together? Wouldn't it be better for you to be here to discuss these things?"

"Don't misunderstand. I am not trying to justify my decision to go... In short... there is no such thing as doing joint work and developing some theses. Everyone should make an effort wherever they are. You can, as well. Serap too. Whoever has a question mark in their mind, no matter the subject, let them try to delve deeper into that problem or the problems. And, as I said, don't overestimate Hasan and me."

"Still, it would be different if you stayed here."

"I don't know how different it would be. Besides, if I stayed, how would I make a living? There is nothing I can do while I live as a fugitive."

"Do you have to work? Can't we look after one person? I'll support you. Serap will support. Hasan will support too. Why do you have a problem with that?"

"Well, that's against me. And let's assume for a moment that I agree. For how long? Your court case is ongoing; you could unexpectedly be in the same situation as me. Are the others different? Yes, their files are segregated for now, but they might be exposed unexpectedly at any moment. What will happen then? It's not just a matter of principle; it has no equivalent in practice. I'm speaking, sparing no words, trusting that you won't misunderstand. It's not a matter of not trusting you all. You know, there are times when I say to myself, 'Look, if I had been an auto mechanic, I would have found a job anyway; did studying at the university help anything?' but what's done is done."

"I think you're exaggerating again. Go and see your Nazli!"

"Yes, that's exactly the point!"

Nevin caught a hint of resentment on Emin's face as he tilted his head slightly to the right and shook it.

"Don't be touchy; I'm just messing with you."

"Anyway... You've finished your drink; shall we order another one?"

"Let's order it; who knows when we'll sit like this again?"

Emin caught the maternal tone that naturally settled into Nevin's voice. It was a rare talent, more commonly found in women in contrast to men, to win hearts with the colour they infused into their voices, even when uttering ordinary sentences.

As soon as the waiter took Emin's cue by raising his empty glass, he got moving. Since the evening crowd hadn't started yet, it wasn't two minutes later that their second double was on their table. "What a love you guys had..." Nevin said, returning to the subject of Nazli. Emin went back to the old days, partly because of the comfort of the drink, partly because he was glad that the topic of "whether to go or not" was over, but mostly because he liked to reminisce about Nazli. Where the memories were in common, one would take the floor from the other and complete the story. Emin felt the need to interrupt the prolonged conversation when he noticed the darkening sadness in Nevin's eyes:

"We could go on till morning, but I think we'd better get up."

They called the waiter. No matter what Emin said, Nevin wouldn't let him pay the bill, so she covered it.

When the night that had just begun for others ended for them, they were walking arm in arm, mingling with the crowd on Istiklal Avenue[29]. Anyone who saw them might think they

---

[29] The street in the European side of Istanbul starts at the northern end of Galata (the medieval Genoese quarter) at Tunnel Square and runs as far as Taksim Square

were lovers. They also wanted the police to think so if they saw them. Emin had experienced a similar but much riskier situation with another friend some years ago.

In the meantime, Emin was thinking,

"I wish I had Nazligül on my arm right now!"

* * *

The night he had a similar experience with another friend, the Association that Emin was the Secretary-General had decided to organise two events together. Firstly, a seminar on Kivilcimli's "History Thesis" was to be held and then, at midnight, they were going to do a poster campaign around Beşiktaş[30]. It had been decided that Emin would give this seminar since it was known that he had participated in the editing of the book titled "Substance of Ottoman History" while studying Kivilcimli's book "History Thesis" intensively.

The meeting room of the Beşiktaş branch of the Association, which could accommodate thirty to forty people, was almost filled up before the seminar started.

After an introduction stating that "As Kivilcimli notes, based on Morgan's discoveries, Engels worked on pre-written history and with his work 'The Origin of the Family, Private Property and the State' he entered a field that Marx had not been able to cover in his lifetime, 'as if fulfilling a will'"; explaining that the term "barbarian" is used in a non-pejorative sense, with quotations from both Engels and Kivilcimli, Emin summarised the distinction between Historical Revolution and Social Revolution and continued:

"Friends, instead of providing an extensive quote from Kivilcimli, I've prepared a summary. I encourage you to refer to Kivilcimli's books for a more in-depth understanding of

---

[30] Beşiktaş is a district and municipality of Istanbul.

this topic. In this seminar, I want to highlight that Kivilcimli's 'History Thesis' aligns with Marx's scientific explanations of how the era of social revolution emerges, as articulated by Marx in the 'Preface to A Contribution to the Critique of Political Economy.' Essentially, Kivilcimli is not presenting ideas contradictory to Marx; instead, he elucidates how the sociological law described by Marx operates in the epoch of historical revolutions.

"At this point, I would like to touch upon how the revolutions, which Kivilcimli defines as 'Historical Revolutions', occurred and what kind of developments these revolutions led to. Although they are caused by the same reasons, revolutions in an environment where social decay is at an extreme level do not always lead to the same results.

"Kivilcimli encapsulates this differentiation under the title 'Two Kinds of Historical Revolutions.' A comprehensive understanding of the details can be gained by reading the entirety of the 'History Thesis.' While he addresses this matter not only in this work but also in others, I want to emphasise that it is under this title that he succinctly elucidates the operational rules of 'Historical Revolutions,' serving as the focal point of the subject."

Emin had filled a large, thick, A5-sized notebook with the notes he took while working on the "History Thesis." Unbeknownst to him then, the ideas he expressed and emphasised during these studies, both in this seminar and later, would become the foundation for the essays he wrote while studying at the university in London in his first year in 1991-92. These ideas gradually led him towards communalism.

* * *

[Flashforward - 1996 and 2013:

"Yes, I think it is precisely from this point, from this distinction we should start. Why were the barbarians in the upper stage of barbarism able to establish a new civilisation, but the others, those at the lower or middle stage, were not able to do so? Why were they surrendered to the old civilisation and couldn't go beyond its renaissance? The answer to this question is indeed mind-opening. Before, when we were working in the Party, we didn't see that answer; we couldn't see that. The society at the upper stage of barbarism, as Dr Kivilcimli puts it, is pregnant with new productive forces. Not nomadic societies, such as those in the lower or middle stage of barbarism. They are highly technical, have a division of labour, and have the appropriate culture and superstructure. They have the yeast to build a new civilisation. The barbarians at the middle and lower stages lack these. They are destroying a civilisation that has reached the stage of collapse and dissolution; however, they do not know what to replace it with. They inevitably adopt both the economic base and the superstructure institutions and rules of the civilisation they have destroyed. This is what happened with the Soviets. It was a renaissance of the old system. A renaissance not only in Russia but on a world scale. Capitalism, in a way, was being forced into a worldwide renaissance by the revolution in Russia. The so-called 'social state' is the result of this. There were also tools for this. Especially the communist parties in Europe and the Second International. But the most important point is that in Russia, there was no infrastructure and superstructure of a new society to build a new civilisation. In the so-called socialist countries, the state was transferred from one hand to another. Those who say that they aim to extinguish the state like a candle provided mind-boggling examples of state tyranny. Why did this happen? Blame Stalin and get it over with! A complete fallacy. Moreover, it is a fallacy that prevents getting to the root of the problem. What is the main issue? It is necessary to go to the roots of social changes. Capitalism was born and developed in the society that preceded it. A new society can only be conceived and developed in the womb of the old society and would be born. It completes its 'nine months' by building its sub-structure, base, and superstructure. We are actually witnessing what Dr Kivilcimli has said in his studies on historical revolutions, which also occurred in the modern age."

"In other words, if capitalism were to develop, it would give birth to its revolutionary forces. Society will progress, capitalism will evolve, and the revolution will occur! Your thesis can be described as a theory of development that even echoes Kautsky's theory."

Upon Aydın's objection, Emin became tense. In a conversation they had before Emin ran away, he was trying to explain that he had developed the thoughts based on Kivilcimli's History Thesis, which had not yet settled at the time. Now, he was attempting to elucidate the foundation of these thoughts. In fact, he was a bit excited about this. He raised his voice without realising it:

"Our labelling is ready, just like our parroting!"

"Shh, calm down. You're not at a rally. There's no need to attract people's attention."

Emin lowered his voice with this warning, silently agreeing with Aydın.

"I'm sorry. It's a habit that comes from the comfort of speaking without worrying about the surrounding environment in Europe."

Emin had lowered his voice, but he didn't back down:

"For God's sake, Aydın, isn't condemning an idea rather than trying to understand it one of the reasons for our unsolved problems? Try to listen and see what I'm trying to say!"

"OK, tell me. But hold on a second, let's order some bread. We're about to run out of cheese; should we order more?"

"That'd be good."

Emin completed the order to the waiter, who came at Aydın's signal:

"Don't toast the bread if it's fresh! The bread is fresh, isn't it?"

"Yes, Abi, it's fresh. As you like!"

"Actually, you know what I miss the most? I mean, one of them... Fresh bread. You can't find the same quality in London. And fatty, soft feta cheese. Not even that! Spread it like butter on the fresh bread, and have a tomato on the side. Cut the tomato in half and bite into it like an apple! Neither the bread nor the fatty, soft cheese can be found, neither the tomatoes. You know that smell of a tomato: there is nothing like it available over there. All are genetically modified. If you try to buy organic ones, you may find them, but they are expensive."

"In fact, you can't find organic tomatoes everywhere here either. Genetically modified vegetables and fruits have become widespread."

"Even the smell is different!"

Emin sniffed the corner of the freshly arrived slice of bread and then attempted to place slices of feta cheese between them. Seeing that Aydın was watching him intently, he felt the need to explain:

"Now, this is how you savour it."

"Shall we order whole tomatoes? They sliced these."

"Nah, no need to exaggerate. It's fine."

"Well, go on, then. Since you objected, I'm removing the political labels, so then you tell me."

"What?"

Emin, immersed in the pleasure of the bite of bread he took from the corner, seemed detached from what he was talking about, as if he had entered another world.

"What will it be? The theory of development!"

"It is not a 'theory of development' or anything like that. Let me explain this from the perspective of Chernyshevsky's 'What is to Be Done?' When adapting the novel for the stage, I argued against the 'theory of development,' contrary to what you say. I stated that 'tomorrow is built from today; those who submit to today trap tomorrow in today.' The main thing is for society to be organised on a communal basis and for everything, from its economy to its culture, to be fermented within the existing order. That is what genuine social revolution is!"

"It's called evolution, not revolution."

"Let's conclude from this that I'm a 'reformist,' would you?"

"You, yourself, said it; I didn't!" Aydın said and laughed.

"Evolution is a revolution itself, and what you called

'devrim' is not a 'devrim' but, it's 'dev-i-rim'. Put a big 'I' between V and R."

Emin was playing with the Turkish word "devrim", [which means "revolution" in English] by separating the first syllable and the second syllable and placing the letter "i" between them, creating another Turkish word 'devirim,' [which means in English, overthrow]. So, for him, what others call "revolution" is not, in reality, a revolution, in the sense of a social revolution, but overthrowing the government.

"I don't quite understand what you're saying, but answer this question first. Let's say you develop Dr Kivilcimli's thesis further. Apply it to our age rather than limiting it to the prehistory period before the Sumers in Mesopotamia. By doing this, you've found explanations for the Soviets, their collapse, and so on. But the author of the thesis, Dr Kivilcimli himself, says nothing of the kind. He describes the occurrence of such revolutions only in prehistory, the barbarian raids, etc. So why?"

"What, why?"

"I mean, why didn't Dr Kivilcimli come up with an interpretation and approach like yours? After all, it's his own thesis!"

"Why couldn't Dr Kivilcimli do that? Honestly, I don't have an answer to that. Yes, I thought about it, and I questioned this too. I can't come up with an explanation. The defence of the 'Socialist Homeland' against imperialism... The concept of 'Socialist Homeland' is also problematic... The moral authority of the Soviet Revolution, its dazzling effect... These factors exist. We cannot deny them. But the truth is, these explanations do not satisfy me either."

Years later, at the end of his essay presented at the Kivilcimli Symposium, entitled "CONTRAVENTION: DR HİKMET KIVILCIMLI AND COMMUNALISM," he would try to answer Aydın's legitimate question:

"1) The yoke of the Marxist-Leninist paradigm in which he is entrenched;

"2) Diving into the vortex of 'daily politics' on the ground imposed by the ruling classes within the limits of the Marxist-Leninist, and the more you dive into it, the more suffocating the chains of that paradigm become;

"3) Defending the 'socialist Homeland' and the 'proletarian revolution' in the face of imperialist aggression;

"4) Not being able to witness events such as Emma Goldman and Alexander Berkman on the spot, which would have given him a chance to get rid of the material and moral burden of these events,

"They were obstacles in the way of Dr Hikmet Kivilcimli bringing his thesis to its logical conclusions and arriving at the Communalist perspective.

"I also cannot help but ask: When Kivilcimli described Darwin in The Power of the Commune, could he also be describing himself? He says, 'Darwin's great error was in the strength of his discovery; he was too carried away by his findings. The human brain is like that: the more it fills up with the laws it mobilises, the more difficult it becomes to open up to other syntheses. Therefore, the only solution is to consider life as a whole, to carry its richness in the brain, and to keep it alive and develop it.'

"What would you say to my recommendation to consider Kivilcimli's statement about Darwin in conjunction with the abovementioned points, especially those in the second and fourth points?"

Emin would formulate these thoughts, documented in 2013, over the years. However, on that day, as he openly shared his dilemma on this matter with Aydın, he also raised his own question:

"Let's say Dr Kivilcimli did not, or could not, carry his thesis to its logical conclusions... For one reason or another. Well, shall we say, 'If Dr Kivilcimli couldn't see it, who are we to dare to do things even he didn't do?' The question is: Would the reasons for the difference between the two kinds of historical revolutions explain what is happening today or not? If they do, should we refrain from taking the History Thesis to its logical conclusions simply because the Doctor did not explicitly state them? Moreover, doesn't this explanation provide clues on what needs to be done and how to do it?

Aydın concluded the discussion with a silent gesture, stretching his arms wide to convey a sense of "I don't know."

Both of them had fallen silent!

* * *

There was not a sound in the hall. As Emin once again emphasised the differences between the 'two kinds of historical revolutions' and the reasons for them, there was a knock on the outer door. After a whispered conversation between the person who answered the door and those who came in, the person who opened the outer door came back to the hall's door and called for Saim with a hand gesture. Saim left the hall. People were chatting quietly in the kitchen, and when the noise of the cupboard doors opening and closing died down, Saim, Ali Atmaca, and a friend from Bitlis[31] took their seats in the hall."

Although Emin found it strange that Ali Atmaca, who was not a member of this branch and whom he had not seen participating in such activities anywhere else, attended the meeting, Emin continued with his seminar.

"Friends, if you look at the mechanism of functioning here, according to Kivilcimli, such civilisations were destroyed at a stage when they were under the complete sway of super-exploitative usury-merchant capital and despotic states. No longer serving the further development of productive forces, the civilisations prime for destruction lacked the internal revolutionary dynamism/collective action capable of reversing the decay of civilisation. At this point, I'd like to quote what Marx says. But if you like, let's take a tea break. Then we would continue."

He wanted to break the stagnation caused by reading quotations, but the real purpose of the pause was to understand what was going on.

He got up where he was sitting near the door and quickly went to the kitchen. He prepared two cups of tea and then walked to the outer door. He nodded to Sami, saying, "I've got tea for you, too," and stepped out of the line where participants were waiting for tea.

When he went to the outer door, he told Sami, who approached him, "Close the door so that we can't be heard." Sami closed the door and accepted the teacup from Emin.

"What's going on? What's all the hustle and bustle?"

"Ali had brought two 'machines.'[32] for security."

---

[31] Bitlis is a Kurdish city in Kurdistan, -Southeastern Turkey-.
[32] 'Machine' was a reference to a handgun. University youth were using such jargon for the sake of secrecy.

He had heard that Ali sometimes carried a gun, usually when they thought there would be trouble at the university, but up until that point, they had never taken such a precaution for any demonstration until that moment. Moreover, it was not a decision that Ali, who had nothing to do with this branch, would have taken on his own. He asked:

"Who asked Ali to do this?"

"I don't know. I didn't ask. I'll get him, and you can ask him."

"No, leave it; now we are out of the door. If we call Ali, it will attract attention. We'll talk about it after the seminar."

They went inside.

When everyone had taken their seats, Emin continued his speech by reading the quotation that he had mentioned before the interval from the notes he had taken from "The Preface 'A Contribution to a Critique of Political Economy' of Marx:

"In the social production of their existence, men inevitably enter into definite relations, which are independent of their will, namely relations of production appropriate to a given stage in the development of their material forces of production. The totality of these relations of production constitutes the economic structure of society, the real foundation on which a legal and political superstructure arises and to which correspond definite forms of social consciousness. The mode of production of material life conditions the general process of social, political and intellectual life. It is not the consciousness of men that determines their existence, but their social existence that determines their consciousness. At a certain stage of development, the material productive forces of society come into conflict with the existing relations of production or – this merely expresses the same thing in legal terms – with the property relations within the framework of which they have operated hitherto. From forms of development of the productive forces, these relations turn into their fetters. Then begins an era of social revolution.

"No social order is ever destroyed before all the productive forces for which it is sufficient to have been developed, and new superior relations of production never replace older ones before the material conditions for their existence have matured within the framework of the old society."

He completed reading his notes and looked at the room from the corner of his eye. Convinced that everyone was attentively listening to him, he continued:

"I had quoted Kivilcimli's words at the beginning. Marx did not have enough time to analyse prehistory, and his emphasis was on social revolutions. Even though this is so, the development process of the social revolution that Marx refers to here and Kivilcimli's process of historical revolutions point to the same phenomenon. Kivilcimli's definition of 'the productive forces stifled, stagnated, and retarded by the old relations of production' and Marx's statement, 'These relations, which are the forms of the development of the productive forces, become their obstacles' confirm each other.' Those who cannot go beyond repeating Marx's words like parrots cannot see the step Kivilcimli took in enhancing the teaching of Marx; they cannot realise that he was a real follower of Marx. Parrots recite; they can and only repeat what is already said. It is necessary to try to understand what one reads, to think about it, to relate it to life, and to try to see its connection with life. We can also call it understanding what you read and making sense of what you understand. I don't want to go into more detail, so I won't prolong it, but there is one more thing I would like to mention in brief that is closely related to the subject."

He paused for a moment. He would as well not have done it. Should he have told what he had to say without attacking the TKP? As some of his friends put it, his contrariness, his 'sectarianism,' became more apparent in such situations. The presence of Sule, who was rumoured to be leaning towards the TKP under the influence of some of her family members and who was said to be 'actually hiding it, but probably a TKP member.' This especially provoked Emin. Although he hadn't heard a single word from Sule to make him feel this way, this possibility was another reason for sticking to the plan he had in mind for the seminar. He had to say what he wanted to express. In fact, it was a behaviour that partly stemmed from the fact that he trusted his friends would tolerate his attitude, even though, as he sometimes admitted himself, it could be called "wilfulness." He decided to stick to his plan and continued his speech from where he had left off:

"Those who fail to grasp Kivilcimli's ideas, such as Sefik Hüsnü, with his nonsensical comment, 'Is the doctor slipping into racism and fascism?' not only demonstrate a lack of understanding of Kivilcimli but also of Engels. They might not have thoroughly read Engels, particularly 'The Origin of the Family, Private Property, and the State.' That's highly possible. While elucidating the development of history in his 'History Thesis,' he did not idealise the Turks. Instead, Turks are depicted as barbarians who have not progressed to the stage of class society and who adhere to the customs of primitive socialism. The primary actors in the rise and fall of pre-capitalist civilisations were barbarians, characterised by egalitarian and communal customs, traditions, and the relations of production of 'primitive socialism.' Turks, along with others such as Vikings, Huns, Goths, Vandals, and Mongolians, belonged to these barbarians. Their actions were attributed to their barbarian nature, not their distinct ethnic identity (Turks, Vikings, Goths, etc.). All barbarian tribes share similar characteristics regarding primitive socialist values, relationships, and the capacity for robust collective action among the ruled.

Kivilcimli explains how the collective action of barbarians, or, in other words, these barbarian qualities, played a role in the initial transition to capitalism in England. He argues that similar phenomena can be observed when examining the Vikings in the north, the Mongols, and other barbarian tribes elsewhere. In summary, Kivilcimli's 'History Thesis,' contrary to what Sefik Hüsnü and the demagogues of the TKP claim, provides us with a powerful ideological weapon to combat both fascism and racism."

He fell silent again for a moment. He deemed it sufficient to conclude with such an emphasis what he had initially intended to explain with a more comprehensive introduction. His mind was preoccupied with "unexpected guests", which had also made him cut his seminar short. He was entirely uneasy about the gun issue.

"Let me leave the floor to friends who have something to add, who have questions, who have comments."

As soon as the meeting, which lasted for another half an hour, was over, he went to Ali.

"Will you come outside?"

Ali followed him with that bully's gait. When they were outside the door, Emin climbed up the stairs. He stopped on the steps in the middle of the two floors and asked in a low voice:

"What's this gun story? what's this all about?"

"Hodja, you know things are crazy. For security reasons. They told me from the Association."

Ali meant the headquarters of the Association. Still confused, Emin pressed on:

"Well, I was there during the day. No one said anything to me. Moreover, we have a clear stance to keep the Association away from such things and not to get involved in such things."

"Well, I did what I was told."

Emin remembered that he had not seen Ferman at the association centre in Laleli that day. "It was probably him if he came after I left," he thought. He didn't press Ali, but he had made up his mind.

"No need for that. Just take the machines back."

"At this time, getting in and out of my dorm is under strict control. How am I supposed to take the machines there?"

"Where were you going to take them after the posterisation?

"I won't go to the dormitory. If everything goes as planned, I'll stay at the house in Ortaköy."[33]

"Take them to the house in Ortaköy, then. We've already arranged our poster-hanging plans, so we don't need your help."

"What if something goes wrong, and anyone gets caught during the poster hangings? Sami and a few others are staying in that house. If any of our friends get caught, wouldn't they reveal the address?"

Emin had called him a "punk" or something like that, but he realised that Ali had a better judgment on these matters than he did. Ali was right, actually. The house in Cihangir wouldn't be the right place either. The situation of the house

---

[33] Ortakoy is a neighbourhood in the municipality and district of Beşiktaş, Istanbul Province.

in Cihangir was not different from the one in Ortaköy. But Emin couldn't think of another safe place to take the guns.

When he saw Sule among those who were leaving the room, he had an idea and decided to try what crossed his mind:

"Sule, can you wait for me for a while. I need to talk to you about something."

When Sule said "OK" and went back inside, she turned to Ali:

"Let me talk to Sule; maybe I can find a solution, but can you join the poster-hanging team to replace me?"

"Yes, of course."

"With his response devoid of hesitation, Ali, in a way, seemed to want to create a good impression on me, knowing that I didn't have very positive thoughts about him. The idea of 'embarrassing me' might not have crossed Ali's mind at all, perhaps. Whatever messages he was trying to convey, it's partly my fault. I've consistently held negative opinions about him, and I should refrain from passing judgment."

When Emin returned inside, he found Sule waiting for him. The only individuals remaining in the association office were those who would take part in hanging the posters.

"I'll be right back; can you wait a minute longer?" he said, then headed to the kitchen where Sami and Aydın were chatting while washing glasses.

"Let Ali join the team instead of me. If Sule agrees, I'll take the machines with her and bring them to their house."

After they agreed to the arrangement, he called Sule to the kitchen and explained the situation. Sule's response was as he had anticipated.

For some unknown reason, Sule, living with Mahmut Aykol, seemed to have reservations about Mahmut's friends.

There were even rumours suggesting she had stated, "I'd rather prefer if no one from your circle came to this house!" Although Sule couldn't be labelled as a bourgeois, she was from a relatively wealthy family, and her older sister lived with a TKP member, leading to the belief that Sule might be influenced by them. According to his friends, this was the primary reason for Sule's somewhat distant attitude. Yet, curiously, she held a favourable view of Emin. "You're a son of an army officer; it's a class affinity," Emin's friends had teased him. Contrariwise, Emin believed that the source of tension was not Sule but his friends. They occasionally jokingly expressed concern that Mahmut might succumb to Sule's influence and join the TKP. Some even suggested it would be better for him to part ways with Sule. Emin's stance remained unequivocal:

"Forget it; if they love each other, we should not interfere. That's not right."

Emin believed that showing respect for their relationship made Sule treat him differently. Having once self-criticised for a similar matter, he was determined not to repeat the same mistake. However, when it came to his own life, he often yielded to the interference of his political circle and considered what they might say. He would later realise that this concession created a precedent for his principles to be violated again, with him indirectly contributing by allowing them to interfere in his personal matters. Then, there you go! History was inevitably going to be repeated in other events!

When Sule said, "Let me put one of the guns in my bag," he refused while placing one on his right and one on his left waist. "A cowboy's only a cowboy with two pistols! All kidding aside, if something happens and we get caught, you don't know anything about that. Here is what you're going to say: We'd just recently met, we were coming back from a dinner as if we had a dinner date, and I was taking you back to your home. Don't say anything else."

"OK. Don't worry!"

As the Indian summer night began to turn cold, Sule and Emin walked from Ihlamurdere Avenue to the centre of Beşiktaş. To conceal the bulge of the guns, he didn't fasten the belt of his coat, and he left the scarf that Nazligül had given him draped over his topcoat as an addition to cover the parts where he put the pistols. The scarf... He hadn't used to wear a scarf even during the winter until he got that one from Nazli. Unaware that he would unwittingly repeat a similar act and utter the same sentence in the future, Emin sighed while purposefully walking arm in arm with Sule to create an impression of being 'lovers':

"I wish I had Nazligül on my arm right now?"

* * *

Ihlamurdere Avenue... and Istiklal Avenue... both held memories of warmth from different friends at different times. Yet, in the present moment, right here and right now, he longed for that friendly warmth more than ever. However, on this night, as he inhaled the cold of Strandja[34], he was alone. While he hadn't felt the chill on that Istiklal Avenue night, thanks to the effects of alcohol, tonight, his feet were freezing as he waited at the Bulgarian customs control shack, uncertain of when and how it would end.

He removed his left shoe and pressed his foot against the radiator. There wasn't enough time for his right foot to get its share of warmth. His solitude was interrupted by the arrival

---

[34] Strandja is a mountain massif in Southeastern Bulgaria and East Thrace, the European part of Turkey.

of a customs official who disembarked from the front door of a bus approaching the shack and hurried inside.

"Get in there," the officer commended, pointing to the small booth. This time, it was the other slim, tall one from the passport control line. This officer, whom he had previously thought did not speak Turkish, had spoken Turkish! His two-word speech was ruder and off-putting than the other officer. Emin had already taken a step towards the small booth when the officer ordered him again:

"Take your suitcase!"

As Emin took his suitcase and the biscuits from the table, he went to the booth with a single chair inside. Another officer entered. Amidst the chaos of shouting and screaming, luggage was retrieved from the bus's trunk and handed to passengers who disembarked under the supervision of two other officers outside, forming an orderly queue. One of the officers outside approached the doorway, organising the passengers in pairs. Inside, two other officers stood behind separate benches, observing as passengers opened luggage on the tables and meticulously examined the contents of their luggage.

Emin was surprised by the meticulous search, especially considering that no search had been conducted on the bus he arrived on and even his suitcase had gone unchecked. Suddenly, his attention was drawn to a hundred Turkish Liras lying near the centre of the window in the booth he was in, which lacked glass. The presence of this Turkish currency, which he hadn't noticed upon entering the booth, disturbed him. "What should I do?" Until then, he hadn't given it much thought and hadn't looked around. Now, however, suspicion crept in. Was there a camera in the shack, particularly in the booth? He glanced around, but there was nothing in sight to suggest the presence of a camera.

"If I leave this hundred Turkish Lira banknote where it is, what if they say, 'Did you put it here to bribe me?' If I pick it up and put it in my pocket, what if I'm accused of, 'There was a hundred Lira there; did you steal it?'"

On the one hand, he argued with himself; on the other hand, he thought, "I must be getting paranoid." The saying "Paranoia: A Heightened Sense of Awareness!" came to mind, and he smiled. Taking the banknote of a hundred Turkish Lira, he rolled it in his palms, creating a lump. With his right hand, he placed it between the two combs of the out-of-order heating radiator in the booth, easily reachable without getting up. However, the banknote didn't stay; instead, it fell to the floor and rolled a little. If one of the officers came to the door, they could easily spot the money on the floor. Not wanting to bend down and pick it up, he pondered, "What should I do?" He waited momentarily at the top of the question, finding a solution to retrieve the rolled-up money. Using his right hand, he took out a cigarette packet and matchbox from his jacket pocket, holding the cigarette packet in his left hand. He stood up, feigning the act of retrieving a matchbox from his trouser pocket while sliding his right foot towards the banknote without making contact with the ground. With the outer edge of his foot, he pushed it, and the money rolled near the back corner, out of sight for anyone coming to the door. Relieved, he lit his cigarette and placed the extinguished match in the glassless window frame instead of throwing it on the floor.

Occasionally, he continued to watch the passengers' luggage being searched as they responded to the questions sheepishly. It had been almost two hours since the search started when the search of the last passenger's suitcases was finished. After he took his suitcase and left, the officer who came in last departed. While the other officer looked around, Emin stood in the booth doorway and asked, "Can I come out?"

"OK, get out," the officer's voice was soft this time. Bringing his suitcase and placing it back in its original position between the two desks near the door, Emin couldn't help but ask the officer who was watching him, unable to overcome his curiosity,

"Who are they?"

"People shopping in Turkey and returning to Romania."

The officer hadn't uttered the famous word "neighbour" when he first arrived, nor now; he was speaking without using the term. Emin was starting to believe that "neighbour" was a sign of sincerity, or vice versa, depending on whether the expression would be used in future conversations.

When the officer left, this time Emin sat on the radiator, taking off his shoes. He placed his feet between the radiator fins. Although the outer sides of his feet in contact with the radiator were warm, the inner sides and Emin's thumbs were still cold. However, he couldn't sit any longer due to the hardness of the radiator and the intense heat. This time, he took the radiator in front of him and tried to warm the inside of his right foot by standing on his left foot and vice versa for the other foot.

Feeling tired, he sat on a bench away from the door, close to the small booth. Having warmed up, he began to feel sleepy. Folding his arms from the elbow down, he placed them on the table and laid his head on them to fall asleep. Just as he was about to drift off, he looked up when Emin heard footsteps coming from outside. An officer glanced at him and left without saying anything. Emin's feet were getting cold again.

"Better cold than hot." One discomfort had triggered another!

* * *

His feet were on fire. Sliding toward the middle of the narrow wooden bench adjacent to the wall, where Emin could barely fit in width, he had been lying on his back for five minutes. He leaned his soles against the cold wall by lifting his feet. The walls, carrying the coldness of January, provided relief for his feverish soles, or at least that's how it felt. He found himself in the cell of the police station in the basement of the eight-story building housing the Bursa Police Headquarters. He had been brought there in the evening from the First Branch, also known as the "political police," situated on the seventh floor of the same building. When the uniformed police officers came and called him in a whisper through the iron bars of the cell door, he was startled at first.

"Don't do that; it's not good. You need to walk. It'll improve your blood circulation and keep your feet from getting blocked up with clots."

The policeman said these words not in a scolding manner but with a compassionate softness. Emin lowered his feet and took a sitting position, leaning down with his arms resting on his legs at the elbows, his eyes fixed on the space between the iron bars. The officer also looked where Emin was looking at. Then he took the keys out of his pocket and opened the iron-barred cell door.

"Come and walk with me."

Emin entered the space in front of his cell and started walking up and down with the police.

"Pity. You're so young. These people upstairs are so unfair."

This uniformed policeman was different.

He was not staging a continuation of the good cop-bad cop deception played out in the 'First Branch,' and he was sincere in his compassion.

This was a conclusion Emin drew not only from the words but also from the way he uttered these words and the expression of his face and gaze. Walking up and down with Emin, the policeman said nothing more; he took refuge in the silence of people who were ashamed of something and kept silent.

The "goodness" of those playing "good cop" upstairs was different. Emin had met four of them at the very beginning of his capture.

After a meeting with the new board of directors following the congress at the Mesken[35] Branch of the association, Emin went to his friend's house, where he planned to stay. Due to their lengthy conversation, they went to bed quite late. It was past nine am when Muhammed, his wife Gülizar, and Emin gathered around a small square table in the middle of the living room. Gülizar's semi-paralysed mother lay nearby. They began to have breakfast together. "I'm late, I'm late," Muhammed complained, quickly finishing his breakfast and heading to the post office to send a telegram to the President of the Republic, expressing concern about the torture suffered by the former members of the board of directors, founders of the association's branch, at the hands of the police.

How have all these started?

---

[35] Mesken is a neighbourhood in Bursa, Turkey, with a population mainly comprised of poor residents and factory workers around that time.

Two days before the congress, three founding board members were detained by the political police under the pretext of an armed clash near the association's building. A day later, the court arrested two of them but released one. The friend who had been released struggled to hold the paper as he read the board of directors' report at the congress. His hands were swollen like drums from torture. This was enough to ignite Emin's anger. Although he had already outlined his speech on behalf of the Head Quarter in his mind, he decided to alter the introduction while listening to the report.

His speech began with a lengthy introduction focusing on the subject of torture. The secret police service in Salazar's Portugal had a name he would never forget: "PIDE". It was easy to remember because the flatbread, especially baked during Ramadan, is also called "pide."

"The Movimento das Forças Armadas" (MFA), led by communist army officers, successfully overthrew the fascist regime of Salazar in Portugal on April 24, 1974. In the aftermath, the working masses of Lisbon flooded the streets, singing songs of freedom as soldiers adorned their rifles with carnations. Factories were occupied by workers, and peasants seized control of the lands. When the PIDE centre, known for years of persecuting people with torture, was besieged, the police opened fire. The people stood firm despite casualties, and eventually, the police surrendered. The rebels gained access to archives, torture instruments, and a warehouse of modern weapons. The people turned a movement that began with soldiers 'throwing down their swords' into a full-fledged popular uprising. During the trial of the PIDE policemen, an incident occurred, the details of which were not reported in the newspapers. The people pulled two policemen out of the car in which they had been brought to court and lynched them.

Emin commenced his speech by vehemently protesting against the torture and arrests of his friends. He concluded this part of his speech with the impactful statement, "Torturers will sooner or later end up in the dustbin of history." His speech, lasting for forty-five minutes, would later become the catalyst for an incident that elicited laughter from Emin himself despite surprising the listeners when he narrated it. The events that unfolded after breakfast at his friends' house in the morning marked the beginning of this unforeseen occurrence.

After breakfast, Emin didn't leave the task of clearing the table and washing the dishes to Gülizar, who had recently undergone kidney surgery. He insisted, 'You haven't fully recovered; don't try to be a housewife!' Instead, he took charge and moved the dining table by the window. Opting for daylight over lamps in those penny-pinching days, he planned to stay in Bursa for three more days after the association's branch congress. During this time, he intended to work on the draft resolution on the Cyprus issue for the Party's General Congress. Besides, he could spend time with his fiancée, who couldn't relocate to Istanbul due to the Party's restrictions on leaving her factory job. Seated at the table with his tea and surrounded by the notes and papers he had brought, Emin noticed a white Renault passing by his friend's one-story house, typical of the workers' quarter. It stopped by the next house, and three people, excluding the driver, emerged and knocked on the door. Emin's intuition told him they were plainclothes policemen. When he turned to Gülizar and remarked, 'I think the political police are here!' their doorbell rang, prompting Gülizar to rise from her seat as he did too.

"You wait, Gülizar. Don't open the door with your catheter bag. Just in case, just in case! You never know what these people will do!" When he opened the door, the man in front of him paused for a moment. This was a moment of temporary surprise for the police officer. The policeman, who was obviously older than the others with a watermelon belly, turned slightly sideways and said to the younger and athletically built policemen behind him: "Look who's here!" and then continued:

"Ohh, we found you on the ground while looking for you in the sky. We had even sent a team to Istanbul for you. Where is Mohammed?"

Gülizar, who was watching what was happening through the door of the room opening to the small corridor where the outer door was located, answered the question:

"Mohammed went out."

"Who are you?"

"I am his wife."

"Did your husband leave you at home with a man and go out? Why don't you open the door?"

She replied defensively:

"My mum is home!"

Emin restrained himself, even though the words "You are speaking according to your profession!" came on the tip of his tongue, implying that you, the police are pimps. He intervened:

"Our friend has just had an operation. She's unwell. I opened it instead of her."

"Come on, come with us."

"Let me get my jacket and identity card," the policeman grabbed Emin's left arm as he attempted to take a step backwards:

While Running Away

"Wait, don't go anywhere. Who knows, you'll run out the back somewhere."

"No, why should I run away?"

"Get his jacket! And tell your husband not to run away, come to our office and give his statement. Otherwise, we'll come and knock the hell out of you all!"

When Gülizar brought the requested jacket, Emin noticed that her face, already pale from the recent surgery, had turned even more yellow. While Emin was taking the coat, he whispered, "Don't worry, it's nothing." He put his jacket on and walked towards the car. One of the policemen standing at the back of the street walked behind the police car and took a seat on the rear left side while gesturing Emin to "Get in" to the rear seat as the other policeman sat in the rear right seat next to Emin. The pot-bellied policeman continued his chatter as he sat in the front of the car:

"Wow, look at God's handiwork. We're lucky today, lucky!" He turned to the policeman driving the car and said, "Irfan, drive!"

The policeman in the driver's seat, sitting with his left side of his back against the door of the car, asked as he put the car into gear, making a semicircle with his right hand:

"Chief, shall we stop by the furniture store and pick up our furniture?"

"Good reminder, I almost forgot. Let's go there first!"

As the car turned left at the end of the street, a strange calm descended on the always excited, quick-firing Emin. "What's done is done. Whatever is going to happen will happen. The strings are not in my hands," Emin thought. Actually, he knew what he was going to experience. He thought of the experiment he used to do with his friends in the hot-baths they used to go to in the study year at the Bursa Institute of Education. They used to compete to stay as long as they could in a tub full of boiling water that came from just below their breasts to an inch below their knees when they sat in it by bending their knees. This was a kind of experiment to endure pain and torture. Despite all his frailty in his appearance, he had always stayed the longest. His friends were surprised by this. "It's not a matter of physical power, but a matter of willpower," he would say, boasting inwardly. "Now, you will face the real torture, and you must come out of it without even saying 'Ahh!' It's time to show that willpower, which I'm so proud of," he had started motivating himself.

The car stopped before a carpenter's workshop, which the police called a "furniture shop". The carpenter, a middle-aged man in a labour apron who came running from inside with his big belly bouncing, stood at attention when he reached the car. "Welcome, chief," came out of his mouth.

The Chief, leaning sideways forward towards the driver's seat, asked through the gap between the policeman driving the car and the windscreen:

"Is our furniture ready?"

"It's almost ready, Chief; the boy will bring it now. Shall I order tea for you in the meantime?"

"Come on, let's have a cup of tea."

"Chief" continued, "Bring a tea for our guest too," without giving the carpenter, who glanced at the rear seats of the police car for a moment, a chance to ask.

"Yes, sir!"

Turning his gaze from the carpenter, who was walking fast back to the workshop, to Emin, the "supervisor" said with a grin:

"Appreciate us. Look, we're getting you tea. And then you'll be talking about how the police mistreated us."

Emin did not change his posture at all. With a tone of voice that matched the calmness that came over him: "Thank you," he said, even though he thought, "Play the role of the good cop..."

The teas arrived in a couple of minutes. As they were about to finish their tea, the conversation between the carpenter and the "Chief" about whether business was booming or not was interrupted by the arrival of a young man in the range of childhood and adolescence with a round stick, similar to a rolling pin but much thicker than a rolling pin. The master carpenter scolded the young boy:

"Son, why don't you wrap it in a piece of paper and bring it; what is this?"

"OK, master," the boy said and turned back but stopped when he heard the voice of the "Chief".

"No need, no need for that."

The carpenter held the stick he had taken from the boy through the open window of the driver's cab. At each end of the thick cylindrical stick, about half a meter long, two neat round holes, about two centimetres in diameter, were drilled ten to twelve centimetres inwards. Emin realised what the 'furniture' was for. After being passed through the holes of the stick, the ends of the twine would be knotted, and the device for "falaka," a method of inflicting pain and humiliation by administering a beating on the soles of a person's bare feet, would be ready to be attached to the ankles of the person to be tortured.

The "Chief" patted the stick he held in his left hand with his right hand.

"Hmm, no splinters. You sanded it well. Thank you for your work. Thank you."

"Thanks, chief. We always do a good job." The car grumbled slightly as the driver touched the accelerator pedal.

That was the signal of "We're leaving now."

The "Chief" raised his right hand simultaneously and said, "Time to say goodbye."

As the carpenter waved his hand and said, "Goodbye," Emin thought, "They didn't even offer him money for the 'good job', parasites!"

Emin never told anyone the full story of what happened after that, from beginning to end, except on two occasions. At times, he provided brief answers when asked, responding concisely. On other occasions, he felt a sense of shame, not wanting to discuss his own experiences, as they seemed insignificant compared to the torture others had endured. One of the exceptions would become a requisite for him years later, and he would share a laughter-filled recollection of the incident at some point in his narrative. In fact, he had smiled when the incident occurred, a moment for which he paid the price at that time. Before that moment, his own voice on the tape accompanying the torture had proclaimed: "Torturers will sooner or later end up in the dustbin of history!"

During the almost forty-five minutes of non-stop beating as his tape-recorded speech at the same length was playing, the policeman, who had the wrist of Emin's right arm, which had been spread out to the side, under his foot, would, at that point in his speech, put the small plastic wastepaper basket in the corner over his head and say, "You didn't put us in the rubbish bin, we put you in the rubbish bin!" The smile he couldn't hold back in the face of this stupidity invited a punch on his nose.

The other exception was that he told his experiences to his namesake, whom Emin had met in Bursa Prison, who would also become his confidant and comrade in the most challenging times there. They had plenty of time to chat in the prison.

After those conversations, time would pass, time would come, and Emin would go through the process of internal reckoning and come to terms with himself. However, both Emin and his namesake had held lengthy chats in the prison, sharing their mutual experiences when the heat of the torture-related events was still on. While Emin and his namesake were chatting, they had moved from one method of revenge to another, choosing from various forms of torture and attempting to find the cruellest one. They were very furious and immature as much, due to their age.

***

[Flashforward– Many years after and before!
What Emin said in an interview with Can Dündar for the TV programme "32. Day" about fifteen years after those days was the result of the internal reckoning he was going through. Although he did not remember the exact words, he would later remember the meaning of what he said:

"Yes, it is true that people who have been tortured need psychological treatment and support. However, the ones who really need treatment are the ones who committed those tortures. Whoever they are, they should be dismissed and put under treatment. However, their salaries should continue to be paid to their families and children, and their families and children should not be victimised."

Following his words, a child on whom the police had closed the gates with iron bars would enter the image. The journalist, Can Dündar, explained the contrast between what is humane and what is hostile to human beings with a skilful visualisation.

He was telling the story, but Emin had an untold process of inner reckoning, and this process had crystallised in a single-sentence essence:

"When you are like your enemy, you've lost even if you've won!"]

* * *

This reality applies not just to individuals but also to social organisations. The way to realise this for individuals, as Kivilcimli pointed out, is through their behaviour: "The greatest of all jihads is the struggle against your own ego." Emin had concluded that inner reckoning was the key to succeeding in this. Without inner reckoning, a person might not just resemble their enemy but, more crucially, transform into their own worst adversary.

Had his namesake, the one he had explored torture methods with, gone through the same reckoning? He would never know for sure. His namesake would later seek revenge on the police commissioner, who had played a leading role in torturing both of them without much harm to his humanity. About thirty years had passed when he met his namesake again. The story his namesake told while reminiscing about those days was a bit cruel but quite funny.

His namesake had ascertained that the retired "Chief," the ringleader of the torturers, frequented a café after his retirement, playing "Okey"[36] in the late hours. After

---

[36] "Okey" is a traditional tile-based game with a long history and many

continuously monitoring the man, one night, precisely when only the retired torturer "Chief" and his "Okey" companions remained, his namesake, along with two friends brandishing fake pistols, raided the café. They swiped everyone's hands through the backs of the chairs and tied them up, along with their bodies, to the chairs. They had done an adverse favour for the 'Chief' by inserting dynamite-shaped candles between the ropes that bound his entire body, including his feet. After gagging everyone and igniting the lengthy fuses attached to the fake dynamites, they exited, locking the door with keys picked up from the café owner. They had watched the fuses burning and the increasing struggle of the retired "Chief" as the flames approached for a while before making their escape.

Yes, Emin had shared the tortures he had experienced with his namesake, but someone who had been sent to prison earlier than him had told the inmates some things he had overheard. Nevertheless, Emin was content to give short answers to the questions that the other inmates asked. He did not want his actions to be seen as heroic.

In those years, the police were required to refer detainees to the prosecutor within twenty-four hours. After Emin was taken to the torture room, the police brought another member of the association, Huseyin Kork, who waited in the next room for his turn. However, Emin was unaware that Huseyin Kork had been arrested and brought there a while later. Huseyin Kork faced the prosecutor, was arrested, and sent to prison before the twenty-four hours were up. The police claimed Huseyin Kork was one of the suspects in the armed clash. Some "minor" confessions saved Huseyin Kork from prolonged torture. Although Emin had been brought to

---

variations. It's hugely popular in Turkey, played mainly in coffee houses by people of every age. It's very similar to Rummy/Rummikub as it is played with the same set of boards and tiles but with different rules

the Police Department earlier than Huseyin Kork, who had been sent to prison before Emin, Huseyin Kork shared with the inmates in the ward what he heard from the next room when Emin was tortured before Emin was brought to the prison.

Emin, who was in Istanbul during the armed clash, could not be accused of anything other than the speech he delivered at the association's congress. However, this speech alone wouldn't have sufficed for an arrest, depriving the police of the opportunity to satisfy their revenge. The police would wait until the evening of the day after his capture to ensure Emin's arrest and then send him to the on-duty prosecutor and judge, who were guaranteed to cooperate with them.

First, he had thought that he was kept waiting for the bleeding in his nose, which he suspected was broken, to stop, even though the twenty-four-hour period had passed. However, on the way from the Political Department to the Kurtuluş Police Station, Emin could understand the real reason for the delay when he heard the police saying to each other, "The prosecutor and judge are on board; he can't get away with this one." He realised they were intentionally speaking like this in his presence. They had wanted Emin to know that he would end up in prison. Then, they handed Emin to the cops from the police station, who would take him to the Bursa Court House and had waited at the Courthouse for a long time for the prosecutor to come. To the prosecutor's question, "What did you do with him?" the two police officers would answer, "We didn't do anything. The Political Branch handed him over to us, and we brought him directly here," taking the words out of each other's mouths. To avoid this question, the police "Political Branch" had deliberately shifted the burden of such questions to the

While Running Away

police station cops. These police officers had indeed treated him well while waiting in the corridor of the Courthouse. One of the police officers had read the referral letter given to them by the Political Branch and asked Emin:

"You don't believe in God, hah?"

The other policeman intervened, "Let it go. Look what they have done to him. The political police have no mercy. Come on, let's see who will jump long. The one who loses in three tries buys the beers," and he took the policeman who asked the question and make him compete in a long jump race in the corridor of the Courthouse where there was not a soul around after working hours.

"Like the police at the police station in the basement of the Police Headquarters, these police station cops must not like the First Branch cops they call 'politicians'. Maybe they are a member of the Pol-Der[37]!" he thought. He smiled crookedly with a swollen face on his right side, remembering the memory of a short while ago.

Experiencing the awkwardness of having a mutual action meeting with the policemen from Pol-Der one night, he remembered how they had organised the hanging of Pol-Der's posters. These posters to be put up in the most populated parts of İstanbul by the members of the left-wing organisations and trade union members taking part in the alliance would be under the protection of the policemen from Pol-Der.

But now, even if they were from Pol-Der, one of the policemen was obsessed with the issue of "being Godless". The Police First Branch had written in the referral letter that Emin was "Godless" but had not written how they had obtained this information.

---

[37] Pol-Der: Association organised by left-leaning police officers in the 1970s in Turkey.

Emin was not able to keep his promise of "I will not even say 'ahh' during torture." When he could not bear the ceaseless caning and let out a relatively lengthy "Ahhh", the policeman, stepping on his right hand with his foot, said, "Stop, stop, he said 'Allah'!" The baton-wielding policeman stopped and asked:

"You heathen, do you believe in Allah?"

"F… your Allah! F… your religion!"

The fact that he swore so loudly was more out of anger at himself than at the police. He had failed to keep his promise to himself. The consequence of his swearing was obvious. Emin, in a way and maybe subconsciously, had punished himself. Huseyin Kork, who was in the next room, heard all these and told it to the other political prisoners. Emin would later realise that the warm welcome he would experience in the prison ward was partly due to this news that had gone before him, although he did not know it at first.

Emin was moved from the observation ward, where he had been thrown upon arrival at the prison, to the ward where the left-wing political prisoners were kept after Bilgin, one of the two association executives who had been arrested earlier, had asked the head guard on duty that night, who was sympathetic to political prisoners, during the roll-call before bedtime, to move him to their ward. As a matter of fact, he should have stayed in the observation ward for at least a day. It was after midnight when he was brought to the ward. A prisoner named Latif, whom he would later learn was on trial for murder and extortion, had woken up to the noise of the welcome in the ward and was grumbling:

"What is this? At this time of the night... You woke me up."

Bilgin responded calmly but assertively:

"OK, OK, OK. I'm sorry. Our friend is here. It's just for tonight."

"Who's here? Who is it?"

On the top bunk in the corner on the right side of the ward door, Latif partially rose from his bed to look down. He must not have seen the new inmate, Emin, clearly, then, as he turned his face toward the wall, dangled his feet from the bars at the foot of the bunk, and jumped down. While putting his slippers on, he looked at Emin.

Bilgin and Huseyin Kork introduced him simultaneously:

"Emin."

"Is it that Emin?" Latif asked astonishingly.

He didn't wait for an answer to his question but continued, extending his hand:

"God bless you, mate. I thought you were a big guy."

Emin also extended his hand, saying, "Thank you". However, he did not like the man's attitude and felt annoyed.

"There have been many instances where my initial positive impressions were proven wrong; in contrast, I have never been mistaken when my first impression was negative. There was an exception where I believed my negative impression was disproven. However, over time, that person revealed his true colours. He was not an exception but a two-faced schemer!" Emin would later recount. Of course, this junkie tramp did not prove to be an exception for him.

"Man, you're petite but valiant. You cursed the cops and yelled at them, saying 'motherfucker' during the torture!"

Emin didn't understand at first.

"No, nothing like that!"

Huseyin Kork jumped in:

"No, not a 'motherfucker.' F… your Allah and religion!"

"Yes, that was true, but how did Huseyin Kork know that?" Emin was puzzled.

"You've done wrong. One does not swear over God or religion," said Latif, dragging his slippers towards the toilet.

Emin had become even more irritated with this man he didn't like in the first place. His namesake, to whom he would later describe this feeling, intervened almost immediately, saying, "Comrade, you must be hungry now. Would you like to eat something?"

Although Emin didn't realise it, his namesake had done it deliberately. When discussing Latif's request to join their commune a few weeks later, he would admit: "I deliberately changed the subject. You glared at him so much that I worried there would be a fight for no reason!"

"No, I don't feel like eating anything now. I don't eat at this time of the night."

He didn't really feel hungry. Strangely, he felt happy, even though he was confined within the four walls of the prison. This happiness stemmed from feeling safe, and it would have been complete if it weren't for the burning sensation in his soles.

* * *

His feet, which were burning that day, felt freezing cold today. Although he noticed the customs officer looking at him, Emin disregarded the scrutiny and reached for his cigarette packet. Lighting a cigarette, he tasted the rust lingering in his mouth. Nevertheless, he took a few puffs. Afterwards, he grabbed two biscuits from the packet and ate them. The biscuits, unfortunately, did little to diminish the metallic taste of rust in his mouth. At that moment, he regretted giving away the tangerines to the people on the bus. "How nice they would be now," he mused. He tossed his cigarette to the ground before finishing it and crushed it with his foot. He noticed that his toes were freezingly cold. Removing his shoes, he attempted to warm them by rubbing his feet, although it didn't help much because his hands were also cold. Eventually, he opened his suitcase and took out another pair of socks, placing them on the radiator to warm up slightly before putting them on his feet. Now, he struggled to put his shoes back on, not only because of the second pair of socks but also because his feet were swollen from not resting for a long time. Emin stretched his legs over the narrow bench, laying them one over the other. Leaning on his elbow, he cradled his face in his left palm. It would be good if he could fall asleep even for a little while. He began to drift off, but as he struggled to maintain balance, his feet slid off the bench, and the sleep he was about to embrace slipped away altogether.

Time, in every respect, wouldn't pass. "Damn world," he said, "it's like you stopped spinning. Don't you miss the sun? It seems you're happy with the darkness you've sucked me into." The dark gloom of falling into the middle of the unknown was blowing inside him. He travelled back to the night before, to the ballad he had sung so loudly. He couldn't do the same here. He didn't feel like it anyway. He started to hum:

"If I were the night of this long night,
If I could be the chimney of a house in my homeland..."

He abruptly stopped humming the song without finishing the rest. Despite being aware of the absence of anyone nearby, he glanced around as if ensuring that no one had overheard him.

He got up, returned to the radiator, squatted down, and leaned against it. Maintaining this position was challenging.

Standing up, he retrieved a sweater from his suitcase, folded it in thirds, and placed it on the heater, half-sitting on it. He also took out a cigarette and lit it, ignoring the taste of rust in his mouth. In a way, he kept himself busy. After finishing the cigarette, a lethargy brought by the warmth settled on him. He returned to the bench to sleep, resting his head on his arms, folded at the elbow and placed side by side, burying himself in his coat with the collar turned up. A passing lorry, its noise interrupting the sleep he had fallen into the depths of, brought with it the first lights of the morning wrapped in the sharp frost of the Balkans.

He reached for the cigarette packet again. He saw the fire of Diyarbakir[38] in the flame of the match. He returned to his thoughts before he fell asleep.

Yes, there were times when he was ashamed to talk about what he had gone through because it was almost nothing compared to other experiences. Especially after hearing from Abdo Orak about what happened in Diyarbakir Prison[39] during their conversation in Selimiye Military Prison in the summer of 1984, he felt deeply embarrassed to share his experiences. Following the mass "falaka" they endured at the hands of soldiers, those individuals who had been hardened by the harsh conditions of Diyarbakir Prison and who had, in their own way, built a bridge of "Sirat"[40] over the

---

[38] Diyarbakir is the largest Kurdish-majority city in Turkey, considered by Kurds as the Capital of Kurdistan.

[39] Diyarbakir Prison is a prison located in Diyarbakir, southeastern Turkey. It was established in 1980 as an E-type prison by the Ministry of Justice. After the September 12, 1980 Turkish coup d'état, the facility was transferred to military administration. What has been called "the period of barbarity" or "the hell of Diyarbakir" refers to the early and mid-1980s; the infamous Diyarbakir Military Prison was the one where the prisoners were exposed to the most horrific acts of systematic torture.

[40] Sirat, according to religious belief, is a bridge that passes from the top of hell. Diyarbakir is a part of "the region of the Euphrates Island", characterised by abundant water and fertile lands. Two major rivers, the Tigris and Euphrates, along with their tributaries and branches, traverse this region.

"Fırat" (Euphrates), would perform a "halay"[41] together each time. This is for boosting their morale, improving blood circulation, and mitigating the damage caused by the beatings on the sole.

In fact, Emin would not tell all these Bulgarians at the customs where he felt trapped. He was determined to give as little information as possible, as much as possible to clarify his own position, limited to what was recorded in the official records in Turkey, for possible interrogation by the Bulgarian secret police from Sofia. Of course, that's if things unfolded as he expected!

"And even then, there is a problem," he continued speculating.

What if they had all the Party's documents? There was no explanation for his attitude towards the "socialist countries" that could save him from being punished by the Bulgarian authorities. Even if he says: "It was Brezhnev I was aiming at," it would not save the situation, even though Brezhnev, too, suffered the fate of every deceased Soviet leader, and his name was crossed out. Because what he wrote was clearly aimed at the entire Soviet system. He could have fallen into a controversy contradicting the one he used to salvage by saying, "It is an honour to live in a socialist country!" He could not deny what he had written. It was impossible in both senses. He couldn't say, "I didn't write it". Nor could he say, "I wrote it, but I was wrong". This would have meant crossing out what he had defended for years at once. His attitude towards the Soviet Union was not among the many things he had to reckon with in his own world of thought because his opinion about the Soviet Union and the so-called 'socialist system' had not changed; in fact, it had

---

[41] Halay is a type of dance indigenous to all people living in Mesopotamia and its periphery. Halay dancers form a circle or a line, often holding hands with the last and first player gripping a piece of cloth.

enriched even more, especially after reading Arthur Rosenberg's 'History of Bolshevism,' a critique from the left." If he would try to explain what it means "to be like your enemy", he would have been deported to Turkey, let alone being allowed to go to Yugoslavia as an "enemy of the socialist Homeland", or worse and most likely, would have been ended up breathing in a Bulgarian prison. "Breathing?!" He was overwhelmed by the gravity of the situation and felt the urgent need to go to the toilet.

"I'll go out and get some air," he said and went to the door. There was no one in sight. The only sign of life was the smoke rising from the chimney of the two-storey building painted grey, a little darker than fog. He walked towards the back of the shack. In the darkness of the night, he noticed the drinking fountain that had not attracted his attention before. About ten paces away, he saw what he needed. When he turned the tap of the fountain, he jumped back a step so that the lush water would not splash on him. He reached out from where he was, turned the tap a little, and reduced the water flow. He leaned over the tap and drank the water that filled his palm. The water was cold yet flavourful, but he couldn't drink much since he was not feeling thirsty. He opened the tap a little more and washed his face with the water he filled in both palms. When he turned off the tap and stood up, he looked at the sun, which did not warm but brightened the day, and the smooth blue of the sky for a short time while standing still. It was as if the clarity of the enlightened sky, hand in hand with the coolness of the water that had just hit his face, had washed away the inner distress. When he returned to the shack with a more energetic stride, his endless stream of unspoken thoughts took on a more positive tone.

"Even if they possessed documents belonging to the Party, they wouldn't open and read them all. Moreover, since my essay on the Soviet Union did not fall into the hands of the Turkish police, it was most likely to be destroyed by Ferman and his associates. The discussions regarding the TKP and the Soviet Union in the documents from the conference held clandestinely before joining the Vatan Party wouldn't present an issue. It was said that the documents from the conference were sent to Bulgarian authorities, who were responsible for observing communist affairs in Turkey on behalf of the Soviet Union. I am not sure about the accuracy of this information. Even if that's the case, it shouldn't be a problem. The speakers were recorded under their pseudonyms. If they ask me for their real names, I will say, 'I don't remember them because I don't know anyone outside my cell closely.' There should be no issue."

The pessimism, which had intensified with the darkness of the night, gave way to optimism with the light of the day. "Damn TKP, wherever I come across you, you have always been the source of negative feelings and thoughts", he said while looking at the two-storey Bulgarian Customs building opposite before entering the shack. In a way, that building symbolised the TKP for Emin.

When he entered the shack, he sat on the radiator again. He lit a cigarette. He looked at the thin smoke coming out of his cigarette and at the density of the smoke rising from the chimney of the opposite building. "The weaker we were, the stronger they- the TKP- were because of the Soviets they had their backs to. Similar to how the smoke from this cigarette stayed separate and distinct from the smoke of the opposite chimney, we also succeeded in maintaining our own separate identity. I did my part, in one way or another." he said to himself.

He was always proud of taking a clear stand on the TKP, although later, as he analysed the roots of the problem, he would see that this was not an adequate answer to the real problem. Nevertheless, no one would be able to find the slightest zigzag in his stance on this issue.

"Zigzag!"

This word triggered memories of another argument Emin had with Aydın.

* * *

"You're wrong about that, and you never understood."

Regardless of Emin's objection, Aydın insisted:

"What's not to understand? Are you going to deny that you've been shifting sides? First, you supported Çelik, then Ferman. After that, you backed Faik Feryat. Subsequently, you railed against Faik Feryat and returned to your old team. Your track record has been full of zigzags."

"Your perception of 'zigzagging' stems from interpreting my approach not as a commitment to the truth but as support for specific individuals. Essentially, I endorsed what I deemed right at different times. If you were to say, 'What you considered right was actually wrong!' that would be a different topic of discussion. Whether it was right or wrong, I would discuss that. I am already having a discussion with myself about what's right and wrong. However, labelling it as 'zigzagging' is not right. Each situation merits individual consideration. Interestingly, some individuals attempted to establish a hierarchical structure in their relations with me, presuming I conformed to their chain of command. After all, they considered themselves the 'authority,' didn't they?

Emin paused for a moment and continued by opening and closing the index and middle fingers of both hands at the second knuckles:

"Put the word 'authority' in quotation marks. Oh, I was going to recognise the 'authority' of these gentlemen! Of course, I do!"

This time, Emin's words were accompanied by a well-known sign, the Anatolian version of showing the middle finger! While Aydın was laughing, he did not neglect to warn:

"You've got carried away again. Keep your voice down so the people around can't hear you."

"It did not take long for them to realise that they had misunderstood me or couldn't understand. For example, when Clark Mahmut accused me of being an anarchist at the last congress, he was actually right within the framework of his own understanding. He had understood my attitude of 'march to my own beat' very well. But you couldn't understand this. Let's start over if you want."

"OK, let's start from the beginning. Didn't you say at the very first [Extraordinary General] Organization Meeting, 'Let's throw out the SVP (Socialist Homeland Party) people,' and then withdraw this proposal at the end of the same meeting? You started zigzagging from day one."

"Stop there. As you may know, I bumped into Fırat on the way to that meeting. He had read the motion I had submitted for discussion at the meeting, the motion in which I had made the suggestion that you are referring to. He had said, 'You were the most outspoken of Ferman's team. You have revealed your intentions that they did not express in their writings.' In other words, when they formed a faction and Ferman's team formed a counter-faction, he saw me as part of it."

"Well, of course you were."

"I'm sorry, but your prejudice has actually become your dull prejudice. And you have always looked at it from there. I have never belonged to any faction within the Party. The most 'Bolshevik' article of the Party constitution was on this subject. I was the 'most Bolshevik' party member in this sense."

Emin paused for a second. He continued with the index and middle fingers of both hands, again making the "quotation marks" sign:

"Just put these words 'Bolshevik' and 'the most Bolshevik' in quotation marks! I have been faithful to this while I have been a 'Party member'. This 'Bolshevik' attitude, the party charter, and, therefore, the Party itself can all be subject to debate. I am questioning it today; my mind is not yet clear. However, in that given situation, my position was clear. I did not belong to any faction. Although the motion I presented for discussion at that meeting seemed nuanced, my views differed from those brought by Çelik and those brought by Ferman. I proposed the immediate expulsion of SVP members. However, during the discussions, when Ferman and his cronies interpreted Kivilcimli's suggestion that the Party should be cleansed of factions by exposing them as meaning that they should not be expelled immediately to make this exposure, and when they interpreted 'exposing as 'after they have been exposed', I stepped back in the meeting and withdrew my own suggestion."

"Was it right that they were expelled?"

"If you ask me what I think now, I would say 'it wasn't'. But I didn't think so at the time and firmly believed that this was the requirement of the party constitution. Couldn't a more flexible interpretation of the relevant article of the constitution have been made? I would still adopt the same attitude if I worked under that party statute today.

Nevertheless, instead of expulsion, I could suggest an intermediate solution, such as removing faction leaders from their positions, making them ordinary members by not giving them positions in authorised bodies, or reducing them to a status similar to candidate membership... However, if he insists on his behaviour, expel him... I don't know, such solutions can be sought..."

Emin realised that he was arguing the issue on the wrong ground and tried to recover:

"The issue is actually connected with the Bolshevik nature of the Party constitution. I can't say' right' today since I cannot work under that party statute is impossible. I have been going through my own reckoning with Bolshevism. In a way, the answer to your question is both, I mean, yes and no!"

"But the idea that they should have been expelled according to the party statutes in the day's circumstances is also wrong. Because in the eyes of the SVPs, the Ferman and his cronies were also a faction."

"But they almost automatically became a faction. Without the SVP faction, they would not have become a faction."

"A faction is a faction. The fact that you want one faction to be expelled while you don't want the same for the others shows that you belong to that faction, or at least that you are in favour of that faction."

"Aydın, that's an Aristotelian logic analogy, for God's sake. What is this? Is this a common characteristic of you, the engineers? Engineers in the Party, including you, Fırat, and others like you, consistently suffer from Aristotelian logic. That doesn't make me a faction member. Yeah, maybe you're right... I should have suggested they should be expelled from the Party, too. I'm not sure. Even if they had been reduced to the position of an opposing faction, they might not have developed another factional mechanism. Since they had already developed such a mechanism, later on, the same mechanism led to provocation. This confirms Kivilcimli's proposition that 'faction leads to provocation'. But on the other hand, could a solution have been found that would have dispersed both factions without provocation? Could this have prevented disintegration? What would have been the way to achieve this? As I said, I don't know exactly, I really don't know. Maybe the ways I mentioned before could have been tried. I don't know. I'm still questioning it myself. But let's make this clear. I didn't participate and work in a faction; I kept trying to work independently."

"Your subjective intentions do not change your objective position."

"It changes. Even the zigzag examples you gave show that this is not so?"

"What sample?"

"The issue of supporting Faik Feryat. If I was in the same faction with Ferman, why would I get up in the middle of the road and support Faik Feryat?"

"Well, then you stood up to him too."

"Yes, I did, but when the idea of knocking on the TKP's door, I broke away from Faik Feryat. Remember: I supported his proposal to reorganise the Party into communal cells and nothing else. Who knows, maybe the disintegration could have been prevented in this way. I saw the 'communal cells' thesis as the ground for the comradeship relations that could not be established until then within such an organisation. Each of the 'communal cells' was to become communes, just like we did in prisons. This could have addressed the deficiency in establishing comradeship relations and influenced various other aspects.

It could have infused dynamism into the Party, aligning hollow and shallow leaders and preventing them from hiding behind the articles of the Party constitution, which they often use as a mere formality to establish and maintain their power. In fact, you and your other friends supported it."

"Yes, I took it in a similar sense. But you should have concentrated on something other than that. You had jumped to other subjects."

"Because of Faik Feryat. The man revealed his true intentions behind the closed doors. I told you then what happened."

"No, you said 'Faik Feryat's intention is to patch the Party to the TKP' and started discussing the TKP and the socialist system."

"Although I did not tell exactly how it happened when I deciphered his intentions and he started to defend the TKP and the Soviet Union, the discussion shifted to that ground anyway. Otherwise, I wouldn't talk about what was said behind closed doors were about. I could have told this detail if he had denied it himself."

"By the way, what did he say to you? I mean, behind closed doors!"

"You're quite interested in the gossip side of things."

"Is it gossip? Well, I can't say I'm not curious, to be honest."

"When these 'communal cells' discussions started, and he saw that I was ardently supporting him, he said to me after a meeting, 'Come on, let's go to our place; we can talk about this in more detail there'."

"He didn't have a house in Istanbul!"

"Yeah, I meant his sister's house. He was staying there. Anyway. We went. Firstly, he listed the similarities he had said at the meeting about the 'communal cells' type of organisation. Then he said that such a structure would really form a steel core, that even if this steel core is small in number, if it enters the TKP, it will reach an effectiveness that will create change within the TKP, how the Doctorist core, which has both the support of the Soviet Union and dominates the widespread organisation and trade unions of the TKP today, can make a revolutionary breakthrough throughout the country and how this will influence other revolutionary parties and movements."

"An exciting portrait!"

"Yeah, right!"

"We know it doesn't excite you!"

"I listened, but when he said TKP, my fuses had already blown. I believe he was unaware of our previous discussions or, at least, of my stance. Or, I don't know; he must have thought that the picture he painted would draw me into this excitement. Anyway... It was the moment of truth. I said to him at that moment, more or less, what I had described in my later writings as a reply. Then, I raised the flag for this thesis at the next "[Extraordinary General] Organisation Meeting. Come on, tell me, where is the zigzag in this?"

"So, you didn't return to the Ferman faction after that? They needed more heads, so they took you back."

"Are you talking like this to push my buttons, or do you really believe what you are saying? I have never had such factional relations with anyone. Why don't you understand that? If I did, I would say, 'I did! It's not like I will run away from this when making harsher reckonings!"

Emin paused. When he started again, his voice was calmer.

"The problem there is actually the problem of 'becoming like your enemy'. The word 'enemy 'needs to be corrected here. Let's say 'opponents'. When you resemble those, you fight; you lose even if you win. How are you different from those you oppose? And why did you oppose them then? You know, they excommunicated him, but he's right. If fascism is necessary, why bother with the copy when you can have the original, he said in a nutshell, for the Soviets."

"You jumped again. Who's that guy?"

"If you wait to see where my words will lead, I'll tell you. Panait Istrati."

"Who's that?"

"Romanian writer excommunicated by communist intellectuals during the Stalin era. Actually, how accurate it is to call him Romanian is another matter. Anyway... After he visited the Soviet Union, he observed the thing over there and said something like what I told you. Even Romain Rolland, closest to him, had distanced himself from Istrati. Although until then, he used to edit Istrati's writings. Romain Rolland edited what Istrati wrote in French."

"You said Romanian."

"He writes in Romanian and French, but his French is not very strong. Anyway. It's about 'becoming like your enemy'. In a way, it's like conquering the conquerors. Dr Kivilcimli describes this as a situation in which barbarians who have not reached the upper stage of barbarism renaissance the civilisation they conquered because they lack the infrastructures and superstructures to establish a new civilisation. It means that the conqueror is to be conquered by the old civilisation they have beaten. They cannot build a new civilisation. What is happening in Russia is similar. It is not possible to establish socialism in an environment where capitalist relations of production have not developed. In fact, the Doctor's 'History Thesis' explains not only prehistory, but even the contemporary history."

"You're going overboard again. You've already concluded that the Soviet Union wasn't socialist, and now you're attempting to find a theoretical justification for it."

"Let's say it is so; what's the big deal? When the apple fell to the ground, didn't asking 'why did it fall?' lead Newton to discover the law of gravity? What I've expressed are unrefined thoughts that require further consideration. The ' History Thesis ' provides explanations beyond merely elucidating the laws of pre-written history.

"If he had, the Doctor himself would have said so. Have you ever come across such a claim from the Doctor? I haven't."

"No, I can't claim that. But that doesn't mean we should stop where the Dr Kivilcimli left off."

"What does this have to do with 'to be like your enemy'? Isn't that an extreme judgement?"

"Isn't this what is called the Renaissance? When you cannot establish your own civilisation, you cling to the mechanisms of the civilisation you conquered. It is the same with factions. Instead of drowning the Party in the whirlpool of factions, everything could have been different if there had been a real search for an alternative. If there is a faction, set up a counter-faction. This is the 'tooth for tooth' approach. Naturally, you end up in the same place. When you think you have won, you realise that you have lost. This is what happened to us, isn't it?"

"OK, maybe for the Party, but it's too much to say the same about the Soviet Union. Gorbachev is trying to transform and democratise the socialist system from within. The system is renewing itself. Once Stalin's bureaucracy is purged, socialism will be able to develop in the direction Lenin showed. Moreover, that Party, the old one, can even be said to have collapsed; it looks very different from what it used to be. Moreover, the Soviet Union is a gigantic power alternative to imperialism."

"Yes, they are standing, but how much of an alternative it could be is debatable. The Afghanistan adventure shows how far they have come!"

"That was Brezhnev's shit. Gorbachev is solving that problem, too. There'll be more."

"I think what it is, the destination will be the establishment of capitalism under the leadership of the Communist Party. The Soviet Union would continue, but capitalism would be restored by the communists. What the Trotskyists call state capitalism will be established now."

"The whole Party is intact. The people have enjoyed the benefits of socialism all these years. They won't let it go so easily. Of course, they would realise capitalism cannot give them free shelter, education, health care, or whatever is needed. The Soviet Union will overcome this. The primary concern now is yourself and your situation; how will you overcome your difficulties? Still, no news about the passport, is there?"

At first, Emin was pleased that the discussion did not continue. Although his emerging thoughts cast doubt on socialism in the Soviet Union, Emin could not actually go beyond a rejection of it and couldn't shed enough light on the issue of the creation of a new society. He was stuck and aware of it. Aydın's question about passports caused another disturbance that superseded his discomfort with the issue they had discussed. "I wonder if the fact that I stayed in his house for so long is making Aydın uneasy, too," Emin thought.

"It is a prolonged waiting. My stay has been extended here, too."

He was generating uneasiness from Aydın's possible uneasiness. Aydın also understood Emin's implication.

"Don't be silly. Even the neighbours have not noticed your presence. You can stay as long as you need. Maybe it's hard for you; it's like a prison. You can't go out or act freely. You can turn the TV on by keeping the curtains closed and the lights off. Be careful with the TV volume so the neighbours can't hear you, and no one will know your presence. And as long as Hasan keeps calling here from the public phone, no one can trace him."

As Aydın said, it was a kind of imprisonment. A sort of feeling of being trapped. But his waiting would not last long. What he did not expect was that he would move from one sense of being trapped to another feeling of being trapped.

* * *

Sleep was creeping in again, fuelled by tiredness, warmth and the feeling of satiety from the four biscuits he had just snacked on. He sat on the bench and lay his head on his arms as before. This time, it was a slightly deeper sleep. He did not even hear the noise of the slowly increasing traffic.

When he heard the click of the tray placed on the table a little beyond his arms and the words "Good morning, neighbour", Emin sat up, looked at the customs officer he had not seen until that moment, and replied with a sleepy sound: "Good morning!" He looked at the tray shown by the officer, who said, "I brought breakfast, neighbour". There was a dark orange coloured drink in a large water glass, which he guessed to be an orange soda with bubbles, a large plate with eight to ten black olives, a small piece of feta cheese, three slices of toasted toast bread and a fork.

"Thank you."

"Bon appétit, neighbour," he said. Emin thanked the officer again as he headed for the door. The accent of this officer was similar to that of the immigrants from Bulgaria to Turkey. "I wonder if these men are recruited from Turkish-speaking people who cooperate with the system?" he wondered. His hunger was overpowering.

He touched the bread and realised it was freshly toasted, even though it was cold. A sip confirmed his guess about the drink. It was sweeter than the orange sodas in Turkey but also had a strange bitterness. A familiar bitterness came to his mouth when he bit the first olive, but the olive was flavourful, not too meaty or dry. He tore off a small piece of cheese with his fork. It was lean, dry, salty, but he still liked the taste. It was no substitute for the white cheese he had specially selected and bought in Istanbul, which was fatty and soft enough to spread on bread. Nevertheless, it was better than eating biscuits again. If there had been a cup of tea instead of soda, he would have had breakfast like usual. From where he was, the earth was facing the sun. He looked at his watch; it was eleven o'clock. "The officers have probably changed their shifts, had their tea and coffee, and then it was my turn," he reasoned. Unlike his habit, he ate his breakfast slowly. He was trying to savour every bite. He swept up everything that was brought. He hadn't left a single crumb, but half of the coloured soda was still there. He didn't drink it all on purpose. He was going to clean the bitter taste that the cigarette would leave in his mouth with soda. He smoked two cigarettes in a row, taking sips of his soda every now and then. When he extinguished the second one, he drank the remaining two-centimetre of soda at the bottom of the glass. He felt pretty good; it was as if his tiredness was gone. "Let me stretch my legs a little," he said, getting up and walking to the door. He hesitated whether to go out or not. Since the arrival and departure traffic had started to increase, he said, "It is better to be cautious. I may come across a wrong officer. I don't want to run into trouble here," as he stood in the doorway and breathed deeply the cold, yet clean air of the outside, he saw the officer coming from the opposite side of the road, who had brought him breakfast. He waited. When the officer came to the door, he asked:

"Have you had your breakfast, neighbour?"

"Yes, I did."

Emin had responded hastily, fuelled by his optimism, hoping that the following words would be, "Come on, come to the office with me!" But they were not.

"Did you like the breakfast?"

"Thanks, that was nice," he said, walking inside, realising from the officer's step towards the door that he wanted to go in.

The officer followed behind him and reached for the tray containing empty glasses, plates and forks. Although he hesitated for a moment, Emin squeezed the offer that came to his mind into a question sentence:

"How much do I owe?"

"No, these are from us, neighbours. You are our guest."

Emin liked this last word, as it provoked his hope. The officer walked to the door with the tray. Emin followed him. Just as the officer was out the door, he turned back and asked:

"Where will you go from here?"

Emin's hope increased. He answered with a vague joy:

"First to Yugoslavia, then to England."

"How much money do you have?"

This time, Emin became suspicious, thinking, "I wonder if they will ask for a bribe."

"Four hundred and eighty marks."

He had counted his money after the night's interrogation.

"It doesn't sound like enough. Do you have a bus ticket?"

"The bus I came on has already left. I don't have another ticket."

"This money is not enough for you!" the officer said, then turned and walked away.

Emin called after the officer:

"I need to go to the loo."

He had meant to say, "I need to pee," but had chosen a more polite way.

"OK, go, but don't go far!" the officer didn't stop; he just turned his head and looked at Emin as he answered.

Emin went to his usual place with joyful steps. His conclusion made him happy: "No, he wasn't asking for a bribe. He wanted to know if the money would be enough for my journey. I think they'll let me go!" He continued talking to himself as he was peeing:

"They probably asked the officials in Sofia. When my information was confirmed in the records, they decided to let me go!"

When he finished, he mocked himself: "What is the old saying? The Turk's mind gets functioning either while running away or shitting..."

He was still smiling when he went to the tap fountain again. After drinking some water, he washed his face once more.

He went back to the shack. "Their Chief must have arrived; the officers can't decide to let me go alone. They will call me soon", he said, frequently checking his watch while making small paces inside the shack, each time turning round by the window. The windows became his companions who paced with him, like an inmate in a prison!

No customs officers were in sight. He grew tired and sat on the bench for a while. As he started feeling cold, he got up and sat on the radiator instead. He lit a cigarette each time he changed his location. When the cigarette he smoked while sitting on the radiator ran out, he resumed pacing. Then he sat on the bench again and, after a while, back on the radiator. He repeated this cycle many times. He observed cars coming and going and occasionally officers walking towards the shack he was in from the opposite side of the road. Still, none of them had come by it.

At a quarter past three o'clock, an officer approached. Emin realised the same officer had brought breakfast and was heading toward the shack. "OK, this time," he muttered, walking to the door. About four or five steps from the shack, the officer spotted Emin at the door and said, "Take your suitcase and come with me, neighbour."

He was aware of his excitement as he bent down to pick up his suitcase. "Calm down, calm down, what will be will be!" he muttered to himself. When he reached the officer's side, he asked, "Have you got everything, neighbour?" Emin replied with a simple "Yes," and they started walking together.

"That's it!" Emin said to himself, "Short answers don't open the door to new questions and don't reveal your feelings."

When they arrived at the door of the building, which he had been observing since the previous night, with smoke rising from the chimney, he had imagined it would be warm and cosy inside. The officer, who opened the door, stepped aside, allowing him to enter. His assumption had been correct; the interior of the building was indeed warm. In the room at the end of the hall, on the left, two grey, artificial leather seats faced each other, providing comfort to some

While Running Away

extent due to their softness. He stopped, waiting for the officer who entered behind him. Emin needed to figure out which way to go. To the left of the entrance, a wall about two meters in length led to a door hidden beneath the stairs leading to the upper floor. Directly across from the entrance, beside the room with the open door, was another closed door that likely led to a different room. Sensing his hesitation, the officer pointed to the room with the open door and instructed him to enter that room.

When he entered the room, he noticed a person in a suit sitting at the far end of a two-seater armchair, leaning against the wall by the door. The opposite seat was empty. About a meter from these seats, a young man in a dark grey suit occupied a single seat behind a large table. He wore a white shirt with a thin black tie, and his clean-shaven face conveyed an air of authority. "This must be the superior I was expecting," Emin thought. The room wasn't well-lit due to the limited sunlight filtering through the partially opened blinds of a wide window behind him, so the lights were on, casting a bright shine on the man's thick black hair. "He must have applied brilliantine to his hair," Emin thought, still uncertain about where to sit. Observing Emin's hesitation, the young man in the suit silently pointed to the empty seat next to the entrance door. Emin took his seat, and the officer accompanying him placed his suitcase on the left side of the seat. The unopened biscuit package in his hand felt like an extra to Emin. He placed the packet on top of his suitcase, leaning it against the seat's edge to prevent it from falling, giving it a slight push.

The Chief said something in Bulgarian to the officer who brought Emin in. After answering him, the officer turned to Emin and asked:

"Can I get you anything?"

159

"If you have a hot cup of tea, that would be nice."

The officer smiled and said something to the "Chief" in Bulgarian, and after a short response and a nod from the "Chief" indicating "yes," he left the room. Being careful not to appear too curious, Emin directed his gaze to the level of the legs of the two-seater armchair opposite him, thinking, "The person seated next to me is also in a suit; they both must be from the Bulgarian secret service." As the room was filled with an awkward silence, he pondered, "Don't let them see me as a snoop."

Turning his head toward the "Chief," he offered a slight smile, knowing that maintaining an air of nonchalance was crucial. He sensed a softening in the Chief's expression, or at least that's how it appeared to Emin. Regardless, he knew he had to exude confidence, not appear defeated. Even though they might be unaware of his current situation, in their eyes, Emin was a member of the Central Committee of a communist party in Turkey, and he needed to convey a sense of equality. While contemplating these thoughts, he couldn't help but look sidelong at the other individual sitting beside him. This person seemed relatively more composed than the "Chief" and appeared to be a seasoned secret service officer. He was older than the Chief and had a notebook in his lap, occasionally flipping through the pages of a magazine without any real intent to read. It was clear that he was merely passing the time.

"Apparently, they're not just going to let me go with, 'Go on, Godspeed!' You'd better take the arrogance in this 'Chief's' sitting posture as an omen of an intensive interrogation to come," he admonished himself. Then, he recalled what had been said about the behaviours of judges in court.

***

Non-political prisoners on trial at the Assize Courts had always said, "If the Judge is tough in his tone, there is no need to be afraid; it is a sign that he will give the lightest sentence. The one to be afraid of is the soft one." His own experience had yet to confirm this.

"I needed to object to the testimonies given by all police officers who participated in the torture, and I had started stating: 'This is one of the police officers who tortured me. I do not accept his testimony.' For the fourth objection, the Presiding Judge of the First Assize Court, Şemseddin Işık, had scolded me, 'Are we judging you or them?' as he had got furious."

Actually, he had been a bit unfair to this fourth one among the seven policemen who were called as witnesses because, during the torture and the next day when his statement was taken, this police officer had simply sat at the typewriter, not actively participating in the torture and refraining from using harsh language. He wasn't going to make this distinction at length in court. Furthermore, the question was limited to 'whether he recognised the witness and if he accepted the testimony.' He couldn't delve into the intricate details, as the question was limited. He left out this detail, convincing himself with an argument: "Shouldn't a police officer present in a location where torture is taking place also be considered a part of that torture, even if not actively participating?"

He continued to raise the same objection against every police officer who came to testify despite the Judge's reprimands. During each hearing, even the Prosecutor requested his release. Still, Semseddin Işık, being rumoured to be a candidate for the Court of Cassation, kept Emin in prison for six and a half months. When the expert report arrived during the judicial recess, the Court's Prosecutor handling his case and the panel of the Second Assize Court, which typically did not handle political cases, were on duty. Considering the favourable nature of the expert report and the Prosecutor's recommendation to release him, the duty court ruled for his release with an interim decision.

In the subsequent hearings, the First Assize Court, having no grounds for re-arrest, eventually decided to acquit him. The stern Judge had insistently pushed for a trial in pre-trial detention. Had that Judge been on duty during the judicial recess, he might not have even considered the Prosecutor's request for release. He would have kept Emin in detention until the regular trial date. Nevertheless, Emin was ultimately acquitted. This situation was a mixed bag, with some aspects fitting the generalisation and others not.

His experiences in the Martial Law Court were more complex. The Prosecutor handling the case related to the association had referred him to the court with a request for his arrest after his testimony. The territorial army judge major had called him directly to the room where he was sitting with the other judges, avoiding the formal courtroom setting, and had taken his testimony. The Judge had been quite lenient, not requiring him to stand but instead asking him to sit. Ultimately, this Judge decided that there was no need to arrest him.

Right after this hearing, another civilian prosecutor in charge of the Party case was to take his statement. He turned out to be a more severe fascist than the previous one. Perhaps the case had been specifically assigned to him, and —probably due to the nature of the case itself— he adopted a harsh stance. The Judge who was responsible for deciding his arrest was a naval captain. This time, he was brought into a small room resembling a courtroom, and the Judge, seated on a raised platform, decided that Emin would be arrested. His file would be re-reviewed on a date corresponding to the fifty-ninth day.

This was a procedural rule specific to the Military Code of Criminal Procedure applied by Martial Law Courts, which had to be complied with if the accused had not been brought to trial within sixty days. If the sixtieth day were not a Saturday, the Judge would most likely have marked the sixtieth day as the date for file review and a decision as to whether to keep Emin in detention or not would have been made on that date. Finally, when the fifty-ninth day arrived, despite all of the Prosecutor's objections, Emin would be released, and he would appear at all subsequent hearings without being under arrest.

While remembering these things, another memory stuck in between made Emin smile.

About a week after his release, he went to Mazhar-Fuat-Özkan's concert with four other friends he had met at bank courses, including Sema, whom he would later marry. Emin's hair, cut to number three a few days before leaving Selimiye, was still short. When they went to the hall at the interval of the concert, he and his friends were smoking cigarettes on his left side. As Emin shook the ash from his cigarette into the ashtray on his right, he simultaneously looked up at the hand's owner doing the same thing. The owner of the hand also looked at the face of the owner of the other hand, reaching for the ashtray he was looking at while shaking the ash of his cigarette. The eyes of those who cared not to burn each other's hands met. A big surprise had appeared in the man's gaze when he saw Emin. "How come the person I arrested two months ago was released?" was the question in those eyes. Emin recognised him as well, even though he was in civilian clothes. When they returned to their seats, the melody from the concert they listened to under the same roof filled the hall: *"Through the roses, my dear / Running, running / Come to me."*

When he attended the first hearing, Emin realised that the Judge who had arrested him was not part of the trial panel. At the very first hearing, this panel had ruled for the release of all the defendants in pre-trial detention unless they were detained in other cases. Moreover, when the "back and forth" to the court reached the edge of the hearing where his interrogation was completed, Emin would ask to be excused from the hearings. The hearing on that day was interesting, making Emin smile again as he swam in his memories.

Since the previous trial, the Judge, having read out some resolutions from the Central Committee Resolution Book of the Party, handed the book via the private standing at the door, like a court bailiff, and asked Emin: "Is the signature under the resolution yours?" Emin looked at his signature on the page of the Resolution Book and gave the same answer every time: "Yes, the signature is mine." Without exception, his signature was on all the meetings he attended. In fact, in one of the resolutions, only his signature appeared. Regarding the last resolution, the Judge again called the private and said, "Take the notebook to the accused and show him this signature." When the soldier took the notebook, the Judge added that Emin had not rejected any of his signatures up to that point:

"I know you'll say 'My signature!' again, but we have to do this as a procedure. You must declare whether or not you accept the signature."

"Yes, it's my signature."

The Judge asked the minutes clerk, "The defendant accepts the signature shown to him under the resolution of the meeting held on the declared date..."

"Do you have anything else to say about this?"

"No, no, Your Honour. I have a different matter."

"Tell me."

Before coming to court, he agreed with his lawyer and listed what he had memorised and uttered:

"Your Honour, as you know, I work in a bank, and it is a problem that I am constantly asking for time off to attend hearings. As far as I understand, my interrogation is complete. Considering my work situation, my continuous attendance to the hearings so far, and my address fixed, I request that I be allowed to be excused from the hearings."

The President of the Court looked first to his right at the other Military Judge of the Court and then to his left at the military member without legal qualification of the Court Panel. There was no reaction from either of them. The answer given by the President of the Court, Major Naci, was an interesting one that did not fit in with the official court discourse:

"Did we ask you to come to the hearing every time?"

In the last hearing, Emin did not attend, and the court sentenced him to eight years imprisonment. Still, it did not issue an arrest warrant for him like the others convicted, even though he had not attended any of the hearings since the day he had requested to be kept out of the courtroom, except for the two hearings in which the Prosecutor read his closing statement and he made his defence.

It had been said previously that this Penal of the Court had acquitted the Workers' Party of Turkey in a decision that did not conform to the logic of 12th September. They had also convicted two torturer policemen.

The generalisation about the behaviour of the judges had fallen flat again.

* * *

The fact that he perceived his time in the warm room of the Bulgarian Customs as a kind of trial led him to his trials in Turkey.

"The human brain is an enigma. It was only five minutes at most! Yet, these five minutes were enough to recall all these memories that followed one another!" Emin thought as he stirred the sugars he had thrown into the large cup of tea that was brought.

"Perhaps it's true that, at the moment of death, one's entire life flashes before their eyes like a film strip, all in seconds... Is the speed of thought faster than the speed of light? It's a possibility." It was time for him to return to reality from the realm of thought.

Earlier, he had unbuttoned and taken off his coat, which he had buttoned up in the cold, neatly placing it under his left arm on the edge of the armchair before settling into his seat. The increasingly meaningless silence in the room was disrupted when an officer entered with a tray containing three large cups and spoke something in Bulgarian. The officer left one cup on the "Chief's" desk, handed the other cup to the second suited officer beside Emin, and the last one to Emin. As he stirred the two cubes of barely melted sugar into the large cup, the two officers from the customs control booth from the previous night had also arrived. Upon leaving, the officer who brought the tea closed the door behind him."

Emin took a small sip of the tea to assess its temperature. It was hot, yet not scalding, allowing him to

While Running Away

take a larger sip the second time. Though it wasn't a perfectly brewed tea, the hot, sugar-flavoured liquid with a hint of tea passed through his throat after many hours, relieving the lingering bitterness in his mouth. The "Chief" pushed the cup in front of him a little forward and got up from his seat, placing the left half of his bum on the right front side of the table and his right foot on the floor. The other two officers who had just arrived took their seats opposite Emin.

While Emin contemplated the possibility that the Chief was attempting to emphasise his authority by positioning himself at a higher spot than the others, the Chief, leaning slightly to his right, began speaking in Bulgarian in a low voice. The customs officer who had sat on the right side of the seat across from Emin and had taken his statement the previous night translated the Chief's words:

"Neighbour, listen carefully now! Our Chief doesn't speak Turkish, so I will translate for him word by word. He says, 'He arrived here with a fake passport, which is a violation under our laws. It carries a penalty of six years in prison. Does he know that?' Do you comprehend, neighbour?"

"Yes, understood."

After translating Emin's answer, the "Chief" continued in Bulgarian.

At first, Emin felt uneasy about this start, but he soon recognised the situation. "The man represents the Bulgarian authorities, and what he's saying is accurate —based on their law or whatever. Furthermore, like any authority, it's natural for him to begin his speech intimidatingly. Authority asserts itself wherever you are in the world."

His thoughts were interrupted by the voice of the officer who was translating:

"Let him answer my questions truthfully. Let him explain everything correctly. If he helps us, we'll help him. OK?"

"OK."

Perhaps because he understood Emin's response, who had become comfortable with his acceptance of reality, or maybe because he did not expect a challenging answer, the "Chief" would continue speaking without waiting for the translation. The other one would translate, and this would continue throughout the night.

"First, tell me your full name, surname, date and place of birth. Then, the names and places of birth of your parents and siblings. (...)"

The questions were the same as the interrogation the night before.

"Then tell me about your life, starting from your childhood."

The customs officer added his request: "Speak slowly with the intervals so I can translate every word of you."

Emin repeated the same things he had said the night before. He stopped every three or four sentences for the customs officer to translate. Emin noticed that the officer beside him was taking notes as the translation continued.

When Emin had finished "talking about his life", the "Chief" said something, and the officer got up and left the room without saying anything. It didn't take him long to return and take his seat.

The "Chief" started talking again, and so the officer translated:

"My Chief says we know that the Turkish police infiltrates every leftist organisation. Who were the moles in your Party? Tell us their names."

"There is no such person I know of or have heard of. We were never confronted with such a person in any police and prosecutors' interrogation or court trial, and there was never such person used as a witness against us."

As his words and the "Chief's" answer were being translated, Emin tried to devise a tidy answer to prevent the issue from dragging on, as he guessed the question would be repeated somehow. His guess was correct. The question was short and straightforward:

"OK, you may not know for sure. Don't you have any suspicions?"

Emin's answer was ready:

"It is our principle. We do not say anyone is a mole without definite evidence or concrete information. We do not make such a labelling or accusation even for those we are most opposed to. No such accusation has ever been made against any party member. This has always been a moral principle our Party firmly adheres to."

That's what he said, but he was thinking while the translation was going on: "Wouldn't I be suspicious? Is it just me? Some of them were the target of other friends' suspicions, too. They had almost parachuted into the Party from the top, those who had black holes in their past. Hasan also shared my suspicions about some people. What would happen if I named them? What would happen is that I would be violating the moral principle I mentioned."

He had told the Bulgarians the truth about this. Indeed, there was no single incident in the Party in which this principle was violated. These were suspicions based on what was told to each other in the conversations between friends who believed in and trusted each other after the dissolution of the Party, not before. There were events one knew but the other did not or instances where one's partial knowledge was complemented by the other to form a complete or larger picture.

It was an "infamous" event that strengthened these suspicions. In this case, too, no concrete data went beyond the limits of suspicion. After all, the Party had disintegrated. Emin could and would not tell these things. Moreover, according to the scenario drafted by his friend and Emin, just in case it was needed during his runaway: "The Party had not dissolved!" He had not told the truth about this and had to continue this lie.

Again, the interpreter's translation interrupted his thoughts:

"Not a single person, you suspect?"

"No. As I said before, our Party is very principled on this issue. I also adhere to this principle of our Party, which is correct.

The Bulgarian "chief" did not press any further and moved on to the crucial question:

"Would you like to defect to us and live here?"

His answer was the same as the night before:

"It is an honour to live in a socialist country. But ..." He kept going on with the repetition.

"Well, how will you get to England?"

"I'll go to Yugoslavia first if you let me go. In Novi Pazar, there are relatives of one of our party members who is from there but lives in Istanbul. They will help me during my stay there. Then I will go to England with the help of our friend in England."

"We can put you on a plane from Sofia. Go to London from there."

For a moment, Emin felt cornered by this unexpected suggestion, which had never occurred. This time, he was lucky; the tea officer had already come with a tray and distributed tea cups to everyone, starting with him. As understood, the officer, who had just gone out briefly, ordered tea. It had given Emin enough time to prepare his answer.

"I've just told you. My mate in England will help. His girlfriend will come to Yugoslavia."

In fact, when Hasan and Emin were exploring the potential risk, they included this possibility in their plan. Emin was not making it up; it was not a complete lie. They considered it a possible solution, especially if he had difficulty leaving Yugoslavia. As Osman's asylum application had yet to be accepted in the UK and he could not travel abroad, the onus was on his girlfriend, whom Emin had met when she had visited Turkey.

Emin continued to talk:

"Since organising the solicitor in England and similar arrangements have been made, we will decide when I will go to London. This is a plan made by our Party, and I have to obey it. As you know, Party members must obey Party discipline and decisions."

The most terrible aspect of this attractive offer, which would, in fact, make his departure extremely easy, was the possibility that the Bulgarians would demand a price(!) for it, just as the offer to live there would be a burden. If the Bulgarians prevented him from going to Yugoslavia, he would inevitably have to accept it. He had tried to push his luck to the limit with his answer.

When the translation was finished, the "Chief" responded in one word: "Utopia!"

"No need for a translator, I understand." Emin smiled and continued:

"Turning utopias into reality is a requirement of being a communist. Our Party is disciplined. Each of us will do our part to fulfil the decisions taken. Our friend in England will also do what is necessary."

He concocted the story again, even though he didn't believe it!

As the "Chief" listened to the translation, He smiled... Emin wasn't sure if it was too early to get his hopes up, but a wave of optimism swept over him. "We are the children of utopias," he thought as the conversation in Bulgarian began between the "Chief" and the custom officer, the night's translator, who was reading from his notes from the night before, sometimes joined by the Bulgarian officer in a suit sitting next to him.

* * *

When he thought that day, "We are the children of utopias", he did not know some years later, he would say, "We need to reconsider the concept of 'utopian socialism'!"

His thoughts, caught in a current like a crab, were in constant motion, pulled between the confines of conventional understanding and a desire to transcend the present reality. Despite flowing in a specific direction, there was a sense of inner turmoil, as if he struggled to navigate beyond the constraints of the moment. "If utopia is a project or idea that is impossible to realise, wouldn't it cease to be utopia if it was realised? Wasn't 'Twenty Thousand Leagues Under the Sea', surpassed by leagues today, a utopia when Jules Verne wrote it? Then, according to whom is utopia a utopia, and according to which time is it a utopia?"

"Hasn't the reality you live in," Emin thought, referring to the Chief, the Bulgarians, and the other socialist countries, "because you have lost your utopias, in the dryness of living for today, turned into the barrenness of mules that cannot promise anything for tomorrow? Hasn't socialism ceased to be the hope of humanity and been reduced to the protection of a state that claims to act 'on behalf of the working class' and the other states around it? Have you not condemned tomorrow to today by submitting to today?"

He had generalised his internal conversation, considering the other person as a representative of the regime rather than a just member of Sofia's secret service:

"Haven't all these massacres and atrocities in the name of 'protecting the socialist Homeland', as you claimed, also condemned tomorrow to today?"

When he said, "Didn't you hang your sieves on your chest as medals after crushing and sifting the utopias of humanity on the millstone of your realism?" Emin was picturing the medals Brezhnev wore. The metaphor of "today-tomorrow", which was shaped in his mind as a repetition of what he had expressed in the "[Extraordinary General] Organisation Meetings", was later introduced to the stage through Lopukhov's mouth when Emin was adapting Chernyshevsky's novel "What is to Be Done?" into stage: *"Society does not change out of nowhere. Life does not stop until society changes. If you, me and people like us submit to the existing situation, how will that society change? Tomorrow is built from today. The one who submits to today condemns tomorrow to today."* While it reverberated as a cry, a distinct emphasis resonated on the stage:[42]

"Tomorrow is built from today!"
"Tomorrow is built from today!"
"Tomorrow is built from today!"

But at the time, when he was trying to get away from the Bulgarian officials, he did not yet realise that these five words, 'Tomorrow is built from today!', would unlock the Leninist shackle on his head later in the future. Although the

---

[42] The theatre piece in Turkish with the same title as Nikolay Chernyshevsky, "What Is To Be Done?" was staged in London in 1997.

reckoning he had begun to experience was once again stirring its mortar while trying to cross the Bulgarian border, he had not yet reached the maturity to untie the knot from where it had been tied off. The borders guarded by the border guards were the borders between 'socialist realism' and 'socialist utopia', and at that moment, his world of thought was on the borderline: 'Isn't labelling every thought and design that goes beyond acceptance as 'utopia' the shortest way of attempting to destroy the hope for tomorrow by deeming it unrealisable today? Isn't this 'utopia' label a 'call to submit to today'? Isn't it, then, a way of saying, 'Sit down, sit down; the honour of living in a socialist country is not enough for you?'"

"Am I exaggerating when I go through all these storms of thought based on a single word,' utopia'? No, one shouldn't back down!"

When the Bulgarian "Chief" started talking to him again, a sentence filtered through life settled in Emin's thoughts: *"Those who cannot dream cannot even pickle."*

* * *

The "Chief" spoke with the smile of giving someone good news, and the softness of his face, reflected in his voice, was not looking at the interpreting customs officer this time but directly at Emin. The officer translated with a similar facial expression:

"We believe that your story is true. We will help you. We will let you go to Yugoslavia. But before you go, we want you to write down what you have told us here in your handwriting, OK, neighbour?"

"Sure, I'll write," Emin said with no objection.

"When you've finished writing, you'll take the bus to Yugoslavia, which passes here every day at midnight."

"OK, thank you."

After the officer finished translating, the 'Chief's' Bulgarian was followed by the Bulgarian of the customs officer. The 'Chief's' Bulgarian filled the room before the customs officer began translating again. Emin, curiously watching the conversation, caught the word "problema" in between. He focused all his attention on the customs officer who had translated before, curious to see what would come from underneath.

"We will inform our customs officer at the Yugoslavian border of your arrival. If there will be problems with your entry into Yugoslavia, go back on foot. Come back to our gate. The officer will inform us. Then we'll come and pick you up. We'll put you on a plane from Sofia. We'll send you to London. OK, neighbour?"

Emin, whose concern first turned into joy, could not stay in the "mansion of relaxation" for long, and although he was worried about "what if I have to go back and they force me to defect to Bulgaria", he answered, trying not to give a sign of his concern:

"OK, thank you."

What else could he say?! As the officer finished his translation and listened to what the "Chief" had said, Emin asked a question to show sincerity and satisfy his curiosity. Still, he waited for the officer to continue translating what the "Chief" had said.

"You will go into the next room. You will write there. Do you want anything?"

"Another cup of tea would be nice. But first, I want to ask you something."

As he waited for his words to be translated, instead of translating them, the customs officer answered:

"Ask!"

"The Turkish police did not realise that my passport was fake. How did you figure out otherwise?"

In contrast to the customs officer who smiled while translating, the "Chief" gave his voice a tone of pre-eminence as he responded. The custom officer proudly imitated his "Chief" while speaking in Turkish, which he had mastered very well:

"We can catch. That's our job. It's a professional secret. We can't tell you how!" While trying to show sincerity, Emin had unintentionally flattered the Bulgarian officials.

As the officer got up from his seat and headed for the door, Emin also got up; he took his coat under his arm and tucked the biscuit packet he took with his right hand under his left armpit. When he bent down to pick up his suitcase, he heard the officer's voice:

"I'll get it, neighbour."

He followed the customs officer, who took the suitcase and walked away. The customs officer opened the door to the next room he had seen on his way in and gave way to Emin. The jalousie curtains of the small square-shaped room were closed entirely on the not-so-large window directly opposite the door. The other room had a smaller table in front of the window. Between the table and the window was a grey armchair similar to the one "Chief" was sitting in the other room, also covered with artificial leather. The light coming from the anteroom disappeared into the light of the room as the officer turned the knob on the right side of the door. Leaving the biscuit packet in his hand on the table and his coat on the armchair, Emin decided not to ask for permission to use the toilet and just inquired, 'Where is the toilet?"

Despite his concern about what would happen if he returned from the Yugoslavian border, his question was a sign of self-confidence, expressing a request rather than a plea for permission. The officer gestured to the bottom of the stairs leading upstairs. The toilet was cleaner than expected, though he dried his hands with toilet paper instead of the towel hanging behind the door. When he returned to the room, he found a wad of white paper, a ballpoint pen on the table, and a large cup of tea waiting for him.

"Sit down, neighbour." He was pointing to the chair, the customs officer with plenty of "neighbours."

"If you need anything, I'm in the next room. Come and let me know," the officer added as he was about to close the door behind him and leave. However, Emin asked, "Is there an ashtray?" He was once again showing an attitude of not seeking permission but rather notifying that he intended to smoke.

"OK, I'll get it now, neighbour, but don't smoke too much. The room is small."

The imperative from the officer and the subjunctive from Emin had collided!

While Emin was placing his coat from the armchair on top of the suitcase, the officer returned, placed a small metallic ashtray on the table, and left the room. Emin was now alone in the warm room with his writing task.

He removed his jacket and hung it on the back of the armchair. He removed a cigarette from the packet in his pocket but changed his mind. Instead, he placed the cigarette back in the packet next to the ashtray, put a match on top of it, and opened the biscuit packet. He had felt hungry, and the bitter taste in his mouth started to return. He moistened a biscuit with a sip of tea. Two biscuits were enough to quell his hunger. The warmth of the tea he drank from the half-empty cup left him feeling content. Afterwards, he lit a cigarette. As he tapped the first ash of his cigarette onto the tray, the metallic tray took him back to July 1984.

* * *

"Light it here; you must have pinched cigarettes from your father. I guess you're used to smoking army officer's cigarettes,[43]" said the Army Captain, tapping the mouth of the packet in his right hand with the index finger of his left hand. Two cigarettes protruded halfway. Emin took one of the cigarettes offered by the Army Captain and brought it to his lips. Anticipating the need for a lighter, the Army Captain pushed his lighter and the metal ashtray toward Emin, pre-empting any need for him to ask. "Tell me, your father was a retired colonel, isn't he?" The Army Captain, trying to establish rapport by offering the cigarette, had Emin brought to the room directly opposite the inner door of Selimiye Prison.

A little earlier, just after Corporal Laz had picked him up, as they were closing the prison's door, he had said, "Alright then, you're getting out of prison." Emin had inquired, "But what about my belongings?"

"They'll stay, so let's go."

The inmates did not like this corporal, the "infamous hero" of an incident that would later make them laugh quite a lot. This ignorant corporal used to misbehave whenever he engaged with them.

---

[43] Special cigarettes were produced for only the army officers in Turkey, with the brand name "Officer."

"There's something dodgy about this!" Emin had thought. "I wonder if they are going to make me pay for making the Istanbul police political branch chase me for twenty days and then surrendering directly to the Martial Law Prosecutor's Office." The fact that it had become a common practice for political prisoners to be taken from prisons and interrogated again by the police after the military coup on 12th September 1980 had brought this possibility to his mind when he heard that he would be released from prison and would not be able to take his belongings. The prisons had not been a refuge for the politically persecuted people from police brutality anymore.

With these thoughts in his mind, as he had passed the other two wards on the right and walked to the door of the administration office at the end of the inner corridor of the jail, situated at the entrance of the prison, Laz corporal had jumped up from his left, had opened the door, and had reported:

"The prisoner is ready for your orders and instruction, sir!"

The Lieutenant Colonel, the Prison Commander, who had once served as the instructor of the 'Tank Introduction' course at the Infantry Training for Reserve Officers during Emin's attendance and whom everyone affectionately referred to as the "Fatherly man," had once again used his paternal tone when addressing Emin, saying, "Come here, Emin." This time, he was fatherly because he knew that Emin was the son of a retired army officer. Upon Emin's arrival for the first time following his arrest, the Commander had noticed his last name and inquired, "Is your brother here as well?" Upon receiving an affirmative response, he continued questioning, 'Is your father also here? Does he know you were arrested?"

Emin had responded with a respectful tone:

"I don't think he knows I've been arrested. I think he's in Selimiye, but I don't know where in the building."

"Gosh, your mum will get upset again. Tell me your home phone number."

After dialling the phone number and finding out who he was speaking to, he introduced himself and continued:

"Your son Emin is with me right now. Unfortunately, he has been arrested, but don't worry. As the Commander of this place, I assure you that we will care for him like our own son; no harm will come to him."

"Come here, Emin," the lieutenant colonel had said following the introduction by the 'infamous' corporal. At that moment, Emin recalled again how the lieutenant colonel was conducting his duties as an army officer in the prison. Unlike the torturer in Diyarbakir Prison, the lieutenant colonel treated the prisoners with respect. The tone the lieutenant colonel called out, "Come here, Emin," also slightly relieved Emin.

Then, he continued: "An army captain on duty will see you. He's waiting for you in the room opposite the door. You will go there with the corporal!"

"The dodginess is coming from the arsehole, who said 'you will be released from prison' to me! "But... We never saw an army captain at any roll call or search in the prison. What the hell is going on?"

These thoughts were going through his mind his mind as his feet carried him to the army captain's room. After instructing the corporal, who was leaving, to close the door behind him, the army captain ordered Emin to "sit down" and gestured toward the chair opposite him. Finally, he had offered Emin a cigarette.

"You are the son of an officer. The prison commander, Lieutenant Colonel, knows you from the Infantry Training for

Reserve Officers and has never seen or heard of your misbehaviour. You had completed your military service without any adverse incidents. Obviously, you've inherited a sense of military honour from your father. Your Party is called the Homeland Party, and it's clear that you love your country. You, as understood, entered politics with youthful enthusiasm. As an honoured officer in the Turkish Army, I wouldn't want to see another honoured army officer's son waste away in prison. Nor would our other army officers, including our Prisoner Commander. In fact, our honourable Army has halted the dangerous path that nearly pushed our homeland to the brink with its revolution. One of the objectives of this revolution is to safeguard the youth to whom Atatürk entrusted our Republic..."

After hearing the word "revolution", Emin was torn away from the Army Captain's speech and fell into his inner dialogue:

"A revolution? It's a coup d'état, and you either don't know the difference or you're speaking with the mindset of the generals. Like 12th March, 12th September is also a coup d'état. A coup d'état, in essence, is the power struggle between the cliques, even if they hold on to power from the edges and those at the top who are servants of the system. Hierarchy is crucial for them. It's done by preserving the chain of command. One form of reactionism replaces another. Revolution, on the other hand, is rebellion. It's the 'enough is enough' of those at the bottom. It doesn't care about hierarchy. It's the right of not only civilians but also soldiers, especially those below, to rebel. It has potential social openings, especially if it joins with civilian rebels. While there are no guarantees, such openings are possible. The more organised the sans-culottes are in mind and body, the more progressive it becomes. It's a matter of 'you reap what you sow.' Otherwise... it's possible to slide into the most unlikely reactionism. Even while indulging in reactionism perversions on the one hand, on the other, it can swim in progressive fluctuations. By looking at the Carnation Revolution in Portugal, which brought down the fascist Salazar, we can see under what conditions and to what extent it can go and whether it can turn into a social revolution. But the one in Portugal was not a coup d'état but a revolution. In short, one should not confuse a coup d'état with a revolution and rebellion."

In response to the army captain's lengthy speech, these thoughts had not been voiced; instead, Emin had pretended to listen, his gaze fixed on the ground. He had remained silent.

When the Army Captain said, "Now, what I want from you is," Emin collected himself. The stream of his thoughts ceased, and the excuse for keeping his head down was no longer necessary. The Army Captain couldn't tell from Emin's eyes that he wasn't paying attention. It was time to listen to the army captain's 'request.' So, Emin listened.

"Tell me about your Party's illegal activities openly. Don't be afraid; it won't be discussed at trial. We will protect you and get you out of here immediately. Furthermore, we'll ensure your acquittal in court. You can then return to work. We will also assist you in securing a promotion at the bank. As a top trainee, you've already completed the promotion course at the bank. Your managers have expressed confidence in your bright future. We'll do our utmost to support you. As the son of an army officer and someone who has completed military service, you understand that 'pacta sunt servanda'—honouring our word is paramount. We stand by our commitments."

The conversation that began with the first-person singular, 'What I want from you,' shifted to the first-person plural, 'We will blah blah blah...' The initial objective of the first-person plural was to compel the other party to surrender. Surrender was not part of Emin's, his own 'self-isolation' period, which he had been living through.

"No matter what I did, I caused harm to myself, but what was it that I boasted about for years, saying that not even a single one of my friends' noses would bleed because of me? Wasn't it really 'pacta sunt servanda' in the end. Does someone who is a puppet of the generals have 'pacta sunt servanda,' or is it the one who rebels against the political generals?" he didn't say. Still, this MIT-style speech had adversely affected Emin, sharpening his stubbornness. He did not say all these, but the speech from the Army Captain, who is obviously an MIT operative, had sharpened Emin's conviction. Even though he was not in a position to express himself loudly, he could have swum in these waters with the sharpness of a swordfish without any noise.

"My Captain," he began. He should have said, "My Commander," according to prison rules. But now that he was out of the prison, the Army Captain had assumed the role of a purchasing and selling officer negotiating on behalf of the state, not as if he were talking to a prisoner. Emin was addressing a member of the "dark forces." At least, that's how Emin perceived it, and he had to speak calmly but firmly to prevent a repetition of such a meeting:

"I have worked as a member and an executive of a lawfully established Party. I have made my most controversial statements and used the harshest words within the bounds of the law, and I have always acted by the law."

He had repeated the word "law" over and over again.

"During this period, I have not witnessed any unlawful or, as you called 'illegal' activities of my Party or fellow party members. I would not have stayed in that Party even for a moment if there were any unlawful activities. Moreover, in the last congress I attended, our Party made a clear-cut decision on the legality issue and shared it with the public. The police were present at that congress, and as far as I know, they even taped the speeches. That decision stipulated that our Party would abide by even the laws it opposed but that all legal means of struggle would be used to change those laws. Our Party was a party that openly declared that it was Marxist-Leninist and did not hide it. Since it believed that legal struggle should be carried out this way, it wanted to show an attitude by openly declaring that it parted ways with all Marxist-Leninists who did not think so. Because we were sincere and honest, we did not hide that we were Marxist-Leninists. Because we believed that a legal party should not have an illegal struggle, we announced our attitude publicly to everyone with such a resolution. The documents belonging to our Party, the Central Committee Resolutions Book, are now in the hands of the Prosecutor's office. All the activities we have done and want to do are written and drawn in those documents."

He had said these, but... Emin had placed ellipses to the flow of his thoughts, letting time fill the gap where the zurna was[44] makes an out-of-tune sound, even though he had placed an unequivocal period at the end of what he had said to the Army Captain.

The Army Captain, whom he had no doubt was an MIT operative, did not try to corner Emin. He pressed his last half-finished cigarette into the metallic ashtray, took the

---

[44] Zurna is a double-reed outdoor wind instrument, usually accompanied by a davul (bass drum) in Anatolian folk music.

cigarette packet on the table with the lighter together, and put it in his pocket. This signalled the end of the meeting, but as he stood up, he uttered his last sentence:

"OK. If you want to tell me something later, tell my Commander, the Lieutenant Colonel; he'll let me know, and I'll come and see you again."

Like the spirals of cigarette smoke in the room, this sentence would disperse into the air and vanish before Emin's eyes. At the same time, the reflection of the moment when the zurna produced an out-of-tune sound would linger in his sight for many years to come.

* * *

[Flashforward - For the following years, years after years and several times:

He would always present an example from the art of "tecâhül-i ârif"[45] **while telling his friends in later years by putting "the miracle of the miracles!" at the beginning of his sentences related to the "infamous" event each time.**

"Miracle of the miracles!" The police don't ask. After hiding for about twenty days, I surrendered directly to the Martial Law Prosecutor's Office. I was not questioned by the police, but others involved in the case were. Which police? The Homeland Party Desk of the Istanbul Political Branch. When I was released from Selimiye Prison, they handed me over to the police station in Kadıköy, and from there, I was taken to the Istanbul Political Branch. With others released from other cases, we were made to wait with our faces to the

---

[45] Same as note: 17

wall and our backs to the door. At one point, the door opened, they called my name, and I turned round.

Emin was talking to his friends, but he was moving from one place to another and from one moment to another while speaking.

"Come here."

One of the two plainclothes policemen in the doorway called out.

"You think you're so smart, don't you?"

The policeman who said this to me turned to the other 'civilian police' next to him:

"This is the brothelgoer who bypassed our Homeland Party Desk and surrendered directly to the Martial Law Prosecutor."

"The Colonel's son?"

"Yes, it is!"

"Let him think he got away with it, Chief. He'll end up here anyway. They're the travellers, and we're the innkeepers. We'll get him anyway!"

"Fuck off, back to your place. You heard you're gonna fall into our hands one day. Then you'll see your midwife's arse!"

Emphasising the repetition of the word "anyway," Emin would always continue to talk in the same way:

"Now, these police officers specialised in the Homeland Party do not ask any questions to the friends they have captured about the "infamous" event. Moreover..."

"The miracle of the miracles! No question was asked about the "infamous" event at the prosecutor's office. They didn't ask me, nor did I hear anyone else being asked.

"The miracle of the miracles! Neither I nor anyone was asked about the "infamous" event during the trial.

"The miracle of the miracles! Even that Army Captain didn't ask about the "infamous" event. He doesn't ask, the Army Captain, and he's from the "MIT", but he doesn't ask!

"The miracle of the miracles! The state ignores the "infamous" event that gives them the chance to bring us down on our knees. Neither on the day when the Army Captain interrogated me, nor before, nor after, from investigation to prosecution, from interrogation to judgement, at no stage has this "deep silence" been broken!

"When it came to their behaviour, Emin would leave irony aside.

"And what did we do? We kept silent. We shared the "deep silence" of the state. This is not an accusation but quite the opposite. We did it right by staying silent on this matter.

"And, doing right that heals being subject to injustice goes hand in hand with being rightful this time. Is this too mystic or too naive approach? I think not. We could not break away from what was right because we were right. Moreover, the right attitude required us to share the enemy's tactic of silence or rather to endure the tactic of silence. It may appear paradoxical, but this was our reality. If inequality dominates society, there is a price to be paid for being right and rightful. We had to bear the consequences of it honourably.

"In one instance, in the corridors of Selimiye, Selda and I were waiting to be called to the courtroom. She said, 'Those guys ran out of Turkey; they saved themselves. We should say at the court, "Whatever was

done illegally was done by them; judge them, not us!" My answer was to remind her of the principle I have always defended, the principle of not causing one of my friends' noses to bleed even if we had parted ways. She closed the subject by saying, 'I was just joking'."]

* * *

As he took his last puff, the cigarette burning his fingers brought Emin back to reality. He stood out from the clouds of the past. While blunting his memories and cigarette in the ashtray that brought them, he placed the point where the rubber meets the road in the back of his mind.

"Stop dawdling," he scolded himself; "Write down what you need to write and finish it as soon as possible. Missing the bus may delay your departure for another day unless another bus arrives. You don't know whether it will come or not," he said, moving from his inner dialogue to the conversation of his pen on the paper:

"Name and surname: ..."

It was not difficult for him to write his story, which he told twice in twenty-four hours. The door to the hesitation of "Should I write this or that?" was already closed. Without thinking about it, he had no difficulty putting what he would write on paper in short sentences as if repeating the lines of a theatre play. The effort to keep the lines aligned adequately on a plain white background was challenging, and it slowed him down when he reached the middle of the third page. After a while, the pen, which he held tightly with the tension, increased by this endeavour; he stopped, especially when the middle finger of his right hand started to ache. He rubbed the middle finger of his right hand, which he took between the thumb and index finger of his left hand, where the tightly held pen had made a mark for a while.

The thought that "If I had a lined paper, I could put it on the bottom and write faster" made Emin get up from his seat and lead to the next room. Even though the second cigarette had turned to ashes in the ashtray rather than being smoked, the smoke from the two cigarettes had already filled the room. The air, saturated with carbon monoxide, slowly drifted towards the entrance hall as Emin opened the door.

Leaving the door wide open and giving the fumes the freedom to "escape en masse", he knocked on the next room's door. Still, Emin entered without waiting for any words of invitation. Even if Emin had waited, he wouldn't have discerned whether the response was "Yes, come in" or "Wait," as he anticipated encountering the Bulgarian-speaking 'Chief' in the room. Unexpectedly, the "neighbouring" officer was reading a newspaper in the armchair where the "chief" had been sitting.

"Excuse me, do you have lined paper?"

The officer looked up from his newspaper and did not understand what Emin wanted. A short gap of silence passed between them.

"Lined paper?"

"I only need one. To put under the white paper. It'll help me write better."

Emin concluded that the officer understood what he wanted from how he opened and rummaged through the drawers. Emin waited.

"No."

"OK, thank you."

Emin was moving to leave the room; it crossed his mind:

"Do you have a ruler?"

The word "ruler?" came out of the officer's mouth as a question without a preposition.

"Yes, ruler. I draw a line on paper and put it at the bottom."

When he realised the funny double meaning of his half-formed sentence, the laughter he had been holding back was reflected as a smile on his lips.

"Wait a minute!"

The officer rummaged through the drawers again, but more quickly. "That's not there either."

"OK, thank you."

Emin left the room and closed the door. "While I'm up, let's go to the loo, too!" He went to the toilet under the stairs to empty three big cups of tea, which he had drunk since he had arrived.

"The teas you drink more than two will force you to go to the loo!" He was inspired by the Mesopotamian proverb: "The dates you eat in the evening will scratch your ass in the morning." The relaxation that came to his body was also reflected in his brain in the toilet. He laughed to himself. The loo could also be called a "mind-blowing centre". He had found the solution he was looking for. He flushed the toilet and washed his hands. The cigarette smoke had almost dissipated when he crossed the hallway and reached the room where a black ballpoint pen summarised his life on paper. As soon as he closed the door and hurriedly sat down on the soft armchair, he folded a piece of white paper first in half, then quarters. He tested it and folded it again in the middle to make it stiffer. His ruler was ready. He started drawing lines almost one centimetre apart on a blank page and stopped halfway down. That was enough. He would place it under the page he would write. As he would complete writing on the upper half of the page, he would pull down it for the rest. There was no need to waste time drawing lines on the other half of the paper. With the help of the lined page, his speed increased as he continued writing from where he left off.

When the "neighbouring" officer opened the door and rushed in with a tray, a bowl, a spoon, two slices of bread and a bottle of coloured soda on the tray, Emin travelled back from the past to the present.

"You must be hungry, neighbour. Here is your dinner."

As Emin pulled the tray, which had been placed in front of the table, aside the papers and moved it in front of him, he thanked the customs officer and lifted the soda bottle. Then, he handed it back to the customs officer and asked, "Can I have a glass of water instead?"

"OK, neighbour, I'll get it. You can keep that, too."

When the customs officer left, Emin murmured, "Soup, but what kind of soup?" as he dipped the spoon into the bowl. Two beans rose to the surface, foreshadowing the blend of carbon monoxide that would mix with methane, hydrogen, oxygen, and nitrogen this time. While spooning his soup, his thoughts drifted to the connection between Bulgarians and the term "soup lovers." He tried to force his memory.

* * *

He seemed to remember. "I think it was in the film 'One Day in a Year'!" he said, entering a new internal dialogue. He brushed aside the chauvinistic messages of the film. The song's lyrics started to harmonise with the melody within him.

"You're a rose that withers before it blooms in my heart."

Had romanticism been an affliction he contracted as he left childhood behind? "No, it's wrong to call it an 'affliction.' Isn't romanticism one of the veins that bring life to the conscience?"

The song played on between his two ears:

"Always gloomy, always sad."

Both sorrow and grief feed on defeat. First, you're defeated in love, and then at the thought of being in love. Love is like socialism. And socialism is like love, too.

Emin himself was nearing the point of expression of the ember, which the poet had declared about three years later to the whole world in just six words.

It was always "her" that was wanted to be reached, tried to be reached even if the name was different, but not found despite sought.

It was always "the one" that he wanted to reach, "the one" sought even if the name changed and could not be found. "The one" defeated and revived while being defeated. "The one" entering and never leaving the life of society and "the one" entering and never leaving the life of a person: The first love...The first love... Its name might have been changing as time passed, but "the one", "the ember", created in dreams, was always "the one" remaining the same.

* * *

[Flashforward:
The poet would tell "the whole story" in six words in 2001: "WHOMEVER I LOVE, IT IS YOU..." [46]
"whomever I love, it's you / astounding
somehow you can't be given up"]

---

[46] It is the poem of **Attila Ilhan**, one of the great poets in Turkey.

While Running Away

* * *

Why is it that people cannot forget their first love?

Is it because of experiencing the unexperienced first time? Is it because it is the person in whom one finds oneself? If so, is it a narcissism?

Is it the meeting with a dream of a mate that s/he has created through life without realising it during that transformation process? That dream, even if it cannot mature and fall into place instantly, once it takes shape, is it the beginning of shaping the future as well?

Isn't the first love the very ember that burns and flares up, even if the height changes, even if its hair and the colour of a pair of eyes changes?

"Hasn't it always been like this for humanity!" Emin was not asking; literally, he was making a statement by removing the question mark and putting an exclamation mark. "Even with Spartacus, even with Sheikh Bedreddin...[47] Even when storming the Bastille... Even with the Paris Commune..."

Soon, he would add to them, "And with Kronstadt rebellion...".

While writing, Emin would link what he had experienced with the history of social development. While writing, Emin would summarise the essence of what he's gone through that he did not comprehend enough at the time they occurred: "That first love, the existence of which has never ceased throughout the history of humankind, one way or another have been part of the life of the society and of the

---

[47] **Sheikh Bedreddin** (1359–1420) was a famous Muslim Sufi theologian and charismatic preacher who led a rebellion against the Ottoman Empire in 1416. He led the revolt against the sultan in the Aegean coastal region of Anatolia. The vital motif of the uprising of Bedreddin and his companions was to share the land equally among people and not to pay the high taxes demanded by the Ottoman government.

human being even though the ultimate union constantly delayed from one spring to another. But delayed for the time being!"

Even after the ideal of the existence of fair, equal, free, fearless people together, but at the same time as an individual, had tasted its first defeat some seven thousand years ago... after the discoveries of Göbeklitepe, now one can say 'fourteen or fifteen thousand years ago'... as Dr Hikmet Kivilcimli put it, "The elements which emerged in a new metamorphosis of social development were always nothing else than the elements of the commune, metamorphosed or simplified by communal laws."

These lines, which he would later read in "The Power of the Commune", had always appeared in Kivilcimli's writings and works, albeit in different sentences and forms. Commune, the communal life, was the first love of humanity. Humanity endeavoured to reach that first love whenever it ran towards a new love. When that didn't work out, humanity tried to find another love like first love. Sometimes, just when it seemed to reach it, it slipped away, but each time, the society tried again and again while enduring so much pain.

He searched his memory to uncover the origins of the term "soup lover." Did it simmer from "cooking" the pain of the people who suffered under Ottoman oppression in Bulgaria? At an early age, Emin had thought that Bulgarians were called "soup lovers" because they liked to drink soup, probably due to the cold. Childishness! Later, he had learned that this term was used for wealthy Bulgarians. Even during the tumultuous times in the Balkans, the Ottoman government passed a law known as the "Çorbacı Code of Practice" to gain the support of Bulgarian peasants, as well as the wealthy Bulgarians known as 'çorbacı'.

"Maybe it was a definition that was later extended to all Bulgarians," he said as he transitioned to a parallel train of thought.

When the productive forces developed by capitalist social relations, which had begun to sprout in the pre-capitalist social order in Europe, pushed and cracked the shell of the old ties, the efforts to close the crack with laws coming down from the top would not be able to prevent the wave coming from the grassroots for a long time. The rupture of the "soup-lovers" from the soup of nations, namely, from the Ottoman Empire, the division and disintegration, which one side considered humiliation and the other liberation from oppression, would occur in bloodshed. The Ottoman rulers were finally forced to recognise those they had called "bloody gangs and bandits" at the end by force of the sword. The divorce process would only be finalised with bloody conflicts.

"This is an inevitable consequence of the process of social development", Emin thought as he sipped the last spoonful of his soup, not knowing that in a few years, the Czechs and Slovaks would divorce without blood on their hands. The flow of his thought was interrupted when the "neighbouring" officer entered with a glass of water and a cup of tea.

***

"I brought a cup of tea too, neighbour; did you finish your soup?"

"Thank you. Thank you very much," Emin said as he emptied the bread crumbs on the table, which he swept with his right hand towards his left palm onto the tray. As the "neighbouring" officer, who had taken the tray, was leaving the room, Emin picked up a cigarette from the more than half-empty packet and lit it up. He was again face-to-face with what he had written and what he would write. After taking two sips of water, he took a deep drag from his cigarette while stirring the sugar cubes he had thrown into the cup, which stubbornly refused to melt.

He had almost reached the end of what he would write when he looked at his watch. The minutes of the evening, most of which were piled on top of nine, were carrying the time towards ten. As he switched from "I will finish before ten" to "I must finish," the pen between his fingers started racing against time. When he put the last dot, he had finished the race only one minute early. No! Six minutes early. His watch was five minutes ahead. He has maintained this meaningless habit since he started working at the bank. Although living five minutes ahead of the events, according to his watch, helped him reach his goal five minutes earlier.

Nevertheless, it had never enabled him to reach the unreachable. The unreachable are detached from time; they are suspended in a void." His thought was interrupted by the sound of "knock, knock" as he tapped the wad of paper he held between the thumb and other fingers of both hands, first vertically, then horizontally and then vertically again on the table. He transitioned from swinging between words and moving toward reality, opening the door he reached after taking four steps around the table. Three steps later, he stood in front of the next door.

As before, he knocked on the room door and entered without waiting for any answer. This time, besides the "neighbouring" officer, the "Chief" was in the room. Although their inquiring eyes found the answer when they looked at the papers in Emin's hand, the "neighbouring" officer, nevertheless, asked his "neighbourly" question in Turkish:

"Have you finished, neighbour?"

"Yes, it's over."

His outstretched hand was meant to say, "Give it to me" without words. This time, after his second step, Emin's outstretched hand handed over the papers to him.

The "Chief" made him speak Bulgarian again. First, the customs officer said something to the "Chief", and then the customs officer threw another bridge from Bulgarian into Turkish:

"Do you want something to eat? Are you full, neighbour? My Chief is asking."

"Thank you. I'm full."

After the soup he had drank, a few biscuits he had snacked on for dessert had truly satisfied him.

The "neighbour" officer translated the words that he carried from the Turkish side to the Bulgarian side, the answer given by the Chief was bossy (!) in both senses of the word:

"All right. Go back to the room. We'll read these. Wait there!"

Emin returned to the room where he came and left himself on the seat with the comfort of someone who had done what he could and got rid of the burden on him. For the first time, he felt the pain that shot from his shoulders to the back of his neck and from there to the back of his head as he sat down. He pressed his neck with his right hand and turned his head from right to left and twice from left to right. He pushed his head back again, then increased the pressure of his fingers on his neck and waited for a while. When he felt better, he straightened up. As he reached for the cigarette packet, his hand stopped halfway. He gave up. He leaned back against the seat, where his back did not meet due to his crooked sitting posture while writing, and closed his eyes. After all the tiredness, coldness, and tension, he did not have to add minutes to minutes to fall asleep, even though it was not deep.

The conductor of the bus, on which Emin was asleep, tapped his right shoulder twice softly with the tips of his fingers. He opened his eyes. First, he saw the "Chief" waiting by the door and then the "neighbouring" officer standing on his right side. The bus and the bus conductor were all in his dream!

"Wake up, neighbour! The bus is here."

When the "Chief" started speaking in Bulgarian, Emin finally managed to close the dream door on the bus and the bus conductor. He was still in the Bulgarian customs building!

"Can I go to the loo?"

Ignoring what was said, the "neighbouring" officer started translating:

"You'll have to pay a hundred Deutsche Marks for the bus. OK, neighbour?" Emin could neither say "No" nor bargain. He didn't even think.

"OK. But let me go to the loo first."

He had wrapped his questioning request in an imperative, getting up from his seat without waiting for the answer. He followed the customs officer, who started speaking in Bulgarian and walked to the other side of the table. Emin had already reached the door before the words of the "Chief," who interrupted him again, were translated. It was clear what the answer was as the "Chief" made way by moving to the side. As Emin headed towards the toilet, the "neighbouring" officer called after him:

"Hurry up, neighbour!"

The officer would not hear him say, "Don't worry, I'll do the small one, not the big one."

While Running Away

At first, he was a little alarmed, but by the time he had urinated, he was both non-sleepy and clear-headed. He mumbled to himself as if he was talking to the officer:

"If you don't let go, can the bus go anywhere?"

Again, this is an awakening point! "The Turk's mind is either while running away or... They didn't ask me any questions after I handed in what I had written. I think they made me bear their burden of laziness in writing while taking my statement by making me write it down. It must have all been just a formality. What's it to you, son? They're letting you go!"

His tiredness was washed away with the cold water hitting his face. As the joy of "I'm getting rid of" spread to his whole body wave by wave, he felt ready to carry his runaway adventure to another stage.

The "Chief" and the customs officer were waiting by the outer door, which would open soon. He looked at his watch; it was half past eleven. Unlike other detentions he had experienced before, this detention lasted for twenty-four hours and would soon end. He quickly returned to the room, put on his coat, grabbed his suitcase, and joined his waiting "neighbours." He had forgotten a packet containing three or four biscuits on the table, which would later leave him slightly upset.

At this point, the "Chief" handed a piece of paper to Emin while the customs officer explained:

"There is an address on it. If you write to this address, it will reach us. Once you arrive in England, send us a letter with your address. We will respond to you."

He overcame the discomfort of "Oh man, they won't leave me alone even where I'm going!" with the thought, "Never mind, I'll tear it up later. They can whistle for it!" He placed the given paper in his wallet behind the money.

"OK, don't worry. I'll write when I get there."

It was another lie that he said to the Bulgarians!

The "Chief" led the way, followed by the customs officer, with Emin close behind. At the exit, the "Chief" moved from the area illuminated by the light above the outer door into the darkness. From there, he stopped under the pale-yellow light illuminating the road. Emin and the customs officer stopped too, before reaching another Yugoslavian bus waiting at the same place where he had picked up his suitcase the previous night, exactly like the bus he had arrived on, with a person, probably the bus conductor, waiting in front of the open luggage door, however, there was something strange that bothered Emin. The bus was facing the Turkish border. Emin felt all his joy tighten into a knot, like a fist in his throat. "Is the bus going to Turkey?" He would try to find the answer to the question in what the 'neighbouring' officer had just said in his inner monologue, with his mood, which had earlier been filled with optimism, now turned upside down, muttering "Damn neighbourliness" to himself".

Don't forget, our customs officer at the Yugoslavian border customs gate knows that you are coming," vocalised the "neighbouring" officer, translating what his "Chief" had said, which was an exact repetition of what had been said during the earlier conversation. The sentence ending with the unspoken question mark, "OK, neighbour?" received a different response than before. Emin, this time, replied to the question with a question:

"Is this bus going to Yugoslavia?"

The "neighbouring" officer initiated his response by addressing the implied question:

"Don't worry, it's not going to Turkey. It will be headed for Yugoslavia."

"Oh, well!"

Seeing them approaching him, the bus conductor, who had been waiting near the open tailgate, approached. As he took Emin's suitcase and placed it in the trunk, the officer translated the orders of the "Chief," who had started giving commands:

"Take out a hundred Deutsche Marks and give them to the bus conductor." As Emin reached into his pocket, the customs officer turned to the bus conductor, translating his "Chief":

"You provide him with the ticket."

The bus conductor paused momentarily, then replied, "Alright, I'll give it to him on the bus. We're already running late."

After double-checking, Emin handed over the hundred Deutsche Marks to the bus conductor.

"Come on, get in, and let's get going. At this speed, it'll be noon before we reach Belgrade."

Although the question about the bus's direction bothered him, Emin didn't utter the words on the tip of his tongue: "But brother, your direction is pointing towards Turkey!" After hesitating momentarily, unsure what to do, Emin extended his hand to the "Chief" and then to the "neighbouring" officer, shaking their hands. He decorated his sentence with a "neighbourly" flower:

"Thank you for your help, neighbour."

In response, he must have repeated what the "Chief" had said, for the officer replied in two short sentences:

"Bon voyage. Remember what we said, neighbour!"

"OK, don't worry, I won't forget."

As if ending a conversation with a friend, he had said, "Don't worry!"

While getting on the bus at the front door, Emin sent a 'hello' to the driver, but that went unanswered. There were no other passengers except a man and a woman in headscarves sitting side by side in the fourth row on the left side of the bus. As he passed by them, he offered them a 'hello' that was also met with silence. With the jolt of the bus making a wide U-turn on the empty road, causing Emin to lose his balance, he fell like a drunk man on the row behind the other two passengers at the windowsill of the right side. Since he set off, he had once again settled on the joy wing of the confusion of emotions oscillating between worries and joys. However, it wouldn't last long.

It wouldn't last long because...

He had been waiting for the bus driver to provide him with a ticket so he could go back to sleep that he had left at the Bulgarian customs building over half an hour ago. He could no longer bear the wait.

Sitting in the left seat of the first row on the right side, the bus conductor was chatting to the driver when Emin called out:

"Excuse me."

He did not give a chance to the bus conductor, who was reluctantly getting up from his seat and approaching him to ask anything:

"Can you give me my ticket?"

"Brother, we don't have tickets. The ticket can only be issued at the coach station."

"But when I was getting on the bus, you said, 'We'll give it to you on the bus,' didn't you?"

"Brother, that's what we said, but we were running late and had to avoid getting into trouble with the Bulgarians!"

The driver's short whistle might have been a signal, and without waiting for Emin to say anything, the bus conductor strode to the front of the bus.

When the conversation between the driver and the bus conductor extended, Emin got up from his seat with his usual impetuosity and approached them. He knew he was in no position to demand, "Give me my money, and I'm getting off," but he couldn't remain still as if nothing had happened.

Upon seeing him approaching them, the bus conductor said, "Abi, take your seat; I'll be back shortly. We'll talk." Involuntarily but inevitably, Emin returned to his seat. The woman in a headscarf was asleep with her head resting on her hands, which were placed like a pillow on the window. But it bothered Emin even more to notice that the man beside her was attentively observing him. Who knows who these people were?

"You've found something else to antagonise. Who's who? Who can do what now? You're not in Turkey anymore. If things go wrong, you can do as the Bulgarians say and try to go to London from Sofia. Don't drag it out!" He had concluded his internal debate with this advice.

When the bus conductor approached him a few minutes later, Emin had calmed down with this thought.

"Abi, look, we can't give you a ticket. Why are you worried about not having a ticket?"

"But what if they ask for a ticket to enter Yugoslavia?"

"They don't ask, Abi. I've never come across such issues."

"Are you sure?"

"What a shame, Abi, am I lying?" said the bus conductor, who had lied when Emin got on the bus at the Bulgarian customs.

"OK, I hope it will be as you say," Emin said as he took a cigarette from his pocket. The bus conductor swiftly lit Emin's cigarette with a lighter before Emin could get his matches out.

"Thank you!"

"Welcome, Abi! Are you going to Yugoslavia for trade?"

"I'm going to visit relatives."

Emin had wanted to brush off the bus conductor with a brief response. Still, it was too late when Emin realised he had inadvertently opened the door to a series of questions. On top of that, he noticed that the other passenger, who was also awake, was watching them intently again.

"Are you from Yugoslavia?"

"Sort of. My grandparents migrated from there."

"Where in Yugoslavia?"

"Novi Pazar."

Waiting for Emin to ask similar follow-up questions, the bus conductor did not return to his seat and remained momentarily silent. Emin was equally stubborn and didn't ask any more questions to end the conversation, but that didn't deter the bus conductor from continuing:

"Are you going to Novi Pazar from Belgrade?"

"Yes."

The contrived, forced conversation took another pause. The bus conductor must have noticed Emin's reluctance to chat, so he hung his words on the closing line.

"OK, I won't bother you anymore. Have a good trip, Abi. Call me if you need anything."

"Thanks. I will." And he would!

He tried to sleep after putting out his cigarette. His eyes hurt, but he couldn't fall asleep. Even though he tried to watch out of the window, the cover of pitch blackness had enveloped the night. The stars and the moon of the night before had surrendered to the dark clouds. Soon, the bus wipers started trying to open the field of vision of the driver, who had slowed down as the rain hastily washed the road.

* * *

What a downpour it was, cutting through the darkness of the night and drumming on the bus's windows! The recurring lightning flashes would now and then part the night's veil, briefly revealing a stunning landscape that he wouldn't have witnessed if he had taken the Bursa route. This time, he was heading to Izmir via Gelibolu/Canakkale without the customary stop in Bursa. Since the Bursa organisation had become part of the new Party, he did not need to stop there. The new Party had affixed 'Socialist' to its previous name, becoming the Socialist Homeland Party (SVP in Turkish). There had been critics of them within the Bursa Provincial Administration earlier, especially among the youth with whom Emin was acquainted. Still, strangely, they were mostly disregarded and overlooked by his Party, the Homeland Party. He would later realise that the Presidium, composed of the two individuals who had parachuted into the Party and Ferman, was preoccupied with something else Emin always refers to as the 'infamous' event, extending far beyond the mere improvement of the Party's organisation.

On his previous visits, Bursa was almost like a respite stop, especially with his conversations with Nurten. In 1972, Nurten's relationship with Nejat was disturbing for the all-male group they were in. Although Nejat was the group's leader, at a meeting Emin and others had held without him, they had concluded that this relationship could pacify Nejat. They had assigned Emin to convey this thought to Nurten, indirectly requesting her to end the relationship. They had thought that since Emin was the closest one among them to Nurten, it would be less disturbing if he would convey this message. In this way, they believed they would show that the group members had no intention of criticising Nurten in atrocious faith but were concerned for the future of the political movement. As Emin struggled to deliver the message, he learned an unforgettable lesson from Nurten, who had defended her relationship and laid bare the absurdity of these ideas. Nurten's statements, which Emin would recall from time to time later on, were precise and unwavering:

"It's not me who should think, but you who meddles in people's private lives!"

Nurten was right, but Emin had to talk to Nejat as part of his duty, given by the group, but it would be a concise conversation. Nejat had also cut it short:

"Nurten said what needed to be said. There's nothing more to say!"

In the face of these reactions, resembling the sharpness of lightning flashes on the way to Izmir, there was only one thing left for Emin to do: Meet Nurten again to apologise and criticise both the groups and his stance. He was going to continue to act in the light of this self-criticism when he encountered similar incidents in the future. When Nurten praised his behaviours later on, Emin would always give the same response:

"What is self-criticism? It is not a confession before a confessor but the ability to correct wrongdoing and avoid falling into it again! This is what makes it the driving force of development in humankind."

He felt that not being able to go to Bursa made him longing for his conversations with Nurten. In the past, during his visits to Bursa from Istanbul, after finishing the meetings with Nejat due to his organisational duties, usually after dinner, the conversations that had begun as a trio would often continue well into the late hours of the night. Nejat, who couldn't tolerate sleeplessness as much as they could, would eventually retire to bed. Nejat was always surprised by the length of Nurten and Emin's conversations, particularly about literature and the books they had read. On one occasion, Nejat had woken up at three in the morning to go to the toilet. Upon his return, he found them still engrossed in conversation. He playfully remarked, "What on earth do you two find to talk about for so long?" while heading to his bedroom, he jokingly replied to their invitation to join them:

"You two city petty bourgeois go on. I've got to get up early in the morning and work to do!"

What Nejat had missed out on was their conversation, which revolved around either Ostrovsky's 'How the Steel Was Tempered' or Chernyshevsky's 'What Is to Be Done?' Emin didn't remember that detail now as he travelled through the wonders of nature gently caressed by the first light of morning. The political struggle had swept the beauties of the friendship aside. It had divided their path, like the road on which the bus was travelling.

Emin resented that he had become emotional; he had duties to fulfil and should concentrate on them. And so, he did. While remembering the past, he wrapped and put asleep the child that was stirring inside him in the swaddling clothes of his thoughts that ordered the plan of his journey, the work he would do, and whom and what he would talk about.

And things went according to plan until, on the way...

After finishing his work in Izmir,[48], he travelled to Aydin[49] and set off for Sultanhisar[50] in the minibus, he boarded at

Aydın Bus Station. About five minutes after leaving Aydın, the person sitting in the single seat next to Emin had got off, but three other passengers had got on in the same place. When Emin realised from the conversation of these young people, one of whom took the seat of the passenger who had got off and the other two were in the back seat, whom he assumed to be students from the way they were dressed, that they were studying at the Ortaklar Primary Teacher Training School, he decided that it was time to "put the Party's resolutions into practice". To his left, a man in his forties sat by the window. He was dressed no differently from any other Aegean peasant. Although he possibly would not react positively, Emin thought he would not show a negative attitude either!

Acting on the Party's resolution to "spreading propaganda wherever there is an opportunity", he took out the newspaper, named "Socialist", from his bag, which was crammed with Party magazines and newspapers. He did not know that Ortaklar Primary Teacher Training School was a school where fascists were dense and dominant. Again, he did not know that he was inviting trouble when he put the newspaper's name in full view.

"Brother, are you a socialist?"

The question came from one of the newly-boarded students sitting in the back row. There was nothing hostile in his expression or tone of voice. Emin thought he could speak freely.

"Yes."

---

[48] Izmir is Turkey's third most populous city, after Istanbul and Ankara, and the largest urban agglomeration on the Aegean Sea. The city's old name was Smyrna.

[49] Aydın: As the reader remembers, this is the name of Emin's friend, but here it is a city (also the province) in the West of Turkey 65 miles (or 105 km) away from İzmir.

[50] Sultanhisar is a municipality and district of Aydın Province.

"Who publishes this newspaper?"
"It's our Party."
"Which Party is that?"
"Homeland Party."
"Homeland Party? Is that party socialist?"
"Yes."
"But its name is nationalist."

For a moment, this insinuation aroused his suspicion. However, given that such labelling also emanated from some leftist circles, it didn't seem entirely unusual. "They, maybe, are from another leftist faction," he thought and attempted to explain. "Our Party is the Party of patriots. Socialists are true patriots. The struggle against imperialism..."

Emin could not finish his sentence when the student sitting at the same level as Emin turned towards him, showing his pistol from under his jacket, which he had just slightly pulled aside with his right hand. The handgun appeared as an integral part of the threat poured into words:

"What the fuck are you talking about? What socialists, what patriots? You're all sell-out communists! Give me that bag."

Before Emin, with his left hand, the same person grabbed the bag from in front of Emin's feet and handed it to those behind.

"Check it out, what's inside?"

"That's not right, but..." Trying to hide his fear, Emin started speaking but didn't know how to continue his sentence, which was also interrupted by a wall of threats again:

"Shut the fuck up. Or else..."

"Guys, what are you doing? Stop it!" The man next to Emin intervened.

"OK, uncle, don't worry," said the threatening student, pulling his hand away to let his jacket cover the pistol at his waist. It was pronounced that he was the chief of the gang.

The minibus stopped, and the driver announced, luckily, that they had arrived at the village café on the outskirts of Sultanhisar that Emin had described before he had boarded where he needed to get off.

The publications were in the laps of the two students in the back, who received another order from their chief, "Give him his bag!". Emin wanted to try his luck while taking his emptied bag, even though he predicted the result:

"Can I take the publication?"

"Get down, what publications? You... What do you communists say? 'Nationalisation!' We nationalised your publications."

Perhaps as a result of being in the midst of so many people, Emin's name was not going to be added to the murders committed by the fascist gangs, which occurred one after the other every day. Still, he also knew he shouldn't insist on getting the newspapers and linger any longer.

Emin alighted the minibus, which he had been staring at from behind. As if the driver wanted to avoid witnessing a possible murder, he had hastily stepped on the accelerator.

When he entered the café, after a hug followed by a "hello", he quickly told İsmail Güldal what had happened.

"Abi, I'm really sorry, I lost the magazines and newspapers you would distribute."

"İsmail Abi", with his easy-going and good-natured attitude, tapped Emin's left shoulder twice with his right hand as if to console him.

"Never mind, don't worry about the newspapers. We'll find a way to get new ones. Be grateful you saved your life. That school is the home of the nationalists. Sit down, have a cup of tea and tell us what's happening at the Party."

İsmail Güldal had realised Emin was scared and had changed the subject with his question.

* * *

The call of Mother Nature brought him back from the memories of another journey to the present one. He knew from the warning on the previous bus that in Bulgaria, the bus would not stop until it reached from one border to another. However, he needed to empty his bladder again, partly because he couldn't fall asleep despite the sleepless night the day before. He called towards the front of the bus:

"Excuse me a minute."

Apparently, neither the driver nor the bus conductor had heard him. When there was no answer, he got up and went to the front, where the driver and the bus conductor were lost in their chit-chat.

"Is it possible to stop somewhere to fulfil an emergency need?"

"Abi, we can't stop until we get to Yugoslavia. If we get caught, the Bulgarians will fine us."

He tried his luck once again, pointing to the deserted road where the bus headlights, illuminating the visibility that had opened up with the cessation of rain, stretched on and on:

"The road's empty, who'll see it?"

"Hang in there a little longer; we'll be at the border in two hours. Let's cross the Yugoslav border."

He returned to his seat helplessly. He had just sat down when he saw the other passenger on the bus get up from his seat and go to the driver. He had not heard the conversation, but since the man, like himself, was pointing the way with his hand, Emin assumed that a similar request had come from him. The man also turned round and sat down.

Despite the darkness, Emin tried to watch the road to linger. A little later, as the bus slowed down, the bus conductor came and said something to the other passengers. When they came to a bend in the road, the bus conductor called out to the seat where Emin was sitting:

"Come on, Abi, get off quickly and do what you need to do, but be quick." Emin got off after the passengers, whom the bus conductor gave way to, by sitting on the seat in front of him. The other two passengers had disappeared behind the bus. He got closer to the bump on the side of the road and unzipped his trousers. With the effect of the bitter cold, he could not immediately respond to Mother Nature's call. Nevertheless, he managed to return to the bus before the other passengers. As he was getting on, he was going to pour cologne from the bottle handed to him by the bus driver -for the first and last time in Europe- into his palm.

As the bus was picking up speed again, he placed his coat folded in half on the armrest of the seat on the aisle side and his head on top of it, stretched his leg bent at the knees to the window side and prepared to sleep, but a little later, when his foot got colder, he sat down again Emin put his head on the side of the seat by the window side, which remained ahead when he tilted his seat by the aisle backwards. This time, he wrapped his coat around his legs. He felt warmer.

When he opened his eyes as the lights of the stopped bus turned on, he saw a Bulgarian customs official in a brown uniform getting on the bus. While he examined and stamped the passports of the other two passengers without asking any questions, Emin had already taken out his

While Running Away

passport and waited for his. Without opening the passport, the officer looked at Emin carefully. Then, he switched on the flashlight and shone it on the picture in the passport. He looked at Emin again. He turned the pages of the passport one by one. When he returned to the page with the photograph, he scratched the edge of the page and then the photograph with his fingernail. "I think he is trying to solve the mystery of the passport he was informed about its forgery", Emin thought. After stamping the passport, the customs officer returned it to Emin without asking any questions.

A little later, they arrived at the Yugoslav customs office booth, where the bus conductor went after collecting everyone's passports. There were only five passports, but it took him longer than expected to come back. When he came back, there were no passports in his hand. He stood between Emin and the other two passengers before he started talking. Speaking in Turkish to Emin, he said, "We are in trouble because of these two Iranians. They won't let us pass. They will send the bus back. But if we give them some money, I will take care of it."

Then he turned to the other two passengers and rubbed his thumb and forefinger together. At the same time, he tried to explain:

"The bus can't get into Yugoslavia. There is no going. I need money." For some reason, when it came to foreigners, everyone had the habit of speaking in broken Turkish!

A male passenger took out his wallet and handed the bus conductor a banknote, the amount of which Emin could not see.

"Not enough, not enough, more, more..." The bus conductor was closing and opening the four fingers of his right hand, which was spread upwards in his palm.

"How much should we give?"

The bus conductor turned his head to Emin to answer his question.

"Forty DM."

"Isn't it too much?"

Emin had remembered the amount they had given to the Turkish police in Edirne.

"That's what they agreed to. They wanted 50 DM per head. I negotiated. You also need to take my effort into consideration. I don't want money; buy me a bottle of whisky at our stopover. I've been working so hard for you."

After counting the money he had received, he reminded Emin once again of the "reward for his labour", pointing to "one" with his index finger in the air:

"A bottle of whisky... A whisky for me."

He went again without waiting long at the customs control point; the bus conductor returned with an officer, opened the door of the luggage storage on the right side of the bus and took the suitcases down. Pessimism knocked on Emin's door once again.

"Oh shit, I guess the money I was given didn't work either. I will probably be at the mercy of the Bulgarians again!"

As he complained to himself in haste, he saw the Yugoslavian attendant squatting down and opening his suitcase. When the bus conductor, standing behind the customs officer, saw Emin looking at them, he spread his hands as if to say, "What can I do?" After rummaging through everything, the customs officer moved on to the other suitcases, which, unlike Emin's, were crammed full. When he finished and stood up, he handed the passports to the bus conductor and walked towards his booths. When the bus conductor returned to the bus, he first threw two passports into the space in front of the steering wheel, then distributed the other three passports to the passengers but did not refrain from reminding them:

"Don't forget my whisky. I want my whisky at the first stopover."

Emin threw a question wedge in front of the conductor's wheel to divert the direction of discussion away from whisky:

"What were they doing with the suitcases?"

"What's it gonna be, Abi? Gun and drinks. But remember, I want my whisky. I've worked so hard. Look... I didn't even make you come down for the suitcase. I did everything myself. Tell me, don't I deserve a bottle of whisky?"

"OK, OK, I'll get it," Emin reluctantly agreed but didn't refrain from cursing under his breath, linking the bottle with the bus conductor's bum.

As the bus wheels were turning towards Belgrade after passing the customs gate, Emin had closed his eyes to go back to sleep when he remembered to look at the passport he had put in the inside pocket of his jacket. He took it out and turned the pages. He turned the pages again and again. There was an exit stamp from Bulgaria but no stamp of entry into Yugoslavia.

"Oh, fucking hell, and now this!" His mouth was all out of order, along with his nerves. When he got on the bus, he added a new one to his consecutive trips to the driver's cab, where the bus conductor was standing.

"They forgot to stamp my passport!"

"What stamp?"

"Entry stamp!"

"Is that so?" said the bus conductor, who took the passport and turned the pages. Then he reached out and took the driver's and his own passports between the steering wheel and the windscreen. The pages of both passports rustled one after the other.

"Neither do ours!"

"What now?"

"Nothing's going to happen. What do you think is going to happen?"

"This could get me in trouble getting out of Yugoslavia!"

"No, man, why would it?"

"There is no entry stamp; what if they say, 'You entered Yugoslavia illegally'? And I don't have a ticket, so I can prove it."

"They won't, don't worry."

"You say so, but what if they say otherwise?"

There were tones of tension in his voice as well as his tone. "Calm down, Abi. We are always travelling back and forth. Sometimes they stamp, sometimes they don't. If nothing has happened to us, nothing will happen to you either."

"You're always travelling back and forth. That's your job. Normally, nothing happens to you, but my situation is different!"

The driver, who had been silent until then, intervened and conversed with the bus conductor in a language Emin did not understand. Then, the bus conductor turned to Emin again:

"Look, we're going to Germany. You can come with us if you want."

"I'm not going to Germany!"

"Where were you going?"

"I told you, to Novi Pazar!"

"It's OK, mate. You can cross the border with us. We'll get you out of Yugoslavia. You'll see that nothing happens; we'll explain the situation if needed. Then you can come back if you want. Then you can get a stamp."

While Running Away

Emin did not know which country they had to pass through first to get to Germany and whether they needed a visa for that country. On the other hand, he immediately decided against it, as it would be costly and time-consuming to do as he was told.

"What kind of rubbish is that?"

"It's up to you, Abi, if you want, as I said. By the way, don't you have a Bulgarian stamp on your passport?"

"I do!"

"It's obvious that you entered Yugoslavia when you left these Bulgarian customs."

The explanation made sense; Emin couldn't object but still couldn't get rid of his uneasiness. They are now far away from the customs point. He returned to his seat with the desperation that no matter what he said, he could not change the situation. As the last puff of his cigarette, in which he wrapped his emotional distress, dissipated in the air and disappeared, Emin disappeared into his suppressed sleep.

When the bus stopped, he opened his eyes to the faintly dawning day. They were in front of a three-storey motel surrounded by trees on three sides. "We will be here for half an hour. You can bring my whisky with you," said the bus conductor, standing by Emin's seat.

"It's all right. Don't worry about it."

When Emin reached the entrance door, which he climbed six steps to, a young hotel porter opened the door and pointed to the cafeteria on the left side with his outstretched hand. Emin, with his thumb and little finger open and the other three fingers closed, put his hand to his ear and asked by placing the sign he made into a single word:

"Telephone?"

Even though he understood what was asked, the young hotel porter hesitated, not knowing how to explain his answer. As Emin gave way to the other two passengers coming from behind, he waited for the bus conductor, who was coming after them.

"Ask the hotel porter if I can phone Turkey from here?"

"You could, Abi."

Following a brief conversation with the young hotel porter, the bus conductor signalled for Emin to follow the young hotel porter heading towards the cafeteria and said:

"Follow this guy, Abi. The phone's inside. Ten DM for three minutes. Oh, and he'll give you the whisky as well."

"How much is that?"

"I don't know, Abi. You two can work it out."

After going down three steps from the opened door, he turned to the right, picked up the extended handset of the telephone on the bar and dialled the number of the house in Istanbul.

"Hello!"

It was his father's voice.

"Hello, Dad, it's me, Emin."

"Hello, son, how are you? Where are you calling from?"

It was a rule he did not call the house directly when he was in Turkey. His father must have been surprised.

"I'm fine, Dad, don't worry. I'm calling from Yugoslavia."

He knew his father, unaware of his plan to leave the country, would be surprised. And he realised from his pause that he was.

"When did you leave?"

"I arrived in Yugoslavia today."

"OK, hold on, I'll put your mum on."

"Emin?"

"Mum, it's me; I'm calling from Yugoslavia. How are you?"

His mother was crying and talking at the same time.

"Thank God, my son, you survived. We are fine, don't worry about us. You take care of yourself."

"It's OK, Mum, don't cry."

"No, it's not that I'm sad, son. You are finally liberated. Are you going to stay there?"

"No, but maybe I'll stay a few days."

"Let me know if you need anything."

"Don't worry. I'll take care of myself. There's nothing you can do from there."

"Let me know anyway."

"Yes, Mum, don't worry. I'll call you from where I'm going. I might have to stay here for a while. Don't worry if I can't call. You have Aslihan's phone, don't you?"

"Yes, I wrote it down. If you need it, I'll give it to you."

"No, no, no. I don't want it for me. Can you call my friend right away? Just say, 'Emin called from Yugoslavia, he's fine. You don't need to say anything else."

"OK, I got it. Don't worry, I'll call your friend right back."

"Mum, I'm putting the phone down; take care, don't worry about me."

"OK, my baby. Kisses. Be careful out there."

"I will be, don't worry about it. I kiss your hands."

As he said his last sentences, he realised his mother had stopped crying.

"She's going to deal with my father's quarrel now. He must have realised that my mum knew about my plans to run away and that she was hiding all this from him," Emin thought.

While in Turkey, he had partially been told about some of the incidents, of which he would hear other interesting details later.

"Your father is not in favour of you living as a fugitive. He says, 'Let him go to jail, we'll take care of him, and it's true what the police say; how long can he walk around with a thorn in his foot?'" Emin was not surprised when he heard these words. It was something he knew and expected. From the beginning, even before the Court of Cassation upheld the conviction, Emin and his mother decided to be accomplices: He would run away. His mother would help him get a fake passport by giving him the money for a piece of land inherited from his grandfather, which she would sell secretly. They would hide his decision to leave the country from his father, not only from his father but also from everyone else in the family, unless circumstances made it absolutely necessary. And so, they did.

When Emin heard the analogy of a "thorn in his foot", he had been once again convinced of the rightfulness of his decision.

* * *

[Flashforward - August 1991:
His left foot ached badly, sometimes so severely that it even caused him to limp. After almost an hour of conversation, Helen Bamber (RIP), who had seen him grimace when he stood up on his left foot by shifting his weight onto it, asked:
"What's the matter, Emin? Are you in pain?"
The conversations he had almost once a month with Helen, the head of the Medical Institution for the Care of Torture Victims, who had been working for torture victims since 1945, had become quite long this time. Emin wanted to skip this pain issue. In fact, Helen was doing a kind of therapy in these conversations. To open

up to Emin, who preferred to gloss over the negativities he had experienced and avoided talking about them, Helen, who had shared her own family matters with years of experience, had shifted the subject to family relations in their last two conversations after Emin learnt that his parents were coming. She encouraged Emin to open up by telling him about her own childhood reactions to her parents' violent disagreements, her son's stubbornness in riding a motorbike even though his foot was still healing after being broken in several places in an accident while climbing in the Himalayas, and how her son had been headstrong since his childhood. Emin was aware of Helen's efforts. He started to tell a little about what he had bottled up, what he had kept to himself. On top of all this, he didn't want to appear like a child whining to his mother by exaggerating a simple ache.

"No, it's nothing important. It's a pain in my left foot. It isn't easy from time to time. It happened when I sat too much and suddenly stepped on it. It will pass when I walk."

"Did you hit something?"

"No, I don't remember. It didn't happen."

"Anything left over from the falaka?"

"I don't know, but I don't think so. It was a long time ago, and it has never happened until now. "

"You never know. These things can suddenly appear even years later. We've just set up an X-ray department here. Let them take an X-ray right away."

"I don't want to disturb you."

"No, no problem at all. Come with me."

She introduced him to the X-ray specialist, briefly told him who Emin was, and made one last warning:

"I'm going to see someone now. If you have time, wait after the X-ray. Let me see the result. If we need to do anything, we'll decide together."

"I won't bother you again."

Helen cut him off, kneading her voice with the timbres of tenderness:

"You do what I tell you to do. Unless you need to do something else, unless you have to go somewhere!"

"No, I don't."

"See you later then," Helen said as Emin entered the X-ray room.

It didn't take long for the X-ray and the result to be received.

"You have a small metal stuck between the tarsal bones of your foot and a calcification surrounding it. Have you had any surgery?"

Although his brain started digging up his memories further, he answered the X-ray specialist's question:

"No, I haven't had surgery on my foot."

"This piece must have been on your feet for a long time. The lime layer around it is quite thick. Take it easy; even use a walking stick for a while. Massage with a painkiller cream. If it doesn't go away, have surgery to remove it."

While the expert talked, Emin remembered what happened when he was about five. His mother had told him about this incident once upon a time, but he did not know the English equivalent of the words. Emin tried to describe it, saying that he had stepped on an embroidery needle on the floor and that the embroidery needle had sunk so deep into the sole that the tip of it was almost coming out of the top of his foot. Her mother had pulled it out from under the sole. The needle tip, which she described by curling the thumb of her right hand, had probably broken off inside.

Helen Bamber had the same reaction as the specialist when he told her about the X-ray results:

"Oh, my God. That must have hurt like hell; how did you stand it?"

"Actually, I don't really remember the moment of the incident. I must have been about four or five years old. I was very young. I know the incident because my mum told me about it later."

When they met again weeks later, he expressed his surprise with his answer to the question, "How is your foot?".

"I have no pain. It's gone."

"So, it's been healed?"

"Yes. When I went home after the X-ray, I examined my left foot thoroughly. There was a slight bump compared to my right foot. I still have it. I think it is because of arthritis."

"Did you have it before?"

"I don't know. There might be, but I didn't notice it. It's a faint bump, anyway. I can feel it more when I touch it."

"How long have you been pain-free?"

"It stopped after Mum and Dad left."

"Did it continue while they were here?"

"Yes."

"Did you tell them?"

"No."

"Why?"

"Especially my mum was very upset about what I was going through. If I told her about it, she would blame herself. So, I didn't tell her."

"Didn't they realise?"

"They did. During one conversation in particular, I grimaced with pain where I was sitting. 'It's because I hit the pedals while getting on and off the bike,' I said to them."

"Is that it?"

"No, it's not. I do it with my right foot. I lift the pedal up with my right foot before I press it. I lied. Lies are always more convincing when they're based on a partial truth. It's not because of that, but I reckon I know why."

"What is it?"

"I mean, that's my opinion. I don't know how scientific it is. It may be psychological, I guess."

"What do you mean?"

"I had told you before my father had favoured my surrender and imprisonment. I was told that once, plainclothes police, possibly from the political police branch, had even gone to my parent's home and had a long talk with my father. They had said, 'How far could he go with that thorn in his foot? Let him surrender as soon as possible and get out while he was still young.' My father had shared this opinion. He told me something while they were here as we discussed these matters. He had had a colonel friend who had been the head of the group of martial law courts. Once, this colonel's son had had an issue related to military service. My father had helped him. When they met while my father was following our court hearings in Selimiye, he had talked about the situation with this colonel, who had shown interest and tried to help, especially during the lifting of my detention. As the trial had reached its final stage, my father had become aware of the news: 'They would convict both of the children. We wanted to save at least one of the children, but unfortunately, it wasn't possible. We couldn't do anything; there were orders from above!' That's what the colonel had told my father."

"You said your brother wasn't punished!"

"Yes, his conviction against him was overturned on appeal."

"They saved him then!"

"No, not exactly. The case was returned to the martial law court for a retrial, asking to reduce his sentence."

It would take about a quarter of a century for Emin to conclude that this rescue had been linked to another person's rescue.

"Didn't your father tell you this before? Was this the first time you've heard it?"

"Yeah. Dad kept it from us. Or from me. It must have been so that I wouldn't run away because he learnt about it before the verdict of the Martial Law Court. After that, the case was appealed. The appeal process took more than a year."

"And then?"

"After that..."

Emin paused for a while. He was hesitating to continue, worried that what he would say would sound strange. But he had already started.

"When my father told me this, I thought about the 'thorn'. If my father had told us what he said earlier, we could have started preparations for my escape much earlier. All of us, all our friends, thought the appeal process would end in our favour, especially given the softening political environment. We had thought the opinion that the verdict would be overturned in an environment where there was talk of abolishing Articles

141-142 of the Turkish Penal Code. We did not know that the verdict against us had already been rendered long ago."

He paused again. He tried to remember the words in that film word for word. Coincidentally, he had watched it at that time, and that scene had particularly caught his attention.

"Have you seen the film The Godfather? The third one?"

"Yes!"

"I don't remember the exact lines. Al Pacino visits the Vatican. He feels remorse for some of the things he's done. While talking to the priest, he experiences the symptoms of diabetes. The priest says, "When the mind suffers, the body cries out!" I supposed mine is something like that! Could it be possible that close to my parent's visit, our conversations about my childhood may have triggered some things subconsciously?

"Could be. Interesting point. It may be the case. Do you think that's why the pain went away after your parents left?"

"I don't know, maybe. For some reason, I thought of it while watching that film. If it doesn't happen again, we can say it's because of that."

Emin would not experience those pains again.]

* * *

On that first day in Yugoslavia, he had no idea that he would later experience foot pain or discuss it. His mind was preoccupied with the payments he had made since he arrived at the Yugoslavian border instead of his father's attitude towards the "thorn in his foot." The charge for the telephone call and a bottle of whisky added to the price of his breakfast, consisting of a pastry called "gibanica" and mint tea, making a total of 50 DM. He didn't know whether to be upset about the diminishing money in his pocket or the suspected overcharging besides the bribe to the Yugoslavian customs officers. The "thorn in his foot" his father had worried about had already lost significance. He had attempted to ease his distress in the "Nana" tea aroma. Yugoslavs had named the mint tea with one letter difference in Turkish, and it tasted pretty good.

After the bus departed following the so-called half-hour break, which actually lasted for an hour, Emin, leaving behind the deceit of the motel, began to gaze at the blue sky with scattered white clouds.

"If it's a cheat, so be it; now I'm travelling freely under the shining sky with a full belly." His mind drifted to the phone call he had made at the motel, "thanks to my mom," he added. The "thorn" on his foot had come out. In fact, he had removed that "thorn" from his foot when he made the "nah" sign with his right hand, which is the Anatolian version of showing the middle finger, while his hand was in his jacket pocket as the bus passed by the police officer who conducted the last check on the bus in Turkey. What wiped the smile from his lips when he remembered this was the recollection of his father's behaviour.

What had happened to the man who had come in his uniform to visit him in Bursa prison, who had then chased after the panel of legal experts appointed by the court to secure his release, who had not left him alone in Selimiye Prison? How had he been convinced that Emin had to serve his time and get out as soon as possible? One memory was connected to another memory. The memory of the argument about the referendum on the junta's constitution came alive.

His father was angry with Kenan Evren for making speeches with the Qur'an in his hand, for 'pontificating on every issue." Still, in the end, it was a constitution brought by the Turkish Army," and he was going to vote "yes."

His father had said, "The envelopes are so thin that they could be considered transparent. What if they see that you voted 'no'? You will get into trouble again. Is it worth it for one vote when there is still a warrant out for you, and you can luckily still walk free? Anyway, there will be more 'yes' votes. What would your vote change?"

Nevertheless, Emin was tenaciously going to object: "Let them realise that there are those who say 'no' to them."

"You still haven't realised the consequences of defying the state. You haven't come to your senses."

The state in his father's mind was the state of the military. The state was equal to the army. To his father, the state was synonymous with the Army — those who had founded, protected, and asserted ownership of the country. From Emin's point of view, he wasn't just arguing with his father; he was confronting a retired military officer who would proudly display a large flag on his balcony during holidays. The lives taken, the tortures inflicted, all these sufferings were for the sakes of that flag... No, not for the sake of that flag... That flag was a cover for the murders, massacres, tortures, and imprisonments. Were the sufferings of thousands of people by the hand of Turkey's dark forces limited to these? What thousands? Hundreds of thousands! He was not the only one thrown from one border to another.

When his maternal grandfather and grandmother migrated from Macedonia, the Greeks were also uprooted from Anatolia and their lands. In fact, in addition to these sufferings, his maternal grandfather's share was also the lands usurped from the Armenians... And Emin himself owed the money for the fake passport he put in his pocket to them, to the victims of the genocide. Although he was still far from realising this fact, which he would comprehend years later, he had already learned that in this geography, in Mesopotamia, humanity first entered the stage of class society called civilisation. There was a one-to-one correlation between the flourishing of the Abrahamic religions in these lands and the infamy underlying all the oppression. It was not without reason that so many prophets flourished in these lands. But then, those religions would evolve into being a yoke around the necks of all the people involved they had emerged to save.

Didn't being the land of prophets also emerge due to the development that reduced human beings to nothing? Wasn't the abundance of prophets in this land the result of the flourishing and rooting in this land of societies that first started by enslaving women to men and then enslaved human beings to human beings? From this perspective, being the land of prophets should be a source of shame, not pride.

All this tangle of contradictions, which first emerged in this geography, had also engraved its traces on his own family history. While his maternal grandfather, who had been torn from his land by those who had the peoples at each other's throats, was eating the grapes of the vineyards belonging to the Armenian people, who had been torn from their land just like him and much more cruelly, he was being driven towards religious bigotry... And Emin's father, who is half Kurdish, was being driven towards the defence of the state, which, as an officer who was the flag-bearer of Turkish nationalism, had stuck a thorn in his own son's foot.

"My rebellion is against my father and maternal grandfather altogether."

While thinking about these things, he realised that he was basing his calculations on the men of the family.

"Isn't it quite natural? While my maternal grandmother was always protective against my maternal grandfather's bullying to make me pray, my mother stepped in to prevent me from going to the prison my father was planning to send me to. Linking our own small stories to the big stories of societies sharpens our consciousness. Yet, it is dangerous. It can become a gateway to megalomania."

He broke away from his thoughts that were tossing from here to there for an instant. For the first time, he was surprised to see the tombstones made of black marble on the right side of the road the bus was going through.

"How can the deceased see the black colour of the stone? What difference does it make to the deceased whether the colour of the tombstone is white or black? Everything that is done for the deceased, including the gravestone, is, in reality, done for those left behind, including respect for the dead. Sharing the pain of those left behind, avoiding words and behaviours that will increase that pain... These are all for those left behind. Then, it makes more sense that the gravestone is black. It expresses the grief of the relatives left behind, expresses their feelings."

Even though he had just added a year to the age at which the poet said, "We are in the middle of life, like Dante"[51], he was still young and, like every young person, he avoided thinking about death, shifting his mind from "Kivilcimli also

---

[51] Referred to a poem in Turkish, written by a Kurdish poet Cahıt Sıtkı Tarancı, which goes:
"35 years! Means half of the way.
We are in the middle of life, like Dante."

died in this country" to "Did Kivilcimli also travel to Belgrade through these roads?".

"According to my calculations, Kivilcimli was to live for about two more weeks in the state hospital in Belgrade, where he was admitted when Tito was informed that he had arrived in Yugoslavia, and Tito had instructed that Kivilcimli be placed in a hospital immediately and receive the same medical procedures and treatment that would be applied to Tito himself."

His thoughts, which he would later record as notes of those days, had once again shifted to the point where the knot was tied:

"When Kivilcimli wrote to Brezhnev asking whether he would hope for 'socialist justice' when the socialist countries closed their doors to him one by one, didn't Kivilcimli himself express the absence of 'socialist justice' in that letter? Sometimes, a word that seems extremely ordinary can take on a very different meaning depending on the context in which it is used. The justice of a 'socialist Homeland', the wisdom of which is unquestionable (!), can be trapped between the 'hoping' and the 'not hoping'. What about what he wrote before the 'hoping' point in the letter, his references to the Soviet Constitution and the decisions of the Communist International? Kivilcimli did not put the words 'communist,' 'socialist,' and 'democrat' in quotation marks without reason, as he not only criticised the absurdity of the Communist Party of Turkey (TKP) but also aimed to question the realm of the so-called 'communist' states, which were both accomplices and protectors of that absurdity. Kivilcimli left the burden of deepening such an enquiry, which he had avoided for years due to his 'socialist responsibility', as a legacy to the next generations."

When "Who Blamed?" and "Letter to Brezhnev" were being prepared for publication, it had been decided that the article in which Emin had expressed these thoughts ten years ago would be the book's forward. Yet, for some reason, by decision of the Presidium, only a paragraph of this article had been placed in the upper right corner as an introductory note:

"Some world tragedies can become flesh and blood as the tragedy of a single person. Of course, this negativity brings with it a positive facet. And comprehending this one individual's tragedy can serve as a clue for solving some of humanity's tragic problems."

"What was the excuse given when the actual article used as a forward was pruned, and only the above paragraph was taken? *'This paragraph expresses everything perfectly; there is no need for more!'* Doesn't this excuse indicate a lack of understanding of what is described in those lines? Wasn't ripping away the abstract reasoning from the entirety of concrete facts, avoiding the actual debate in a way running away from the actual confrontation?"

While Emin was thinking about all these, the road passing under the bus's wheels, on which he kept his eyes fixed, erased the upheavals in his mind. He fell into a cloud-light sleep.

* * *

"What are you talking about? The Presidium? Nope, it was Laz Ismail.[52] He's the guy who pruned your foreword. And if you're having doubts, check it out for yourself. They're in a meeting, and guess who's there? Yep, Laz!"

---

[52] Laz İsmail, who used to be the Secretary General of TKP, influenced the 'socialist countries' under the SSRC to deny entry to Kivilcimli, who was in the final stages of cancer and running away from the fascist military junta. However, Tito did the otherwise!

While Running Away

Emin rose from his seat ragingly and followed the direction indicated by Aydın's finger, which led from the party meeting hall to the Central Committee room. Without bothering to knock, he grasped the doorknob of the closed door and barged in. Laz Ismail, grinning with his prominent "horse teeth," occupied the chair at the far end of the Central Committee meeting table, which stretched from the door's entrance to the opposite side of the room. To Laz Ismail's right sat Çelik, and beside him was Faik Feryat. Emin instantly recognised them as they were facing the door. However, the two individuals on Laz Ismail's left remained obscured, their backs turned to Emin.

One of these two was Ferman, who initially didn't notice the door opening. However, when Laz Ismail, Çelik, and Faik Feryat shifted their attention towards the door, he also turned his head atop his nearly non-existent neck to look. That's when Emin recognised Ferman's round face. Yet, the presence of Ferman's sturdy frame obstructed Emin from identifying the short person beside him.

"Come and sit down, comrade!" The invitation came from Laz Ismail. Emin accepted the call and sat in the first chair before him. At the same time, he started getting angry with himself. "What am I doing?" He didn't know whether curiosity or the impulse of the tradition of being kind to the guest made him sit down on the chair. However, his anger grew as he sat down. He was angry at himself for not being able to react instantly.

"How dare you come here? Who do you think you are?"

As Emin uttered the final words hissing through his teeth, his eyes shifted from Laz Ismail, the intended recipient of these words, to the others. To his astonishment, he realised that the other faces had blurred and become unrecognisable.

"If you are hoping that those who previously attempted to hand over this Party to you will now, in a different manner, achieve what they want through these means, you will surely be left empty-handed."

Neither Çelik nor Faik Feryat nor Ferman were there anymore. Since he was behind Ferman when Emin entered, he couldn't also see the fourth one, whom he couldn't recognise.

Suddenly, he felt embarrassed. He was sitting in his swimming trunks. After leaving the sea coast, he hadn't stopped by the tent to pick up his shirt, and as soon as he heard what Aydın had said, he had stormed into the Central Committee meeting room. Now, he was feeling cold. But how had he travelled half naked from the natural beach near Silifke to the party building in Aksaray, Istanbul?

When he woke up by straightening his head from his coat, which he had made a pillow by leaning against the window, he felt his right arm freezing from his right shoulder, which was leaning against the window, almost up to his elbow.

"It was all a dream. Really, who was that person whose face I couldn't see, who was hiding even in a dream?" he said, trying to warm his right arm, which he patted up and down with his left hand, as the bus left the outskirts of Belgrade behind and headed towards the station.

* * *

"Do you know which side of the terminal the buses to Novi Pazar are?"

"No, Abi! We don't hang out here; we only pick up and drop off passengers."

"Can you help me by asking someone?"

While handing the suitcase to Emin, the bus conductor looked around. When he couldn't see anyone near the bus parked at the station entrance, he said, "Let me ask the driver," and went to the open front door.

After talking to the driver, he spread his arms halfway to his sides and said, "Abi, he doesn't know either. He says, "It's somewhere inside!" Emin responded with a "thank you" and walked in the direction where the buses were parked parallel to each other.

In the chaos of buses, Emin spotted someone standing in the doorway of the second one from the right and decided to try his luck. When he uttered the second word, he realised that he had started his question to the man, who was almost the same height as him and had short, tobacco-blonde hair, by speaking in Turkish.

"Excuse me..." He stopped and reduced his question to three words.

"Novi Pazar, bus?"

Emin couldn't tell whether the man, whose language he didn't understand, raised his shoulders in a manner that meant "I don't know" or "I don't understand."

After giving up on asking and deciding to carry out his search alone due to lack of local language, about half an hour later, he realised that his almost non-existent sense of direction and the distraction caused by fatigue led him to pass the same places two or three times. Faced with this challenge, he eventually abandoned his attempt to "search without asking anyone."

No one showed him the way the second, third, fourth, or even the fifth time. As he tried to communicate with the last person, using just three words, someone who approached them gestured with their hands, indicating, "Come with me."

He followed this guide until they arrived in front of a ticket office.

After the man had finished what he had said to the ticket seller, he repeated his question:

"Novi Pazar, bus?"

As the man at the ticket office raised both hands and showed ten fingers, he caught the last word of the sentence in a language he did not know.

"Mark?"

While taking out his wallet and handing over ten DM, Emin asked first in Turkish and then in English:

"When? When?"

When Emin finally understood from the ticket agent's hand gestures that the bus would depart at 14:30, he thought of the Turkish-English dictionary in his suitcase.

While signalling "one" with his right forefinger, he again relied on his Turkish:

"Wait a minute!"

From the dictionary he retrieved from his suitcase, he quickly found the English equivalent of the word "before":

"Before!"

"No," the ticket agent continued, once again speaking in a language Emin did not understand, shaking his head from side to side and laughing. When Emin saw that the person who had brought him to the ticket office was laughing, too, he joined in. He didn't grasp whether there were no available buses or if there were buses but no available seats. Nevertheless, he didn't push for further explanation. In the end, the outcome remained the same.

Emin's "OK!" sounded like a question to the ticket agent:

"OK?"

"OK, OK!"

After Emin's double answer, the ticket agent placed the ten DM, which he had held in his hand until that moment, into the drawer in front of him and then proceeded to the well-known "unpleasant" question:

"Passport?"

Emin felt relieved when he observed the ticket agent using the passport to write down his name on the pre-printed ticket without asking further questions.

After getting his passport back with an accompanying ticket and placing both in his pocket, Emin thanked the agent and began heading towards the passenger lounge to find a seat. Then, he felt a hand had grabbed his right arm—the man who had brought him to the ticket office. The man responded to Emin's questioning eyes with an international hand gesture involving the thumb and forefinger rubbing against each other.

Emin gently put down the suitcase and picked up five DMs from his wallet. Imitating Emin, the man thanked him in English, saying, "Thank you."

Emin smiled and replied, "You're welcome", even though he felt like saying, "Fuck off!"

Although it resembled a bus garage in any Anatolian city, the passenger hall was spacious and not crowded. Emin had plenty of time. And the time stuck in the brevity of minutes while rushing for something would surrender to the prolongation of the day when stuck in the stagnation of waiting. There was nothing to do but kill time with sleep as he regretted not taking any books. His overly cautious behaviour was partly to avoid attracting attention when leaving the Turkish border, but "How useful a book would be now!" he thought.

He turned and looked at the ticket office where he had bought his ticket as he let himself down in the nearest row where no one was sitting. Although Emin thought that he should go to the ticket office again to ask for the platform of the bus that he had forgotten to ask a moment ago, and said with the weariness of fatigue, "Later," he said, "I will go when the departure time is near."

Emin could have straightforwardly realised that someone had come to the bench he was sitting on if he was going to sleep, but he still tucked his suitcase between his legs. He crossed his arms over his buttoned coat. If a pickpocket attempted to swipe his wallet or passport, it would turn everything upside down, even though he had half his money tucked into his socks. This thought was enough to keep him awake despite his exhaustion.

He followed his self-advice: "I should at least close my eyes so that my eyes can rest."

* * *

He actually liked travelling. He was on the road, even if it was a journey imposed by necessity... His favourite type was the train journey, especially the one by the steam locomotive that moves while puffing and chuffing. He didn't know why, but Emin liked the smell of a steam locomotive burning coal. It was different now, but he was on the road...

Bus journeys had become bearable for a long time since he didn't need pills to prevent motion sickness. His efforts to overcome the motion sickness during the bus travels that had plagued him since his childhood with the medicine he took had become unnecessary from the day he and his friends went to Niğde Prison to visit Çelik. He had forgotten to take the small pill box from the safe deposit box he had given when entering the visit, and he could not find a pharmacy at the coach station before boarding the bus on the way back. He hadn't felt the slightest nausea during the journey and hadn't taken any pills against bus sickness after that. Was it the repeated discussions in his head about his conversations with Çelik that diverted his attention away from his stomach?

It wasn't a minor annoyance; he had been genuinely bothered by Çelik's ongoing critique of the decision not to join the TKP and his disagreement with the conference's resolution. He couldn't comprehend Çelik's inability to come to terms with a decision that went against his own thesis within a movement he led.

"But," he said, talking to himself, "Isn't that called careerism? Shouldn't someone more advanced than us all have already overcome all this? Isn't that putting oneself above the Party?"

These questions that Emin was contemplating jumped from local issues to an international disaster.

"Was it not careerism, which Kivilcimli defines as 'ambition and pride for position' and which the Constitution of the Homeland Party considers as a reason for expulsion, that caused so much trouble for the great Bolshevik Party? Was it not the main and fundamental reason for the lives taken by Stalin's despotic rule, 'careerism'? Didn't humanity watch how careerism and bureaucratic organisation fed each other and led to painful experiments? OK, careerism could flourish even without the bureaucratic structure. Amen! But could careerism and careerists survive, take root, and completely dominate a movement without that party bureaucracy? Even a structure that ignited the most revolutionary dynamics in human history has been entangled in the nets of reaction by the anchor of bureaucratism."

Emin's questioning around the period of his first visit to Çelik in Niğde was limited to the practices of Stalin, the cruel tyrant and his fluctuating accomplices.

He had moved further since then. And... Once upon a time, as far as Emin was concerned, "There was Lenin!" Like his other friends, he was also mired in the short-sightedness of "Lenin found the solution when he suggested making more workers members of the Central Committee". If Lenin said something, even the flowing waters would halt, which means "not disputable"! There was no questioning, no cross-questioning, but always acceptance without questioning.

He arrived at the point to say, "Lenin was also a human being; he could be wrong" on an autumn evening in Istanbul when his previous unquestioning acceptance mingled with the flowing waters of the Bosphorus. Again, on that day, he remembered a determination of Marx. Although he knew what Marx said, Emin had not sifted Lenin's solution through the sieve of Marx's determination until that day.

He had climbed the hill in Ortaköy, where the foot of the Bosphorus Bridge was nailed, to watch the Bosphorus. For some reason, even in his most troubled moments, watching the flowing waters of the Bosphorus was a relief for him. During his university years, he used to sit on the coastline of the Bosphorus between Ortaköy and Kuruçeşme and take refuge in the flowing waters of the Istanbul Strait to disperse his inner distress. Later, he discovered the magic of the view on this hill in Ortaköy. And once, while watching the Bosphorus from that hill, it was a starting point for his thoughts on bureaucratism, which had become as labyrinthine, like his own inner world, as he was, when he remembered Marx's words, which he had known for so long, but which had remained dormant and idle in a corner of his mind:

"It is not their consciousness that determines the material conditions of life, but it is these material conditions that determine their consciousness."

"If," and there was a lot of "if" here, "Marx was right about this; the candle Lenin lit would not give light to the bottom," he said. "Suppose that not only the majority but the whole of the Central Committee was composed of these people from production and that these people continued to work in their factories. However, those in other organs, especially Politburo, would inevitably break from production and become Party professionals. Wouldn't the poisoning of power eventually begin to circulate in the veins of these people as well?"

When he thought he had left the labyrinth, he found himself in another maze. If "Lenin's proposal", which he had seen as a solution for so long, was not a solution, how could this problem be overcome?

Inspired by the flowing waters of the Bosphorus, when he intuitively drew horizontal parallel lines, which intersected by the vertical parallel lines with a piece of a branch in his hand on the ground between his feet, another lived experience emerged from the nooks and crannies of his memory.

The wire mesh windows, filled with vertical and horizontal parallels, came to life in his mind. On one side, where the prisoner stands, and on the other, where the visitor stands, these double wire mesh windows in the visit cubicles of Bursa prison intervened between the visitors and the prisoners.

* * *

"Abi, they changed after they became the management committee members of the city branch."

"In what way have they changed? What are they doing or not doing?"

Emin was asking these questions to the young people who complained about the Bursa Branch Management of the Party. He was drawing a parallel with what he had heard during the visits of the Bursa Management Committee of the Party while in the Bursa Prison. What did they say to Emin?

"This is not a party organ; we cannot discuss everything. We would pass on only whatever you say to the Central Committee. If a message from the Central Committee needs to be conveyed to you, we will convey it. We can't answer your questions. We cannot discuss Party matters with you."

"Aren't you here to liaise with me as the Party's provincial organ? Don't you discuss among yourselves the matters that I ask?"

"We talk, but we talk only in our management team's meeting."

"Then talk to me too!"

The namesake among those who came to visit Emin would break his silence in the face of this request with a demeanour he had not seen in him before:

"You're not a member of the Bursa Management Committee!"

"I am a Party member, and as the provincial organ, you are responsible for my relationship with the Party! Who am I supposed to talk to if not you?"

The protracted discussion had not yielded any result on that visit. Now, Emin was trying to understand the impressions and thoughts of the "young people". After all, the "young people" were his friends who were five or six years younger than him, aged seventeen or eighteen, whom

While Running Away

Emin knew from the branch of the Association and who had recently joined the movement, but his dialogue with them was different. They and Emin had no hierarchical relationship, neither because of the age difference nor the tasks they had undertaken. The distance that did not exist between him and the young people had started building up between him and his old friends from the Bursa Branch Management Committee, whom he had known much earlier, except for one.

On that Tuesday afternoon, he was going to implement the decision that he had made after what the young people had told him. He ignored the insistent announcements, "You have a visitor; go to the visiting area!" When his namesake from prison came back from the visiting area and said, "They are from your Party, including our namesake, they are anxious. I interrupted my meeting because of you. Stop being stubborn and come there!" Emin resisted this call, too. His namesake went back to the visiting area and came back a few minutes later. "There was a friend of yours called Samet among them. He said, 'Give him my name, ask him to come!' are you coming?"

"Say hello to him. Say that I will see him when he pays a visit alone!"

He did not overshadow his stubbornness, but in the meantime, he tried to convey that Samet's place in his eyes was different from the others. Actually, that was the case. In fact, this tiny woman Samet would later marry, whom they called "Bicir" (which means "chattering" in English), was friends with Emin's fiancée, and that was one of the reasons for their close friendship. Another reason was that Samet was more open-minded than the others. Samet would utter the words that would make Emin uncomfortable but angry when someone else said them:

"Are you trying to organise the youngsters around you [against the management]?"

"What are you talking about? When did you see me doing such a charade?"

"It looks a bit like it!"

"Image and reality are not the same thing. If you are deceived by the image, the spoon in the glass of water is broken. Is it really broken, or is it an illusion?"

"I look at the glass from a bird's eye view, not from the bottom!"

"Come on, you can only look at Bicir from a bird's eye view."

The atmosphere, which had been tense for a moment, suddenly relaxed with the warmth of sharing the "some sort of privacy" that this reference described.

"Hey, you're all talking about it and pulling my leg by it."

"It's not like you can't get mocked! You were up in the tree, meowing. Even though we've already left March behind." Emin was joking with it, but it was born from the truth that Samet did climb a tree in the garden on the night of May when all of the Party members in Bursa were gathered for a wedding party.

"It's because of you that everyone noticed!"

"Maybe you didn't realise it, but you always kept your eyes on Bicir when you talked and tried to sing a ballad. So, people noticed naturally. Besides, no one was there for me to talk about such matters. There was only Nurten that I was close to talking about such things, but I didn't say anything to her either. I don't think Hüsniye said anything to anyone either, except Bicir. You didn't realise what you were doing because you were drunk!"

"No, I didn't drink too much."

"You drank, you drank... I mean, I drank, too. Everyone drank under the pretext that it was a wedding, but there was another trick."

"What trick?"

"Nejat and I threw sugar in the wine glasses!"

"Nejat doesn't do such things. It should be you!"

"That's what you think! He's your leader; doesn't he do that sort of thing? Doesn't he? Oh, let me tell you... He does! Besides, the idea didn't come from me; it came from Nejat."

"Let's not derail the actual conversation. You'd better watch your behaviour with youngsters. Whatever your intentions, that's the impression you make!"

"Is that what you think, too?"

"I don't think you were, but that's the impression."

In a way, Samet's statement "the impression" was confirmed by what the youngsters told him during the visit and that they could freely and easily talk to him about their discomfort. He did not censor what was on his mind during the visit of the youngsters, regardless of Samet's warning and even though appearance triumphed over intention:

"I think you are right, guys. That's the impression the Party management has given me. I'm in prison and don't know what is happening outside, what they do, how they behave. I speak from the attitude they adopted and the behaviour they showed when they came to visit me. You have to criticise the matters openly at the meetings with sympathisers of the Party. Both careerism and bureaucracy destroyed the great achievements of the October Revolution. We in Turkey are the ones who can learn the best lessons from this. Doctor Kivilcimli has left us a solid legacy. We are better equipped than any other group. We can prevent this from the beginning, but as I said, we need to criticise openly."

"What can we criticise? They all support each other. No matter what we say, they're not accepting any criticism."

"Then you can go to Istanbul and tell the Central Committee."

"Isn't that against the Party Constitution?"

"If the provincial administration does not pay attention, you have the right to complain to a higher body."

The "young people", who were not convinced by his suggestion, would repeat the same complaint when he travelled to Bursa again shortly after his release while they were chatting in the association building.

"Abi, look around, if there is anyone from the management? They wrote and printed the leaflet, but it's almost three o'clock, and they're not here. The buses to the factory's site leave at half past three for the night shift. We have to leave soon. There's no one but us."

They were all young men, the oldest of whom were nineteen or twenty.

"Where are they? Why didn't they come?"

"There's a management committee meeting."

"The management committee meeting could have been held later," Emin thought but refrained from saying that. "I have to do something that should reassure the young people rather than demoralise them," said the voice inside him.

"OK, it's fine. It's not a big deal. I'm here. Come on, get up; we're going together."

He was pushing the limits of party rules. He was not supposed to go with them for security reasons. He had just been released from prison; he should not have participated in any activity in Bursa without informing the Party. He was taking the initiative, and from the discipline point of view, it

While Running Away

may be considered that it was "irresponsible" to some extent.

When the police arrived during the leaflet distribution, everyone, including Emin, had managed to run away, with one exception. When Bülent, who was only seventeen years old, was caught, Emin would go to the police and try to get him released as he thought that he couldn't leave a minor alone" and would say to the police: "This is a legal party leaflet. I am responsible for it on behalf of the Party."

The police had taken him in, too, just as they had not let Bülent go. After the detention, which was limited to a few slaps, he was released after the prosecutor rejected the police's request for arrest. When he returned to Istanbul, he would face Ferman's criticism of him as "irresponsible", but according to Yakup, Ferman, the Secretary General of Homeland Party, Ferman had earlier said behind Emin's back, "He just got out of prison recently, and now he's jumping out, and in Bursa no less. In fact, he is trying to be a hero." Emin rejected it fiercely and bluntly: "It is full of craps and bullshitting!"

When Yakup's words came to his mind, he remembered his argument with Aydın:

"I'm being arrested, and my photo appears that shows my smashed face in the local newspapers in Bursa, on the front page, clearly documenting the fact that I was tortured. Even though I am the Secretary General of the Association and the editor of its newspaper, the guy, I mean Ferman, objects to reporting both the torture and the arrestation in our newspaper. His justification is similar to the other incident: 'Our newspaper is for voicing the people's problems. Not to create heroes!' He sees the issue from an angle as to whether or not I am a hero. This bloke, who is so full of shit as to claim that I was trying to be a hero by getting me arrested by speaking provocatively about the torturers, even though the cops taped the conversation, when Yakup, whom you dislike, insists he finally accepts that it should be published as a short news item in a single column, but definitely not on the front page. So, Yakup is not the problem; people like Ferman are the ones we should really be concerned about. They managed to hide their careerism behind the rhetoric of: 'Responsibility' and 'Party discipline'. As long as they were accepted to be a 'head', no matter the head of what, be it an onion head! In fact, it was people like us who were the problem. We couldn't say 'Enough!' to these people."

"Wait a minute, I don't understand. OK, Ferman is a careerist, but what does that have to do with what he said about you?"

"It's a long story. The issue's root lies in the division of labour in the Association's management before we participated in the Party. It's about how I became the Secretary General of the Association. He was uncomfortable with that. It's, in a way, a power struggle for Ferman, but that's not the real problem. It's the bureaucratism behind which he hides his careerism. Party Constitution, party discipline, etc., are all excuses. That bureaucratic hierarchy has become a tool behind which all kinds of disgrace, especially careerism, are hidden. And we were supposed to be following in the Doctor's footsteps. We were under the roof of a Party that should be the most resistant to all these. Since we were like this, think about the others, I mean the other socialist organisations. It's not about me, Ferman, this or that."

"Maybe that's it!" beginning with this, Aydın put the final dot to his objection by quoting the Dr Kivilcimli's words:

"The clash of the petty bourgeoisies!"

"You're taking the easy way out. Let's say it is. But these are the Parties of working-class..."

"Or claims to be!"

"OK, it happens in a Party that 'claims to be of...' But didn't something similar happen in a Party that succeeded in the first working-class revolution in the world? And in a bloody way!"

"The larger the entity, the greater the challenges it faces. If we had come to power, wouldn't we cut off some heads, too? Maybe your head would have been among the first to go." Aydin laughed ironically and continued: "Maybe the coup d'etat of 12 September saved you. Now you will go to Europe and lead a better life!"

"Don't water it down. Do we have to stay stuck in this bloody stalemate? The hierarchy and the bureaucracy are pulling us down by our legs. And in a Party with a solid constitution like our Homeland Party?"

* * *

Followed his self-advice of "I should at least close my eyes so that my eyes can rest."

Upon obliging his self-advice, his eyes had rested to some extent! However, he could not give his brain rest. His thoughts, starting from his love of travelling, were skidding in the mud of bureaucratism-careerism again, stopping by the memory stations in the Party years.

Suddenly... "Why didn't I think of it until now?"

When he opened his eyes, experiencing the joy of finding a solution to the dilemma he had described as being "stuck," even within "a Party with a solid constitution like the Homeland Party" while talking to Aydın, he found himself face to face with two pairs of closed eyes. On the opposite bench, a couple, either in their thirties or thereabouts but certainly younger than him, were kissing. The six- to seven-month-old baby on the woman's lap was sound asleep and smiling, wrapped up in the couple's cocoon of love. Emin also smiled spontaneously. He felt embarrassed and looked away from them as he returned to his thoughts.

"Why didn't I think of it until now?" he asked himself, adding a paragraph ending with a big exclamation:

"While the party program introduces a mechanism for recalling those elected to govern the country, applying this rule to intra-party elections would be a decisive measure that would rescue us from the dilemma we were stuck in. Instead of Lenin's formula that led to the transformation of workers into bureaucrats, this method could hang over the head of bureaucratic tendencies like the sword of Damocles!"

The smile he caught from the baby grew with the joy of what he thought was the answer he had been searching for years. Emin believed he had it, or so he thought until he could pinpoint the genuine source of the problem.

He had initially averted his gaze, which carried an endearing envy. But when he heard the mother murmuring something to her baby in their native language, he briefly glanced at the couple once more. Lowering his head to the ground, he looked away again as he retrieved a cigarette from his pocket. The mother had raised her sweater, preparing to offer her breast to her baby.

Emin's memories began to flow along the paths drawn by the cigarette smoke he gazed at with his head bowed.

* * *

While Running Away

Nazli was sitting on the floor, swinging her baby on her feet, while Emin had thought, "That could have been our... the child of both of us." Was it jealousy? "Even if it was defined as jealousy, it was a different feeling of jealousy," he would tell Aydın.

"I was never jealous of her relationship with Yakup. It wasn't sexual jealousy. I didn't have that feeling."

"You're fooling yourself. You're self-deluding yourself because you think it should be that way. In reality, you've been jealous, like a dog. You've hidden it even from yourself."

"I'm hiding my feelings from myself! What non-sense. I've never really experienced such a feeling. What's more... This is a chat between us. Let's keep it that way. We all have sexual dreams sometimes. You probably have them, too."

"Leave me out of it."

"Whatever. I'm just saying it's natural. You know, I've never had a sexual dream about Nazli. You know... When she met me in 1983, she said, 'You're still in love with me because I didn't sleep with you'... Actually, I should have told her what I told you at that time... She came to my bed once in my dreams. She was stroking my hair, sitting on the edge of the bed. 'OK, I'm here now. Don't cry.' I woke up, my eyes were wet. That's all. Also, I told you what went through my mind while she was rocking her child at her feet."

Aydın finally exclaimed, "The masochism of platonic love has also entrenched itself in your dreams. You deserve it, suffer!" and burst into laughter!

He had not told Aydın that evening, but now, while waiting for the bus to Novi Pazar, it came into his mind.

"If it's masochism, that's what I had in common with Nazli. So, she had this masochism, too. Was keeping the postcards I had sent merely retaining a memory? Then what it is, you do put them in the buffet with a glass door, where you can see them at all and any hours of the day!"

He had been back to the scene where Nazli was swinging her child on her feet. He remembered that two postcards he had sent from Bursa Prison to Paris, tucked away in the glass door buffet behind Nazli as she sat on the floor.

Despite her objection, 'You wrote them to me, and they are mine,' he had initially taken back the letters to burn them. However, Nazli remained adamant and refused to return these two postcards, choosing to keep them.

Emin had partly agreed with her objection but had reasoned with her. "Yes, maybe you're right, but I don't want it to be used for political purposes if it gets into anyone's hands in any way."

Nazli was persistent in her objection: "Who's going to get it? Yakup already knows what happened between us."

"I don't mean Yakup. I mean the police and so-and-so."

Some in the Party were hidden in that "so-and-so". In particular, in 1976, when Nazli was flying to Paris, Emin did not go to the airport himself - *he was in Bursa, busy retaliating for Nazli's escape from an unfulfilled relationship and blocking the way back for himself with that step he took*; Nazli said to those who came to see her off, especially to one of them, "Emin did not come, if he had come I would have had something to say to him" and according to that specific person, who was one of the persons hidden in the "so-and-so", Nazli was so upset.

Emin's response to what was recounted about that day was very brief:

"I've closed that book!"

Emin was trying to convince himself of this, and he wanted to close the door to the gossip that the one who passed Nazli's words to him would create. He shouldn't have given any leverage. Letters could also be a trump card.

He had finally taken the letters from Nazli, and moreover... he had burned them.

"We didn't be like the couple at the opposite bench," he thought as he once again felt the regret he later expressed whenever the subject came up. "We didn't kiss even once. We didn't hug each other tightly even once. We could hold hands only once, but only once for a brief moment, squeezed between two minutes. After listening to Ahmed Arif[53] at the Cinematheque as we were leaving!"

How had those who had been afraid of touching each other for years reached the point that "one brief moment squeezed between two minutes"? He rewound his memories again.

When they could not find a seat in the hall they had entered late, they started listening to Ahmed Arif standing up. As the verses rang out in their ears, "Spring onions from my visitor", Emin, leaning over, asked in a low voice:

"Are you, as well, going to bring spring onions?"

In the hall's silence, Ahmed Arif's voice was pouring out as verses while Nazli's response was pouring out of her eyes as tears.

When they left, instead of walking straight from Siraselviler Street to the taxi stop in Taksim, they turned into the darkness of Meşelik Street and headed towards the exit of İstiklâl Avenue. Spontaneously, without talking, just like that... On their way to the Cinematheque earlier, they met in front of the French Consulate, where Nazli had gone to borrow books and taken a shortcut to Siraselviler. This time, they crossed the street where it intersected with Istiklal Avenue, but Nazli stopped as soon as they stepped onto the

---

[53] Ahmed Arif was a Turkish-Kurdish poet.

pavement. Emin, afraid that both of them would break the intensity of emotion shackled by silence since they had left the Cinematheque, was silent, unlike usual. He would pour the words into himself one by one and stay above the words. He would not crush his feelings under the words. Nazli, who paused on the pavement, was the one who broke the silence.

"OK. Let's get engaged."

Emin had broken his silence by softly taking Nazli's left hand in his right palm. Their hands, untied while getting in the taxi at the taxi stop fifteen or twenty steps away, would never reach each other's warmth again. Emin did not know this when experiencing only a week of happiness.

Hadn't he watched for years how their relationship, whose physical intimacy had been limited to this, now brought tears to his eyes like the smoke of his cigarette and gradually disappeared?

"No, that's a false analogy," he protested to himself.

"She didn't blow this relationship into the air, nor did I! Whatever the excuses we created, we somehow kept it alive within ourselves, even if we ran away from each other. No... Maybe she didn't, but I did. Most of them, by placing the sin of this escape on my eyes in silent tears. And she, Nazli, thought she was the one who cried all the time. She thought I made her cry. I kept this relationship alive inside me without hiding it. Me! Me! Me! Isn't that unfair, just saying: 'me'? Isn't it unfair for a person who, in 1983, accused me with these words: "You ruined not only the lives of the two of us, but also the lives of four other people!"? That was the sign that she kept this relationship alive inside her and a sign that she missed it. Even if she is not like me, hasn't she kept this relationship alive in his own way? Every person lives and keeps a relationship alive in their own way. Their own way, even when they are together. They are different colours of the same feeling. If they can come together, they turn into a magnificent riot of colours. We failed... We ran away from each other... By experiencing the inability to escape while running away..."

"She once asked me, 'Why do you use the ellipsis so much in your writings? I couldn't explain it; I was not able to explain it. I didn't really know either... Did I say, 'I feel like it'? I think I did. Yes, I felt that way. They were sentences I couldn't finish. Sentences that I didn't want to finish. Sentences that I wanted her to complete. They were the questions asked without asking. Each time, it was a way of running away, ending in failure. 'Running away'... From what? From unescapable?! We try to fit life into words. Would it be possible? That's why we are lost for words when life is beyond words. Yet, it carries an irony in it. The irony of trying to fit life into two words, 'Running away', when life does not fit into so many words! Could it fit into? That's why we have the phrase 'Where words fall short'. Even if the past closes with these two words, 'Running away', the future would be opened with the same two words. Because there is an after... these three dots hold the promise of more, ready to unfold beyond what we've enclosed within them! If I had those letters with plenty of ellipses, I could reread them now. What a fool I was to burn them. She, Nazli, didn't resist for good. She gave in to my request. Yet, haven't I witnessed, at times, the stubborn resistance anchored in her own silent and calm depths? Whether she has a share or not, I'm the one responsible. I took those letters back. I burnt them. Can I describe what I experienced in those days with the same warmth? I burnt them! There's not a single letter left. She had kept these two cards, which had quietly remained in their place behind the glass of a buffet over time. Is it possible that, despite their silent presence, these cards did not trigger memories? Were they removed after she found out I was divorced? What difference does it make? While I burned the letters, she preserved the cards. Perhaps she was creating her own justification to accuse me. Her accusation...It was true, even if debatable, even if it was one-sided. I must reflect on the account I need to settle. I can't shift it onto someone else, nor can I settle it with someone else's account. People harbour their greatest secrets within themselves. They conceal themselves from themselves. The answer that one will find only by asking oneself is within oneself."

* * *

[Flashforward - 2016:
"The Answer Given to the Letter from Paris before the Forty Years had passed!"
"I had heard the news about you. I walked down the Champs-Elysées from the Arc de Triomphe de l'Étoile to the park. I threw bread to the ducks in the pond, humming songs," you had written in your letter.

I had never asked what songs they were. Your favourite song was "Be patient, heart, one day this longing will end". And your favourite ballad was "Earlock Had Poured on the Face." Whenever I listen to it when I am alone, I get lost in the dream of your hair falling from right to left.

I don't know if you still like these songs... There's something else I don't know. The first song, OK, liking that song was understandable... but it was surprising that you liked Neşet Ertaş's folk song, considering the environment you grew up in... I never asked... Actually, I had so many questions to ask about you. I was running after other questions. I could neither reach you nor the answers to the unasked questions. They remained there as they were, like unopened letters in the non-existent envelopes.

On the other hand, your opened letter, opened and read by the prison officer, would come while squatting in the warmth of the May sun at yard time, inhaling spring with the smoke of my cigarette. The other Emin (my namesake) was sitting next to me. The days stretching from 1 May to 6 May were behind us. We were weary and silent because of the prison riot that occurred on the night we commemorated the execution of Deniz Gezmiş and his two friends, along with the events that followed.

For a moment, I was disconcerted by the voice coming from the loudspeaker, which read your last name as your first name and your first name as your last name instead of mine. "Mete Nazligül, Mete Nazligül, come to the hall. You have a letter," the announcement said. The year was 1977. You know how they say, 'I was caught off guard!' It was like that!"... I went... I picked it up...

A pale blue, elongated envelope with the word "international" written in printing letters. On the envelope, enclosed by blue and red slashes with gaps in between, your last name came first as the sender, followed by your first name. Did you write it that way so it wouldn't be recognised as coming from a woman? I assume that you didn't know that in the prisons, incoming letters were to be opened, read and then given to recipients in the jails.

The longest part of your letter was Aragon's poem "There is no happy love". I read it for the first time. I never asked afterwards, "Did you translate it?" I think you translated it, you, who didn't like poetry before. When you said you didn't like poetry, I gave you Ahmed Arif's book[54] as a gift... and... I had read a few of his poems to you. During those days of separation in the past, you liked the poems I read and said, 'If only Emin were with me and could read them."

I don't know if you remember the night when we listened to Ahmed Arif reciting his poems at Cinematheque. It was the moment when the poet recited the lines 'Spring onions from my visitor, my cigarette smell of cloves.' I leaned into your ear and asked, 'Are you also going to bring spring onions?' Your response was tears silently streaming down from your eyes. How much had you realised that this was an imminent and genuine danger? Those were the times when I was summoned to the prosecutor's office one after the other.

You were far away when I was getting used to pacing back and forth in prison, not because of the articles in the newspaper I testified one after another, but because of a speech I delivered. Neither the spring onion had arrived, nor did my cigarette smell of cloves. You were in Paris, and I was in Bursa... But your letter had arrived. And I kept reading it over and over.

In your letter, there was a small sprig of lily of the valley, on which I saw your face when I looked at it, dried between who knows in which book. I didn't know it then, but I learnt later that on the streets of Paris, a

---

[54] Referring to the book titled "Through My Longing for You, I have worn out fetters" by Ahmed Arif.

sprig of lily from the valley is always presented to relatives and often to strangers as a gift. It turned out that the Lily of the Valley and 1 May were associated. I was told that even if the world were split in half, the Lily of the Valley would not be sold on the streets of Paris except in the last week of April.

Another sentence in your letter was engraved in my memory: "You are there, and I am here in prison. I experience this feeling in Paris." After the ward door closed on us at night, I lay on my bunk and tried to imagine Paris on the ceiling, reading your letter over and over again. "I, too, will go to that pond... I'll throw bread to the ducks," I said, picturing the pool on the ceiling a metre above me.

Now I'm by that pond. I can't throw bread to the ducks... They don't come to the edge of the pond... And they're not the same ducks...]

* * *

When Emin paused from flipping through the pages of the past and lifted his head, he saw the woman gently, but with a clear rejection, push to stop the man from attempting to kiss her again. She was still breastfeeding her child. The maternal instinct had locked the door on all other emotions.

Emin looked at his watch. There was almost half an hour left. He headed towards the box office where he had bought a ticket, buttoning his coat as he walked out of the waiting room door.

"Bus?"

Even though Emin did not understand, the man at the box office spoke, pointing with his hand to the other bus on the right side of the bus, standing at the box office's level. He must have realised Emin's hesitation, looking for the word he didn't know to be sure, so he opened the door of the box office and went out. He called out to the man standing in front of the bus he was pointing to with his hand. The man, shown, taking one more step before dropping his cigarette to the ground, inhaling another breath, and ensuring with his right foot that he had extinguished it, lazily took another step with his left foot towards the ticket booth. As he approached, Emin raised his right hand toward the man and added, 'OK!' Then, the man gave up coming.

"Toilet?"

Upon Emin's question, the man, who was about to return to the ticket office, gestured towards the waiting hall. Although he first intended to go towards the bus to give his suitcase, Emin changed his mind and returned to the waiting room he had just left. He didn't hand his suitcase, fearing "Will they go through while I'm in the toilet?" What would happen if they did? There was nothing but a pair of trousers, a jacket, a cardigan, a sweater, a set of pyjamas, two pieces of underwear, two shirts, four pairs of socks and a carton of cigarettes. This was the only thing he had that was valuable in poverty. He had not changed his socks since he left Istanbul. When he came out of the toilet, he felt his feet were relieved with his clean socks.

When he approached the bus, he could not find anyone to give his suitcase. Without going into the question sentence, he said "Hello" in Turkish to a young passenger, who seemed to be in his twenties, who was getting on the bus. The bus was going to Novi Pazar. A Turkish town. This young man should speak Turkish too! He must not have spoken Turkish; he just smiled and nodded in greeting. Emin replaced the question "Have you seen the bus conductor? Do you know where he is?" with "Do you speak Turkish?".

Again, when the arms stretched out to the sides to express "I don't" were accompanied by an answer in a language Emin didn't understand, he went back to the ticket office. While pointing the bus with one hand to the man at the counter, he lifted his suitcase with the other. "My Tarzanish is improving!" he mocked himself as he followed the man who left the box office without saying anything towards the bus.

Sitting in his seat after his suitcase was placed in the trunk, he felt a sense of inner peace, thinking, "It's easy from now on!"

"When you arrive in Novi Pazar, go to the booth at the garage, and the people there will help you get to Suleyman. He's a policeman, so everyone knows him. It's a small town anyway. After that, you won't have any problems."

If Eşref said so, he could leave his worries at the Belgrade bus station. The hard part of his runaway was complete. Was it? It didn't even occur to him to ask himself that. He would ask the man next to him, then the one on the other side of the corridor, the one sitting behind him, the same question:

"Do you speak Turkish?"

When the negative answer he received from the bus conductor, starting from those sitting in the direction next to him, travelled around the whole bus and came back to him, he folded his question and tucked it into the corner of his mind. He planned to retrieve it in Novi Pazar.

While trying to watch the Sava River flowing in the centre of the city, the houses with miscellaneous dimensions around it, from the gap between the large body of the man next to him and the seat in front, he turned his head to the other side when the bus crossed a bridge and took the river on its left side.

For a moment, his gaze met the gaze of the two on the same row next to his left, whom he guessed to be about his own age on the other side of the aisle. He responded to the smile of the woman sitting by the window with a smile, and at the same time, the man next to her smiled. When the woman handed him a slice of pastry from the napkins she had just opened, Emin gently tapped his chest with his right hand, "Thanks, no thanks!" The man next to the woman took the pastry from her, crossed the small corridor between them, and touched it to Emin's hand resting on his heart. Emin accepted it graciously, expressing his gratitude with a "Thank you, thank you" while bowing his head.

The first piece he bit into, which also made him feel his hunger, had a flavour that did seem quite familiar. It was similar to the pastries made by his maternal grandmother. Although he could not identify the herb inside, he recognised the flavour of the cheese. He nodded his thanks again, showing that he liked it, to his companions, who were still looking at him. They smiled at each other again.

When he finished the pastry, his travelling companions, whom he glanced at out of the corner of his eye, were still busy feeding themselves. The road was now flowing outside the city. Returning to his own world, he gave up watching the outside world. 'In a foreign country where you don't know the customs and ways, the last thing you need is to stir up trouble, especially while travelling with a fake passport, right?" he warned himself. After that, he avoided looking at his travelling companions.

"If you were to take the passengers, mostly men, on the bus with almost all the seats occupied and put them on a bus in Bursa on their way to any of the towns with their clothes and light-coloured skin, they would not seem foreign at all. They might not seem foreign, but this is more due to their resemblance to the migrants in Bursa rather than their Turkish origins. How accurate is it to call these people Turks? Even if there were people who came from Anatolia and settled there in Yugoslavia, they must have been mostly Slavs who converted to Islam during the Ottoman occupation. What could be more natural than the similarities between societies that have lived together for hundreds of years and intertwined due to migrations? Our pastries will also resemble each other. Then, a wave of nationalism came and turned the whole geography into a bloodbath. Now, we must put passports in our pockets to cross borders in the same geography. Mine doesn't even belong to me. Forget all this now. Go to sleep."

He fell asleep. He woke up. He could have slept even more if the man next to him hadn't said something in his own language and touched Emin's shoulder. As he gave way to the man who stood up from his seat, the bus stopped in a town the size of a village. He went to the window and made a pillow with his hand on the glass. "There is still time; let's go to sleep again," he said, but the spell didn't work. He returned to his thoughts before falling asleep about two hours ago. When the bus reached the exit point of the town where it had completed its passenger exchange, he saw the black tombstones in the cemetery once again. They were similar to what he had seen before.

* * *

"Could it be the experience of war upon war, uprising upon uprising for nearly two centuries that turned these tombstones black... The Balkans... The perpetual bleeding geography of Europe in the last century. Although it has nothing to do with it, the blackness of the tombstones...

Maybe I might have gone overboard again... Hasn't the suffering caused by being in a region where the usury-merchant civilisation collided with capitalist civilisation driven people to despair and made them wear mourning in black? In these lands, where European capitalism is struggling to take root despite this region's relative backwardness, haven't the societal uprisings triggered by capitalism led to movements in the ever-expanding and increasingly unwieldy territories, stretching from Anatolia to the Middle East, and worsening as one moves further east because of usury-merchant profiteering? Weren't the elements of the Ottoman Army that rebelled against the Palace the ones in contact with the West? Thessaloniki was their main hub! We could say, "The city where capitalism with all its elements knocked on the Ottoman door," couldn't we? "And there you have it, "liberty-equality-fraternity" for you! In Europe, the bourgeoisie seized power by rallying the masses with these slogans but gradually became more reactionary and established their own tyranny. But, here, the reactionary forces established their own despotism in no time. Those who revolted against tyranny established their own tyranny as soon as they came to power. Even if there are only crumbs of it in the West, who could find even a speck of 'liberty-equality-fraternity' here. Furthermore, they acquired the capital for their capitalism by plundering the property and possessions of the ancient peoples of Anatolia while annihilating them. This is an alliance between the Ottoman usury-merchant capital and the usurpation capital created by the state. Two minarets. One of them is cloaked in religiosity, the other in nationalism! They called this the Turkish-Islamic synthesis. The coup of 12 September 1980 was a response to the social awakening that posed a threat to this. Isn't this wind forcing us to flee to Europe that has brought the country back to where it started? This is yet another story of being unable to run away while running away! How will this vicious circle be broken? The antithesis of the reactionary usury-merchant establishment is the youth, with the prominent being the military youth! Yet, this youth sings the ode of nationalism from the other minaret. Even 'socialism' has, in the end, become part of these notes of this anthem in this country. Moreover, isn't socialism itself suffering from this ailment? Those who maintain the boundaries among themselves that the Doctor rebelled against..."

He stopped at that point. He was so confused, remembering that Yugoslavia was the land he travelled through.

"The Doctor is right in his idealisation, but what can Yugoslavia do? When it tries to establish socialism independently, it has to defend its existence against the Soviet Union."

The borders of Yugoslavia had hit the limits of Emin's thoughts, even if he was unaware of it.

"Maybe by living here, I can find the answers to what I'm looking for."

He remembered that they had excluded this alternative. Isn't that what they, Hasan, Eşref and himself, had talked about it.

* * *

"Let's hurry up. We're getting late!" warned Hasan. "Eşref Abi is disciplined. If we are more than fifteen minutes late, he doesn't wait; he leaves. He brought his communist discipline from Yugoslavia."

"Really, I don't know that. When did Eşref Abi come to Turkey? Has he ever lived in Yugoslavia?"

"Well, I don't know. Every now and then, Eşref Abi goes to visit his relatives. Once, he stayed for a long time for a treatment of his lung. Although it was said that he stayed because he had a girlfriend but... I don't know. One way or another, he's a disciplined man. He never misses a beat. Say, it is the discipline of the Homeland Party!"

"You mean I don't have that discipline?"

"Don't be touchy. You've got it; I know you've got it. You've synthesised your father's military discipline with Bolshevik discipline, but let's not sway!"

They were not late; they arrived at the meeting place on time. They thought they had arrived before Eşref. As soon as they sat down, Eşref arrived.

"We came before you, look," Hasan teased Eşref.

"You're on time. I was in a hideout, watching the entrance of this place from the waiting room in front of the ticket counter. Let's order tea first."

With the sign Eşref made by raising his long matching his tall stature, the waiter in front of the tea house broke off and came at a run. The teas were ordered.

"So, you finally decided to run away!" asked Eşref in a half-questioning manner.

"What can I do? The appeal has been failed. There's no point in sticking around! I'm on my own, after all!"

When this word came out of his mouth, Emin realised the blunder he had made.

"I mean, I'm not alone, but we are not a part of an organisation. There is no Party behind us. When there had ever been one, that's another matter. How long can I survive here relying on individual friendships? Thanks to my friends, they support me. But they could also face a similar threat at any moment. Besides, I may have brought an additional risk for them."

"I think you're doing the right thing," said Eşref.

Before Hasan started, the waiter who brought the teas intervened with his arrival. He left the teas. Hasan took the floor with the waiter's departure.

"Everything is ready for Emin. We thought it would be better for him to leave the country by bus, as there are stricter controls at airports.

"Where will he go?"

"It would be good for him to go to England to Osman. Osman will help him there, and they can work together."

"Yeah, that's better, I guess."

"The only problem is that he can't go via other European countries. Can he get on a plane from Yugoslavia or Bulgaria and go to England?"

"Why?"

"According to refugee law, he can only seek asylum in the first safe country he enters. The socialist countries don't fall into the category of safe countries, so it's not a problem. Yet, if he visits others, such as Austria or Italy, he has to seek asylum in the first country he enters. It is also not appropriate for him to hang around in Bulgaria. We thought Yugoslavia would be best. That's why we wanted to meet you. Can you help us? We thought you could, at least, give us some advice."

"I got plenty of advice to spare, you know! Said Eşref half-jokingly and then asked, "How long will you stay in Yugoslavia?"

Emin's response of "One week!" was corrected by Hasan:

"At most one week. If he stays for more than a week, his asylum request will not be accepted according to the immigration rules. In the meantime, Osman will arrange for a solicitor in England. When all is ready, Emin will get on the plane."

"When's the trip?"

"As soon as possible," Hasan responded.

"I think you shouldn't linger too much in Yugoslavia. It's not very safe."

"Why, Abi? If something goes wrong, I'll seek asylum in Yugoslavia. Although Hasan isn't very keen on it, it's still a last resort."

"Hasan is right. If you stayed in Yugoslavia, what would you do there? The people in Yugoslavia are trying to get to Germany. There are a lot of illegal Yugoslavian immigrants. After those from Turkey, Yugoslav and Spanish labourers are the most numerous there. And it is not only a matter of labour. Muslims are anxious in Yugoslavia. I mean our people. There was tension the last time I was there. Don't even think about this possibility."

"What if I get stuck?"

"Then you'll either go to Austria or Switzerland. Forget Yugoslavia. Go to our people in Yugoslavia, who will help you there. Suleyman will help you. He's my aunt's son. He's a policeman in Novi Pazar. Go to Novi Pazar and stay there until things are sorted out in England. If things don't work out, he will find a way for you to go to Switzerland or Austria. Germany maybe, but the others are easier."

"Is Novi Pazar far from Belgrade?"

"It's not far. About five hours. Depends on your bus. When you arrive in Belgrade, take the bus to Novi Pazar from the same bus station. Arrange your departure to arrive in the daytime. There is a bus to Novi Pazar every two or three hours during the day. When you arrive in Novi Pazar, ask anyone at the bus station; they'll recognise Süleyman because he's a policeman. Ask one of the officials there to call him. On the phone, tell him you've come from my side. Don't say too much. I mean, that you're on the ran! You can discuss these things face to face."

"Thank you, Abi. This is a huge help. I don't know how to thank you."

"Don't be ridiculous. There's no party left, but we're still comrades. Just let us know you got to England safe and sound. That would be the greatest thanks. Be careful there, I mean, in Yugoslavia, don't get drunk. They drink a lot there. And they have beautiful girls; don't fall in love with one!"

"What's love at this age?"

"I'm teasing you; I'm joking."

"Let's drink here if he can't drink there."

Following Hasan's suggestion, they said their goodbyes in a tavern a little further away from the tea garden, following Eşref's warning, "You shouldn't drink too much in these situations", and fitting their farewells into a 35-litre bottle of raki.

* * *

Emin did not know that it was the last time he would see Eşref when he remembered his warnings about Yugoslavia. He was about to meet one of the beautiful Yugoslavian girls who had not yet appeared before him. The bus had to take a lunch break for that.

When he entered the restaurant where they had taken a break, he felt his hunger intensify as he caught the rising aroma of food. He sat down at the first empty table in front of him, yet within two minutes, the table was crowded with two men and a woman from the other passengers coming behind him. He listened to the waiter standing over them without understanding what the waiter was saying. While his tablemates were reciting in the same language, the waiter wrote down what they wanted in the small notebook in his hand.

"Menu?" he said. The waiter explained that he didn't understand or that there was no menu, spreading both hands to the side. They both led to the same door. Emin touched the waiter's arm with his thumb as he stood up and pointed to the kitchen behind the glass two tables away. He followed the waiter and walked toward the kitchen. As the waiter opened the door, he attempted to convey, once more through a hand gesture, the question, "Can I enter?" He complied with the gesture that signalled "Come in!" and stepped inside. With the arrival of a stranger, the heads, which he couldn't quite count, whether they were five or six, turned toward him with curiosity.

At that moment, brown, semi-sad smiling eyes caught his attention. The woman, with her blonde hair, gathered and a portion elegantly left loose at the front, secured by a knotted headscarf at the back of her head, her hair cascading over her shoulders, perhaps from the rush, perhaps from the heat of the kitchen, perhaps from her own nature, or perhaps from all of these combined... smiled for a moment, her dimples blossoming on her rosy cheeks that burned with a blush. Then, she continued to slice the bread in front of her.

A large plate filled with clotted cream was standing next to her. Emin made up his mind when he saw the steaming bread in the big bread baskets behind her while looking around for jam or honey. When he saw the honeycomb and the honey jar, he pointed each of them one by one. In addition to a round whole loaf of bread, almost big enough to fill both hands, fresh clotted cream smelling of milk and honey, there was the tea he wanted in a small teapot. He tried his luck:

"Limón?"

The waiter smiled and nodded, saying, 'Okay!' Emin squeezed a few drops of juice from the half lemon that was brought and added it to his tea, all the while under the watchful glances of those at the table. His smile travelled around the table. Actually, he was craving a meaty dish like the others on the table; still, he was not sure what meat it would be, so he decided to save his appetite for Novi Pazar. Since they were Muslims, pork would not be served there anyway. Here, he wouldn't know. The fresh, pure clotted cream that he spread on the slice of bread, fresh out of the oven, and the honey, which he determined to be unadulterated by examining its flavours and colours, gave Emin more pleasure than he had hoped. When he had devoured it all, he drank his last cup of tea with his post-meal cigarette. The taste of rust had settled in his mouth since he set out on the road was gone. He enjoyed his cigarette immensely. The bill was also fair. Regardless of what was written on the bill, the waiter showed his five fingers when Emin said, "Mark, Mark". When he took it out and handed over five Deutsche Marks, the waiter said, "Danke!". Emin repeated, "Danke".

There was a lively atmosphere among the passengers returning to the bus after lunch. While everyone was talking, he listened, wondering if he would catch a familiar word. Alas! He soon gave up this endeavour. His thoughts went back and forth between honey-coloured eyes and shaped hands cutting bread.

It was the hands and the eyes that first caught his attention in a woman. It had to be the eyes, those of the woman in the kitchen. Perhaps it was just his imagination, but he had seen a semi-sad smile in those eyes, much like

Nazli's. The tangled web of memories began to unravel thread by thread once again.

* * *

Nazli's stories had become a pain in him.

"I was little when we lost our father. After that, my brother became the man of the house." Emin concluded that his brother was trying to prove he was the "head of the house" through his domination over Nazli.

"When he was angry, he would come and hit me on the head. Sometimes, I didn't even understand why. Although he doesn't do that nowadays, he shouts at me whenever he wants and interferes with where I go and what I do. But no matter what he says, this time..."

Nazli's "this time" was the first time she would participate in a political action.

They had left their classes upon hearing the news of a revolutionary youth named Kerim Yaman being shot by the fascists and the subsequent occupation of the University's central building in protest. He had gone all the way to the Galata Bridge with Nazli. Except for the period of the disagreements they had during the on-again, off-again phases of their relationship, they had made a habit of these farewells at the pier where the ferries to Heybeliada, [55] where Nazli lived, departed.

The first time, Nazli was in a hurry; she had to catch the ferry.

"Okay, I'll go with you!"

"To the Island?"

---

[55] Heybeliada is the second largest of the Princes' Islands in the Sea of Marmara, near Istanbul, Turkey

"Was it an astonished question or an expectation? I couldn't figure it out at that moment. In fact, this dilemma did not even occur to me at first. When I think about it, it seems like an expectation to me. But since I felt the joy of being able to accompany her even as far as the Galata Bridge, I gave a short answer: 'As far as the pier!' She said nothing but 'OK'," he would later recount in a conversation.

Even though they went by bus that day, in reality, these farewells would actually turn into walks stretching from Findikzade to Galata Bridge if the weather was good. These farewell "rituals", which would be repeated as the only times of shared solitude on days when Emin went to school and had no errands to run after school, were the moments when the unnamed relationship between them was silently and knot by knot.

The ritual would be repeated that day, ending with Nazli getting on the ferry. He thought so. Until Emin, who was already ready for the answer "No!" and clad in a black parka against the cold of January, a cap on his head, timidly asked, "Come along, if you want... to the occupation". He was met with an unexpected answer:

"Wait, let me phone my mum."

Nazli put the token in the phone under the bridge and dialled the number. Emin didn't look at first. Then he started to watch. 3, 5, 1, 8, one number, one more number and finally the last number. She didn't wait long to speak.

"Mum, can I not come today? I'm staying at the Munevver's house to study."

There was no objection; Nazli jumped up and down gently when she hung up the phone.

"Okay, let's go."

They had just come out from under the bridge in front of the pier and were about to head towards the stairs of the Galata bridge when Nazli paused with a sullen face:

"My brother!"

As Nazli stepped towards the slightly taller, slender man, Emin paused.

"Abi, hello."

Then, another step. Emin was left behind. He didn't hear what was said in a low voice. At some point, Nazli turned towards Emin, and so did her brother's gaze. Emin sent a vague bow of the head and a "Hello" that went unanswered.

Whenever the person who answered the phone first to the one his sister talked to at length was himself, Emin felt the gaze of the man who gave the short reply, "Nazli is not here," lingering on him for a while. It was like, "So, that man was this man!". Each time, Emin had dialled the numbers with the wish, "I hope Demet, Nazli's sister, picks up the phone if Nazli doesn't pick up". Demet would answer with a sentence ending with "I guess", which was later dropped from the sentence but added at the beginning:

"Wait a minute, please... Come here, Emin is on the phone."

On the rare occasions when her mother was the first to pick up the receiver, she was willing to accept the woman's call "Nazli, telephone!" in a cold voice, as if saying "that man again" without saying anything to her, but Demet's answer was different. Even though they had never seen each other, there was a warm approach in Demet's voice, which Nazli confirmed.

"Mum and my brother have negative feelings towards you, but Demet is different."

He would see that difference on a Saturday afternoon, 2 July 1983. But there were still years and ways to go until that day.

On the day when the first university occupation after the 12 March 1971 coup was set to occur, as they walked together from Galata Bridge to Istanbul University's Central Building in Beyazit, Nazli narrated what had happened on the other end of the phone, both on that day and in the past, to Emin, who had been unaware of these events. But before narrating these, there was a task to be done: Getting rid of her brother. Although Nazli had tried to respond to her brother with her head slightly bowed, Emin was witnessing Nazli's stubbornness, which she was displaying for the first time, unknowingly and without realising it. Emin will understand later; he will still taste the pain of this silent stubbornness.

Emin walked in Nazli's direction as his older brother headed for the ferry.

"My brother is going to tell Mum that he saw us. The good thing is there are no telephones in Munevver's house."

After a long silence, the conversation that Emin would remain silent for a long time started like this. With an inaudible voice, Nazli opened the pages of her life that she had not opened to Emin until that moment, leaving them piece by piece on the cobblestones of Sultanhamam. How her mother had devoted herself only to her children after the loss of her father... She talked about Demet... and her brother... with a sad look in her vaguely misted eyes on their walk. Nazli and Emin had taken the long way around Sultanahmet instead of going through the Grand Bazaar.

Somehow, it had come to that, he couldn't remember: Nazli had said that her favourite ballad was Neşet Ertaş's "Earlock had poured on the face." Emin also loved this folk song, very much. Whenever he listened to it, since the date when she entered his life, Nazli would come to his mind's eye with her hair falling over her face. And his other favourite song: "Be patient, heart, one day this longing will end." They had never talked about their favourite folk songs and songs before, and Emin had never mentioned that he also loved the ones she loved. It was spontaneous... and... Emin was surprised that someone who had grown up on one of the Princess islands, who lived off some property inherited from his father, who could read and write French, who could be called an elite "city-petty bourgeois", so to speak, was in love with a ballad from the heart of the steppe. This was what they called "prejudice, blind judgement". "There's no point in fudging; I've had my share. But I couldn't learn a lesson even at that moment, so a few years later, I couldn't stop myself from talking nonsense with the same prejudice and blind judgment. One doesn't get rid of these things just by saying, 'I did!'"

Whether it be the song that Nazli loves or the ballad, no matter from which perspective Emin looked, what Emin had seen was the hidden sadness in Nazli's eyes.

* * *

After the lunch break, Emin positioned himself by the window where his fellow passenger had gotten off. As he watched the road, delving into memories, his eyes got misty, and he tried not to let anyone see the mist inherited from Nazli, particularly from Nazli of those days. The sadness in the eyes of the woman in the kitchen brought back the ballad of Neşet Ertaş from years ago.

"Wander in these lands... oh my

Be a scribe and write... oh my oh my."

While Running Away

The words halted here as the first tear dropped onto the semi-closed fist in his mouth. He caught a second one with the bent index finger of his right hand at the corner of his eye.

"This moment, this space, they're no boundaries for emotions!"

Can time and place indeed confine what's felt within? "They must," would be the reply!

"We should put ellipses in these now..."

Nazli had asked, too. "Why do you keep putting ellipses at the end of sentences in what you write, all the time?"

"What answer had I given to that question? Don't start again. Did you put the ellipsis only in your emotional life?" He was trying to transition to other aspects of life with this question. Still, it had gotten stuck at Galata Bridge instead.

The Galata Bridge... Almost three years after experiencing the bitterness of the past in Yugoslavia, he would say about the burnt old Galata Bridge: "They burned my Istanbul! They burned down a whole history, along with my own little history. If I ever return one day, I will be going to a diminished Istanbul.".

"I'm a wobbler who slips on the ice and can't move forward."

* * *

However, he was not wobbling as they were walking on the Galata Bridge towards the stairs going down to the pier. It was a day when the sky was as clear as the memories of that moment. Warmed by the sun without scorching. "Before reaching the stairs, he had stopped her with a touch of her fingertips over her long-sleeved blouse, being careful not to disrupt the privacy between them.

"Look, this is the third time I've told you this. It will be repetition, but... Look, this is the third time I'm telling you. It might happen again, but..."

Nazli had initiated the conversation in which Emin expressed his discomfort with these sentences.

Nazli started by conveying her conversation with Cengiz, ending with the sentence, "They are not like you. You are different."

"When you were there, he said to you, 'Yes, you're right,' but after you left, he said, 'Emin doesn't know the programme of the Homeland Party, he's just making it up.' Cengiz was going to badmouth you in his mind, but I also heard what he said in your presence. How could he say such a thing to me after you left? Does he think I'm stupid?"

"I think it'll be better if you should do your own search, read and come to conclusions by yourself rather than what anyone says, including me."

"You may be right, but I don't see anything different from what you've told me in what I've read. Besides, you are what you are. The people who badmouth you are not like you. You're unique. And, moreover, you were right in warning about this person."

Despite his objection to Nazli's words, Emin was inwardly ecstatic. Cengiz, the antihero of the incident that had made Aydın say to Emin, "You're pretty stupid when it comes to Nazli," was finished in Nazli's eyes. After the university occupation, Cengiz took Nazli's arm, whom Emin had left behind, saying, 'Maybe you will be uncomfortable with me taking your arm; let me go to the front row.' Actually, Emin was afraid that she might think he was being opportunistic for physical intimacy if he acted differently. After this incident, this man showered his interest on Nazli like hail, always coming to her during the class breaks of the other school they shared a courtyard with. Nazli was finally annoyed by him, and Emin was actually pleased.

Was that the only thing that made him so happy? What about Nazli's gaze at that moment, "her gaze with a sparkle that replaced the shadow of sadness?" Nevertheless, Emin tried to keep his inflated ego under control. He endeavoured to keep the danger that could end their relationship, which constantly made him feel its fragility, at bay, with a warning that was connected to each other, but trying to open two separate windows:

"It may be a repetition, but... You're turning me into something like an idol. You'll smash me smithereens if I ever make a mistake or do something wrong someday. And it will be a mistake or error you'd consider perfectly natural if someone else did it. Bring me down to earth; see me as a human being."

Did Nazli understand the dual emphasis in the words "see me as a human being"? Emin was not entirely aware of it either, but he hadn't had the opportunity to ponder it.

Nazli was silent and headed towards the stairs first. Then she turned around and made her call in a cheerful voice:

"Come to the Island. If you have time. And I'll tell you one more thing."

With a bit of curiosity and a willingness to prolong the happiness he often experienced but couldn't quite put into words, they were ready to engage in a conversation deepening amidst the coffee grounds in the second tea garden lined along the shore right next to Heybeliada pier. It all began with Nazli's stories from the ferry.

"I didn't say it before; I know you don't like MeHeBe, but his approach is similar to Cengiz's. One day, after you left, he told me, 'This one pretends to be a 'Doctorist', but he doesn't know anything about Dr Kivilcimli and his theories'.

As I told you when you came to the Island for the study notes, we visited bookshops in Sultanahmet one day after this conversation. When he saw Kivilcimli's books, he said, 'I want to read one of the books by this man. Everyone is talking about him. I wonder which one of Kivilcimli's books I should buy?"

"The man is trying to follow fashion, as he told me. 'Socialism is necessary for him to do journalism,' he tells him. At least he's more honest than Cengiz. At least he told me that openly."

"What I meant was different. MeHeBe had told me, 'Emin doesn't know anything about Kivilcimli!' Then, without realising it, he admitted that he hadn't even read a book by Kivilcimli," she clarified.

"I had already told you, so nothing is surprising. But, as I mentioned earlier, you should read Kivilcimli's books and draw your own conclusions. Moreover, Kivilcimli is an exception in a country like Turkey, where parroting is considered theorising. An exception sacrificed to prejudices and blind judgements. And because he is an exception, prejudices and blind judgements can come into play quickly and immediately. Let me tell you how I became acquainted with Kivilcimli's works. This is an example of my own prejudices and biases. When I first saw his newspaper called "Socialist" in Kastamonu[56] during my high school years, I bought and read it because of its name. I was interested in what I read but don't remember what was written. It was before the 12 March 1971 coup. Two rallies were organised for the villagers on dates close to each other. I can't remember which one was the first. It was either a rally for hemp or garlic producers in the village. Dev-Lis[57]

---

[56] Kastamonu, formerly Kastamone (Greek: Κασταμονή), is a small city in northern Turkey.

While Running Away

and Dev-Genç[58] members had attended. We had formed a revolutionary group in the city before. But, anyway, we had no knowledge of left-wing factions or anything like that. When one of them asked, I told him that I liked the newspapers called 'Socialist'. In a way, this person had lectured me about the Doctor being a 'coup plotter', using incomprehensible language, being difficult to read, etc. They're coming from Ankara... They're coming from an organisation like Dev-Genç. Naturally, we're overestimating them. They were from that group called PDA[59], and they even handed me a magazine. It was published by that charlatan, you know, the one Dr Kivilcimli called a 'CIA socialist,' Perinçek. Then, I went to the Bursa Institute of Education. Again, we were ignorant of Kivilcimli. Then I came to Istanbul. It was after I started our Uni. A friend called Salim -*Emin hid the fact that Salim was a cell leader and that he was in an organisation's cell, and Nazli didn't ask questions that couldn't be voiced even if she sensed it-* had brought Kivilcimli's book '27 Mayıs ve Yön Hareketi Sınıfsal Eleştirisi'[60]. 'Read it, then let's talk about it', Salim said, but he also warned me, 'Kivilcimli writes in a language that is difficult to read'. You know, I had heard the same thing before. I started reading it, fearing that I would read it and not understand it. It was not difficult; I enjoyed his use of language as I read it. It was very different from other

---

[57] Revolutionary Students of Lycées
[58] Revolutionary Youth, the members of which were the University students.
[59] PDA, which stands for Proletarian Revolutionary Light, was a group organised around a magazine with the same name, led by Doğu Perinçek. In the late 1990s and early 2000s, this group ironically transformed into a political party, with retired army officers participating in its leadership, promoting a form of national socialism.
[60] The book title in English is "27 May and Class Criticism of the Yön Movement", and it is about the military coup of 27 Mays 1960 and the magazine Yön that claimed to defend the idea of the progressive role of the young army officers' role in the society.

theoretical works. I mean, in terms of language. In terms of content, too... Anyway. It's about language. A lively language. When I met my friend again, he asked me, 'How are you doing, are you having difficulties with the book?' I said, 'Sometimes there are old words I don't understand, but it's an incredible language. It's not difficult at all; on the contrary, it stimulates my appetite for reading,' and he was surprised. 'This is the first time I've had such a reaction from someone reading Kivilcimli for the first time,' he said. For me, it is the opposite. I still don't understand why people cannot understand such a colourful language."

Was it only the language that was not appreciated?

* * *

[Flashforward - 2014:
Emin was telling Zafer about his first acquaintance with Kivilcimli's works while trying to explain that what was not understood was a problem beyond language.

"Kivilcimli's '27 May' was the first work I read of his. He narrated how those 'dynamic forces' swam around like bewildered ducks because they lacked the leadership of the working class. It wasn't a glorification of 'the army will make the revolution, and we will snatch it out of the air.'

"Those who haven't read Doctor appropriately, falling for the propaganda of some charlatans, have mistakenly believed that Kivilcimli advocated making a revolution through the military and therefore considered him a 'coup plotter'. Naturally, the parasites exploited this ground for their demagoguery to hide their dishonesty. They used it to attack Kivilcimli's 'History Thesis.' There have even been self-proclaimed 'communists' who have

dared to claim that Kivilcimli had 'made things up' and that the quotations from Ibn Khaldun did not actually exist. I pluralised the conversation when talking about the person. Let me correct it. Someone did this. That person, while ostensibly praising the Doctor, was able to depict Kivilcimli as a coup plotter in his novel. He managed to deceive others. I'm not surprised that someone whose life revolves around making films, like it's said in an English proverb, 'when the cat is away the mice will play', would also try to 'direct a film starring himself' as the opportunity presented itself. What surprises me is that those who call themselves 'Doctorists' swallow this crap.

"Let's say they didn't understand the History Thesis, I mean the 'Doctorists', of course. Well, Kivilcimli explains at length in the introduction of '27 May' that socialism is not statism. Moreover, the further one moves away from the state and statism, the closer one gets to socialism. Did they not understand this either? There is more. Look, let me read you a sentence from the same book: 'The vacuum created in the field of economics due to the mass population exchanges known as the 'population exchange,' and in the field of politics due to World Wars and the War of Independence, as well as the human casualties in revolutions, had opened up opportunities for livelihood and employment, albeit in an adverse path, for the unemployed and those in need after 1920. The expulsion of the 'non-Muslims' who held a monopoly on all the resources of the prosperity of Anatolia eventually provided ample opportunities, although temporarily, to the indigenous elements, and even opened up a looting ground for some opportunistic Muslims.' In these statements, we can find shortcomings and aspects to be criticised. This is a separate issue. I want to look at ourselves from the perspective of not comprehending what was said.

"Let me draw your attention to this definition of 'the negative, adverse path`. The connection between the phenomenon of 'raising capitalists by the state', which Kivilcimli insists on pointing out, and what he says is what he calls 'the negative and adverse path' is obvious. How much have we understood, and how much have we been able to make sense of what we have read? I leave the other leftists. Look at ourselves, those who wear the epaulette of 'Doctorist'... I said that!... Then I turned to myself, I clung to the needle of 'leave others, look at yourself first'. I put the sack aside and just took a needle. I also have an intriguing clue.

"The vineyards and gardens of my maternal grandfather... He was an immigrant. The ones who came during the 'population exchange' in 1924-25. He had no share in what happened to Armenians in 1915. But when he came... I don't know whether or not he proved it, but when he came, he said, 'I have this much property', and he owned those vineyards and gardens. In other words, the government gave property to those who migrated in proportion to their wealth in the place they came from. Who owned these properties before? Did we ask this question? When I asked myself this question, I came across the cyphers of the social dramas we are experiencing, in this tyrannic state. The extreme nationalism of the migrants must have a very economic and material basis. When one of the cornerstones of the capitalism created by the state was this extortion economy, it was necessary to cover it with nationalism.

This is the basis of the nation-state. The nation did not create the state. The state actually created and formed the so-called nation. Kivilcimli explained this in his own style. Let us criticise many other things, such as his propositions on daily politics and his tactical orientations. He, himself actually calls for this. But when we get to the heart of the matter, we see that Kivilcimli offers us a rock-solid foundation. However, the parrot culture has prevented us from going beyond repeating what is presented to us instead of taking this foundation and developing it. At this point, I gave up being a 'Doctorist'. I don't think the Doctor was a 'Doctorist' either. Just like Marx was not a Marxist.

"I am not a 'Doctorist,' that is to say, I am now free from such ideological definitions based on the name of person/s. On the other hand, the foundation of my current thoughts is rooted in Kivilcimli. My starting point is Kivilcimli 's History Thesis. Although Kivilcimli did not do it, I believe carrying the History Thesis to its logical conclusions is necessary. I may say this, but to what extent does the madrasa or parrot culture allow it? Add the 'Who do you think you are?' as well.

"Should I say that I have a bit of luck... It's not... No, it's not... We're used to entering the conversation this way. After arriving here in London on flight number TCK-141[61], which I owed to the Martial Law Court, I had the opportunity to study at university again. I majored in accounting, but I studied it alongside German. By delving into German history, language, politics, and so on, I had the opportunity to read and discuss different things. I made this choice on purpose. For example, the

---

[61] TCK-141, in this context, refers to Turkish Penal Code 141, which was in effect at the time of his conviction by the Martial Law Court.

lecturer is anti-Marxist. We are having a discussion. During the semester, I took 'Utopian and Scientific Socialism' as one of the essay topics. As I said, the lecturer is anti-Marxist; he claims that 'the claim of scientific socialism has collapsed! My essay on this subject was a continuation of my previous work on the Paris Commune.

"In a way, the first work was a turning point for me. There, I attempted to elucidate the defeats of both the Paris Commune and the Soviets, drawing on Kivilcimli's 'History Thesis. I repeated it in the second one, but at that time, I was still, for example, looking at Robert Owen's experience through the narrow window of the concept of "utopian socialism". Starting with Engels' Utopian Socialism, I looked at some of the relevant works in English, quoted from them, analysed the subject from the perspective offered by the History Thesis, and tried to explain what happened to the Paris Commune and the Soviets from this perspective. The excitement in me is also about capturing a different and new approach. The lecturer may draw a cross on my writing and say, 'come off it'. Frankly, this was what I expected. I wouldn't be surprised if someone who has never heard of Kivilcimli reacts this way. In the end, I was surprised! In his note on my paper, that anti-Marxist lecturer stated -I quote- this: *'An interesting paper. Some of your arguments needed further elaboration and more careful wording.*

"Nevertheless, your work good use of empirical evidence. Overall, an interesting approach.' Look, here is what he wrote. It is one of the folders where I kept some of my works at the University...

"But what about us, what is happening in Turkey? Let me tell you what an 'Althusserian', who is now lecturing at a university as a professor of economics, who at the time was very 'knowledgeable', who had 'devoured' Marxism, was spouting.

"Interestingly, it is the same period. That man, Sedat, was severe: *'Lenin was an arrogant, presumptuous. Lenin intended to make fun of Proudhon. He supposedly criticises an important work of Proudhon, such as 'The Philosophy of Poverty', by writing something called 'The Poverty of Philosophy'. If it relies on an ideology created by adding this man's name to a master like Marx, of course, the Soviets will collapse!'* That's what he said. He has heard the book's title but doesn't know who penned it! Such people are out there!

"Alright, we're laughing now, but the difference between universities that educate such individuals in Turkey and the one here is this!"

"What did you say to him?" asked Zafer.

"What did I say to that guy? What else can I say? Did he say something that can be corrected?... So, to 'poke fun,' what else could I do? I said, 'Hey, Sedat Hodja, let's not leave our conversations to chance like this. Let's get together, even once a month or something. I want to benefit from these enlightening discussions!'

"Actually, when I decided to run away, I wasn't considering the opportunities and environment I would find here. However, in the end, this environment provided the opportunity for me to develop my thoughts. Especially, seeing the parallels between David McLellan's interpretation of Marx and Kivilcimli's interpretation – which, them being aware of each other is absolutely impossible – was both enlightening and gave me hope that even on the other side of the world, people, despite being unaware of each other, can reach the same conclusions.

"Again, for example, I was chatting to Esen. It was in the early years of my life in London. He looked at what I told him about my questions and asked, 'Do you follow the Russian New Left?' I said, 'No.' He said, 'What you say sounds very similar.' As I told him, I wasn't even aware of their existence, let alone their thoughts.

"In short, whether it's what I wrote while I was in university, my desire to adapt the novel, titled 'What Is to Be Done' for the stage to carry these ideas to a broader audience later, or the criticisms I directed towards both BSP and ÖDP during their formations, at the core of it all lies Kivilcimli's ideas. My starting point is Kivilcimli. It's what Kivilcimli wrote. In the past, I had tried to study Kivilcimli by reading. Still, after leaving the Party, I acquired a severe difference in perspective. Questioning, not content with understanding but trying to make sense of it, has a significant share in this.

"Yes, of course, other sources have been eye-opening. Although some of my other readings have influenced me, Kivilcimli is still the basis of my thoughts today. No one in Turkey has yet uttered the term 'communalism', and I am not aware of Murray Bookchin or others. Imagine that until 2001, I was saying 'alternative society' or something like that, as I had given up using the term 'socialism'! Inspired by the Russian Social Democrats' break with the concept of 'Social Democracy'. More precisely, inspired by Lenin. He was right in his own way. I thought it should be done like that then, but I couldn't replace the concept of 'socialism' with anything else. I don't know the word for

'Ümmetçilik[62],' so I looked it up in the dictionary. What did I come across? 'Communalism!' The penny dropped...Communalism instead of communism! I was in a 'Eureka! Eureka!' mood... I said to myself, 'Wait,' and I went online. There are lots out there! Stunning! I had been clueless about the world!

"Of course, there's also the matter of productive forces, connected to this. As you transcend the boundaries of the paradigm you're confined within, you start questioning the concepts you know and have learnt. But it is still inspired by Kivilcimli. Kivilcimli's interpretation of the productive forces is far beyond Stalinist interpretations. Even a comparison cannot be made. Anyway, let me not go on and on. The subject is 'What happened in the Soviet Union? Let me quote this part from what I wrote about the ÖDP."

This time Emin reached for another folder. He was rummaging through the folder while continuing to talk.

"The foundational ideas for what I've written about ÖDP were shaped during my university years, particularly in my dissertation on the German Greens... Ah, I found it! I dated it 8 May 1996. Almost a year and a half after the dissertation."

Emin started reading:

Capitalist production relations impose a dreadful technological 'development(!)' on humanity. At this point, capitalist production relations suffocate and destroy the geographical productive forces. Mother nature cannot renew itself. Let's pause here and recall the materialist conception of history!"

---

[62] Some dictionaries now include the relatively new word "Ummahism" as a translation for "Ümmetçilik."

Emin looked up from the paper he was reading and paused reading.

"By the way, let me draw your attention to the fact I don't use the term 'historical materialism'. You know that concept we use often, Marx doesn't have it. David McLellan says that Marx never used this term and preferred to say 'the materialist conception of history' because what was put forward was a method, an approach rather than a fully developed system of thought. This is not a nuance. This distinction actually delineates, even constrains, the boundaries of our thought world, or if you look at it from the reverse perspective, it breaks its chains. It is very much connected with the issue of whether or not to carry Kivilcimli's 'History Thesis' to its logical conclusions. I believe that perceiving the History Thesis as simply an explanation for the period before written history (or better to say 'pre-written history') and overlooking the method behind it originates partly from the concept of 'historical materialism,' using that term, leading us to a mindset of 'it's done and done, mashallah!'"

Emin continued to read from where he had pressed his finger tightly:

"In the Preface to the Contribution to the Critique of Political Economy, Marx presents his materialist conception of history very succinctly: 'At a certain stage of development, the material productive forces of society, operating within the hitherto existing framework, come into conflict with the existing relations of production or - and this is merely a legal term for the same thing - with the relations of property. These relations cease to be a structure enabling the development of the productive forces and become a structure stifling them.' This law set by the materialist conception of history has been limited to Marx's application to his own era. Furthermore, it has been paralysed, especially by Stalinist dogmas. The conflict has been addressed exclusively within the confines of human productive forces and the working class, which is specific to Marx's era, as well as capitalist relations of production -along with their legal superstructure of capitalist property relations. But hasn't one of the parties in this conflict now yielded its priority to another among the productive forces today?

"The conflict between human productive forces among the material productive forces and capitalist production relations has now been replaced by the conflict between another material productive force, namely, the productive forces of geography, and capitalist production relations. Capitalism is currently engaged in a struggle to preserve its existence by destroying nature. It requires this to maintain its grip on the face of the working class. It must provide something, not only for its own working class in the metropolis, as crumbs from the exploitation of underdeveloped countries but also, to some extent, for the masses of the exploited countries, although not as much as for its own masses. The propaganda it has been pumping into the countries labelled 'socialist' for years with the help of developing communication technology has affected this target group as well as the masses of underdeveloped countries. The only way for finance capital to sustain its system, based on profitability rather than morality, was to develop technology at a formidable but terrifying pace."

Emin looked up from the papers in his hand.

"Here, I mentioned the relevance of the nursery rhyme 'social progress'. Let's skip this part."

He turned the page.

"I went on to say: 'The law set forth by the materialist concept of history stood, and the conflict between the productive forces of geography and capitalist relations of production took precedence. Capitalism, to survive, was destroying nature in such a way that it would never be able to renew itself again, and this was a problem that no other system had ever imposed on humanity. The destruction of nature was at the top of the agenda not only as a problem of a class but as a problem of the whole of humanity. The problem has gone beyond being just an issue of exploitation; it has become a matter of life and death. What falls upon us is to set aside idol worship – whether it be the idol of the working class or any other – and instead, bow to the laws presented by the materialist interpretation of history – which are the laws that impart scientificity to socialism, not everything Marx or Engels said on every subject – and apply them to our present-day.' I think this is enough. Are you bored?"

"No, I'm not bored, but I wonder where you will connect it. Besides, these are topics open to debate. Moreover, you need to delve deeper, or as the anti-Marxist university lecturer pointed out, your arguments needed further elaboration!" said Zafer.

"Why should I do it alone? The production of theory should also be communalised. It shouldn't be left solely to individuals we might label as 'theorists.' Just as you said, 'It should be debated!' This is necessary for the communalisation of theory production. Knowledge should be spread to the broadest possible audience and discussed on the broadest possible basis. Theory production becomes communal in this way. As for what I wrote... I accept that there are issues open to discussion. I distributed what I wrote to the people I could reach. I even gave it to someone from ÖDP who came here so that they could take it to the ÖDP administration. I don't know whether it reached them or not. I didn't hear anything from anyone."

Emin paused for a second and then, continued:

"Let's be fair; back then, Gün Zileli was around here, and I gave it to him, too. Later, when we met, he said, 'You've been quite inspired by us!' I replied, 'I have no knowledge of exactly what you're saying, but my source is Kivilcimli,' and tried to explain. That's all. As I said, we can't hold a reasonable debate! Why is that? Do you know what lies behind our inability to hold a reasonable debate? Prejudices and blind judgments. What I'm trying to do, above all, is struggle to purify myself from stereotypes, prejudices, and preconceived judgments. I can't say 'purification,' but it's a struggle for purification!"]

* * *

Although the incidents he shared with Nazli about prejudices and blind judgments often saddened or angered him, some moments of such incidents made him laugh. After approximately three years since his conversation with Nazli, he added the events in Bursa Prison due to a small trick he played to the list of funny incidents.

"You've got a lot of books again! Will you give us some to read?"

Emin gave an unhesitant response to the cheerful H.F. Afacan, one of the three 'Dev-Genç' members who had a warmer relationship with themselves compared to the other four:

"Of course. Look, we'll give you the ones you want. But let my mates from our commune pick them first."

The days when his namesake would oppose Emin's favourable judgment about H.F. Afacan had not yet come. His namesake had said, 'Fuck it, he's a useless coward and a con man,' following the uprising in the prison. Many years would pass before 1988 when Emin would realise the fallacy of his favourable judgment, confirming what his namesake had said about that person.

To shed the naivety of imprisonment, where even the slightest glimmer of humanity appears like catching the sun, Emin would eventually encounter the setback that this person would throw his way in 1988, utilising a commercial cunning befitting his surname, Afacan, one of the meanings of which is 'crafty.' He would reveal his true nature by exploiting Emin's predicament during the escape preparations. Only about eleven years later would he fully comprehend his namesake's warning.

Before reaching those days that had not yet come, Emin would go through the books given to the commune a week late, along with H.F. Afacan. Most of them were the works of Kivilcimli, and there had been no demand for them.

"Can I have this?" asked H.F. Afacan.

"What is Dialectics in Science and Philosophy?", written by Ali Kızılırmak, was the one requested.

"I'll read first. Then, my namesake, I mean Emin Karakulak. After that, we'll give it to you guys."

At first, he did not tell anyone except his namesake that the book's author was Kivilcimli.

"Emin, you are not prejudiced against the Doctor, but the others are. So, don't tell them who the real author is; it is between you and me."

His namesake got curious: "Okay, but why?"

"As I said, it's a matter of prejudice. It's a small book, and it's also about dialectics; let the other inmates read it, so let's wait; let's not say anything until the book comes back to us."

Emin would later rejoice at the way the book was passed from hand to hand among the "Dev-Genç" people, who would shortly afterwards call themselves "Dev-Yol"[63], and at their reaction to it:

"How beautifully he explained dialectics. How clearly and simply he explained thesis, antithesis and synthesis."

"Yes, very useful. It transcends scholastic accounts of dialectics."

H.F. Afacan, who had not understood Emin's reference to Stalin's "Dialectical and Historical Materialism,' which he had almost memorised without naming it, was to act as an emissary:

"You're not on good terms, but the Maoists want to read it too. Shall I give it to them?"

Emin looked at his namesake, and his namesake looked at him... The exclamation of sarcasm settled on their lips as a smile to keep their secrets a little longer. They agreed without speaking!

"Sure, I don't mind, but you are responsible for bringing the book back to me, not them."

These Maoists, whom Emin and his friends belittled by calling them the 'People's Relatives,' and who had no connection to Perinçek, nevertheless, with a wholesale

---

[63] Devrimci Yol (Turkish for 'Revolutionary Path,' shortly DEV-YOL) was a Turkish political movement with a nationalist tendency (as opposed to a tightly structured organisation) that had many supporters, mainly youth and students at the time

approach, Emin was equating them with the 'CIA Socialist' and his team. Let them stay away... Was... Was it really?! This reflected the attitudes he had opposed, the "prejudice and preconceived judgement" he had argued against, which he thought he was against. Dialectics was not smoothly transitioning from knowledge acquired from books to manifest in his behaviour.

In the end, it came full circle, and the book returned.

"Would you like to read the other books by the Doctor?"

Emin, realising they might not have grasped the meaning behind his question, continued with a subtle hint:

"For instance, in the 'History Thesis,' Kivilcimli deconstructs history using the dialectical method he narrates in this book."

"So, Ali Kızılırmak is Dr Kivilcimli?"

"The Doctor published it under that name."

"Why didn't he use his own name?"

"I don't know either. Either to avoid censorship of such a work or for fear that it will not be read with prejudices and preconceived judgements... I don't know."

* * *

Upon looking at his watch, he instantly detached himself from the memories associated with the prejudice and blind judgments he had immersed himself in on the roads of Yugoslavia.

"We've been on the road for almost five hours; how much longer?"

His eyes searched for the bus conductor. He had to poke his head into the aisle to realise he was lying on the rear seat. When Emin came to the conclusion that the bus conductor wouldn't be able to see him, he got up and went to him.

While asking 'Novi Pazar... When?' he expressed his question through body language by pointing at his watch with his right index finger and opening the palms of both hands in the air.

The question was understood, but the answer was again given in a language he did not understand. The bus conductor, who had risen from his seat, rummaged in his pockets. He drew a long line on a piece of paper with a pen. After placing Belgrade at one end and Novi Pazar at the other, he put a dot near the last end and made two signs with his fingers, showing his watch.

Emin repeated the bus conductor's actions before going to his place, completing them in Turkish:

"Two hours."

The bus conductor nodded.

The bus, going through the darkness of the night, was travelling through villages and towns, stopping at some of them. Emin could no longer see the details of the houses he had captured in daylight. Their silhouettes under the pale lights told that they were not different from the ones he had seen during the day.

In Thrace or along the Aegean coast, no one would find it strange to see single or two-story houses, similar to those in Yugoslavia, nestled in the shadows of minarets or church steeples, or even both. Even though some of them were maintained, these houses were singing the sad songs of poverty to Emin, mostly with their walls where the clay plasters were falling off in places, wooden balconies were attached to the walls, ready to throw the boredom of the room's troubles dissipate into the air despite all their wear and tear. Or, they were sad songs suitable for Emin's mood, which also contained tenderness. Even though there was a church in one of them and a mosque in the next, in a few, these two could coexist in these places where people could put their heads under a roof.

When he brought these images back to the time before he fled, he observed not only the similarities but also the differences.

"Once upon a time, it was like this in Anatolia. Then, the magic of coexistence was broken. Because of capitalism! In this respect, can we say that capitalism represents an advanced stage? If this is societal progress, shouldn't we reconsider this concept?"

As weariness weighed on his half-awake eyes, grappling with the night's darkness, his thoughts drifted into the profound depths of sleep. However, when all the bus lights turned on, and the activity and chatter of the remaining passengers filled the surroundings after more than half had disembarked on the road, his half-awake slumber was abruptly disturbed. They had arrived in Novi Pazar. Not only the words that the assistant said to him that he did not understand, but the fact that he came and tried to say something to him meant that the journey was over.

Beneath the pale lights of the lampposts at the small coach station, bathed in the moonlight's embrace, he waited for the bus conductor to hand over his suitcase, far removed from the hurriedness of the other passengers' journeys. As most passengers headed toward the exit directly across from the bus's entrance and a few passengers got into taxis with their large suitcases being loaded, he walked towards the building, where no one seemed visible despite it being lit up inside.

When he moved to approach the closed door on the left side of the booth in front of him, instead of the door that opened into the building directly across, he waited for the young blonde woman, petite and with a smiling face framed by delicately trimmed eyebrows and bangs falling over her forehead, to open the booth window from an unseen side door. He awaited this moment with hope, ready to voice his question before asking:

"Do you speak Turkish?"

The young woman's thin eyebrows, raised in surprise, and her head turning a few times to the right and left with short movements silently conveyed that they did not share a common language. Emin tried to find a shelter by uttering the name of the police whom Eşref had told everyone would know:

"Suleyman (...) Police!"

In response to the sign of not knowing, Emin pointed to the pen in front of the young woman, mimicking holding it with his right hand and making a writing gesture in the palm of his left hand. Emin repeated the writing sign when the woman handed the pen through the bell-shaped glass gap. The young woman handed over a blank piece of paper, casting a gaze mixed with some curiosity and suspicion upon it. He repeated what he had just said in capital letters so that it would not roll into the chaos of his messy handwriting.

"POLICE SULEYMAN (...)"

He wanted to avoid any suspicion or misunderstanding arising from the word "police" by putting "Police" in front of the name.

The young woman, whose eyes, hands, and raised eyebrows were saying, 'I don't know... I don't know", lifted the telephone receiver to dial the numbers. She spoke with someone while looking at the paper Emin had given her. Even though Emin couldn't hear, he understood that the woman had asked someone about 'Süleyman.' When the conversation ended, the reiterated gestures indicated that this attempt was fruitless, too. There was no other way left but to go to the town and try his luck there.

"Taxi?"

The young woman clung to the phone once again. As she finished her conversation, Emin couldn't discern whether she had gestured "Five minutes!" with her hand or signalled "Wait!" without putting a handcuff over the duration; nevertheless, he had no choice but to wait.

He again took out the cigarette pack and was about to pull one out, but he paused for an instant and offered it to the young woman first. Emin understood, more or less, the "No, I don't smoke" response beneath the shawl of her smile. The cigarette he had lit was not halfway through when a taxi, which had just entered the exit gate where the passengers were dispersed to the town, made a "U" turn in the bus station and stopped, facing the direction from which it had come. Although Emin intended to go towards the taxi, he waited when he saw the woman at the counter coming out with the paper he had just received from Emin. The driver had already got out of his car and was coming towards them. The young woman showed the paper in her hand and explained something. In addition to the repeated name and surname of the policeman, there was one more word in the story: 'Turski.' The driver neither knew the policeman nor spoke Turkish. This was the conclusion Emin drew from the raised shoulders.

Nevertheless, in a desperate effort, he asked, 'Do you speak Turkish?' The driver's shoulders rose again.

"What a question I was asking! When the woman mentioned 'Turski,' consider the question I was posing to the man who did not try to speak Turkish with me." He had

While Running Away

found the person to be angry with. Not for no reason, Aslihan, his old-time friend, had said, "You're the man who fights with his own shit!"

"Motel or hotel?" He directed his question to the driver. At that moment, he wasn't sure whether he had thought it himself or if the driver had said so while pulling Emin by the arm. Did he say "Haydi!"? He would later discover that "haydi" in Turkish was "hayde" there. He placed his suitcase in the back seat and himself in the front seat.

The driver said something Emin did not understand but finished his sentence with an understandable question:

"Istanbul?"

Emin confirmed, "Istanbul!"

When the taxi stopped after a less than five-minute journey, Emin looked around but could not see a building resembling a hotel or a motel. Next to the single-storey, side-by-side shops with no light and closed iron-fingered doors, the driver got out of the car, pointing to the place with the light on and the windows fogged with the breath of the people inside, and gestured for him. Desperate, Emin got out. When the driver opened the door of the place they were heading to together, Emin was confronted with a familiar sight.

"It's a coffee house! We're in a country not so different than ours!"

The crowd of men, engrossed in their noisy conversations that drowned out the television's music, halted their game, of whatever the game was, upon noticing the stranger beside their friend who had saluted them at the door. Following a brief silence, the clamour resumed with sentences interwoven with unfamiliar words, apart from 'Turski,' 'policeman,' and 'Süleyman (...),' none of which Emin recognised, yet all connected to each other. Then, they returned to their own royal throne after completing their answers. No one spoke Turkish, and no one knew Süleyman. The taxi driver grabbed his arm again, dragging him into the car, leaving Emin even more bewildered that no one seemed to speak Turkish.

When the car started moving, the driver was talking, saying "Turski, Turski" every now and then. It didn't take long. Around three minutes. Again, they stopped in front of a similar building. Again, the driver saluted the crowd of men, opened the door and spoke loudly. Again, a hum.

While trying to convey to the driver his destination by repeatedly saying 'hotel, motel' and gesturing towards the taxi, Emin thought, 'There will be some people who speak Turkish; if not, I can find English speakers. I can understand them with the help of a dictionary anyway!' In the midst of this chaotic attempt at communication, Emin suddenly noticed a young man rising from his seat and approaching them.

After finishing his talk with the driver, the young man turned to Emin and saluted him in Turkish:

"Hello."

During his journey, Emin asked this question formally in Turkish with the second-person plural suffix. As he felt a sense of joy when he encountered someone speaking Turkish, he adjusted his question with the second-person singular, informal suffix, infusing a friendly tone:

"Do you speak Turkish?"

"So, so. Not a lot."

Emin found the young man's pronunciation a little bit odd, and though he was speaking broken Turkish, it was still understandable.

"It's all right. That's good. Do you know Suleyman (...)? The police?"

"I know Suleyman, the policeman. Father's surname. But mum's surname," he added without saying 'by,' giving another surname. The driver joined the conversation, saying something in their language. At the end of the conversation, the young man turned to Emin, pointing to a hilly place at the back of the car:

"The house up there," he said, pointing to the hill. "Sulayman brother Ibrahim there. His mum there. Go with taxi. Ibrahim may not there. Come back. Come back here. I'm at the café. You and me go hotel. Don't give money. Ibrahim at home, Ibrahim gives money to taxi. Otherwise, come back. Don't give money."

He must have repeated the exact words to the driver because the taxi driver, nodding his head in response as if to say "yes," opened the car door and invited Emin into the taxi.

"Thank you very much, thank you very much." Unconsciously, he had started speaking incomplete sentences in the same language as the young man. "Thank you."

Emin held out his hand and shook the young man's hand, a smile of joy on his face.

The taxi slowed down as it left the slope and entered the road, curving to the left. The driver honked the horn at the end of the muddy dirt road. When a young man emerged from the door, bathed in the filtering light, the driver exited the taxi, gestured with his hand, asking him to approach, and threw a sentence, including 'Ibrahim,' toward the young man at the door. The young man, approaching swiftly, turned to the barking dogs behind him and uttered something. Whether he said, 'Shut up' or 'Go to your place,' the barking, which had turned into a growling, ceased, and the dogs retreated.

After the driver said a few words, the young man extended his hand to Emin.

"I'm Ibrahim. Brother Süleyman. Suleyman is not here."

Not knowing how much Turkish Ibrahim understood, he started telling his issues to him.

"I'm from Istanbul. Eşref Abi told me to come here and find Süleyman."

"Eşref Abi. Dobra... Dobra[64].... No Süleyman. It's all right. Come here."

"Dobra" was a word Emin remembered from his childhood. He had often heard it from his maternal grandmother, even though he didn't know its meaning at that time. However, he knew the term "dobra-dobra konuşmak," which meant speaking openly without beating around the bush.

"How much is it?" Emin asked the driver in Turkish, seeking refuge in Ibrahim's interpretation. Ibrahim reached into his pocket.

"No, no, no. Not you." Emin tightly gripped Ibrahim's arm, thinking he should prevent Ibrahim from misunderstanding.

"Not you. I'll pay. Ask how much it is."

The driver understood. He showed the ten fingers of both hands twice, making the sign of twenty and formed a sentence in which the word "Mark" was stuck in the middle. Ibrahim's tone of voice was telling Emin that he was objecting. The driver laughed and showed ten fingers this time.

Emin took out fifteen Marks from his wallet and handed them over. He declined the five DMs the taxi driver tried to give back, ignoring Ibrahim's repeated "NOs". The man had not only been a driver, he had tried his best to help. Emin had felt indebted for his efforts. Like Emin, the driver was

---

[64] Dobra (in Serbian): Good

While Running Away

also happy, albeit for different reasons; he went and took the suitcase from the back seat of the car and handed it to Ibrahim. Emin hesitated for a moment. If he tried to take his suitcase, it might create the impression that he did not trust Ibrahim; on the other hand, if Emin did not, he would be making someone else carry his own load. "The latter is better than the former", he said to himself and did not object.

As they were walking home, Ibrahim suddenly stopped. "Stop. Dogs." Without waiting for Emin to answer, he sped up and dropped the suitcase in his hand inside the door. Calling the dogs after him, he tied them to a tree about twenty steps away, then came back to the doorway and called out:

"Come."

He gave way for Emin to come in. They both took off their shoes at the doorstep. Ibrahim took the suitcase and walked ahead in the narrow corridor of the house. Emin followed him.

In the room, there was no one except for an older woman sitting at the far end of the couch that extended along half of the wall. Ibrahim introduced her:

"Ana!" Instead of "Anne", which means "mother", he had chosen a casual tone reminiscent of people in Anatolia.

Emin went over to the older woman, took her outstretched hand, kissed it, and placed it on his head. He had not asked Eşref what the customs were, what to do and what not to do. Thinking, "They can't be that different from ours, anyway," he had repeated what he knew, mixed with the bewilderment of not knowing what to do!

The woman listening to Ibrahim's words patted the spot next to her, indicating for Emin to sit down. He complied.

After finishing what he had told his mother, Ibrahim left the room, returned in the blink of an eye, and tried to talk to Emin in broken Turkish.

"My Turkish weak. Eşref Abi sent you."

"I fled from Turkey. Eşref Abi and I were members of the same Party."

"Party?"

Emin tried to match Ibrahim's broken Turkish:

"Political Party. Socialist. But I got a penalty. A prison sentence.

"Jail?"

"Yes," Emin replied, crossing his wrists, and it seemed that Ibrahim understood what had been said.

"Eşref Abi said, 'Süleyman will help you'."

"Suleyman is cop. Him no. I will help."

"Thank you."

"Suleyman is a cop. Not good for him. You sleep at night, but just one night. Then motel. Otherwise, the police need a record. It's a problem."

"OK, thanks. I'll go tonight if you want. I don't want to create a problem for you."

"Nema problema.[65] Go to bed tonight. Hotel tomorrow."

"Thank you."

At this moment, a young woman of the same age as Ibrahim, with her hair falling onto her forehead and the rest covered by a scarf, entered the room with a tray in her hand. Ibrahim stepped aside a little and made room for the tray on the sofa. The woman greeted Emin with a nod and placed a tray on the sofa, bearing a glass of hot milk, a small plate with granulated sugar, and two pieces of bread.

"My brother's wife."

"Suleyman's?"

---

[65] Nema problema: Not a problem.

While Running Away

"My other brother. I have a brother in Germany. Suleyman has another house."

"Dinner's over. Sorry. Milk and bread."

"Thanks, I don't want any food. I'm full."

When does a person lie, even if they dislike lying, even if they proclaim, like Emin, "A harmful truth is better than a useful lie!" It was such a moment when Emin felt compelled to lie. With cushions and rugs on the floor, an old cover resembling a wall tapestry with a deer motif hanging behind the couch, and walls with peeling paint, the house was already depicting all its poverty. The hot milk he drank, refraining from adding sugar to reduce his burden, was enough to satisfy all his hunger.

"You're tired, go to bed..."

They started to communicate with half-finished, half-formed sentences.

"Oh, yes. I'm sorry to have inconvenienced you. I'm sorry."

"No. no inconvenience."

"May Allah give you peace," Emin said, using the customary Turkish phrase, to the house's mother before turning to Ibrahim, who got up and took his suitcase. Although he didn't understand a word other than "Allah" in her response, he accepted it with a slight bow and a smile. When he reached Ibrahim, waiting by the front door, he condensed his question into a single word:

"Toilet?"

When Emin opened the door of the wooden hut twenty-five to thirty steps away, which was directly opposite the outer door that Ibrahim pointed to with his arm, the toilet, which was of the type called "alla-Turco", was almost identical, including the pitcher on the right side of the pit where the need was met by facing the door and squatting, to the one in his grandmother's courtyard, which he remembered from his childhood! When he came out, he hurriedly washed his hands at the tap on the side, where the water flowed from a shallow trough. The coldness of the water added to the cold of the February night, which took away the warmth Emin had wrapped in the room a moment ago, making Emin abandon the thought of "Should I wash my face as well?". With quick steps, he tried to take his suitcase when he reached Ibrahim, who was waiting at the top of the wooden stairs to the right of the outer door from the front. Again, there was no permission. He did not insist; he climbed the stairs after Ibrahim.

After passing through the door that opened when they went upstairs, Ibrahim opened the door to the right of a small hall, where they stepped with a thin creaking of the boards, left the suitcase right next to the entrance, and turned on the light.

"This is your bed."

The bedding was new, with its shining iron bars at the head and foot ends. The smooth flatness of the bed, covered by a milk-white duvet cover, ended in a slope rising towards a large mound extending from one end to the other at the head.

"From where I stand, what is the end is actually the beginning. Our perception depends on where we look at the world. It is as if this room was prepared for a guest to come or always kept ready in case a guest came." His thoughts that began with "From where I stand" were drawn to the freshness and cleanliness of the items in the room. Realising that Emin looked slightly surprised, Ibrahim felt the need to explain.

"My brother and sister-in-law's room. The wedding night room." Ibrahim paused. He repeated the news he had told while talking downstairs.

"Just got married."

"The bridal chamber, then," Emin corrected in his internal conversation before attempting to decline the offer, a sentiment he did not know how to express.

"The bride's room... I won't disturb."

"Nema problema. My brother not here. Sister-in-law stays with my mother. Here, there is water."

Ibrahim pointed to a glass jug filled with water on the bedside table next to the bed, with a lace cover underneath it and the spout with a lace cover. An overturned glass cup was next to it, on top of a more minor lace cover.

"Thank you. I've inconvenienced you."

"No inconvenience. Good night."

Ibrahim, trying to warm a room without a stove in the cold of February with the warmth of hospitality, came out of the door, which he slowly closed behind him. As he descended the stairs, Emin walked to the window. He opened the curtain, on which the floral embroidery was brand new, and looked at the chilly night with its frost. The stars in the cloudless sky and the moon's brightness were heralding a sunny day in the morning.

The stars in the cloudless night sky and the moon's brightness were heralding a sunny day to come in the morning.

He liked to sleep in a cool, even chilly room, but it was pretty cold. He lifted the duvet cover from one end. When he saw the quilt, he went back to his childhood, to the childhood to which he had just been taken for a moment by the outhouse toilet in the garden.

It was the kind of quilt under which he would never again be able to crawl, although he didn't know it at that moment. He softly moved his hand on the smoothness of the lavender-coloured satin, which was embellished with stitches resembling slices of baklava and centred in the middle of the rectangle; the white, fine sheet, sewn by hand on all four sides, cradled by three sides more expansive than the other, equally measured ones at the top. He also caressed the smoothness of the lavender-coloured satin where the lace ended at the end of the milky white coverlet, which was threaded onto the very high pillow under the quilt, the end of which it curled. He inhaled deeply the smell of the freshly washed bedding. He recognised this smell that took him to his childhood and childishness.

His mother would move all the furniture in the room to the sides and sew the quilt, which he placed on the sheet spread over the opened area, from all four sides with a large quilt needle. No matter how fast she sewed, it wouldn't be finished quickly. Emin would do somersaults on the quilts being sewn with his brother whenever he had the opportunity. At the same time, his mother was busy with this work, which took up a large part of the day. It was a game for Emin and his brother. Since all the quilts were dismantled, washed and sewn together again, towards the end, his mother's scolding, which was initially joking, would become severe. They would lay down on the other quilts, sewn and folded on the side and smelled clean, and watch his mother complete her work with rhythmic hand movements.

That clean smell also came from these quilts and pillows, but he could no longer linger. He recovered from the chill created by the cold.

"Come on, come on. This is not the time to journey from one time to another time, from one land to another land, from one memory to another memory. This is no time to get sick!"

He stirred with the warning he gave himself. A feeling of happiness spread throughout his whole body as he put on the pyjamas hastily retrieved from his opened suitcase. He dressed in the joy of knowing he would sleep in a bed after two nights of fitful naps, but the cold was becoming more pronounced. He decided to put on his jumper, too. He pulled the duvet over his head after he turned off the light and got into bed. He wouldn't sleep like this. His head should be out of the duvet when he slept, but first, he would warm the duvet with his breath.

Between the moment he raised his head onto the quilt and the deep, dreamless sleep that lasted until the early morning hours, except for just before waking up, he tried to cram in some planning for the tasks he would undertake the following day.

"I should leave this house early. First, find a hotel, then phone Hasan and Osman. The most difficult stage of the escape is over; the rest is easy."

It was easy for him to fall asleep with the comfort of thinking that things had become more manageable. Suppose he had known and could have anticipated what he would experience. Could he have fallen asleep so quickly despite all his exhaustion? Or would he have kept tossing and turning, chasing sleep from one side to the other? Especially when there was not even a single book that could tear him away from the moment he lived in and help him sleep!

* * *

While Emin was making a plan for the next day, saying, "He should phone Hasan and Osman", he was not aware that Hasan had been in a rage since the morning of that day.

When Hasan learnt from Aslihan that Emin's mother had called and said that Emin had called from Yugoslavia and said "Hello," he went out and called Osman, but no one answered.

"I don't know how many times I telephoned after that. No one answered me day or night, even though I called every chance I got all day. There is no number to call you either. I don't know where you were staying at that time. I can't call you either. It's a complete uncertainty," he would later tell Emin.

Hasan got up from the bed where he had been tossing and turning with the stress of rolling around in questions, took out his cigarette from the packet on the bedside table and was going to light it. However, he gave up and littered his lighter in the living room to avoid disturbing Aslihan's sleep.

"Look here, they're putting wood in the cigarettes!" He was muttering to himself. He got more and more angry. After taking two puffs, he pinched his cigarette, waiting between his fingers for a short moment, but was unable to inhale when he brought it to his lips again, between his thumb and middle finger and threw it out of the half-opened window. The wave of cold air hitting his face with the opening of the window sobered Hasan up.

"This guy is trying to fool us as usual, isn't he? We asked for a passport, and he sent a refugee travel document. He says that the police raided the printing press of the people he was going to get passports to in London, and that's why he couldn't send passports. He says, 'I have such and such relationships... We can even start a newspaper here, and it will be easier when Emin comes,' but he can't even arrange for a passport. You can't establish connections when you call, and he doesn't even call back unless you remind him multiple times."

He examined the Samsun cigarette, which he softened by kneading the tobacco from one end to another between his fingers, removing and smoothing out the protruding tobacco. When he concluded that there was no dry tobacco vein he referred to as "wood," he lit it. He took a deep puff.

The cigarette he had just thrown away without smoking a quarter of it took Hasan back to the "days abroad" when they could not even think of such extravagant behaviour. They smoked cigarettes in numbers. Sharing them with Osman. Selamettin Oksuz didn't smoke. This became his excuse when he was caught buying ham sandwiches and eating them secretly without their knowledge, despite their limited money. Osman was more sharing... On the one hand, Hasan was saying this, and on the other hand, he was puzzled by the contrasts between what Osman had said and what he had not done since he went to England.

"At the time, he was sharing, but I don't know whether this was a necessity brought about by his eagerness and excitement to live abroad or not and whether it was related to the helplessness arising from the fact that he couldn't find any other support in unfamiliar environments. I suppose the justification of my reactions to Selamettin Oksuz's selfishness, combined with the fact that Osman and I are fellow townsmen, prevented Osman from adopting a different attitude. To this should be added the effect of feeling incomplete in my presence due to his education, which was limited to the Evening Trade High School."

Hasan's memories went back to the moments when Osman expressed his surprise with exaggerated expressions when he took him to the canteen of the Political Sciences Faculty. *"Abi, one day I'm going to enter this school too,"* Osman had said with an ambition mixed with envy. Hasan knew that he held a distinct place in the eyes of Osman, who had to leave Turkey during those turbulent days as life hurtled towards the coup of 12 September 1980 without the chance to fulfil his aspirations.

He would tell Emin more later on the phone:

"Underlying his obedience to what I say is the sheikhdom passed down to me from my father as the eldest son."

"I am aware of such relations among the Kurds, but... I cannot say that I am not surprised that this plays a role in the dynamics among revolutionaries."

Hasan laughed at Emin's reaction.

"You wouldn't understand. It's a hierarchy that develops spontaneously in the environment we, I mean Osman and me, grow up in. It exists even if we don't speak it, and sometimes it works."

As Hasan extinguished the last cigarette of the night, pregnant with the developments that would lead to this conversation a few months later, and went back to bed, Emin was deep in sleep in his bed, covered in white sheets that smelled of freshly scented soap.

* * *

"Get down!"

He didn't even ask the policeman why. The officer had opened the bus's rear door, and his steely gaze was fixed on Emin. As he rose from his seat and descended the steps,

Emin fumbled to button up his coat while pondering what to say. Finally, he heard the command,

"Give me your passport."

Emin handed over the passport he had retrieved from his jacket pocket…

He opened his eyes. First, he saw the daylight filtering through the thick curtains, then the brightness of the freshly painted walls of the room. With the thought of "Let me sleep a bit more," he pulled the duvet up to his nose, also taking in its scent.

Sometimes you wake up. You don't know the reason, but a tranquillity has enveloped every cell in you, carrying a bubbling joy inside." If he hadn't seen the dream just before waking up, he would have woken up with these feelings. With the daylight dispersing that nightmare, Emin was transported to the feeling that waking up without a dream brings. The curtain of sleep had lifted. He had also forgotten his dream.

The dream did not forget him. Later on, for more than two months, almost every morning, right at that moment, as he was handing his passport to the police, it was the first time he would see the same dream that would wake Emin up repeatedly. Each time, he would say, "It was just a dream," and get relaxed. After going to the bathroom to become even more relaxed, he would attempt to go back to sleep. However, he would start his day instead of returning to sleep each time. But this time, he didn't have the luxury of returning to sleep. His thoughts jumped from "Let me sleep a little more" to "Is it time to sleep?".

The daylight seeping through the curtains was a harbinger of a sunny day, and the sky he looked at through the curtain he opened from the edge confirmed it.

He opened his suitcase and put on the clean socks he had taken out. Then, he quickened his movements, replacing the pyjamas underneath his sweater with a shirt while putting the sweater back on. After putting on his pants, he neatly folded the pyjamas he had previously tossed onto the bed and went downstairs with the suitcase he had settled into. Ibrahim had also opened the door at the house entrance to greet him, holding a towel in his hand. He had heard the noise of the doors opening and closing while descending the stairs.

"Good morning."

Ibrahim answered Emin in his own language:

"Dobro jutro."

Later, he would look it up in the dictionary and learn the spelling of the word he had heard as "yutro": "jutro." Ibrahim had spelt the "j" as a "y".

He repeated Ibrahim's "Good morning": "Dobro yutro." They laughed.

"I'll go to the loo."

"OK."

He left the suitcase by the door. He hung the towel that Ibrahim had handed him around his neck and walked towards the toilet. After attending to his needs, he repeatedly washed his face with cold water, this time without rushing. He also drank a bit of water.

He took his suitcase and left it behind the closing door, as he was following Ibrahim. The mother was sitting in the same place when they entered the room. Emin repeated the newly learnt words again:

"Dobro yutro."

The woman's face lit up as she returned Emin's morning greeting with the exact words.

Ibrahim gave way, pointing to the sofa with his arm:

While Running Away

"Sit down."

"No, I won't. Let's go if you wish." The phrase "if you wish", the conditional statement, had slipped out of his mouth.

"Eat bread, then."

"No, no, no. Don't bother. Let's find a hotel and then have breakfast together."

Ibrahim didn't object to Emin's request, which stemmed from his effort not to be a burden. Upon this, Ibrahim recited the words of his own language aloud in the direction from where the milk had come the previous evening.

A female voice responded briefly. It must have been the "bride" from last night.

After a brief pause, Emin repeated what he had done when he arrived the night before, kissing the mother's hand.

"Goodbye. Thank you!"

Following the mother's incomprehensible reply to Emin, Ibrahim told her something, and they left the house.

While trying not to sink too deeply into the mud that hadn't dried despite the sun, they continued along the path Emin had taken the previous evening. The view Emin saw from the house above the town until he got down to the road was no different from that of a typical Anatolian town.

"There's a nice hotel. But expensive."

Emin's attention was distracted from the view of the town when Ibrahim started talking.

"How much?"

"I think, maybe fifty DM."

"There's only one hotel?"

Emin's question also signalled that he found it expensive.

"No, no, no. There are small motels."

"Are they cheaper?"

"There's one. It's close by. Thirty DM. There's one a little further away. Twenty-five DM."

"Let's see."

There was no vacancy at the first motel they went to. Emin was pleased. He was looking for a place to sleep for a few nights. The cheaper, the better.

There was availability at the one further away, and breakfast was included in the price. One of the two employees at the reception desk took the suitcase, said "Come" in English, took Emin upstairs and showed him the room. In addition to two separate beds, there was a wardrobe and a bathroom with a toilet, separated from the room by frosted glass. Emin checked the radiators. It was warm.

"OK."

He took the suitcase from the hand of the motel employee waiting just inside the door and put it next to the bed by the window. Then, they went downstairs.

Ibrahim was sitting at the table closest to the counter next to the buffet where the kitchen was served, chatting with another employee.

Pointing to a phone he saw on a table at the back of the dining buffet, rather than on the foldable counter where no phone was present for service, Emin asked:

"Can I phone Turkey from here?"

Ibrahim translated the question, and both of the employees shook their heads in the sense of "no!" which told what the answer was, but Ibrahim explained it anyway:

"No, international telephone, post office. No calls. But someone from other countries can call the motel."

"Isn't there anywhere else but the post office for international telephones? Only the post office?"

"Just the post office."

"OK, I get it. Let's have breakfast. You order."
"What do you want?"
"Tea, bread, cheese, olives, anything!"

He carefully observed the conversations between Ibrahim and the workers. Still, he didn't understand anything except for the word "çay," which means tea in both languages, Turkish and Serbian. It was not about picking up a few words from an unfamiliar language but the curiosity to grasp common words.

A little later, the table was set with plates with a glass of milk, cucumber and tomato in addition to what they wanted. When tea arrived in a porcelain teapot, their breakfast was ready.

"Do they have any lemons?"

He had spoken to Ibrahim, but the motel worker answered.

"Limón?"
"Yes."
"Yes."

When they finished their breakfast and lit their cigarettes, another motel employee, whom they hadn't seen until that moment, came over along with the one providing service.

Emin picked up words again: "Passport."

Ibrahim tried to explain his struggle with his Turkish:

"Give your passport. It stays with him. You go, he gives back."

"But when I go out, if the police ask me on the road!"

Ibrahim's look of incomprehension prompted Emin to explain differently.

"I'll go to the post office from here. Passport if the police ask for it on the way."

"No, he won't ask."

He repeated his question because he was surprised that the obligation to carry an ID in Turkey did not exist in Yugoslavia:

"Won't he ask?"

"He won't ask. Bring it here."

"If he asks, I'll tell the police to come to the motel."

"Yes. But he won't ask."

While Emin was taking out his passport and handing it over, Ibrahim explained what was being discussed to the others in his own language.

The motel employee, to whom he had given the passport, returned a little later and handed Emin a business card-sized piece of paper. It contained the motel's name, address, and telephone number, all neatly printed, similar to a complimentary slip.

"I've got work. I have to go. Yeah?"

"I'll go out with you. I'll go to the post office. Can you show me the post office?"

"I'll come to the post office, then I'll go."

"You don't need to come. Lead the way."

"No, I'll come. It's close. I'll talk at the post office. They won't understand you."

Emin gestured with his hand, requesting the bill from the waiter standing by the counter. When he said "no" with his eyebrows and eyes, he also waved his hand as "goodbye" and said something to Ibrahim.

"No breakfast money. Breakfast is free."

Breakfast was included in the motel price, but they had just arrived. He gladly accepted this extra treat, considering the limitations of his money. He didn't refuse. As he was putting on his coat, he remembered another breakfast that was free of charge but surprisingly unprecedented.

While Running Away

* * *

They worked day and night at the Party. After a bomb was planted at the door of the Party headquarters while the Central Committee was in session, it was decided that someone would be on guard every night. Even though he couldn't make sense of the decision made after this incident, which resulted in a few people getting injured, he had to abide by it. How could someone inside prevent a bomb from being placed outside the door? Furthermore, in the event of a raid, what could someone armed only with a dinner knife do other than become a victim? No one objected to this decision taken by the Presidium immediately after the attack. Neither did Emin!

"I didn't object, I couldn't object. I suppose it was for the same reason that others couldn't object: 'Emin's scared!' 'He's avoiding work and responsibility'." This is how he would explain his reasons to Zafer years later.

When he was on one of those night shifts, he opened the door to Selo, who rang the doorbell in the early hours of the morning with his bag in his hand, who knows for what business, bouncing his belly, a little breathless from climbing the stairs of four floors.

"Did I wake you up?"

"Nah. I was folding newspapers."

"Is there tea?"

"No. I was waiting for someone to come so we could buy some tea and brew it. Do you have money? Let's have a 'simit'[66] each."

"There's money, don't worry, but let's have breakfast downstairs."

---

[66] Simit, also known as a Turkish bagel, is a circular bread typically encrusted with sesame seeds found across the cuisines of the former Ottoman Empire.

"There's no one here; how can we leave?"

"It's next door to the apartment block entrance. We can see who's coming and going."

They got down and closed the entrance door of the building tightly. Following Selo's suggestion, "Let's have a hearty breakfast", they ordered their breakfast of butter, sour cherry jam, feta cheese, soft-boiled eggs and tea at the small artisan restaurant, which served chicken over rice, haricot beans over rice, dried beans, and other meals, and so on, and whose owner they were almost sure worked for the police.

When they finished breakfast and got up, Emin opened the exit door and waited for Selo to pay the bill. Selo asked the restaurant owner for his pen as he checked every item on the receipt one by one. He crossed out and corrected the number of eggs on the receipt, reducing the price from four to three. He had eaten two eggs, and Emin had eaten one egg. He adjusted the total cost and reached into his pocket. The restaurant owner objected and kept claiming that four eggs had been eaten. As Selo persisted, the restaurant owner said what he shouldn't have said:

"Then don't give me any money!"

As he put the money back into his pocket, Selo intended to speak with Emin, giving him a gentle push rather than responding to the restaurant owner.

"Come on, Hodja, let's get out."

Emin expressed his discomfort to Selo, who closed the door behind him and left while opening the outer door of the apartment block:

"It's a shame!"

"What shame? He tried to rip us off. Besides, he's working with the police, that pimp. Forget it; you won't let such people ask twice."

He hadn't hesitated much, and what was peculiar was that the man hadn't come after them to ask for his money either.

***

"After all, breakfasts are included in the motel fee. If they had given an extra breakfast, they should count it to their hospitality," Emin thought, who had also not hesitated this time, was taken away from the memory of the past by Ibrahim:

"The post office is near. Three-five minutes. I won't come back today. I have work. I'll come tomorrow morning. No work. OK?"

"Suleyman?"

"My brother works. It's not good for you to see him. It's not good for him. I'll help you. Not him."

Emin felt disappointed when the possibility that Süleyman would help him, which he had been happy about when Eşref had told him, had disappeared. The hope that getting help from a policeman would make things easier for him had been dashed.

"Beggars can't be choosers!" Emin murmured.

Since blurting out what crossed his mind didn't go beyond a whisper, Ibrahim didn't understand, so he asked:

"What did you say?"

Emin couldn't say what he was actually murmuring.

"You know best. I'm not from around here. I'm a guest. Whatever is convenient for you, you know best. Of course, I don't want to cause any trouble for your brother. I hope it won't be a problem for you either."

"No problem for me. Don't worry. My brother is a policeman. It may be a problem for him."

"OK, thank you." They went inside the post office. Recalling the conversation at the motel, Emin remarked, "Another Turkey again!"

A scene resembling that of a small town or a small city's tiny post office in Anatolia. An L-shaped counter. Two clerks on the long leg of the L-shaped counter and one on the small leg, opposite where three telephone booths are located. The chairs lined up opposite the counter are empty, waiting for customers. Ibrahim approached the clean-shaven clerk wearing a loose jacket on his slender body directly across from the telephone booths. On the other side, two clerks, one male and the other female, had interrupted their conversation when Emin and Ibrahim entered. They were now staring at the incoming stranger without pretending at all.

After a short conversation with the officer, Ibrahim told Emin what to do, using his fingers:

"One, you call from the booth. Two, give the officer the number. The officer will phone. Then go to the cabin and talk."

"OK, thank you. I'll call now."

The officer pointed to booth number one when Ibrahim asked. Ibrahim said, "I'll come tomorrow," and walked to the door while Emin entered the phone booth. He took out his wallet and dialled the number of Osman's house in England. Silence. A long silence.

"In Turkey, you can find a telephone booth every two steps and use it only at the post office here. Years ago, in Turkey, when it came to making long-distance calls, we used to have to go to the post office, or if you wanted to call from home, you had to have the post office connect the number. We used to wait for a long time! Now, here is the same technological backwardness. Wait. Be patient!"

While Running Away

He counselled himself and waited a minute for a voice, but nothing was on the phone. He hung the receiver back. After a moment's hesitation, he decided to redial the number. Again silence. This time, he waited longer. Fruitless. "I can't get through!" Finally, he came out of the booth. He showed the number in the phone book to the post office clerk.

"Telephone. England!"

The clerk, realising from his gestures rather than his words that Emin wanted him to connect the number, put a small piece of paper and a pen on the counter without saying anything. Emin wrote down the number and turned the paper one hundred and eighty degrees before placing the pen beside it. The clerk continued his work without looking up. Emin waited. Finally, the officer took the paper and showed Emin the chairs opposite the counter, near the telephone booths. There was nothing he could do but have to wait.

* * *

"Waiting, defeat and sacrifice."

In the days following another phone call, he remembered the opening sentence in the preface of the novel "The Tartar Steppe" that he had read.

"Dino Buzzati had defined life as 'waiting, defeat and sacrifice' in his novel."

From a conversation that started with a call he made in a telephone booth before the previous meeting, Emin had lived the relationship in the "waiting" tunnel, even though he tried to get out of it from time to time. Every attempt of him to get out of the tunnel had been met with Nazli's resistance, and they had had resentments following his effort. It was a strangeness that would be repeated later on. In the previous one, if he had found the excuse to meet again, in the next one, Nazli found it. Not once, twice, or thrice. It had been repeated countless times until that call. It would repeat many times later, except for that call. Contrary to usual, it would not be a week-long falling out but a months-long one.

The day before that call, again on the phone, Nazli had told him she had a crush on someone else and had gone to talk to him about it. Emin had ended their conversation with the confused indecision of not knowing what to say.

"I don't know what to say. Let's talk later. I'll call you later!"

He hung up the phone without saying anything else after Nazli had said "OK".

"The waiting ended in defeat... Now you will sacrifice... Where is the sacrifice in that? What are you sacrificing? The woman has given her heart to someone else. There's nothing you can do... There is... They're both your friends. You sacrifice your feelings. You'll suppress them... Wait a minute! Nazli didn't say what Fikri said or how he reacted. Did I even ask? What a strange world! Fikri, in cahoots with Tevfik, was the one who pushed and encouraged me into this relationship."

In the days when Emin kept his emotional turmoil to himself, he remembered, word by word, how he reluctantly accompanied Fikri and Tevfik to the island. They went to retrieve her statistics lecture notes from Nazli and the playful banter he had with Nazli there. Emin recalled the moments when they left Nazli and boarded the ferry, reflecting on what both Fikri and Tevfik had said.

"Don't you get the message, Emin? What is the girl saying to you? 'MeHeBe, whom you dislike, is showing interest in me, sharing his thoughts, taking me to the bookstore and all, but you're not interested,' she says, right? Come on, she tells you, 'Pay attention to me!' And she's giving you a signal of closeness, jokingly saying, 'I can throw you into the sea from here.' It seems you're not indifferent either, but you're not showing it. Instead of acting like high school sweethearts, go talk to Nazli."

"Their words encouraged me. Indeed, during that banter, Nazli had grabbed my arm with both hands and jokingly pretended to push me into the sea when we were near the pier."

He remembered these things, but he still could not overcome his confusion.

"You have a crush on one of the two people I'm best friends with in the class. What did Fikri say? I can't phone Nazli again and ask her!"

He had wavered amid the ebb and flow of the dilemma about whether to talk to Fikri for a while. Given their close proximity, the question remained: what could he say?

"Actually, Nazli's approach is quite right! Well, is 'right' the suitable word for this matter? Not right, but it's more accurate to say 'natural.'"

On one hand, he was engaging in such an argument within himself. On the other hand, he was oscillating between whether to turn back or not as he walked towards Fikri's house.

"Both Fikri and Tevfik are the children of a family of medium-sized business owners trying to become bourgeois. What did Tevfik say: 'What Marx tells us is that the petty-bourgeois with a small manufacture is struggling to become bourgeois and be part of the finance capital....' Indeed, no one but us, the 'Doctorists' among the leftists, use the term 'finance capital'. They don't know Doctor Kivilcimli, but the knowledge of reading Marx... They analyse the situation of their fathers well... 'My father is a business owner buried in debt in the interest spiral of finance capital. But he is doomed to fail. So is Fikri's father!' Fikri agreed with Tevfik's assessment."

With these two, who did not participate in political discussions in the classroom, Emin found a closeness from finding someone who had read Marx and Engels. He could engage in conversations with them that went beyond the slogan-like assessments of the others, calmly and without shouting.

"Is that all? Tevfik also has a more coherent view of love and sexuality. 'People confuse sexual impulses with love. It is one thing to experience sexuality in love and another to mistake sexual attraction for love.' I had read these statements of Tevfik somewhere before, but I hadn't really thought about them. Tevfik's example was also interesting: 'If you can still hug and sleep with the woman after you have made love with, instead of turning your back on her and going to bed after everything is over, it means you love that woman'. They can live like that. I mean, they can have lovers or whatever it is called. If we did, we would be criticised by those around us. Let alone outsiders, even our own friends. Theirs is a 'bourgeois culture?' It's natural for Nazli to be interested in someone like that. But isn't the issue where her relationship with me also tangled the same thing? Suppose it is a matter of similar class-based tendencies. Isn't Nazli also considered conservative in experiencing love physically, unlike Fikri? One way or another, her heart has fallen for Fikri. Handsome guy, moreover. Compared with me, he's even taller and sturdier."

He found himself before Fikri's door while floundering in these thoughts. While he had come, he couldn't resist knocking on the door. And he didn't resist. He didn't need to bring up the topic. Could he keep it to himself? He couldn't. He felt relieved with the response he received:

"What can be said? Maybe she has such a feeling on her own, but I'm with someone else, and I don't have such an emotional closeness to Nazli. Don't pay any attention to that. Maybe it's because you don't show her the closeness she expects from you. Remember our talk on the island ferry... you were the one running away. Who knows, maybe she's doing it to make you jealous. Women are better tacticians than us. Wait a while. There's no such thing for you to get out of the way, right! Besides, even if I had such a tendency, you're not in the middle of anything; two people have gotten close to each other, and whatever is happening is between them. Wait a little longer... Let's see what Nazli will do... Let her come to you this time and seek peace with you. You know, you two are playing a childish game, just like high school students."

Emin had been relieved when he left Fikri's house, but he still could not overcome the feeling of defeat inside him.

"Let's say Fikri had such a tendency, would I not be able to make sacrifices like Lopukhov?"[67]

On that day, he was getting ready to play the role he would play on the stage a quarter of a century later when Chernyshevsky's novel, which Emin adapted himself, was staged in London. He remembered those moments as he was on the run, those moments that would make his eyes misty while 'writing on', those moments that he had not yet been able to digest while 'living on'.

What about those moments…

When he telephoned the next day, he poured his thoughts into the most harsh and hurtful words and did not

---

[67] Lopukhov is one of the main characters in Nikolai Chernyshevsky's "What Is to Be Done?" He steps aside when the woman he loves falls in love with his closest friend.

hear Nazli's silent crying at that moment, which she would later tell. Nazli, whose jawbone had cracked while having her molar extracted, was in no condition to speak.

Due to their prolonged resentment, they were going through a much longer wait than usual, this time not limited to a week.

.

* * *

Emin's current wait ended with the post office clerk's call that didn't leave room to remember what would happen at the end of that wait in the past. He headed towards the number two telephone booth.

When he picked up the receiver, he heard the other phone ringing. He waited for an answer but only waited. Finally, he hung up. He went and gave another number to the clerk to call. This time, he was having Hasan in Turkey called. Whether out of pity or because he had nothing else to do, the clerk did not make him wait this time. Emin entered the booth in the middle, number two again.

When he heard Hasan's voice, he felt a sense of refreshment, akin to someone reaching an oasis in the desert and taking a drink from a small lake, as often described in novels and films. He had experienced this feeling about six months ago.

"Hi, what's up, how are you?"

"I'm fine, thank you. Everything is going well. I met up with my friends."

He had deliberately pluralised it to avoid any special meaning the singular might bring, anxious to be listened to.

"Did my parents call?"

"Yes, Aslihan told me. Your mum called. You had a good trip."

"Yeah, it went well."

"There's nothing wrong, is there?"

"No, no. But I couldn't reach Osman. I called him a while ago. No answer. I thought I'd call you while I was at the post office."

"Are you calling from the post office?"

"Yeah, from the post office. The motel I'm staying at doesn't have international calling capability, only from the post office. But I couldn't reach Osman. He's not answering his phone."

"Could be. Osman and his girlfriend might be at work at this hour."

"Oh, I see."

"Call him later. Call at a later hour."

"OK, I'll see what I can do. I'll try to call."

"Don't say 'try', call him! If you need anything, he will assist."

"OK, I understand. If the post office closes, I may be unable to call late. It would be nice if Osman could call me."

"How can he call?"

"I'll give you the number of the motel where I'm staying. Making international outgoing calls from the motel is impossible, but incoming calls can be received."

"Give it to me, then."

"Just a minute."

Emin took out the small piece of paper given from the motel. While telling him the number, he realised something was missing.

"They didn't put the country code here. Why don't you look it up?"

"OK, don't worry, I'll find it, but you call as late as possible."

"Yeah, I'll call him."

"Anything else?"

'No, thank you. Say hello to everyone."

"I will. Keep me posted. Take care of yourself."

"OK. I'll call you as things progress. Bye."

He was pretty relieved when he hung up the phone. He went to the clerk and asked with hand gestures how much he would pay first while extending 10 DMs at the same time. The clerk, who took the money, multiplied and divided the numbers on the paper in front of him and then handed Emin a lot of Yugoslav dinars in coins besides banknotes. Without counting the money, Emin put them in his pocket, pointed to the door, and asked about the closing time, raising his hand and forming a question mark. The answer he got was "six o'clock", which the clerk indicated with the fingers of both hands. He went back to the motel to avoid attracting attention from outsiders.

When he went to his room, he once again regretted not bringing a book with him. There was no television in the room. If he went downstairs to the motel restaurant, he would have to eat and drink something, which meant money. A magazine on the bedside table between the two beds caught his eye. He flipped through the cheap yellow pages of the thin, glossy-coloured magazine cover while lying on the bed.

He skipped the first page, filled with Cyrillic letters he could not understand, and turned to the second page. A black-and-white photograph of uniformed men with a display of medals on their chests with crowded shoulders occupied a quarter of the page from top to bottom. The first quarter of the adjacent third page was also filled with the same Cyrillic letters. Still, after the page had been split in half, the right-hand quarter was completed with another black and white photograph. A photograph of a young woman about to walk lightly, clad in a tiny bikini that left parts of her body half-naked.

***

[Flashforward - 1996:
"At the time, I found it strange that in that magazine, there was a young, beautiful, half-naked woman on one page and party bigwigs in uniform on the other. I thought, 'Well, This is probably a reflection of the uniqueness of Yugoslavian socialism.' On the one hand, I tried to find solace in the optimism of whether we could call it a libertarian approach and brushed it off.

"This is my second time watching Emir Kusturica's 'Underground'. For some reason, I suddenly remembered that magazine at the motel I saw in February 1989. I don't know if such a connection can be established. Still, it struck me that there was a parallel between that magazine's impression on me and the lives of the party leaders depicted in the film. I wonder if Emir Kusturica is trying to show that the double life of the party leaders, who were always men, in their relations with women was not limited to this area of life."

"You're going overboard again, Emin!"

"Why? Couldn't Kusturica have made such a reference?"

"That's not what I'm saying. It's connecting the pictures you see in the magazine and the film."

"Come on, let's say it is. I mean... I'm going overboard again, making a connection like that. Did I get this impression out of nowhere? But that's not what

I'm saying. Is Kusturica's implication a product of my imagination or fantasy?"

"Perhaps there is such an aspect."

"Perhaps?"

"OK, let's say there is. Party leaders indeed have a double life, or even more accurately, a hypocritical life. But this is a human being. Is a party leader a robot? Can we skip the human phenomenon? This is the existing material."

"What material!"

"The struggle, carried out, must not be underestimated."

"It's not condescension. Glorifying the struggle is leading to ignoring how the parasites were created in that struggle. And the inevitable result! Because the parasites dominate. Why is that? The problem is the mechanism that provides a breeding ground for parasites."

"Party!"

"Yes, the Party. And the state, which has become an apparatus of that Party. Strip the woman so that she is seen as a sexual object, and decorate the man with layers and layers of medals so that these decorations symbolise power. Is there no connection between these?"

"To draw such conclusions from those two magazine pages in a small motel room, wow, that's far-fetched! "

"That magazine evoked the subjugation of women as the first step in the division of societies into classes, turning them into the sexual objects of men, and the reflection of that reality in our present day. This discrimination continues even in a so-called 'socialist' system. The aftermath is obvious!"]

***

He put down the magazine, not understanding a single line. Despite a sound night's sleep, he could not wholly get rid of the exhaustion of the journey; he fell asleep.

At five o'clock, when he dialled the house phone in London again at the post office, he had the freshness and calmness brought by the sleep, the shower and the coffee drunk in the motel bar. Emin preferred to make the call himself this time instead of asking the clerk. The line was not dead, and the bell rang, but he waited in vain for a long time. There was no answer once again. He hung up and called again. The result was the same. He left the post office and walked down the street. When he reached the edge of the stream flowing through the town, he sat on the mound ahead and lit a cigarette. He wasn't able to think of anything. He loaded the despair of not knowing what to do on a tree branch, its origin unknown, that was slowly but silently rolling through in the stream, and watched it until it became invisible.

"That's what's missing, self-pity," he scolded himself, then warned: "Stop talking rubbish, get up and call again."

He thought out loud this time. He looked around; there was no one nearby to hear him. After leaving behind the cigarette he crushed with his foot, he headed for the post office. Again, the same! Fruitless!

It didn't matter what he ate. When he sat down at the motel's restaurant to satisfy his hunger from not having eaten anything since breakfast, he didn't have the language to express his wishes, nor did he have a menu of dishes. His hunger had intensified the disquiet that occurred due to the failed phone call attempt. The waiter who came by attempted to explain the restaurant's dinner offerings. Still, Emin, in addition to facing a language barrier, hadn't paid enough attention to what the waiter was saying. Finally, he obeyed the call of the waiter behind the counter and went to look at the food in the glass-fronted buffet. He didn't prolong it. He pointed at the long plate of neatly arranged meatballs and the salad bowl. Then, he showed the beer bottle on the buffet to the waiter, who asked what he would drink by bringing the open thumb of his closed fist to his mouth.

He returned to sit in his chair, facing the buffet, with his back to the door. The waiter, while pouring the beer into the glass he had brought, called out to someone entering through the open door:

"Ahmed."

When Ahmed approached the waiter, he listened to what was said, then turned to Emin and greeted him with a 'Hello' in Turkish. 'Hello,' Emin responded, pleased to engage in a conversation in Turkish, even though it was just the beginning.

"You're Turkish?" Ahmed inquired.

"Yes, I'm from Turkey."

"I know a bit of Turkish. How are you?"

"Thank you, I'm fine. Won't you sit down?"

As he took a seat in the chair to the right of Emin, Ahmed said something to the waiter standing by, then turned to him:

"When did you arrive?"

"This morning."

"Did you come to go sightseeing?"

These were routine questions, but still, Emin felt a sense of restlessness.

"Sort of."

The waiter, who brought another bottle of beer, started talking to Ahmed, which interrupted Ahmed and Emin's conversation, and the call out for the waiter from the counter interrupted their discussion in their own language. When the waiter came back to the table, he placed a plate with a bowl of rice along with neatly arranged meatballs and a basket filled with slices of fresh bread next to the salad plate in front of Emin and then returned to the kitchen.

"Bon appétit."

"Join me."

Emin, who showed his plate with his hand, realised that he had made a half-hearted invitation and finished his words in a hurry with a sincere sentence:

"Tell them to bring you a fork."

"Thank you. I have already eaten… At home. Bon appétit!"

Trying to cover up his embarrassment, Emin lifted his fork and showed it to the worker at the counter, trying to convey that he wanted one more. After a while, Emin pushed Ahmed, who didn't reach for the fork placed in front of him:

"Take one. It's nice."

Ahmed didn't refuse this time. Emin was the first to act. He tucked the meatball at the end of his fork into the corner of the bread.

"This is how the meatball tastes better."

Emin caught a glance in Ahmed's eyes, not understanding what was being said.

"I mean, it tastes better to eat meatballs by placing it between the slices of bread."

"Yes, I think so."

After swallowing a big bite of his bread, Ahmed lifted his glass:

"Cheers."

"Cheers."

Then silence. Ahmed and Emin didn't speak until Emin finished eating.

In front of the buffet, two rows of four tables were arranged parallel to the kitchen, followed by five rows of three tables each, right up to the window. All of them were for four people. There was enough space between the tables for one person to pass through. Besides the two tables in the centre, customers were at the three tables by the window. One could ascend to the rooms on the upper floor from the stairs next to Emin's table. Upon descending the stairs, just before reaching the entrance door directly across, there was a door on the right leading to the toilet. Pointing to the middle one of the tables by the window, Ahmed started to tell Emin:

"Few here speak Turkish. The man sitting at that table with his back to the door speaks good Turkish. He worked in Istanbul for two years. Let's call him over. You can have a chat. OK?"

"It's up to you."

"Mirza", Ahmed completed his call in his own language.

Emin turned slightly to the side and, from the corner of his eye, saw Mirza, a person at the table he was glancing at, make a gesture by raising his left arm as if to say, "screw it." Emin chose to ignore it, but at the same time, he briefly experienced that initial negative feeling towards people, which always turned out to be correct."

Ahmed tried to explain.

"They drink. They have their own conversation. Mirza won't come."

"It doesn't matter. Don't worry about it. I'm also tired; I'll pay the bill and go to bed."

"You're staying here?"

"Yes."

Meanwhile, Emin made the usual gesture of asking for the bill to the waiter with his hand, drawing a circle to indicate the entire table. He had thought, 'If only he had also eaten a meal, I couldn't have offered it; it would have resulted in a hefty bill. By paying for the beer, in a way, I'm covering my embarrassment!' as he made this gesture.

He paid the bill. He was happy. It was very reasonable, even cheap. When the waiter brought the change, he returned the plate as it was without taking the change.

Ahmed said something to the waiter, grabbing Emin by the arm as he tried to get up and forcing him to sit down.

"Another beer. On me."

"No, that's not OK."

"Sit, sit, it's on me."

"No need!"

"It's like this here. One beer on you, one beer on me."

Whether it was because he saw Emin attempting to leave and thought to catch him before he left or whether it was to get another round of beer- a question Emin would ponder later- Mirza placed a chair he had brought from the adjacent table between Emin and Ahmed as the beer bottles were being placed on the table, and then he sat down.

"Hello."

With a sly smile on his clean-shaven round face following his thinning, greasy hair combed back from the left, Mirza extended his hand to Emin from the sleeve of his dark, smoked-coloured suit on his white shirt with a dirty collar without a tie. The negative impression Emin formed when he first saw Mirza intensified and deepened as he reluctantly extended his hand.

"Hello."

"Where are you from?"

"Istanbul."

"I lived in Istanbul. What part of İstanbul?"
"Kadiköy."
"I lived in Laleli. Do you know where that is?"

Emin, trying to keep the conversation short, didn't say, "I know it very well," but instead said, "I don't really know those parts. I know the Anatolian side." However, Mirza had no intention of ending his questions.

"What do you do for a living?"
"I was working in a bank, but I quit."

It was Mirza's cleverly disguised inquiry, delivered like a ticking time bomb, that prompted Emin to realise he had inadvertently revealed his actual occupation. It was then that he remembered his passport stated "marketing."

"You defrauded the bank, and now you're running away. How much money did you swipe?"

Emin managed to contain his anger, which had swelled enough to provoke him to say, "Fuck you!" He responded with a counter-question to buy some time since he didn't know how to reply to Mirza's words.

"I don't understand what you said?"

Even though Emin tried to formalise the conversation as much as possible, Mirza paid no heed:

"You stole the bank's money, and you're running away, right?"

The thinking speed of the human brain came to the rescue, and the time-buying mutual questioning that took ten to fifteen seconds helped Emin find an answer that connected his passport profession to banking.

"Where are you getting such an idea? I used to work on the bank's marketing and advertising affairs. I didn't have a role that involved handling money directly. I'm divorced from my wife and going to London to meet my English girlfriend."

As soon as he finished his sentence, Emin realised he had forgotten that "married" was written in his passport, but despite being bothered, he didn't care; it was a gap that could be comfortably dealt with. Furthermore, the man couldn't have examined the passport he handed to the motel unless he were a police officer. While Emin was thinking about these things, Mirza put the increasing dose of his arrogance into words:

"You're telling fairy tales!"

Emin's characteristic of remaining cooler than ever, let alone panicking when he saw the danger coming at him, surfaced to the forefront once again. He took out his wallet and, showing the photo of his daughter inside, attempted to steer the conversation onto safer ground.

"Look, this is my daughter. My wife and I were not getting along. I met an English woman who was an advertiser when she came to Istanbul on business..."

Emin was up to his storytelling antics once again!

Most of the time, just for fun, especially when watching Turkish movies at home, he used to improvise on the spot by taking inspiration from the scene and creating on-the-fly scenarios to mock the film...

* * *

Emin no longer liked family outings, which he loved as a child because they spiced up the monotonous winter nights, which were not much fun except for listening to radio theatre. Television had entered their lives in those days. Moreover, he had books, especially those he read secretly from his father. It could have been Dostoevsky or Tolstoy. The fact that the author was Russian was enough for his father to classify a book as "harmful" and "communist" publications, and it was necessary to be read clandestinely. Keeping them at home using different covers was not enough to solve the problem, especially if some books had the book's name and author on every page. The best times for reading were when his mother and father were not at home. He eagerly looked forward to the opportunities created by family outings, especially if it was a kind of book that he was excited to read.

"You're still in front of the television. Leave the movie already; we're running late. Are we going to pay a visit to stay overnight?"

At the warning of his father, who was waiting dressed in the doorway, his siblings reluctantly got up from their seats. With unfulfilled desires in her heart, his little sister begged and pleaded:

"Abi, you keep watching and tell us the rest when we return."

Was it Eşref Kolçak or Ahmet Mekin? It could have been Cüneyt Arkın[68], but he couldn't remember. Whoever, who was! The 'hero (!)' was handcuffed, walking between the gendarmes toward the waiting train, the locomotive huffing and puffing. However, the "main girl" had not yet appeared in the film when his family left.

With the door closed, Emin retrieved his book from under the bed and lowered the television volume. Although he occasionally glanced at it, he had detached from the movie.

As the time for the household members to return neared, he put his book away, took a harmless(!) book, and then lay down on the couch. The movie had already ended.

When the door opened and the family members crowded into the house, he quickly got up from where he was lying

---

[68] Eşref Kolçak, Ahmet Mekin and Cüneyt Arkın were all famous leading actors in Turkish cinema at that time. s

and sat down. In the presence of elderly family members, especially the father, lying down or even stretching one's legs and crossing them was considered inappropriate as it went against family etiquette.

His sister asked as soon as she entered the room:
"What happened after we left?"
"I read a book."
"Haven't you seen the film?"
"I watched it for a while, then I got bored and stopped."
"What happened during the parts you were watching?"
"Where did you leave it?"

Although he knew, he was taking his time. Both to write his own scenario in his head and to make her sister more curious.

"You know, the gendarmes handcuffed him and took him to the train..."
"Oh, I remember."
"What happened, what happened; did the girl make it in time before the train's departure?"
"She arrived at the last minute."
"And then?"
"Just as they were getting on the train, the girl came with a bundle in her hand. Gendarmes didn't want to take it, but when they saw the girl in tears, they couldn't resist and accepted it. The gendarmes were romantic boys too, you see."
"Abi, come on, don't play the giddy goat. Tell me properly."
"Anyway, as the train began to pull away, the boy waved from the door's window with his handcuffed hands. Once they were settled in their carriage, he carefully unwrapped the bundle, revealing the girl's headscarf with delicate crocheted edges—a cherished souvenir she had lovingly

given him, along with her homemade meatballs snugly tucked inside half a loaf of bread."

"You're taking the mickey out of me again."

"No, I promise, cross my heart. The boy sniffed the meatballs, then wrapped the bundle again. He didn't eat those meatballs all the way. They slept at night. The next day, he opened the bundle again after entering the prison ward. The people in the ward said 'welcome' and brought tea. He ate the meatballs without speaking to anyone.

Someone from the ward said, 'How cruel these gendarmes are; I guess they didn't let you eat all the way, brother!

The boy replied with his mouth full, 'No, no. The gendarmes were good people, but I didn't want to eat before them

.' People in the ward asked, 'Why?'

The boy explained, 'The meatballs had onions. If I ate them, my breath would stink, and it would be embarrassing in front of the gendarmes!'"

"If you're going to tell a story, tell it properly. You're making fun of me again."

"This is my script. It's so realistic!"

* * *

He should also write a realistic script for Mirza so that it would be convincing. He continued.

"I filed for divorce after I met the British advertising girl. I will meet her here, and we will go to England together. After I improve my English, we will work in the advertising business together. Everyone says I can make better money there."

"Why are you meeting here?"

"What the fuck do you care?" crossed his mind, but once again, Emin didn't say it out loud.

"It depends on how soon she can get a break and come here or in Belgrade!"

"Why did you come here?"

"Fuck you, fuck you, fuck you, fuck you." Once again, Emin didn't say it out loud.

"My grandparents used to live here, but they migrated to Turkey. While waiting for my girlfriend, I thought, 'I have time; let's go and visit these places.' I was curious."

At that moment, Emin found relief in Mirza's following question, which indicated his belief in the presented story.

"What about the child? You abandoned her."

"No, no. I'll get my daughter to come as soon as I've sorted things out. Besides, if she studies in England, she'll save her future, too."

"Saves your what."

"Her future. She'll have a good future and go to good schools."

Emin started his own barrage of questions, thinking, "Since my made-up story now appeared convincing, to prevent Mirza from probing further with more questions, I have to change the course of the conversation."

"How long have you lived in Istanbul?"

"Two years."

"You had relatives there?"

"No!"

"Did you go on business?"

"Yes."

"What did you do?"

"Trade. "Bringing and taking goods back and forth. I used to buy here and sell there, buy there and sell here. Let me order a beer."

Emin was about to ask, "What were you buying and selling?" when Mirza interrupted the conversation with a beer offer, which gave Emin a chance to leave the table.

"No, I can't have any more to drink. I've already had two. Moreover, it's getting late, and I'm feeling tired. I've had a long journey, so I'll head to bed. Thanks."

"Tomorrow night. We'll drink then. I come here often. These are my friends." Intentionally or unintentionally, Ahmed had come to his rescue, saying, "These," as he pointed to the motel staff with his hand.

After saying goodbye to everyone and Emin went up to his room, muttering to himself, 'Damn, what a trouble I have got into!' He was unaware yet that Mirza would later cause even more trouble.

"This scumbag, who knows what tricks he was pulling in the name of trade, and he thought everyone else was just like him."

Without realising that he was thinking aloud, he continued to grumble. The words of his friend, the President of PIM[69], came to his mind.

"As Hacı Dal said, 'Everyone sees the world through their own eyes!' Anyway, I got off cheap. Not just in terms of the last-moment made-up script I wrote but also money-wise. The guy will buy three beers, even though unwittingly, I'll have to buy them in return. There you go, that's three beers worth of money."

Actually, it wasn't late; the clock had just struck ten in the evening. Despite having taken a nap earlier in the day, the combination of the beer he had consumed and the sudden

---

[69] PIM is an abbreviation of the Association for the Struggle against Costs and Unemployment. Association organised by the followers of Dr H. Kivilcimli in the 1970s.

change in weather bore down on him. With little effort, he succumbed to sleep.

* * *

"Get down!"

He didn't even ask the policeman why. The officer had opened the bus's rear door, and his steely gaze was fixed on Emin. As he rose from his seat and descended the steps, Emin fumbled to button up his coat while pondering what to say. Finally, he heard the command,

"Give me your passport."

Emin handed over the passport he had retrieved from his jacket pocket."

Once again, in that recurring nightmare of the moment of failing in the attempt of running away he would later experience numerous times, a persistent knock came at his room door, having interrupted him intermittently for three minutes."

"It's a dream again," he said to himself, "OK, I'm coming," he said to the person knocking on the door as he got out of bed. In his haste, he took off his pyjamas, put on his trousers in a hurry, and opened the door without even buttoning the shirt he put on.

The woman at the door, with her light brown hair styled similarly gathered, a portion elegantly left loose at the front, secured by a knotted headscarf at the back, reminiscent of the woman working at the roadside cafe they had stopped at on their way from Belgrade to Novi Pazar. Her eyes shared the same honey-coloured hue. She wore a knee-length dress and held sheets and towels in her hand, giving the impression of a woman in her thirties. When the woman whose eyes caught his also looked into his eyes, Emin lowered his gaze to the towels.

Obviously, the woman had come to tidy up the room. Still, due to the lack of common language, it came down to body language again. After indicating with his watch that he wanted the woman to come back in thirty minutes, as she nodded, the woman said "Okay" in her own language and left. Emin stepped into the shower and thought, "Are all the women working in this country the same model in height, build, eye colour, clothes, and how they tie their hair?"

However, he had noticed one distinction: 'There was no sadness in this woman's eyes, or at least, I didn't see it.'"

And years later, he would encounter another woman who resembled these two, with the same hint of sadness in her eyes as the first one and with light brown hair like the second one. Still, just like both, her eyes were a shade of honey. It would happen in another Mediterranean country. The season was once again the same.

* * *

[Flashforward - February 2012:
Anita's saying, "Let's eat Turkish pizza", momentarily surprised Emin. They were in Nicosia, and it was natural for dishes like "lokma tatlısı"[70] and lahmacun[71] to be made here. He asked her with the Turkish word he had inserted into their English conversation:
"You mean lahmacun?"
"Yes, yes, 'lâmajun' That's what they call it."
"OK, the Greeks do it too."
"No, not Greek."
"Do the Turks have a restaurant here?"

---

[70] Lokma tatlısı is fried sweet dough balls soaked in syrup.
[71] Lahmacun or Lahmajoun (Armenian) is a round, thin piece of dough topped with minced meat, minced vegetables, and herbs

As it is commonly known, they were only three hundred meters away from crossing the border, dividing the city in half, going from Nicosia to Lefkoşa, the occupied part of Nicosia by the Turkish Republic. However, it was nearly nine o'clock, and it was not feasible for them to make the trip back and forth at this late hour.

"No, they're not Turkish. They are Armenians. There's a bakery. We'll get a takeaway from there. We can eat on the way. It'll be cheaper."

Those who paid their employees nearly a quarter of the wages in London charged their customers almost the same bill as they did in London. He had reached this conclusion after a conversation with an employee in the café where they had been sitting earlier.

For a second, Emin was surprised to discover an Armenian bakery in Cyprus, where Anita suggested they could dine affordably, but then he remembered Anush.

A friend of his was running one of the places known as a "social club" in London, but, in reality, it operated just like the coffeehouses in Turkey. Emin, determined not to connect Turkish TV channels to his home, would visit there during significant events in Turkey when the internet was not yet widespread.

There was someone else who used to drop in from time to time: Anush. Whether it was because her Turkish was poor or she did not want to talk, she did not answer Emin's questions about her family and 1915, which he had met twice or thrice. It was the mid-1990s. His friend, the owner of a "social club" who knew her better, did not know much either. Anush did not tell him anything other than that her family had somehow survived the "Great Catastrophe" when the genocide reached its extreme and had taken refuge in Cyprus via Syria.

Coffee, as always! This woman in her fifties used to drop by this "place" on the way, which made good Armenian coffee upon request.

It remained unknown, but it was speculated that her occasional visits were driven by the combination of having coffees, the legacy of her ancestral lands passed down through generations, and listening to the haunting melodies of those distant, lost lands—the sorrowful songs playing in the coffeehouse. Even if it was in a foreign land... Even if it was in Turkish, a foreign language for her... Particularly the songs performed by a Kurdish singer Ahmet Kaya, called 'Ağladıkça' in Turkish, but its original name was "Picture", and composed by a famous Armenian musician, Ara Dinkjian. Remembering Anush reminded Emin that Cyprus was one of the homelands where Armenians took refuge.

When they arrived at the bakery in the centre of Nicosia, just parallel to the main street, they saw it was not only a bakery. On the side, kebabs were also being grilled over charcoal. From time to time, a woman, who was much slimmer and slightly younger than the person kneading the dough, was topping the dough with the mixture of herbed meats and vegetables. Then, when the lahmajouns, thrown into the oven by a man with a shovel, came out, she and another man collecting them would offer the wraps they made to their customers, taking their money afterwards.

While topping the dough, it was as if the young woman's shapely, slender, long fingers were pressing on the invisible keys of a piano.

"This Armenian woman might not have been as young as those two women in Yugoslavia, as they were in their twenties then; however, she is now younger than them. She should be around forty. Those in Yugoslavia must be in their fifties by now. It's been more than twenty years since I saw them, but in my memories, they still exist at the same age as they were. Memories are like that; people age, but the people in memories never do; they always live at the age they were in those memories!"

It was Anita's question that plucked Emin out of the memories that were travelling on the woman's piano virtuoso fingers:

"What are you thinking?"

"Nothing. I was only watching that woman preparing lahmajoun. Isn't she good at it?"

"Yes, she does it very fast."

This woman, a child of the Filipino people, compelled by poverty to work around the world, looked from her own window at the children of other people who had managed to escape the genocide committed by bloodthirsty oppressors and had also been scattered around the world: Diligence!

Emin, who thought like this about Anita's evaluation, was looking at the Armenians he admired for their artistry through his own perception beyond their diligence: Beauty! He saw artistic beauty even in their preparation of lahmajouns.

Later, during the hours Anita worked during the day, he went to eat lahmajoun again. The Armenian woman,

who worked with the same beauty, hid the sadness in her eyes behind her smile and thanked Emin in English as she gave him the wraps and took his money].

* * *

He had forgotten to lock the door after sending the woman from the motel away, asking her to return in half an hour. In the bathroom, he had stayed under the hot water for a long time and had lingered a while to dry his hair before going out into the cold air. Did the woman arrive a bit early; didn't she?

When the woman clicked the door once and entered, Emin, who was wearing only his undershirt and shorts, grabbed the pants he had placed on top of the radiator under the window, then hopped onto the bed next to him, and from there, he reached the shower door with two leaps. While he hurriedly did these things, he noticed the woman smiling. He quickly put on his trousers. He was laughing vaguely himself. When he walked round the foot of the bed and went to get the shirt that he had put on the chair, he showed the bed with his hand to the woman standing two steps from the door and signalled that she could start her work. He smiled at the smile of the woman who had her eyes fixed on Emin, and although he responded with a smile, he was embarrassed to be standing in his undershirt. He averted his gaze from the woman, whom he thought had sparked a faint flirtatious spark in her eyes. He was neither in the mood to flirt nor to analyse the behaviour of a woman he saw for the first time.

Moreover, he was not fully dressed. As soon as he took his shirt, he quickly headed towards the door; after getting closer to the door, he turned his back to the woman, put his shirt on his back and tucked it into his trousers. While taking his jacket, he noticed that his suitcase lid was open. He closed it. Before taking his coat under his arm and leaving, he signalled to her with his hand that he was leaving. Emin chose to avert his eyes and ignore the light in her eyes when he looked up and saw the smile of the woman looking at him.

The table where he had sat the evening before was set with the same breakfast dishes as the morning before, including a quarter of a lemon sliced into wedges. He looked around to see if Ibrahim was there, but no one was there except the two people sitting at the table by the window where Mirza had sat the night before. Emin sat at the table facing the door this time, with his back to the kitchen counter. Tea and bread also arrived without the need to ask for them. Since Ibrahim hadn't mentioned when he would arrive, he began having breakfast with a somewhat contradictory slowness, thinking, "Let him also catch up to breakfast."

When two other people at the table opposite clinked their glasses, he realised that the men had been drinking. It was nine o'clock in the morning. He pretended to be looking at the door, and out of the corner of his eye, he glanced at the tables of those clinking glasses. There must have been white cheese on the plate and nothing else. And bread. Even though the colour resembled beer, it couldn't have been beer since it was in a pitcher. He wondered. "I'll ask when Ibrahim comes," he said to himself.

He felt the need to go to the toilet before he was halfway through the cigarette he lit following his half-hour breakfast. Since he had set out on the road, he hadn't experienced such a necessity. However, this was his daily routine every morning for years. He restrained himself until he finished his cigarette. Ibrahim was still nowhere in sight. When he lit his second cigarette and stood up, the waiter came to clear the table. He touched the waiter's arm with one hand and made a "let them stay" gesture with the other hand, all the while spitting out some English:

"My friend, Ibrahim. OK."

Pointing to the waiter, he patted the coat hanging on the back of the chair twice. He wanted to say, "I'm leaving it here". With the waiter's "OK", they reached an agreement. He went up to his room. The place was tidied up, and the woman was gone.

It didn't take him long to get downstairs, but Ibrahim was nowhere in sight. Emin couldn't wait. He had to phone England. Who knows when he will get through the phone line? He went to the counter at the entrance of the kitchen. The waiter who had just served him was already in the kitchen. He smiled when he saw Emin. Emin realised that he had not asked the name of the man serving him since yesterday. He asked in English:

"What's your name?"

"Jusuf."

He did not need to mention his name, thinking, "They would have seen it on the passport anyway".

"Jusuf, I'm leaving." Waving his hand towards the door, he underlined his sentence and continued:

"Ibrahim. My friend is coming. Tell him to sit here." He pointed to the chair.

He couldn't remember the English verb "to wait". "Come", "go", "sit", "get up", "see", "give", and "receive" were the first words that came to his mind. At this moment, the word he sought was no longer a concern worth his contemplation.

"I'm going to the post office. Telephone. I'll be back. Ibrahim should sit down." He pointed to the chair again.

Jusuf threw his "OK" once again, along with a nod. Emin, convinced that his intention was understood, headed for the door. Jusuf lifted the counter lid and walked behind Emin to collect the table left behind by his drinking customers. When Emin realised that Jusuf was heading to the table of the other customers who had left the restaurant, not Emin's own table, he turned to Jusuf. Then, he attempted to convey with hand gestures that he could also clear the table where he had breakfast. The waiter understood.

"OK"

Unable to overcome his curiosity, Emin pointed to the other table and gestured to inquire about the drink:

"What's that?"

"Rakia."

"Raki?"

There was astonishment in that one word, like who drinks raki early in the morning.

Jusuf repeated:

"Rakia."

Emin thought he understood and said goodbye.

"Bye."

As he walked from the motel toward the post office, his astonishment at having "rakı" with breakfast lingered.

"Raki," he said, but it looked more like beer. Suddenly, the intense house wine they had drunk at Çatal Fırın[72] came to his mind. It was a pleasantly drinkable wine with a surprisingly strong profile. However, the colour was a bit like the colour of "Rakia" that he saw. His memories travelled back to those days as he walked towards the post office.

* * *

---

[72] Çatal Fırın was a district in Bursa that was popular for its authentic taverns at that time.

At Çatal Fırın area, five young people studying at the Bursa Institute of Education, Emin among them, walked to the sound of music coming from one of the taverns lined up side by side as they turned left from Altıparmak Street.

"Didn't I tell you they've already started?"

It was Ali K.'s discovery. It is not known when he came on his own when he sat down and got drunk. Unknown, because they were boarding school students and always hanging out together. Especially Ali K., Fatih and Emin. Three of the central five figures of the political organisation began to take shape within the school. Among this group, only two people, Nejat and his girlfriend, who were day school students at the same institute, would not participate in their nightouts. Especially after their discovery, they would visit this tavern at least once, if not twice a month, on Saturday nights. It also suited their wallets. The menu, per person, consisted of one portion of anchovies, the white bean salad, plenty of bread, and a bottle of strong house wine.

The routine of such nights was more or less the same as their first visit. On their arrival, the waiter said, "Upstairs, youngsters!"

As these youngsters, who were experiencing the first year of their twenties, ascended the stairs to the upper floor, those playing the tanbur and oud were tuning their instruments at a low sound for the songs they would sing, with the participation of some middle-aged men like themselves, as the introductory violin solo approached its final. As he and his friends settled and placed their orders, Emin perked up his ears to the "nihavent maqam"[73] song,

---

[73] **"Maqam"** is a system of melody types used in Turkish classical music. Each "maqam" specifies a unique intervallic structure and melodic development.

which sounded familiar, composed by the Armenian musician 'Kemani Sarkis Efendi Suciyan,' with lyrics by Ihsan Raif Hanım.

> "I do not complain to anyone; for my affairs I get weepy,
> I shiver like the one guilty when I look at my destiny.
> The curtain of darkness is drawn; I fear my destiny,
> I shiver like someone guilty when I look at my destiny."

After the songs downstairs and the glasses upstairs followed each other, and the players took a break, the voices of the youngsters filled the night:

> "Izmir's poplars
> Shed their leaves
> 'Çakici,' they call us
> My darling, my willowy
> We tear down mansions."

The songs they sang were lined up until the sounds of the instruments downstairs could start. The youngsters fell silent. It was the turn of older people. The music passed from upstairs to downstairs and then from downstairs to upstairs, filling the tavern's atmosphere with notes throughout the night, even if some were off-key as they moved from tipsy to drunk.

Near the end of the anthem, they had started with, "At dawn, we all awakened / To trenches we headed," the waiter placed the bill on the table and began clearing the plates. When the anthem ended, the final whistle came from the waiter, who had also collected the last plates, saying:

"Nihavent" is one of them.

"Come on, guys, you've had too much to drink. We'll be closing soon."

In fact, the night, which had ended for older people but had not even reached its midpoint for the youngsters, continued on the road with the young ones.

They walked with slight swaying, first through the bustling streets of Bursa in silence. When they reached the deserted school road from Duaçınar, they once again uttered, "To the trenches we headed."

On one of these nights, Emin drank too much. When he reached his locker to change, he saw Besir closing his locker at the opposite end of the row.

While making their school choices in Kastamonu, Besir was among those who chose the Bursa Institute of Education with them. The goal of forming a revolutionary group at the school they selected succeeded considerably, and four of them, including Besir, scored enough for the accession. Although the other three, like Emin, were not part of the core group in Bursa, they initially participated in the sympathising circle. Later on, Besir gradually shifted towards supporting the CHP[74] (Republican People's Party) and eventually aligned with nationalist fascists. Emin found this particularly challenging to digest due to a personal reason.

Besir's inclusion among them had been suggested by Emin when determining the choices earlier in Kastamonu. However, in their lycée years, Besir wasn't part of their political activities. Despite this, the families of Besir and Emin, originating from Marash and residing in the same neighbourhood in Kastamonu, had fostered a friendship. Seizing the opportunity, Emin had invested considerable effort in 'winning him over' to socialism. While Emin's friends

---

[74] CHP (Republican People's Party) is regarded as the founder Party of Turkey.

initially didn't include Besir in their political activities, deeming him insufficient, they had eventually accepted Emin's proposal to include Besir in determining their choices for the Education Institute preferences.

Riding the clouds of the night's wine, Emin vented his frustrations towards Besir through spoken words.

"You're a bastard. You are despicable. Fascist dog."

"Are you talking to me?"

"Who else is there? You, of course."

Indeed, no one else was in that row of cupboards on that floor.

"Say it again, say it again!"

"You're a vile, fascist dog."

With two long strides, Besir reached Emin's side. Towering over 1.80 meters, weighing more than ninety kilos, and boasting well-developed biceps, Besir, in stark contrast to Emin's relatively short and thin stature, delivered his final warning by grabbing Emin's lapels.

"Take that back, you treacherous commie!"

Taking his word back would be out of the question for Emin, no matter what, even though his feet were more or less off the ground.

"You fascist dog, I'm not taking it back. I'm not scared of you!"

Emin, who had a habit of not backing down from a fight even when he knew he would get beaten, couldn't recall what happened afterwards. Beshir had lifted Emin and thrown him to the ground. Two months ago, Emin had collided with a friend they had raced on the school road while taking a curve and the collarbone of his right shoulder was broken. When Besir threw him, he fell again on his right shoulder, and his collarbone broke from the same spot.

Seyfi was at his bedside when he opened his eyes in the hospital in the morning.

"What happened? Where am I!"

"You're in hospital with a broken shoulder."

"What hospital? Why did I break my shoulder? It was broken two months ago. It was healed."

He attempted to move from his place, but with the sharpness of the incoming pain, he surrendered himself to the bed.

"Don't move! The fracture hasn't been set yet. They were waiting for you to regain consciousness. Don't you really remember?"

"What?"

"That you had a fight in the evening!"

"What fight?"

"You had a fight with Besir upstairs."

"I don't remember."

Seyfi, who had worked together with them in Kastamonu and was part of the group that had come to Bursa and who had also maintained his moderation while drinking at the tavern the night before, became anxious this time:

"Wait, I'm going to get the doctor."

First, he went to find a doctor, then called the school. The summary of what he told them was five words:

"Emin has lost his memory."

* * *

Leaving the memories that the colour of the drink in the motel brought out from the depths of his memory outside the door, Emin entered the post office. After gesturing to the clerk and receiving a confirming nod, he again entered the number one booth to use the telephone. He dialled... but there was no sound. He hung up and called again, but there was no sound. He dialled again. This time, the line was responsive, but there was no answer to the ringing phone. In vain, he decided to call Hasan again!

"Hello."

Emin did not recognise the voice.

"Hello, can I speak to Hasan?"

"Hasan Abi is not here; he went out. Who's calling?"

"Abuzittin."

"Who?"

Hasan and Emin had agreed on a made-up name that was not used much, to be used when Emin needed to call the office. They had decided to use the name "Abuzittin" as a code. Hasan occasionally chose not to answer the phone directly to avoid specific customers.

The person who answered the phone most likely repeated the question again to gain time and be able to tell Hasan who was calling.

"Abuzittin. I'm his friend. Write it down so you don't forget."

Emin deliberately prolonged the conversation, giving time to the person on the line, thinking that if Hasan was there, they could inform him of his call. And he was right.

"Wait a minute."

"Hello, Abuzittin."

"Hi, how are you?"

"Good, what's up with you?"

"I can't get through to Osman. He's not answering his phone."

"Hey, you guys in Europe can't even reach each other, and you're hoping for help from me here. What kind of things are you two dealing with?"

"I can't make calls from here whenever I want. I tried calling last night, but there was no answer. What can I do? If you get the chance to call from time to time, you might reach him. Finding him at home in the evening is easier since he doesn't answer when I call."

"All right, all right. Who knows what Osman's up to again! Call back late this afternoon."

"OK, I'll call you, thanks."

"Take care of yourself."

"Thanks, you too. Goodbye."

When he made his payment and went out the door to go to the motel, he saw Ibrahim waiting on the opposite side of the road.

"Dobro Jutro"

"Dobro Yutro. No forgetting."

Ibrahim smiled, referring to the fact that Emin had not forgotten to say "good morning" in their language.

"No, I didn't forget. I waited for you for breakfast this morning. But I couldn't wait any longer so I wouldn't be late for the phone."

"I had work at home. I'm late."

"It's all right. I mean, I couldn't wait any longer; I'm sorry. Did you go to the motel?"

"Yes, I went. The waiters said 'Post Office'. I came."

He did not ask Ibrahim why he was waiting outside, considering that he might not have wanted to attract the people's attention at the post office.

"Did you wait long?"

"No."

"Telephone. England."

"Yeah, yeah, yeah. There is a problem. No answer."

When they started talking, Ibrahim began to walk towards the stream, and Emin kept pace with him."

"Where are we going? We should go to the motel and have lunch."

"Nah., I ate. You?"

It was too early for Emin, but he wanted to invite him to lunch to express his thanks.

"Where are we going?"

Ibrahim pointed to the stream with his hand.

"To the stream!"

In addition to the English words squeezed in between, they had become quite adept at understanding each other through hand gestures.

"No one's there. We talk."

The area would later be enclosed with walls and transformed into a promenade. Still, at the time they started walking along the edge of the stream that used to flow freely, Ibrahim asked:

"Problem, England."

"Yeah, problem. No answer on the phone."

"What will you do? How long will you stay?"

"In Novi Pazar?"

"Novi Pazar!"

"I don't know. I'll phone again later. In the evening. I can't stay long in Novi Pazar."

"I have a son of uncle. He has a truck. He's a driver. He comes on Friday evening. He goes to Germany on Saturday. Let him take you."

Ibrahim tried to explain by adding English and Turkish to his own language.

There was a new common word: Truck! Emin tried to ask what kind of truck it was, but even if they couldn't communicate, he gave up with the joy and relief that this new option brought:

"Is that all right?"

"Yes."
"There's Austria?"
"Austria, OK."

Emin wanted to say, "There is Austria in between", but Ibrahim thought he wanted to go to Austria. They lit the cigarettes Emin took out. The faint murmur of the flowing stream that was going through the emerging silence. Emin was thinking, and Ibrahim was giving him time to think.

"Why not? Who was there? Mahmut Aykol is in Austria, I think." Emin's different attitude towards Mahmut's relationship with Sule, unlike the other friends, had brought a unique dimension to their friendship, but... Mahmut was "a devoted fan of his namesake Mahmut SUzer". It had been said that he even was the right-hand man of Clark Mahmut.

* * *

[Flashforward - 1997:
"Clark Mahmut?"

Emin replied to Nurten's somewhat bewildered question, feeling the need for an explanation, "Your leader at that time...".

"He was your leader, too, but whatever!"

Nurten was referring to the days before the split. Emin kept his objection to himself: "I never considered him a leader!" He didn't want to divert the subject.

"Aziz Nesin has that one. He describes it as 'making a Clark'."

"Yes, Aziz Nesin wrote a story like that, but..."

"I was inspired by it."

Realising Nurten's questioning pause, he wanted to clarify what he said.

"You know how to make a Clarks, don't you?"

"How?"

"You'll raise one eyebrow in the air and smile flirtatiously, just like Clark Gable. Did you ever notice him doing it? I observed it during the '[Extraordinary General] Organization Meetings,' but I didn't realise it was deliberate behaviour. I learned that later, which is when I made the connection."

"Like what?"

"Most importantly, he would adjust his tone of voice to convey authority and confidence, and he would complement the authoritative expression on his face by raising his left eyebrow."

Emin tried to imitate, raising his right eyebrow. They both burst out laughing.

"God, how do you come up with such things?"

"But he used to raise his left eyebrow, not his right, like me. I can't raise my left eyebrow!"

Nurten also got caught up in the mood of the conversation:

"It's normal. He is the most leftist leader; of course, he will raise his left eyebrow!"

"See, I hadn't thought of that."

"But he didn't smile."

"If you're going to flirt with women, you can smile. If you're going to engage in political seduction, it's different. You have to be authoritatively stern and swagger!"

"You're the real deal!"

"Wait, I'll tell you how it came to my mind. This eyebrow lift caught my attention, but, you know, people have certain tics and gestures that they get used to, and I attributed it to that. As I said, I didn't attribute any special meaning to it, even if his arrogant behaviour was repulsive. Anyway. While on the run, I went to Izmir for about a week. I stayed with Ismet. Ismet's wife, Tuna, is Clark Mahmut's sister-in-law. His first wife's sister. Before Ismet stepped aside, Clark Mahmut was still married to his first wife during those times. They were very close then. Tuna told me about it when I was in Izmir. On one occasion, this guy said, 'It's not just about what we say but how we say it. We should know how to influence people with our tone of voice, gestures, and style.' Although my recollection might not be verbatim, she told me something along these lines. I, then, said, 'The actor, I mean the big brother, was giving us a Clark.' We burst into laughter!"]

* * *

Emin started tending cold to asking for Mahmut Aykol's help because of his closeness with Clark Mahmut. He was also unsure whether Mahmut Aykol was in Austria or Switzerland? He didn't find out, even if he tried to probe the depths of his memory.

"It doesn't matter anyway; there will always be someone who has emigrated from Turkey. There are human rights organisations where I can get help; I can go to one."

When he realised that Ibrahim, whom he had forgotten while immersed in the past, was looking at him, Emin reaffirmed his acceptance of the suggestion:

"Yeah. Yeah. Yes. Austria. But wait. I'll phone England tonight. If not, Friday. Wait! And Saturday, decision. OK?"

"We, you and me, talk tomorrow."

"Yeah."

"My uncle's son. Give money."

With the naivety of his inexperience in these matters, it had never even crossed Emin's mind to ask this question.

"How much?"

"Other people, one hundred, one hundred and fifty DM. You give sixty DM. For my uncle's son."

Others were making a hundred or a hundred and fifty DM. Was his uncle's son going to make sixty DM, or was the son of his uncle showing friendship by reducing it to sixty DM for him what he made a hundred or a hundred and fifty DM for others? He knew that Turkey ranked first in providing cheap labour to Germany. The Yugoslavs were in second or third place after the Spaniards. Eşref had told him that many workers from Yugoslavia went to Germany illegally. Ibrahim's uncle's son must have found his way there too! He didn't mind. What was it to him!

"OK, yeah."

Emin was delighted. Absolutely delighted! It was much cheaper than he had expected, and he had enough money. He had already calculated that he would have around ninety, perhaps even a hundred Marks left after covering the cost of the motel, which was expected to be the most substantial expense, along with other costs such as phone calls and meals.

"Visit elsewhere, you want?"

"I don't know. Where can I?"

"There is a monastery. But it's far. The car."

"Do you go by car?"

"Yes."

"I phone England in two or three hours!"

He started to speak Turkish like Ibrahim again.

"No time!"

"Yeah, no time. Let's go and have a beer."

"No, I don't drink."

Emin pointed to the stream and said, "Then let's walk here".

"OK."

"Novi Pazar is beautiful."

"Yes, good."

"Good. There are mosques and monasteries. Muslim, Christian. All together. It's beautiful."

"Good, but problem."

"What's the problem?"

"Christians don't like Muslims!"

"Muslims like Christians?"

"No, they don't!"

"Don't you like Christians?"

"Me, nema problema!"

Emin didn't bother to analyse what he meant by "nema problema". He shifted the conversation to a less delicate topic, steering it towards the personal by asking, 'Does Ibrahim have a girlfriend, fiancée, or any intention of going abroad?"

Once again, after talking about "Austria", "sixty Marks", and "Saturday", they headed to the post office. While Ibrahim continued on his way uphill, Emin entered the post office. It was nearly four o'clock. After Emin signalled that he would make a phone call, the post office clerk pointed to booth number one with familiar gestures.

The call had gone through on the first attempt, which surprised Emin.

"Hello."

"Hello, is this Osman?"

"Yes, it's me. Emin, is that you?"

"Yeah, yeah. How are you?"

"I'm fine, thanks. How are you?"

"Thanks, I'm fine."

"Hasan said you had been calling me for two days; sorry, I wasn't home. I work from morning until afternoon. I also had overtime for the past two days. What have you been up to? What's the situation?"

"I'm in Novi Pazar. I'm stuck here."

"Hasan hinted indirectly, but he told me to speak to you about it."

"The only phone I can use here is the post office. Did Hasan give you the phone number of the motel?"

"Yes, he did. I'll try to arrange something; let me talk to Rachel in the evening. Then I'll get in touch with you. If I haven't called you, call me tomorrow afternoon, around two o'clock. That would be around three o'clock your time there."

"That's fine, yeah, I'll call you."

"Oh, look, there's a Yugoslavian girl. I met her at an English course here. She lives in Belgrade. Her father is high up in the Communist Party. I'll tell her to contact you if I can reach her."

"Can she be of any help?"

"I don't know, maybe. It's good to keep in touch."

"Can I call her?"

"No, have her call. I'll give her the motel number. She doesn't know you. Plus, you can't explain it. You don't speak much English."

"No, I don't."

"Does anyone in the motel speak Turkish?"

"No."

"Then it may be difficult for two of you to communicate with each other."

Emin remembered what Ahmed had said the night before when they said goodbye.

"Someone speaks Turkish and comes to the motel's restaurant in the evenings. If it happens when the person who speaks is around, he might be able to help."

"OK, we'll look into it. But there's no guarantee. Maybe I can't find the Yugoslavian girl. Maybe she can't do anything. But we'll give it a shot."

"I understand. I can't call Hasan again from here. Can you call him and let him know that we've talked?"

"I'll call, I'll call him. He also had asked me to call him. Don't worry. Take care, speak to you again."

"Thanks. Speak to you soon. Say hello to Rachel."

The pessimism and loneliness he had fallen into were swept away by a brief two or three-minute phone call. In an unfamiliar land where he didn't know anyone, uncertainties about the next steps bred pessimism. The absence of someone to talk to about all this, even if that person couldn't solve the problems he faced, was causing a profound sense of loneliness deeper than pessimism. He had encountered this feeling before, during the initial days of his life as a fugitive in Kuşadası.[75]

* * *

Emin narrated the story nonstop to his friends upon his return when they asked about his days in Kuşadası.

"There was no one to talk to. I wouldn't and shouldn't phone anyone. There were no other books in the house. I hadn't even asked if there was. I had only taken two books with me. Mornings were fine. I would go to the sea early, and the sea was calm. Around twelve o'clock, I would return home to escape the scorching sun. The few biscuits I would snack on when I got up lasted until then. Hunger would take

---

[75] Kuşadası is a beach resort town on Turkey's western Aegean coast.

While Running Away

over, you see. That's when I would have the actual breakfast; it also means lunch. Then, I would read a book, and it wouldn't take long before I would fall asleep. It's partly the effect of waking up early, the relaxation that comes with eating, and the book. I've been using books as a sleeping pill for years! It's not the books I'll work on, study, or take notes from, but it's a novel or something. I wouldn't go to the sea in the afternoon; the sea was wavy due to the wind. I would go to the city centre in the evening, just like the other tourists. They set up small kiosks on a street near the city centre. Three or four tables in front of each one. Their prices are the same and reasonable. They cook kebabs on big barbecues placed on the side of their kiosks. Salad, ayran[76] and plenty of bread as usual. I had got into the habit of eating there for dinner every day.

"The first time I went, I ordered my dinner at the second kiosk with an empty table. Then, I started going to the same place every evening. But one evening, I realised there were no empty tables. They were all full. Only one couple was sitting at one of the tables. Typical Aegean villagers with their clothes. Both of them are shorter than me and considerably overweight. I said, "Bon appétit, can I sit down?"; no answer. The man stared at me, and the woman was busy with her food. 'What rude people!' I said in my heart, but I hesitated whether to sit down or go to another kiosk. The man who owned the kiosk called out: "Welcome, brother, sit there, it's OK." The people at the table fell silent once more, savouring their appetites. The woman had only a glass of water before her, and the man was drinking beer.

"I ordered the usual: salad, bread and ayran. In the beginning, I ate the salad and bread bit by bit; otherwise, it

---

[76] Ayran" is a traditional Anatolian yogurt-based drink. It is made by mixing yoghurt with water and often a pinch of salt.

was not possible to get full with the small portion of kebab. The man beside me unexpectedly asked me in English, pointing to the ayran: 'What is that?' 'Ayran,' I said, but at the same time, I was thinking: 'I spoke Turkish when I first arrived; why do our Aegean villagers think I am a tourist and try to speak English? They didn't look like tourists either.' The man repeated his question after I said, 'Ayran'. Again, in English, he pointed to my glass. This time, I said, 'I think he's asking what's in it.' 'Yoghurt and water.' I had said yoghurt for yoghurt. I didn't know what yoghurt meant in English and wouldn't need to anyway! But I said water in English. He showed me the beer bottle in his hand. He asked if it could be drunk after the beer. I blasted my English again: 'Yes, very good, very good!' The man ordered an ayran. And he liked it. By the way, I got curious.

"They are foreigners, but where are they from? The answer to my question was 'Samos'. 'No ayran, Samos?' I was surprised because I knew that the Greeks also made yoghurt. Whoever makes yoghurt also makes ayran, right? No! Anyway. The woman tasted the ayran and grimaced. The man pointed at her and tried to explain: 'She likes wine. Not here.' The kiosk was only serving beer. We started chatting.

"I call it chatting, but it's just a figure of speech. The man would ask, 'Do you know Zülfü Livaneli?' I'd reply, 'Yes, I know. I like him.' Then he'd inquire, 'Mikis Theodorakis, do you know him?' I'd repeat my previous answer, adding, 'A great man.' I didn't know how to express it; whatever English words came to my mind, I used, or rather, the English words I knew. A smile, an expression of closeness, appeared on his face. He put the thumb of his right hand in the air and said, "He is a communist!" tilting his head slightly towards me in a voice close to a whisper. While I put my finger to my mouth and made the silence sign, I, of course, did not neglect to say 'I know' while I rolled my eyes from left to right, signalling a warning: 'Don't let it be heard around!' I tried to change the subject by asking where they were staying.

"I was told they had come to Kuşadası to shop and would return to their island the next day. We couldn't sit there for hours. When the bills were being paid, the man asked: 'Kuşadası, music, casino, where is it?' I replied, 'I don't know, I'm new," Momentarily, I thought of what he had said about her: 'She likes wine.' I told them, 'I have cassettes of Zülfü Livaneli and Mikis Theodorakis at my place. We'll buy wine. Let's go to my place.' They accepted without a push.

"Then, we went to a shop and bought two bottles of wine. I refused their offer to pay for the wines with a firm determination. 'You are my guests; it is rude if I let you pay', I said or, more precisely, tried to say! Upon my direction in Turkish, the shopkeeper refused their money and took mine. I had to be economical when I spent money, but it was impossible in such a situation!

"When we left the shop, I asked: 'Fifteen-twenty minutes' walk, five minutes minibus?' They understood my question, expressed it in uninflected English, and signalled their response by ticking the second option, pointing at their bellies. They were trying to say, 'It is good to walk after dinner'. That's how I translated it myself, and then we walked towards where I stayed.

After leaving the city centre, the semi-dark road had only a few pedestrians, with passing cars being the predominant presence. At the end of our Tarzanish chat, I learned they had no children and resided in Pythagoreio on Samos Island. The town, which used to be called Tigani, was named after the Hellenic mathematician who was born there, and it is the most touristy settlement on the island.

I'm narrating this story quickly, but you can envision how the conversation stretched over a long period. I'll share something amusing about that day, recounting it precisely as it unfolded, as that's how you might appreciate it."

He paused briefly while transporting his narrative back to that day. It was as if Emin would relive that moment while sharing the next part with his friends in conversation.

"Christina and I, your house, wine. Thank you. You, come, Pythagoreio. One mile."

"Yes, come. Our house!" This time, it was Christina who repeated the invitation.

"I can't come!"

"Why? Come, come!"

"No passport. State. No passport!"

Stavros stopped. He was not walking.

"You like Livaneli! You like Theodorakis! Nah, passport."

Meanwhile, Stavros broke his left arm at the elbow and proceeded to slap the bicep of that same arm with the palm of his right hand.

"I am not exaggerating; he did 'Nah' exactly as we do it, accompanied by this movement. Just like we do. I echoed his words and gesture: 'Nah, passport!' We burst into laughter—Stavros and I. But Christina, in a different mood, asked inquisitively, 'Why!'

"I didn't want to talk in the middle of the road, even though no one was passing by. I tried to say, 'Later, we'll talk at home; there's a dictionary.'

"Whether it was an attempt to reassure me or the result of the rapprochement, whatever it was, they also told me that they were Communists, members of the Communist Party in their country. While on the run, one looks at everything and everyone with some degree of suspicion, a state of being on edge. Believe me, I didn't doubt their sincerity for a moment. I just trusted them. Anyway... We came home, opened the wine bottle, and the cassette started spinning on Zülfü Livaneli's songs.

"As soon as we clinked glasses and took our first sips, Christina reminded me of her question: 'No passport. Why?'" I didn't hesitate to tell the truth; I tried to explain what had happened with the help of the dictionary at home. I had bought an English-Turkish dictionary and had thought that I would study English, or rather would learn English words before going to England. I showed them but can't explain the word 'fugitive'. Their English was short, too! I tried to get help from Western films like 'Wanted'. Christina started saying 'hero' and 'hero'. But this time, I didn't understand. Dictionary again... She said, 'Hero,' and I replied, 'No hero, this is Turkey, it's normal!' I objected, but she was insistent. I felt bashful.

"As I contemplated how to explain it, the memory of the civil war they lived through crossed my mind. Even though they weren't the children of that era, they knew their history anyway. I attempted to convey, 'They, your comrades, were the heroes.' Then I added, 'Me, I'm nothing. Just a prison sentence. No hero, it's normal.' Despite being the offspring of a country scarred by civil war, for them, it was history. They were members of a Communist Party working within the legal framework. It appeared distinct in their perspective compared to ours.

"When I was trying to explain that Kivilcimli, our leader, had served a quarter of a century and that other people had served much longer than the sentence I had been given, Stavros interrupted me, straining his English: 'We will help you!' I was surprised. 'How?' I asked, 'We will go to Samos.

We will come back. Motorboat. You will come to Samos!' he said. The question "Could it be?" momentarily crossed my mind, but my answer differed. As I tried to explain that I had been waiting for a fake passport and closed the subject by thanking them, they strictly instructed me to write to them after I ran away from Turkey. Stavros wrote his name, surname and address on a piece of paper. On the way back to their hotel, they took the minibus at night. The minibus we stopped had to wait a while because Christina was hugging me as she cried and making me cry, too.

"As I told you, I was willing to bear with Semra. You know, even with Semra, who, on the night of the day when the Martial Law Court delivered its verdict, I had said to her, 'You don't have to go through this with me; you can get a divorce,' and she had said without hesitation, 'Yes, I will get a divorce, but we have to wait a while, we just got married.' Such a strange feeling of loneliness. This was precisely my state of mind when I experienced these things with these two Greeks. I can't tell you how emotional it makes me feel. A kind of gratitude!"

* * *

[Flashforward - 2015:
Years later, Emin finally bought his ticket.
As soon as he arrived in London, he waited a long time for a response to the letter he had written. Stavros would find someone who knew Turkish to write his letters. At first, there were sporadic correspondences, then the phone calls that didn't go beyond "How are you? Are you well? Let's speak again sometime" had stopped. The "Come to Samos" invitations made during

each phone call had been hindered for a long time, primarily due to economic reasons and timing issues.

"Michael, I have friends in Samos; I want to phone them, but their English is very poor. Can you help me?"

"Of course. Call me when you need me!"

With the help of his Greek friend at work, he had managed to explain to Stavros on which day and at what time his plane would land in Samos. Stavros was insistent that Emin shouldn't stay in a hotel. Otherwise, he and Christina would be upset and wouldn't talk to him again. Emin agreed, albeit with a lack of enthusiasm. For the sake of the memories that held so much emotional intensity for him, every time he recounted them, he was willing to endure the discomfort of feeling like a burden on people and give up the freedom to live without daily obligations on his vacation.

Stavros and his cousin Kostas, whose English was good, picked Emin up from the airport.

When they arrived home, Christina greeted Emin at the door and hugged him, tears in her eyes again. Emin started laughing, even though his eyes were moist when Kostas translated what Stavros had said in the meantime:

"Christina doesn't hug me like this, as she would to this stranger!"

When they came in, they immediately sat at the table Christina had prepared. All the vegetables were from their own garden, and the wine was of their own making.

With Kostas' help, the questions ranged from how Emin fled to his life in London and politics.

To Christina's words that they were sorry for the collapse of the Soviet Union, Emin gave a response that they did not expect:

"The collapse of the Soviet Union, the socialist system, was natural and inevitable. I am not sorry that it collapsed."

Emin fell silent, waiting for Kostas to translate.

"Imperialism has won. How can you not be sad?" Stavros asked, his facial expression revealing both disapproval and surprise.

"It's not a question of imperialism winning. Were Soviets communists?"

"Of course, they were communists!"

"Maybe yes. But I'm not a communist!"

Kostas translated, but before the others had a chance to speak, he pronounced his own judgement:

"You are apostátis!"

"What does that mean?"

Emin didn't understand the non-English word. Kostas tried to explain with another word.

"Traitor!"

When Kostas translated, Emin read the displeasure on Stavros's and Christina's faces.

"One moment, one moment! It was actually them who betrayed. The Bolsheviks betrayed! The Bolsheviks betrayed the ideal of a classless society. I'll explain, but you translate first. Let them wait. I will continue."

Emin waited for his words to be translated and then tried to explain them in simple sentences, pausing for Kostas to translate every two or three sentences.

"When I met you in Kuşadası, I already had doubts. I had voiced my belief that the Soviet Union was not truly socialist in discussions within our own Party. Although my thoughts weren't as clear back then, I was questioning. After I went to London, I continued to question and analyse. I started to read the criticisms and revolutionary criticisms of the Bolsheviks from the left. What I read about the Kronstadt uprising was a turning point. They had defended the real Soviets. The Bolsheviks betrayed the revolution. They suppressed it in blood. Why? For power! In class societies, the state mechanism is centralised, bureaucratic and militaristic."

Emin couldn't express himself the way he wanted to. The language was challenging. It would have been easier if he could speak in Turkish. At that time, he could have used the analogy he often used and said:

"There is a saying in Anatolia -learned later that is similar to an English idiom-: *'One nail drives out another.'* The Bolsheviks supposedly opposed the centralist, bureaucratic, and militaristic state by creating another centralist and bureaucratic party structure. They sunk deep into militarism. Such an organisation could not establish a decentralised, non-bureaucratic and non-militarist social structure. Yes, the nail had driven out the nail, but it was itself a nail."

He didn't say, "In 1921, in Kronstadt, they eventually became the nails hammered into the coffin of the Soviet structure." He also couldn't explain Murray Bookchin's views on what the Party should be like and how it should be. He tried to make a shortcut:

"The Bolshevik state is a copy of the centralist, bureaucratic, militarist state they destroyed. The state has passed from one hand to another. That was what Marx was against. Why did it happen this way? The Bolshevik Party, a centralist party organised from the top downwards, saw coming to power as its main goal. Once in power, a Party with this goal would seek to preserve its power at all costs. And indeed, it did so. Therefore, it is the Bolsheviks who betrayed. But this was already in its nature. Moreover, every new form of society is born and develops within the old one. Capitalism has developed its own substructure and superstructure within pre-capitalist society. They were built on this. Revolutionism is to reorganise society on a communal basis. A party that considers itself a saviour cannot lead a revolution or be genuinely revolutionary. Who will save who from whom?! We will be saved if we get rid of our saviours! The first name of the Bolshevik Party was the Social Democratic Party. Then Lenin changed this name because the term social democrat had come to denote reaction. For me, too, the concept of communism means giving up the ideal, the ideal of a classless society. I renounce the concept of communism and the thoughts of communists. I am not a communist; I am a communalist. I call myself a communalist because I believe that society should be organised on a communal basis. The organisation of society on a communal basis is not something that a party can start to do when it comes to power; it is a process that can start now, right from today. It must be organised within the existing system. It is like the development of a child in the womb."

Kostas interrupted Emin's speech with a laugh:

"You're saying, 'Fuck the system!'"

Emin started laughing at these words, also used as a slogan by some anarchists in England.

"Yes, 'Fuck the system!' Only if society is going to get pregnant with the new system! Otherwise, it's not a matter of demolishing it! I am aware that I can't explain it appropriately. It's hard to explain in English. I want to write on this matter in the future. Then I can explain it better when I write. In short, I am not 'apostátis'."

Was he able to express himself? He didn't know. What he realised was that cold winds were blowing between them. While Christina cleared the table, their conversation was interrupted when Kostas got up, saying he "had to go". It was already siesta time for Stavros and Christina. They showed Emin to his room and advised him to rest, too. After they got up, they went for an afternoon march. The Communist Party had organised a protest against NATO. Emin agreed to go with them, even though he did not feel comfortable marching under the banner of the Communist Party. Emin had nothing to do with staying at home and wanted to avoid the unpleasantness of not joining them. He would also have an opportunity to go down to the city].

* * *

The first meeting in Kuşadası, which momentarily lifted Emin out of the loneliness and pessimism that had enveloped him, was like a refreshing drink, despite its limitations, to someone with a parched throat who was unaware of what would happen at the end of almost three decades. About six months later, he was experiencing a similar feeling once again. His conversation with Osman had pulled him out of the similar pessimism that had started to fall into in Novi Pazar. Despite his doubts and concerns, a glimmer of hope had emerged.

"Besides, let's say nothing comes through with Osman. I'll go to Austria in the worst-case scenario, as Ibrahim suggested. Whatever will happen will happen! It'll be clear tomorrow."

He was relieved with the thought that the uncertainties were coming to an end as he headed towards the motel.

He took a short nap in his room until dinner. When he woke up, he felt a bit groggy. Washing his face with cold water didn't help either. "It must be the room's stuffiness," he thought and opened the windows. He stood before the window for a while, taking deep breaths of the fresh air.

When he went down, he sat at his usual table with his back to the door. The restaurant was more crowded than on other evenings. A rather fat policeman in uniform, sitting with his back to the door at a table one row back from his own level by the opposite wall, attracted his attention. His collar was open, his tie was off to one side, and his hat to the other. Unlike those sitting at the following table, he was chatting quietly with a plainclothes man opposite him. Emin did not find it strange that two people sitting at the table next to the wall, like the police desk on the same level as him, were talking loudly. In fact, the way the conversation was held at the policeman's table was an exception.

Emin decided to have fish and asked if it was available. Luckily, it was! He then requested yoghurt to accompany the meal, using hand gestures to convey to the waiter that he could be called on the motel's phone.

While trying to enjoy the fish, which had few bones and a name he did not know, he thought, 'I wonder if it tasted so delicious to me because things seemed to be going well today.' With that, he severed his connection with his surroundings and delved into his inner world. His joy did not last long. In the seconds before he lifted his head and looked in the direction from which the noise was coming, he thought that the waiter had dropped the tray he was serving, the clinking of forks and knives accompanying the sounds of glasses and plates falling to the floor and breaking. What he saw when he looked made him forget to swallow the morsel in his mouth for a moment.

When he entered the restaurant, he took his usual seat, where he had grown accustomed to the cacophony of conversations in an unfamiliar language. A man was seated with his back to the door and facing the kitchen, causing all the commotion. This individual, appearing to be in his thirties, had a relatively larger build, and his unironed trousers were complemented by a jacket. Emin hadn't seen the first move, but he understood, 'This man probably was the one who pulled the tablecloth, which he is still holding, from one end, scattering whatever was on the table onto the floor. Neither he nor the man in front of him said a word in a moment's pause. As Jusuf and the other motel employee who had come out of the kitchen quickly moved towards them, the man threw the tablecloth on top of the pile of plates, glasses, etc., scattered on the floor and headed for the door as if nothing had happened. When Jusuf tried to go after the man, the other man at the table grabbed him by the arm and stopped him. All the noise in the hall had stopped. What surprised Emin even more was that the policeman, sitting with his face turned towards that table. He had undoubtedly seen the whole thing in detail and probably heard the arguments, but he did not seem to mind. It was as if no such incident was taking place or that policeman was not there! It wouldn't have been possible in Turkey. The other employee came out of the kitchen and spoke to the man at the table while Jusuf picked up what was scattered on the floor. The hall returned to the usual noise of before the incident.

Emin had lost his taste. He accelerated his eating with the thought of finishing his meal and going to his room as soon as possible. The phrase "A guilty ass gives itself away", which he would have laughed at any other time, came to his mind, but he couldn't laugh. If the police came soon and tried to take everyone's statements, Emin, as a foreigner, might attract their attention. It was the best way to avoid the probability of facing questions like the night before. However, he didn't get the chance. Ahmed arrived before he had finished eating.

"Good evening."

"Good evening. Come on, join me."

"No, I've eaten. Bon appétit."

"Thank you."

"You eat yoghurt with fish?"

Emin smiled at Ahmed's question, the implication of which is obvious: 'You can't eat yoghurt with fish".

"Yes. Unusual combination?"

"I don't know. We don't. It's not right."

* * *

Emin had learnt that "It's not right" was wrong when he was in high school in Kastamonu, from Huseyin, who came from a village in Taşköprü with a "communist" head of the village and was the closest supporter of the head of the village. He couldn't remember the name of the village exactly. "Ortaköy, I think?" Another thing he could not remember was whether that meeting was before the rally for hemp or the rally for garlic producers. Still, the rest was somehow engraved in his memory.

While Running Away

There were two outsiders from the city in the rally to support the producers: The revolutionary youth group consisting of students from Kastamonu Abdurrahmanpaşa Lycée and Gölköy Primary Teacher Training School. Emin, who was keen on reading, had met Alev, a civil servant whom he had been seeing more often due to book shopping, before the rally:

"I'll introduce you to Huseyin today. He's in town."

"Huseyin from Izzet Aga's village?"

"Oh, but don't refer to the mukhtar as 'Izzet, the landlord' when talking to him. They will be offended. That's what his villagers say, but if we call him 'the landlord,' he will get upset."

"Isn't he a landlord?"

"No, it's not. Izzet Aga has the village behind him as an 'Aga/landlord'. After he and Huseyin founded the TİP[77], he was especially sensitive about this issue. After all, the TİP fights against landlordism. You know what I mean!"

"OK, OK; don't worry. Will Izzet Aga come to the meeting?"

"No. Huseyin came alone. I told him about the effort to organise the people here. He was particularly curious about you, 'How could an army officer's son become a revolutionary?'"

"Where are we going to meet?"

"There's a small tavern on the other side of the river, in the alley; he'll come there."

"You mean he is getting drunk."

Since Alev was often getting drunk, Emin couldn't say, "Do revolutionaries meet in a tavern?" however, Alev caught the implication.

---

[77] TİP (The Workers' Party of Turkey) was a political party in Turkey in the 1960s and 1970's.

"Meeting there would be less conspicuous."

When they arrived at the tavern, Huseyin had already set the table. There was yoghurt with the "raki-fish" duo. Emin was surprised. After a bit of chit-chat, when the subject of the frictions with the nationalists in Kastamonu came up, Huseyin, who was tipsy with the effect of a 35lt bottle of raki; he was nearing the end, leaned towards Alev and Emin and made his suggestion in a low voice:

"Let's storm the place where they're gathering!"

Alev objected:

"It will lead to major conflicts."

"So be it. Let them see that we have power."

In addition to counting on the mobilisation arising from the peasants' discontent, Huseyin placed reliance on the over three thousand votes that TİP had garnered in the November 1969 elections in Kastamonu despite the strong dominance of reactionary forces.

Alev continued to object:

"Huseyin Abi, both you and Izzet are well-known names. They'll come for the TİP."

"We, Izzet and me, don't need to be there. The villagers, whom they don't know, deal with them."

Emin, who, like Alev and much under his influence, emphasised mass actions rather than such actions, interjected:

"Won't it harm the rallies? What matters is the people's movement."

Alev completed Emin's words:

"If a large crowd gathers and they see us there, it will already be a threat. Add to that the people coming from Ankara and Istanbul. They will see that we are not without backers."

Huseyin withdrew, although he did not wholly abandon his proposal:

"If you say so, so be it. But if you get stuck, give us a shout. We'll send youngsters from our village."

Emin moved the conversation to the subject that had intrigued him from the beginning with his question:

"Huseyin Abi, you eat yoghurt with the fish; isn't that dangerous? Won't it poison you?"

Huseyin laughed and teased Emin.

"You are an educated man, but you don't know such things. No, on the contrary. If the fish is stale, yoghurt prevents poisoning."

* * *

As he always did after that day, Emin had yoghurt alongside the fish in Novi Pazar, and this time, he shared with Ahmed the information that he sold to those who were surprised every time.

"If the fish is not fresh, it could poison. Yoghurt prevents poisoning. That's why I always eat yoghurt with fish."

When Ahmed, who had only come "to say hello", declined the offer of a beer, Jusuf brought the bill on Emin's signal. He, through Ahmed, could not overcome his curiosity and asked Jusuf the nature of the incident that had occurred a few minutes ago. Ahmed again translated a few short sentences.

"It doesn't matter. These people, quarrelling, are relatives. Sometimes, they confront each other like this."

Emin was relieved with this answer that erased the possibility of the police coming. When Ahmed left, he retreated to his room, tossing and turning on the bed. Emin couldn't sleep. Turning the possibilities over in his head, he had finally fallen asleep when there was a knock on his door. He got out of bed in his pyjamas, grabbed his trousers from the chair and opened the door. İt was Jusuf.

"Telephone, telephone."

In a drowsy stupor, Emin answered Jusuf's one-word words in Turkish and pointed to his trousers:

"I'll put my "pantaloon" (trousers) on and come back."

"Pantalone. OK."

He had learnt another common word from Jusuf's repetition. For some reason, without putting on his socks, in the absence of which he felt naked, he put shoes on but stepped on the back of them and went downstairs, but he was disappointed. The phone had been disconnected.

He agreed with Jusuf's suggestion, who showed him the chair and told him to sit at the other table between the kitchen buffet and where he always sat, even though he did not understand a single word in the conversation. It seemed that Jusuf and the other motel employees had also read the emotions he had never been able to hide from his face. It was the second half of the night, or, more accurately, the first half of the forthcoming day, and the Kosova Motel employees were ending the working night by drinking at the table they had set up for themselves after closing the door. Jusuf placed a glass in front of Emin and promptly poured the beer he had opened without giving him a chance to object.

"Wait. You might get a phone call again," Jusuf and others were saying with the signs they added next to the words.

Who was the caller? Since the Yugoslavian girl was unlikely to call at that hour, he tried to ask Jusuf, thinking, "I must have been called from England.":

"Is it English? Telephone, English?"

Jusuf turned to the one sitting opposite Emin, the one who seemed to have answered the phone, and echoed Emin's words:

"English, English."

Dino Buzzati came to Emin's mind once again. He was at the "waiting" stop once more! Now and then, the people at the table tried to include him in their conversation after clinking glasses with him, but Emin was mute in front of them. Occasionally, he responded to what was said by spreading his hands to the sides and making "I don't understand" gestures. Finally, they left Emin on his own. He was mute; he also remained deaf to the conversation. It had been over half an hour since he had arrived, and the caller had not called again. When he gave up hope, he stood up and put his hand in his pocket to pay for the beer he drank. Jusuf grabbed his arm.

"No problem."

As he continued with words in his own language, the others joined him in chorus:

"No, no, no, no."

He tried to express his thanks as well as his request in English:

"Telephone. Come in. Me, come."

Thinking that he might be called again, He went to bed with what he was wearing, instead of pyjamas, so as not to waste time getting dressed again. When he got up to go to the toilet after dozing half-awake for about two hours, convinced that he would not be called, he put on his pyjamas before going to bed again.

He was awake but lingered in his bed in the morning. When he heard footsteps, signalling a knock at the door about to arrive, he got up and got out of bed. When there was a knock, he reached the door and opened it. As he expected, the housekeeping lady was standing at the door.

"Dobro yutro."

"Dobro yutro."

The woman, whom he prevented from entering by standing in the doorway, said something in her own language. Emin, who thought that she was trying to explain that she either wanted permission to enter or that she would make the bed, said, "Nema problema, nema problema," and tried to explain with gestures that he did not want the sheets to be changed or the bed to be made. When the woman pointed to the towels on her arm, he said, "OK," and gave way to the woman. The woman put the towels in her hand on the edge of the bed, collected the used ones and left.

He went to the toilet and returned to bed, intending to sleep. But he couldn't. Starting from the thought "Everything will be determined today" and trying to turn the possibilities over and over in his head, his sleep was utterly disturbed. He could have smoked a cigarette to concentrate on his thoughts. His hand went to the packet, but remembering that he hadn't had breakfast, he changed his mind. He had made it a rule not to smoke in the morning without having a snack, even if it was just two mouthfuls.

Wasn't there an exception? There was one in a thousand. Emin travelled towards the memories of that morning in 1976.

* * *

All night, they talked about "their relationship, what are we doing?" in the student house on the top floor of the seven-storey apartment block in Cihangir. Yakup, one of their friends who had stayed in the other room and left Nazli and Emin alone, knocked on the door and stuck his head out.

"Time to say good night. I'm going home to Ortaköy."

"It seems like I have disrupted your usual order, haven't I?"

Yakup replied to Nazli's apologetic words without leaving Emin a chance:

"No, don't think like that. I have to go to Ortaköy anyway. I'll see you at the print press in the morning."

"Do you have five minutes?"

Thinking about the coldness of Nazli's addition of "five minutes" to their conversation, which was interrupted by Yakup's arrival, Emin was annoyed, but there was nothing he could do.

"Of course, I do," Yakup replied.

"If Emin doesn't get angry, I have a question."

"If you have something to ask, you should ask, why should I be angry?"

"Yakup, you're our friend who best knows our situation. He's been telling you almost everything," Nazli said, with the tone a mix of statement and inquiry.

"He tells me things, but I don't know if it's everything."

Emin jumped in:

"Even if I didn't tell you all the details, you know the gist, I did."

This time, Nazli turned to Emin:

"That's what I'm saying. Yakup knows the problem, knows what's going on between us."

"Sort of."

Yakup corrected Emin's ambivalent answer in his own way:

"Yes, I am aware of the problem, to the extent Emin told me."

"There's something I want to ask you. What do you think about our problem; do you think Emin is right?"

"This is a matter between the two of you!"

"Well, as a third person, you can look at it more objectively. Don't hold back!"

Yakup looked at Emin, who did not interfere in this part of the conversation and kept silent. Emin felt the need to speak when he caught this look.

"Yeah, what do you think?"

At first, Emin was annoyed that the intensity of their conversation might be disturbed. Nevertheless, he was ultimately glad that Nazli asked this question. Although he knew what Yakup was thinking, he had never mentioned it to Nazli. His joy was because he would hear it directly from Yakup's mouth. If it had been up to him, he would neither have asked Yakup this question in Nazli's presence nor relied on the answer to help untie the deadlock in their relationship. Moreover, Nazli might have thought that Emin was asking a question to which he knew the answer and was staging a scenario he had prepared to draw her to the point he wanted. The wall of the deadlock would collapse on the deadlocked relationship. The wall they built hand in hand without holding hands! Now, the situation was different. Nazli had brought up the subject herself. Emin was thinking about these things, but he did not realise that Nazli was looking for a lifeline, trying to find a pillar to implement a decision she had made in her head.

In his conversations with Emin, Yakup said that he did not understand Nazli and that her saying, "I could live in the same house with you even if you get married, and of course, if your wife agrees", was "nonsense that goes beyond arabesque", and gave the answer Emin expected by putting it in the politest mould:

"Emin is right, Nazli. If a relationship is to be lived, it should be lived in all its dimensions. What could be more natural than that?"

"That's what I'm beginning to think, actually," said Nazli, who lowered her head and avoided eye contact with Yakup and Emin while uttering these words.

"OK, I'll go now. It's hard to find a minibus anyway. It's late."

After Yakup's departure, there was a long silence between Nazli and Emin.

Beyond not knowing how to approach the matter with certainty, Emin was waiting for Nazli to finish her words. He had determined not to yield to his usual dash of hasty behaviour this time. And he didn't. Nazli was the one who pulled the curtain of silence apart.

"I've been thinking... I've been thinking a lot... I mean, I've been thinking for a while... I even told Cevat... To overcome the problems between us..."

She meant Cevat and his fiancée.

"If you want, we can..." Nazli paused once again. Her hesitant gaze was trying to read Emin's reaction. "...we can sleep together."

For someone who wanted to experience the relationship in all its dimensions, presenting a proposal with the condition "if you want" had only one meaning for the two who knew each other well. It was beyond being an "if" beyond a conditional clause. It meant, "I will be together with you because you want it." Emin didn't hesitate to dig deeper, even though he knew the possible outcome.

"Are you going to be with me just because I want to?"

He had skipped the second part of the sentence in his mind and couldn't say, "Not because you want to, but..."

Nazli answered Emin's question briefly with a mixture of tension and worry on her face.

"Yes."

"No! You should have known what answer I would give to such a question. Of course, no! If you will be with me just because I want to... then, of course, no."

There was not the slightest trace of ambivalence in his voice.

Another seven years would be added on top of 1976, and in 1983, he would adopt the same attitude when he sensed a similar approach. Even though it might come up in a different context, the essence of what they would experience between them remained the same. In both incidents, while Emin had not put it into words when talking to Nazli, he had always emphasised to Aydın, Nevin, and Serap when recounting the events: "Sexuality should have been the crowning of the love we had. I'm not saying this for the sake of literature; this was my feeling!"

Although Nazli could not grasp his emotion, her facial features had been softened by Emin's answer, "No!"

"You know, Cevat and his fiancée were right."

Emin did not understand. With a question mark in his eyes, he was listening without saying anything. Nazli continued, unaware of the upheaval and feeling of humiliation inside him.

"Cevat and his fiancée were right. When I shared this decision with them, they said, 'Emin will say 'No!' to you. The 'Emin' you told us about will definitely say 'No!' to you.' It's now proven that they were right."

Emin did not say, "They have figured out who the 'me' is based on what you told them about me, but you, yourself, have not understood." He didn't voice these thoughts, even if they crossed his mind! All he wanted was to rest his bewildered head on her lap.

While Emin, who had forgotten to be 'the impetuous Emin,' was looking for ways to prevent the distance between them, which had been gradually decreasing all night, from suddenly widening again, Nazli wanted to put an ending sign to the emotions experienced during the night, unaware that it was just a semicolon:

"Shall we sleep now? I'm going to the printing press early tomorrow. Let's sleep for at least four or five hours."

As if she wasn't asking a question, she got up from the bed next to the door where they were sitting, the one Emin always slept in, and moved to the other bed without waiting for Emin's answer when he said, "OK." Emin had tried to hide the resentment in his voice.

Nazli got into the single bed set up in the centre of the living room next to the stove, wearing a sweater and trousers, her head facing Emin's side. Emin also turned his face to the wall when he entered the bed. It was as if, by not seeing Nazli, Nazli wouldn't exist in the room. He couldn't fall asleep. As he got up to briefly use the bathroom, he noticed that Nazli's back was partially covered by the blanket, bathed in the moonlight spilling into the room on that chilly night.

Years and years later, Nolina, unknowingly, would remind Emin of that night as she shared a part of her story:

"Love is also about safeguarding my man's sleep from the sunlight, lost in my most intimate darkness! Or vice versa! Or the other way around, it's the vanishing act of my man, whose sleep I shield from the sunlight in my most intimate darkness! But…"

Years and years ago, Emin did something similar to what Nolina would do when she was on the other side of the world.

He gently pulled the blanket and covered Nazli's back to protect her from the cold.'"

* * *

[Flashforward - August 2014:
In May 2010, Emin voiced his reaction in two languages when he inhaled the tropical heat that would envelop his whole body as soon as he left the airport gate in Manila, even though it was midnight:

"Oh, for fuck's sake! Fucking hell!"

Only when a young black woman said, "Welcome to the Philippines!" with a smile he realised that he had uttered the words, which expressed astonishment rather than complaint, in a way that those around him could hear. Although she didn't resemble a Filipino, the man beside her did. He was also anxious not to encounter the greeters as soon as he stepped out of the gate, so he slipped through the door for the chat, hoping to find someone to help him, forgetting Anita's warning: 'Stay away from people you don't know at the airport exit!

"It's so hot!"

"Is this your first time here?"

"Yes."

Realising that he had been imprudent in giving such an answer to the man, whom he assumed to be Filipino, who had asked the question, Emin quickly added:

"I've got a friend. She was supposed to come, but..."

There was no need for Emin to complete the sentence he didn't know how to finish; the young woman had extended a helping hand:

"The greeters are on the other side of this road. Follow us."

This was how his friendship started with Eban and Nolina, who would be taking the same taxi to the same hotel, by also taking Anita, who had returned to the Philippines for a vacation about ten days earlier. However, Emin did not recognise Nolina's voice when she phoned him in London in August 2014.

When they met in the hotel lobby where Nolina was staying, the sadness in her beautiful eyes first caught Emin's attention.

The answer he received to the question, "Where is Eban? Hasn't he come?" explained the sadness in Nolina's eyes. When they first met, Emin had learnt in Manila that Eban, whom he likened to a Filipino, was a native of Hawaii, although his ancestors were Filipinos. It was Eban who had been arrested during a protest against the American occupation and had not survived the police station where he had been taken.

Nolina seemed as if she hadn't heard Emin's words coming out of a struggling attempt at voicing comfort. After wiping away her tears, she broke her silence:

"Let's make a plan. Where can we go today?"

She wanted to spend the first day with Emin rather than travelling on the tour she had come with. The first stop Nolina and Emin chose was Tower Bridge, where Nolina was leaning on the railings, admiring the scarlet sea created by the poppies spreading all around from the window of the Tower of London.

"It's probably representing the sea of blood in the First World War. It's very well done. Meaningful. They're not real poppies, are they?"

"No, they're not. You're right; it's meaningful. Yes, it depicts the sea of blood in the war."

Emin's mind focused more on the poppies emerging from the tower than the sea.

"The more interesting part is where the poppies are emerging from. They come from inside the tower and exit through the window."

Trying to understand what Emin wanted to say, Nolina dug further:

"So?"

"In England, the cradle of capitalism, many were imprisoned in this tower. Those who fought for freedom. William Wallace, for example."

"Is this the tower from the film Braveheart?"

I think so! It's perhaps an irony, but in England, the cradle of capitalism, this is the centre of the bloodshed caused by imperialism. The source is this tower! And it's as if the tableau they've created with poppies is telling their own story about the blood they have shed."

"That's a fascinating point. I mean, what you just mentioned."

Emin was swept up in the current of his thoughts, and Nolina's reaction only fuelled his exuberance further.

"In a way, imperialism says, 'I will cut off your heads, I will shed your blood if you do not submit to me'! More precisely, capitalism says this, and at the stage when it evolves into imperialism, the same bloodshed manifests itself not only inside but also outside."

Nolina had tears in her eyes once again. Emin didn't know what to say, so he kept silent. He realised that he had reminded Nolina of Eban's death. For a moment, he gently took the young woman's right hand resting on the bridge railing in a friendly manner and gave it a gentle squeeze. This was how he wanted to express his support when words were not enough. They stood on the bridge without speaking, their eyes fixed on the poppy field, until Nolina broke the silence:

"How is Anita?"

"She's good. In the Philippines."

"She's not coming?"

"No. Anita's over there, too busy."

"What's she doing?"

"Let's go to that nearby pub I told you about. The one decorated with full of flowers. I'll tell you about it there."

"OK."

Emin was about pondering what and how he would tell as they headed to the pub.

They sat outside to enjoy London's rare day when the sky was sparkling, and the sun was warming them up. After taking their first sip of the red wine Emin had brought, Nolina repeated her question:

"Come on, tell me, what's she doing there? How are things between you two?"

Emin told Nolina about what had happened in Anita's village near the seaside resort where Nolina and Eban had stayed for a while. He talked with evident excitement about the merging of neighbouring fields and Anita's efforts for the communal structure in the village, but he didn't tell them everything. He kept the true identities of Joel and Rochelle Ann hidden. These two young people, whom Nolina had also met at the seaside resort, had joined the commune with some friends coming down from the mountain. He avoided using the words "from the mountain" or "coming down from the mountain."

In the context of the progress made in the peace talks that had been intermittent since 1980, their organisation had allowed Joel and Rochelle Ann to go into the countryside. Their organisation saw the move from communal life in the mountains to communal life in the countryside as a new experience. They viewed the issue not as guerrillas adapting to civilian life but as civilians adapting to the lifestyle of guerrillas. Communal life in the mountains was a voluntary necessity. The necessities of life in the countryside had played a role in attracting the peasants to communal life as well.

He skipped some of all these details, Emin. Still, since he found someone who would listen, he endeavoured to explain how communalism would undermine capitalism in the womb of which it flourished.

"In a way, those villagers in the Philippines are trying to transfer what is described in Thomas More's 'Utopia' to life in their own way, according to their needs. That Thomas More is the same Thomas More who was imprisoned and beheaded in the Tower of London. His blood mingled with the bloodstream described by the poppies."

"Interesting... but is it possible everywhere? Like in Hawaii?"

"Why not? It doesn't have to be the same everywhere. Everybody has to find the most appropriate way according to where they are. The way to expel imperialism from Hawaii is to defeat capitalism by establishing alternative relations of production and an alternative life. Otherwise, someone will leave, and someone will come. The British leave, and the Americans come."

"You know, Eban's ancestors were from the Philippines. They came and settled in Hawaii in the 1850s!"

"Eban had mentioned it when we first met in the Philippines, but I don't know the details."

"Between 1830 and 1850, land was distributed in Hawaii, but only one per cent was claimed by the natives."

"So, at that time, there was no concept of 'land ownership' among the people?"

"No, there wasn't. Besides, the land is to be cultivated, but there is no one to work. So, labourers were brought from China, Korea, Japan, and the Philippines. Eban's ancestors were among them. Then they became natives."

"As far as I understand, land ownership hadn't had much meaning to the people until those dates. The present-day natives are not the same as the natives back then. The original natives merged with newcomers to form today's native population. These are subjects worth pondering and dwelling upon."

"If Eban were here, who knows what he would tell you now?"

The conversation had circled back to Eban. Emin listened to Nolina all day, her heartache still fresh. How they had met, how they had experienced a passionate love.

And, of course, with tears in her eyes, she told the story of the day when she closed the curtains again, saying, "'Love is also about safeguarding my man's sleep from the sunlight, lost in my most intimate darkness!'" The story of Eban's last day. The protest would reach its climax the next day. What struck Emin the most was its final sentence:

"My man, whose sleep I protected from the sunlight, is lost forever, not in my most intimate darkness, but in the darkness of the police station."

Nolina paused when she saw that Emin's eyes were also filled with tears.

"I've upset you too. I'm sorry."

After searching in her bag and not finding a new one, she handed Emin the tissue paper with which she had dried her eyes.

Then, thinking it was necessary, Nolina changed the subject.

"You were talking about Anita. Go on. What's going to happen now? Are you going to the Philippines, too?"

"I don't know yet. Let's see what the days hold."

"It seems like she has gotten involved in these matters under your influence. Shouldn't you be with her, by her side?

"Whether I'd be with her is another matter, but it cannot be said that she has been doing what she's been doing only under my influence. The environment was ready. I tried to give an idea of a different way of accomplishing what she wanted to do. It's a long story. Ultimately, whether I'm there or not doesn't make any difference. Besides..."

There was more, but Emin again chose to keep what he knew to himself. What happened to Eban was similar to what had happened to Anita's brother. In the

Philippines, Anita had only told Nolina and Eban that her brother was no longer alive, nothing else.

Anita was thinking of joining Joel and Rochelle Ann, who were also her brother's friends, to seek revenge on the unknown perpetrator - though actually known-.

However, first, she had to open a small shop to provide a living for her parents and to achieve this, she needed to earn and save some money. To pursue this goal, she went to Cyprus to work. Meeting Emin opened the possibility that she could seek her revenge differently.

Emin's approach was persuasive enough for Anita: "The best way to seek revenge on the corrupt, authoritarian system is not by taking lives, but by preserving our own, by upholding the right to self-defence, by living, and by creating opportunities for others subjected to poverty and oppression to thrive."

Emin had added something more to encourage Anita: As a woman, alongside Rochelle Ann and other women, she could lead the communal organisation in her village and exact revenge on the corrupt system through the new life they would establish. Women would and should lead society! Emin did not go beyond sharing these ideas; that was the extent of his role. Anita and her friends were carrying out the actual actions.

Emin had mentioned none of these. He weeded out the ones he shouldn't talk about, including how Anita's brother died, which might reopen Nolina's wound once more. Emin continued his chat from where he had paused by saying, 'Moreover...' and linked his words with Aragon's famous verse.

"Moreover... There is no happy love!"

Emin knew Nolina would assume he said it for her relationship with Anita. Yet, in fact, he had said it for Nolina, too. Additionally, what he hadn't mentioned to Nolina was his platonic relationship with Nazligül, who had included these lines in her letter to Emin back in 1977.

Emin felt embarrassed by his thoughts. His own experiences couldn't even be mentioned compared to what Nolina had been through. If anything, at most, his own action of pulling the blanket over Nazli's back so she wouldn't get cold could have resembled the act of Nolina drawing the curtains to shield Eban from the sunlight.]

* * *

When Emin returned from the toilet after covering Nazli's back, he saw that Nazli had pulled the duvet over her head. Not a single strand of her hair was visible. He resented this, thinking, "She's hiding herself from me." What he didn't realise then, he would come to ponder the next morning when reflecting on the events they were about to experience: "Perhaps what Nazli was concealing were her tears."

He checked his watch when he noticed the sunlight coming into the room through the curtainless window. It was approaching eight. He went to wash his face, intending to wake Nazli when he returned. Nazli had also risen and was sitting at the edge of her bed when he returned.

"Good morning."

"Good morning."

It was as if it wasn't the two of them who had those arguments and tensions that night. It was as though they hadn't lived through that night but had just met.

"Let me wash my face, too, and we'll go out, OK?"

"Yeah."

When they went down the street, cool but sunny weather awaited them. They started climbing the cobblestone ramp of Siraselviler Street.

"Let's have breakfast somewhere."

"No, I'll be late for the printing press."

"But you'll be in the printing press all day. You can't work hungry. At least let's have a toast in Taksim."

Nazli did not answer; instead, she turned her face to the left, away from Emin, who was walking on her right, so he wouldn't see her. Emin took a broader step forward and leaned slightly towards Nazli, trying to catch a glimpse of her face. And he succeeded. The silent tears falling from Nazli's eyes had washed away Emin's pessimism from the night. A hopeful smile appeared on his lips, which Nazli noticed as well. However, it would later be revealed that she interpreted this smile differently. She thought Emin enjoyed it when she cried. Unbeknownst to her, each teardrop of Nazli fell like a molten glass bead in the fire somewhere deep within Emin. He smiled at the sight of her tears, experiencing a peculiar sense of joy, which he would later note this feeling down:

"My smile was for the love wave flowing from you to me, even though those tears hurt me inside. The love I lived in my own way crystallised within me, thinking that you loved me despite everything. Otherwise, how could I possibly enjoy seeing you cry?"

Although it wasn't his usual habit, that morning, he took out a cigarette and lit it. It was one of the one-in-a-thousand exceptions, defying his self-imposed rule of not smoking in the morning without a snack.

* * *

This time, there was no excuse for exception. Emin withdrew his hand from the package he was reaching for. He got out of bed, dressed and went to breakfast immediately. A new day was starting in Novi Pazar, one that would determine the course of his life, one way or another.

Jusuf, sitting in Emin's usual chair, got up when he saw him coming and made room for him to take his place at the table equipped with breakfast dishes.

They exchanged "Good morning" in Jusuf's language.

He waited for the teacup to arrive to start his breakfast. Someone was enjoying a drink at the two tables by the window this time. Emin took his time once again to kill time. Unlike usual, he chewed and chewed his morsels and lingered in his mouth. He added two cigarettes together when he finished his breakfast. He took one last cup of tea and went up to his room.

He lit his third cigarette before settling onto the toilet while enjoying his smoke. It was customary to smoke in the toilet, but the image of Nasreddin Hodja's joke popped into his mind as he sat with a teacup. He laughed, "You can eat in the toilet, but... if someone sees you, they might think you are eating something else."

Then he stood under the shower for a long time. He dumped his dishevelled suitcase on the bed, from which he had randomly taken his underwear and shirts, hastily pulling them out earlier. He folded everything one by one in a very organised way and put it back. Still, time did not pass. He didn't know where to go, and the worry of not attracting attention by wandering around prevented him from going out and walking around.

He went back to bed and tried to sleep again. And he did. "This night will be my last night here. After that, one way or another, I will take a step towards a new life," he clung to the thought again. He felt a sense of comfort and relaxation, partly since he had eaten and had a hot shower.

When he woke up, it was already noon, but he still had more than two hours to make the phone call. For some reason, he felt that he would be forced into the position to place the phone call himself. Deciding to stroll down the deserted road leading to the upper town as if heading to Ibrahim's house, he got up. He got dressed after tossing and turning in bed for a while. He took his time while getting dressed. Just as he was about to open the door and leave, he gave up with the thought of "What if the phone call comes?" and decided to go downstairs and have tea.

When he descended the stairs, he saw Mirza in the restaurant and changed his mind again. He used hand gestures to inquire if there was a phone call. When Jusuf responded with a hand sign indicating "No," he pointed to his room with another sign to convey that he would be there. Jusuf had understood and said "OK". He returned to his room, not knowing what to do but determined not to deal with Mirza again.

He just took off his jacket and tossed himself onto the bed. He tried to recall poems from memory. Only one of them was coming to the tip of his tongue. It was the poem Serap had interrupted time and time again on their last night in Istanbul, never allowing him to read it in its entirety.

"As usual, she was trying to be the centre of attention again, as if she were the one who was going to leave. This time, no one could interrupt," Emin said. Then he recited

Enver Gökçe's verses one after the other in a murmur he could hear himself.

"FUCK OFF, MAN!
I am on the go, brothers.
And also, sisters

I'm on the go,
None left
All forbidden
This earth roofs
These trees
These stones.

"The 'Apat', that is called—
Is an inflated car tire—
And a raft,
Made of a few planks,
A float,
Float on water."

Son, kid and my wife
Says the wolf
"Fuck off"
Says the bird
Says the snake
"Fuck off",
A scorpion, too.

Hey brother
What kind of wound is this?
Bleeding from every part of me

I've been beaten,
Cursed,
Exiled,
Told, "fuck off,"
From my own homeland,
Like a partridge
I'll take myself and go away.

One more... One more... He repeated it again. Again, it was as if he would never repeat it. Indeed, the poem would stay in the motel room in Novi Pazar, never to be performed again. This decision was influenced not only by a change in his mood but also because he considered it too self-pitying, more than just partly, but significantly so. Then, this poem would fade from his mind, but it helped him pass the minutes at that moment. He kept repeating it, emphasising one verse after another.

As he had assumed, nobody called. He was going to call. He was trying to slow down as if reining a horse whenever he realised he was speeding up. Nonetheless, he arrived early at the post office. He passed the time with a cigarette outside and then went inside. When he dialled the phone, there was no problem; the answer came from the other side without delay:

"Hello, Osman"

"Hey, what's up?"

"It's good. What about you?"

"We're fine too. Listen, Rachel is getting ready to head to the airport right now. We just booked her a flight to Belgrade over the phone, so she'll be there tonight."

"To here?"

His question had a tinge of joy, and he hurried on.

"Good then, I'll check it out if I can… I'll leave for Belgrade on the first bus."

"No, no, no. Don't move. Rachel will be there. You stay put."

"Shouldn't I go to Belgrade?"

"No, it might be challenging for the two of you to find each other there. You'd better wait there. Rachel will call you when she lands in Belgrade."

"Fine, it's up to you."

"I've told Rachel what you're going to do. Whatever she says, you do it. I'll get the solicitor ready in the meantime. Rachel will tell you all about it when she is there. Now, let's not drag this out on the phone."

"What time does she get in, Rachel?"

"She'll be in Belgrade around 7pm. Then she'll call you from there."

"OK, thank you so much. I don't know how to thank you."

"It's OK, it's OK. You wait at the motel. Rachel is now getting ready, and we'll go to the airport soon. How's your money situation?"

"I assume I'll have seventy or eighty Marks left after I pay for the motel."

"It's too little, but don't worry, Rachel will take enough money with her."

"That's fine, thank you. We'll sort it out after I get back."

"Don't worry about that now. Let's get you out of there. Like I said before, do whatever Rachel says! Leave everything to her."

"All right."

"See you later. Take care."

"OK, see you later. Say 'Hello' to Rachel."

He left the booth. His hands and feet were quivering with excitement. He didn't even realise how he had paid for the

While Running Away

phone call. He poured his Yugoslav dinars from his pocket onto the counter. Also, he took out ten Deutsche Marks, keeping it in his hand, considering it was a more extended call than usual. After the clerk took the money from the counter, he pushed the remaining coins towards Emin. He didn't need to exchange Marks.

To overcome his excitement, he went down to the stream. He lit a cigarette, clenching his right fist and swinging his arm, bent at the elbow, parallel to the ground, inwards, saying, "It's done, it's done!" When he threw his cigarette into the stream and took the first step back to the motel, he repeated the same movement and words:

"It's done!"

Emin thought he should be calm now, even though he felt like ringing bells and dancing, even though he was useless when it came to dancing. He put on his composure and walked towards the motel with slow steps. He entered the motel's restaurant, where most tables were occupied, with only two or three left empty. Unaware, he stepped into a night that would be full of events, a day that had remained uneventful until the phone call that freed him from the constraints. The table where he always sat was also occupied. He looked around, then spotted Ahmed seated in the next row, two tables back. Ahmed faced the stairs, with the door to his left and the kiosk to his right. Ahmed, too, noticed Emin's arrival.

Emin went and sat at the same table, with his back to the door and his face to the buffet, to Ahmed's left, to keep an eye on the kitchen where the telephone was. Toward the buffet, on the right side, two tables away, she saw Mirza. He was sitting in the same place as the afternoon, but two other people were with him this time. Emin pulled his chair to the right, attempting to stay out of Mirza's line of sight, positioning himself where Ahmed stayed between him and Mirza.

"Hello."

"Hello, Ahmed. How are you?"

"Thanks, I'm fine."

The halved meatballs on Ahmed's plate reminded Emin of his hunger. Catching his gaze, Ahmed's call of 'come in' was answered with a nod, and he pointed to Jusuf, who was approaching their table.

"Thank you. Enjoy your meal. I'll order another one now. You go ahead and keep eating!"

"Same thing, plus salad," Emin ordered.

Jusuf repeated:

"Salad."

"Yes, salad."

He added to what he ordered, making two signs with his fingers.

"And two beers."

"I have," Ahmed had objected, but Emin insisted:

"It's OK; you can drink it when it's over. There's only a little left. Ahmed, please tell Jusuf that I'll receive a phone call. A woman will call around half-past seven or eight."

"Seven thirty, eight o'clock."

"Yes, around that time."

Jusuf, listening to what Ahmed was saying, gave an "OK" and then continued in his own language to Emin. Ahmed translated:

"Jusuf says, 'Don't worry, we'll let you know.'"

"Thank you. Thank you too, Ahmed."

"Is your friend coming?"

"Yeah, my girlfriend, she is coming."

They were both referring to the conversation they had two nights ago. Ahmed's meaningful smile was met with a smile from Emin, through which he had tried to imply, "What I told you last night was true."

When Emin felt İbrahim's hand on his shoulder, which he did not see coming because his back was to the door, he raised his head and stood up. They shook hands.

"How are you. Any news?"

"Thank you, Ibrahim, I do. My friend will come tonight. OK."

He said this in a low voice, even though his back was turned to Ahmed.

Pulling the chair to his left, he gestured for Ibrahim to sit down.

"Come, we're having dinner. You eat too. This is Ahmed. He speaks Turkish too."

They greeted each other with nods in their own language, but it was clear that İbrahim was not keen to sit down.

"No, I ate."

"What a shame İbrahim, you always say, 'I ate." Let's sit down and eat together."

"No, I ate. I came to look for you. There's news. No problem. I'll come tomorrow morning. OK?"

"OK, OK. Have a beer, at least."

"No, I don't drink."

Emin couldn't figure out whether he wouldn't drink at all or if it was just for the moment. Still, Emin thought, 'Perhaps he doesn't want to reveal his connection with me. Maybe that's why he seemed uncomfortable, which I just noticed.' This realisation prevented him from insisting.

"Well, come over for breakfast tomorrow."

"OK. Have a good night."

He had started to nibble on the meatballs after the beers, salad, and bread when Mirza raised his hand in greeting, but he ignored it even though it brushed against the corner of his eye. He tilted his head a little more forward and tucked the meatball on his fork between the slices of bread, creating a sandwich. He was trying to give Mirza the impression that he didn't see him, as he was solely focused on eating. Mirza didn't give up. He added a loud 'Hello' to his gestures. Helpless, Emin slightly bowed his raised head and silently accepted the greeting with his empty left hand while holding the bread in his right hand. When Mirza beckoned, "Come, come," he pointed to his plate and tried to explain that he was busy eating. Mirza was insistent. He got up and came to their table.

"Come to our table."

"I'm eating."

"Well, we'll take your plate there."

"No, thanks, it's fine here. I'll come back after I've eaten."

"OK, come back when you've finished eating."

"Alright, we'll see."

As Mirza turned away with a sulky expression, Emin sighed and said to Ahmed:

"What kind of guy is he?"

"He's drunk. Never mind. Is your friend coming from London?"

"Yes."

"Then you'll go to London?"

"Yes."

Thinking that he was giving short answers to Ahmed as if brushing him off, he attempted to explain so as not to cause offence.

"First we'll go to Belgrade, do some sightseeing. Then we'll go to London."

"I'm going to Belgrade too."

"When?"

"Midnight tonight."

While Running Away

"We can only go tomorrow. Are you going sightseeing?"

"No, I am going to see my brother."

"Does he live there?"

"Sort of. My brother is in jail. I'm going to visit him."

"Tomorrow is visiting day, I think."

"Yeah, yeah, yeah. It's visiting day every Saturday."

Emin was curious but couldn't ask Ahmed why his brother was in prison. It had become a habit not to ask unless the other party volunteered the information. A habit that had been acquired from the days of illegal work! He had developed such a manner during the political struggle.

"Haven't you ever been out of it?" Emin asked himself, recalling an incident he had experienced. He wasn't sure where to place his behaviour in that incident in this context. Would it be considered as being out of it?

* * *

At that time, Emin couldn't make sense of Selamettin Oksuz's invitation to the sympathiser group for the Party cell meeting, even though the subject was a common concern for both the Party cell and the sympathisers. Selamettin had explained his reasoning similarly, but holding a joint meeting went against the principles of operating clandestinely. Consequently, it had revealed who was a party member and who was not. Despite feeling uneasy about it, Emin wasn't able to object. He consoled himself, thinking, "The people at the top must have had a purpose for doing so."

At this joint meeting, Selamettin Oksuz explained in detail why it was decided to join TSİP. According to the decision, everyone was to apply for membership. He said "everyone", but he was not among this "everyone", and Emin and

Selamettin's wife Selda were to coordinate the work in the Beşiktaş district of TSİP.

"Aren't you going to become a member of Beşiktaş District?"

Emin's question was based on the assumption that he would also become a member but would work elsewhere.

"No."

"Since TSİP is a legal party, there is no harm in asking," Emin thought. And he asked!

"Where will you work? In which district?"

"Nowhere."

"So, you're not going to become a member?"

"No, I won't."

Emin was not convinced that Selamettin had excused himself from the decision to join the TSİP, which he justified at length. Although he did not hesitate to ask the question "Where will you work?" because it was related to the legal ground, asking "the reason for not becoming a member" would have been a question that would have pushed these limits, but Emin could not resist asking.

"Why?"

"We'll talk about it later."

Emin attributed this answer to the fact that Selamettin didn't want to talk about it in the presence of sympathisers, saved his question for later, and repeated it on the motorboat with Selamettin and Selda as they crossed from Beşiktaş to Üsküdar. Selamettin's answer was the same.

"Talk to you about it later."

Emin couldn't understand this answer. They were sitting in the stern of the engine, out in the open, and there was no one else but the three of them. Yet, Emin didn't press on.

Two days later, when he went to Selda's house, which was very close to his own, for a meeting about their Party work, Selamettin was also at home. The living room, accessed through the entrance door, opened into the room at the other end. Through the half-open door, he saw Selamettin working at his desk. After a formal handshake followed by some pleasantries, Emin repeated the question that had previously gone unanswered. He was stunned by Selamettin's roar:

"You're making a provocation! You're making a provocation!"

"What did I say? What did I say?"

His voice was shaking. Not just his voice? His hands and feet, too. He was facing an unexpected and grave accusation. Selda took his arm and dragged him into the other room, but Emin was still repeating the exact words.

"What did I say? What did I say?"

"OK, come on, let's get down to our work. You can talk about that matter later."

That "later" in Selda's "later" would never come. He would have to wait until 1989 to see the filthy sediment of the leader's sultanate lying at the bottom of the "later" well, even though Selamettin made the same fuss that he had accused him of making in 1978, this time at a meeting of the Central Committee of the Homeland Party, and used it as a cover for his political escape.

Emin was not sure if it was a question that pushed the limits of illegality.

Nonetheless, thirteen years later, he would learn the answer to the question he could not find that day.

* * *

[Flashforward - Autumn 1989:

After Leyla Feryat told the stories about Faik Feryat's disappearance, she brought the subject to the discussions in the "[Extraordinary General] Organisation Meetings" and Emin's attitude.

"I think you were unfair to Faik. He was trying to rally the Party with his suggestions."

"My objection was not to his proposal. In fact, I supported the idea of organising the Party into communal cells. I believed it could serve as the foundation for building comradeship that couldn't be established otherwise and could spread gradually from one circle to another. The problem was that he approached me with the proposal to join the TKP behind closed doors, likely because he saw me as a supporter of the 'communal cells' thesis. I can't say who was aware of how much. Still, I think the "[Extraordinary General] Organisation Meetings" were the most democratic process experienced by an organisation, not only in our Party but perhaps in the history of the Turkish left. It made it possible for every Party member to be heard without getting lost in the labyrinths of hierarchy. Faik Feryat could have done the same instead of whispering to me behind closed doors. It was as if he wanted to make me battering ram in kind. That's how I felt. Besides, I was one of those who had the clearest stance on the TKP. I had and have always been against it. In this sense, he bit off more than he could chew."

"The TKP issue was not as you know it!"

"What was there not to know? After all, what else was it but a means of establishing power over the movement and monopolising the struggle by taking refuge behind the Soviet Union? Shouldn't those who call themselves

'Doctorists' have learnt this from Doctor Kivilcimli, even if they learnt nothing!"

"Yours is the same sectarianism as before. Political struggle requires considering the conditions of the day and the environment. Whether you accept it or not, the TKP was massed, unlike in the Doctor's period. Besides, this is not the main issue. As I said, there are things you don't know."

"It's massified, etc... It was the reasoning that was also voiced at the time. It's not something I don't know."

"That's not what I meant when I said you didn't know."

"What don't I know, then?"

This wasn't a stance Faik took on his own, and it wasn't a stance taken just during those days, either?

"What do you mean?"

"The attitude toward the TKP results from a decision made during the exit process following the coup of 12 March. Faik Feryat, Selamettin Oksuz and Alp Öktem took this decision together on behalf of the movement after the coup of 12 March. Faik would convince the friends working in the workers' organisation abroad, especially in Germany. Selamettin Oksuz had the task of convincing the cadres in Turkey and ensuring domestic organisation. Since he failed, Faik wanted to use the "[Extraordinary General] Organisation Meetings".

"I never heard Selamettin Oksuz suggest joining the TKP even one day."

"It's normal; he must have tried to resolve it at the top. Once he convinces the leadership cadre, the rest follows."

"It wouldn't have worked that way either. Even if he could convince the so-called leader cadre, he couldn't convince the militants. If he could, Çelik could. Selamettin Oksuz was no more effective than him. Was it only him? None of the others, who thought they were leaders when they gathered five or ten people around them, would have been more effective than Çelik. I don't know if you heard when Çelik brought this proposal to the conference where the decision to join the Homeland Party was taken... He had sent a lengthy statement of justification for his stance. Salim, who was in prison with him at the time, also wrote a one-page, primitive justification, 'The name TKP belongs to them; joining the TKP is our duty,' and so on. This proposal was overwhelmingly rejected. None of them could be a greater authority than Çelik. As I said, even he had rowed in vain. Thanks, actually, it's good to know what you said. Some things are clearer to me now."

"Like what?"

"Selamettin Oksuz's cries of 'Provocation!' have gained meaning. As it turns out, whenever he got stuck in this issue, his cry of 'Provocation!' became his refuge. You know how he left the Party. At the Central Committee meeting, when it was asked to clarify the situation of union presidents in DİSK who were party members but had concealed their relationship with the Party, as well as to provide explanations about the Party's connections abroad and links with workers' organisations in Germany... and even these issues were brought up by Hasan, who was, funny enough, in his own faction, Selamettin once again cried, 'There is provocation here!' and left the meeting, and subsequently, the Party. In other words, issues related to the TKP once again... The man hides his behaviour even from his own faction; what kind of relationships is he in."

Emin also summarised to Leyla Feryat the story of the 'provocation' he had experienced, pushing the limits of illegality.

The reason for Selamettin Oksuz's run away had become apparent. It was the same as the others: Love for the TKP!

Emin, at that moment, made a mockery of him, too, by singing the first verse of a "Hüzzam maqam" song:

"What a love, ah, what an agony!"]

* * *

Beyond his habit from the illegality days, Emin had another reason for not asking Ahmed about his brother's reason for being in prison at the Kosovo motel's restaurant. He believed that such questions may lead to developing further friendliness, which could open the door to counter-questions, which was a situation he didn't want at all. The sound of the phone ringing shook Emin out of his thoughts. Standing up, he waved at the waiter from the kiosk, who was already heading towards the phone, and tried to make himself visible. It was the first time he had heard the phone ring since his arrival. He felt excited. When the waiter answered the phone and, with a hand gesture, indicated that it wasn't for him, he returned to his seat. His disappointment faded as he checked his watch, which still displayed seven pm.

"It wasn't for me."

In response to Ahmed's contented smile, Emin's smile froze when he saw Mirza approaching their table.

"Come on, you've finished eating; come to our table and have a beer."

"Darn it, if I don't go now, this guy will get upset, and then he might go to the police and explain his twisted scenario. I'd better keep a cool head to get through this night without any trouble," he murmured under his breath, then went after Mirza willy-nilly.

He sat in his chair directly opposite Mirza, who was sitting with his back to the kiosk, directly opposite Mirza. To his right, a man about his own age, with greasy long hair parted in the middle, unshaven beard and moustache, a junkie type with an open collar, whom Emin would later liken to a glue-sniffer-type fascist intellectual - the only thing he lacked was glasses - was sitting across from him, a younger man with a brown neck sweater, shaved face and neatly cut hair. A few minutes after Mirza called out to Jusuf, four beer bottles were on the table. Emin, who did not even have the opportunity to object, was trying to calculate the cost of the following four beers, thinking it would be his turn to order in the next round.

"Şerefe!"[78]

Mirza, who had begun to speak in their own language, must have explained its meaning to the others as the other two repeated the same word:

"Şerefe!"

"Şerefe!"

Amin reluctantly went along with them.

Mirza started to introduce the others. He only mentioned the name of the neatly dressed young man on Emin's left and started talking about the long-haired one.

"This is my uncle's son Nihad. But he's like my brother. We grew up together. He's a gallant lad."

---

[78] "Şerefe" means "cheers" in Turkish.

The first thing that caught Emin's attention in this "gallant lad" was the unevenly cut, long nails holding the beer glass. The filth-filled nails disgusted Emin.

***

[Flashforward - February 2014:
Exactly a quarter of a century later, Emin would recall this scene and the feeling it created. The phone in his hotel room would ring at eight in the morning. It was the director of the foundation they had travelled with to Hawler/Erbil, the capital of South Kurdistan, which had been under Iraqi occupation.

"Good morning, Emin; are you awake?"

Even if he had not woken up before, he would have woken up with this phone call. Emin answered without caring about the absurdity of the question.

"I woke up; I was about to go to breakfast."

"Come and see me before you go to breakfast."

"What happened? Are you OK?"

"Not really; I'll tell you when I come to my room."

"He must be suffering from a hangover," Emin thought, since the night before, in another hotel in Hawler, one of the few hotels that also sold alcoholic beverages. They had stayed until past midnight, and his CEO had downed one whisky glass after another. The problem was indeed drink-related, but not as Emin had imagined.

The CEO aimed to explore opportunities for the foundation to undertake initiatives in Southern Kurdistan, utilising the network of contacts. Emin would later gain an understanding of the nature of that network. Originally from Northern Kurdistan, ceded to

Turkey by Western powers led by British colonialism after the First World War, Emin was brought along by the CEO, who said, "You are familiar with the customs and traditions there; you will be of help." Initially assuming Emin could speak Kurdish, the CEO learned that Emin spoke neither the Kurmanji dialect in Northern Kurdistan nor the Sorani dialect in Southern Kurdistan. Nevertheless, the CEO insisted, "Come anyway," thinking the institution would benefit from the positive image created by having a Kurd among its staff.

Playing a dual role, this former trade union lord, besides succeeding in infiltrating the "Coalition to Stop the War", was also a friend of Tony Blair's—According to Emin, the CEO was a typical example of the yellow trade unionist, and Tony Blair was a war criminal; the relationship of these two hypocrites was rooted most probably in the CEO's trade union years. The CEO had also established a connection with the leaders of the United Workers Union in Hawler, for whom he organised a meeting with Tony Blair in London during the Iraq intervention. He hoped to utilise this network of relationships to get some work for the charity he ran.

The CEO's preparedness to establish multifaceted schemes would not be sufficient to prevent him from facing an unforeseen situation. The man's distress, who would be a bit angry with Emin for not warning him, would manifest itself when he opened his knocked door.

"Good morning, Emin; come in. You didn't warn me either, and I forgot to buy alcohol while going through customs. Plus, you've booked a hotel that doesn't sell alcoholic beverages. Get on my laptop and finish this

Excel spreadsheet; I can't type now. After breakfast, we'll print the presentation; I'll have it done at the hotel's printer before we head to the morning meeting."

Emin did not understand what was happening for a moment. He grasped the situation that he did not know when the hands with unevenly cut dirty nails and crooked and shaking fingers opened the Excel table. Until that moment, Emin had not realised the extent of alcoholism in the man, who, suffering from the inability to drink alcohol, not only struggled to focus but also couldn't type with his hands shaking. Emin would witness more of it with the events of the whole day. The man, who had barely completed the morning meeting, would ask the Kurdish trade unionists to take him to a restaurant serving alcohol for lunch. The Christian neighbourhood in Hawler, where alcoholic drinks are available, is quite far from the location of the afternoon meetings. Moreover, it would take a long time for the man to satisfy his craving for alcohol.

One of the meetings would be postponed because of this. Since the postponed meeting coincided with the other one, Emin would go to one meeting, as he would go to the other separately, even though they had attended all of them together. This led to the dilemma of whether or not to visit the refugee camp near Hawler for Kurds from Rojava in Syria, the last task of the afternoon. Emin emphasised and insisted on the importance of observing this camp for a potential project that would cover ten other similar camps. Consequently, they decided to visit the Kawergosk Refugee Camp as well.

Emin, as he put it, "didn't give a fuck" when, at the end of the visit, the CEO complained that they were late for a drunken dinner. After all, he had seen with his own eyes the miserable life that the Barzani gang offered to the Kurds of Rojava in another part of their homeland in Kurdistan.

Emin also managed to discreetly take a photo, exposing this disgrace. He seized the moment when the translator, sent by the Barzani gang to capture images portraying the camp in a positive light, was occupied with the CEO. He could have complained as much as he wanted, given that he was delayed in getting his whisky and cigars to be held by his hands with unevenly cut filthy nails.]

***

Emin quickly averted his eyes from the filthy nails that had disgusted him and turned his gaze to Mirza, who continued with his dodgy, flattering talk. Emin's suspicions were stirred further, and he once again murmured under his breath, "Birds of a feather flock together, and you're just like one of those troublesome rascals."

While Emin was only half-listening, Mirza kept on, explaining that Nihad was not a bachelor like him and had married and had three children.

"So, are you staying at this motel?"

Before starting to talk to Emin again, Mirza, who had a long conversation in his own language with the others, surprised Emin with his question. At first, Emin was taken aback by the thought, 'What am I doing here if I'm not staying here?' But his surprise faded as he remembered that none of the restaurant's customers, except himself, were staying at the motel.

"Yes, I'm staying here."

"How much do you pay for this place?"
"25 Marks."
"How many nights have you been staying?"
"Two."
"It's a lot of money. They're robbing you!"
"It was the most convenient."
"This is not acceptable. This can't be done to a Turk. We are all Turks. We need to look after each other. These things are wrong, wrong!"
"Motel will make money, that's normal."
"No, no, it's not. A Turk has no friend but a Turk. Look at what they are doing. Is it befitting Turkishness?"
"But this place is good. The staff is hospitable. I'm happy staying here."
"The staff are good guys, I know that, but it's expensive. They're ripping you off. We'll get you out of here."
"I'm happy, no need."
"Why should you pay so much money for them? Nihad has a big house. It's empty. His wife was not home and was visiting the village with the children to see her mum and dad. I'm staying there now. You can stay too. You can only buy the booze, and we'll get drunk there. It'll be cheaper for you, too."

"Chasing a free high," Emin thought. His naiveté again took hold, and he hadn't even thought beyond.

"No, thank you. I'm happy here."
"No, no, don't. Grab your suitcase and settle the bill. OK?"

Mirza continued his sentence without giving Emin a chance to say anything. "Jusuf!" he called out towards Jusuf, who had instantly appeared by their side. While signalling to Jusuf with his hand, indicating "no, no," Emin continued to object to Mirza:

"It can't be like that. Let Jusuf go. I must stay here; I'll tell you why; let him go."

During this argument, he decided to explain to Mirza, whom he was trying not to contradict, the reason for his stay in the motel, confirming the story he had made up during their first-night encounter.

"Tonight, my lover from London is coming. She'll be here. I can't go anywhere else. She should be in Belgrade by now. I'm just waiting for her phone call."

"She's coming all the way here for you!"

"That's what we agreed. My girlfriend wants to visit the nearby monastery as well. After all, she's a Christian. She's eager to see historical sites. Then we'll go to London."

"You're a lucky man. Life is better over there."

"Yeah. Yeah. I told you the other night. We're going into advertising business together."

"You're going to be rich!"

"Let's see, inshallah!" Emin was using such words deliberately to ease suspicions.

"Your parents don't mind you marrying an infidel?"

Relieved that the subject had shifted to this topic, Emin slumped in his chair with his left arm over the backrest. He tried to continue the conversation in the same vein, not realising that his watch, whose strap was a little too loose on his wrist, had caught Mirza's attention, all while thinking to himself, "Keep pigs flying." He was fabricating a story again.

"You know, they're from the old generation, after all. They may not be thrilled, but they still say, 'You know what is right!' They say, 'Your happiness is the main thing.' However, they hope that the girl will convert to Islam. At one point, they asked me, 'Will she convert to Islam?'"

"Will she convert?"

Emin had noticed Mirza asking his question casually; his gaze was fixed on Emin's arm hanging from the back of the chair. However, Emin thought Mirza was looking at someone at the back table and answered the question.

"I don't think so. I don't know. Maybe my girlfriend will. She'll convert if she wants to. It's not that important to me."

"Get her to do it. You have to convince her. You'll earn good deeds. It's an honourable task."

Emin wanted to say, "A moment ago, you were trying to uphold the honour of Turkishness, and now it's about Islam. The Turkish-Islamic synthesis has truly become a part of your soul." But he kept his sarcasm to himself as he replied.

"It's an honourable task, but as you know, there's no compulsion in Islam. If she chooses to do it willingly, it's acceptable. Therefore, it's up to her."

"What do you mean by 'acceptable'?"

"It means valid, good, true."

"Sometimes my Turkish falls short."

"Don't worry; your Turkish is quite good."

"Thank you."

Emin, aware that the bottles were running low, was contemplating whether or not to order new ones while Mirza and Nihad were chatting. Then, Mirza switched to Turkish:

"You have a nice watch."

Emin looked at his watch on impulse. It was ten to eight pm. "Yes, it's a good watch."

"How much did you pay for it?"

Since it was a gift, Emin didn't know the price, so he tried to buy time.

"It's been a long time. I don't remember exactly, As DM…" Emin replied, feigning uncertainty. He pretended to calculate it in his head. What should he say? They might think he was wealthy if he gave a high figure. On the other hand, as a bank marketing man, he couldn't keep the price too low.

"I think twenty-five or thirty in Marks!"

"Can I have a look?"

Emin put his left arm on the table. It was one foot in front of Mirza when he looked down.

"Five stones, I think."

"I don't know, I don't know that much."

"Why don't you take it out so I can look closer?"

Emin paused, unable to make sense of this request.

"Why?"

"He's an expert, understands such things." He was pointing at Nihad. "Let him take a look."

Despite his initial hesitation and commitment to avoiding confrontation, Emin took out the watch and handed it to Mirza. Mirza brought it close to his eye, then gave it to Nihad after a curl of his lip to indicate that he didn't understand. Nihad turned it over several times before saying something to Mirza in their own language.

Mirza said, "That's not how it's understood. He means you need a tool." Mirza brought his thumb and forefinger together in a circle, mimicking a magnifying glass. Realising that the "tool" referred to the magnifying glass used for the watch and electronic repair, Emin reached out to take back his watch.

"OK, then. Give it to me."

"We have the tool at home. Let's go take a look and come back."

Mirza and Nihad had just stood up, and coincidentally, the phone began to ring.

"Wait a minute, wait a minute, wait a minute."

In the meantime, due to the language barrier, Emin couldn't understand what Mirza and Nihad were saying to each other. But what was being told to Emin was also unclear to him. His attention was directed toward the waiter who was answering the phone. The waiter gestured to him, and without waiting for the counter to be lifted, Emin walked under it and picked up the phone. It was Rachel on the other end. Emin tried to signal Mirza, heading toward the door, asking him to come back with hand gestures, but Mirza ignored him and left with Nihad.

"Hello."

"Good evening, Emin. Hello."

Rachel was trying to speak Turkish, and Emin responded joyfully, noting her pronunciation of the undotted "Ş."

"Good evening, Rachel."

"Emin, I'm at the coach station. It's half past eight, and there's a bus. Me is coming. You got it?"

Emin looked at his watch. It was five minutes to eight. Rachel probably meant the bus time when she said "half past eight".

"Got it, Rachel."

"You have to wait there. I come there."

"OK, Rachel. I come to Novi Pazar station to meet you."

"No, no, don't come there. Me... get a taxi."

"OK, you come to the Kosovo Motel."

Emin's Turkish had faltered again, this time following Rachel's example.

"OK, I know. Osman wrote it."

"OK, thank you very much."

"Good evening. You wait, Kosovo Motel. Don't go to the coach station."

"OK, I'll wait. Kosovo Motel."

"Me... will close up now. Bye-bye."

"Bon voyage."

"Thank you."

When he replaced the receiver, half-snorting laughter escaped his throat as he tried to suppress his chuckle. His joy mainly made him laugh, even if it partly related to Rachel's Turkish.

"Thank you, thank you."

His repetition of "Thank you" to the waiter emphasised the sincerity of his gratitude. This time, after passing through the open counter, he swiftly headed toward the table where Mirza and his friends had sat. The third person was still at the table. "Where are they?" Emin asked, pointing to Mirza's and Nihad's empty chairs. "Sit down, sit down," the young man said with his hand. When Emin took his seat, this time, he opened both palms to the side, lifted his shoulders and tried to ask, "What's going on?" The answer was that the man waved his right hand up and down his wrist twice calmly. "Calm down," he wanted to say, as Emin understood it. Again, with gestures indicating the door, he tried to explain that those who had left would return, accompanied by sentences that Emin did not understand except for the names "Mirza" and "Nihad".

Meanwhile, the young man responded to what an older man from the next table said towards them. The conversations that Emin did not understand lasted for a minute or two. As Emin drank the last sips from his drink, he objected to the young man who lifted the empty bottle and pointed to the waiter:

"No, no."

Emin didn't want the beers refreshed. The young man didn't insist either. Then silence. Emin felt stuck. He got up and went to the toilet. As he sent most of the two beer bottles back to nature, he thought, "What if this guy runs away too?" He stopped what he about to do and zipped up in a hurry. As he opened the toilet door without washing his hands, he came face to face with the young man who had put on his coat and was about to leave the restaurant.

The young man staggered a bit as Emin lunged forward, grabbed his arm and threw him backwards.

"Where are you going?"

His shouting in Turkish immediately silenced the hall. Everyone was looking at them. Jusuf came running over. Ahmed, who until that moment had either not heard or did not want to get involved in what was happening two tables away, got up from his seat and joined them. As the young man staggered, Emin, who had stepped in front of him so that he was between him and the door, pointed to his left wrist with his right hand and said, "Watch, watch."

"They took your watch?" Ahmed asked.

Emin quickly summarised to Ahmed, who asked the question, and Ahmed translated to Jusuf what he was told.

Ahmed translated the conversations that went from Ahmed to Jusuf, then to the young man, and back to Ahmed to Emin:

"Jusuf says, 'Let him go. This one's father is sitting at the table next to you."

Jusuf pointed to the older man who had just spoken to the young man. Ahmed continued telling Emin what Jusuf told him:

"It's eight o'clock now. Twenty minutes. They will come back. They will bring your watch. If they don't, then Jusuf will call the police. His father will stay here, they will come, his father will go."

Although Emin was uneasy about the police, he took the fact that the young man's father was there as a guarantee, so he was relieved that it wouldn't come to that. He is also convinced he shouldn't have made a scene, either. With these thoughts, he stepped aside and gave way to the young man who hurriedly exited the door. Then Emin ordered two beers from Jusuf while walking towards his chair, following Ahmed, who had guided him to sit at their previous table.

"Thank you, Ahmed."

"OK, brother, I'm sorry."

"You don't have to apologise. You've done nothing wrong."

"It's OK, you're a guest; it's a shame."

Jusuf said something to Ahmed as he put the beers down and waited.

Ahmed translated of Jusuf again:

"Jusuf says, 'I'm sorry.' And he says, 'Don't worry, the watch will come.' OK?"

"OK, thank you."

Emin was about to reach for the glass that Jusuf had filled when he remembered that he had not washed his hands.

"Ahmed, I'll wash my hands and come back. Tell Jusuf to keep an eye on the young man's father. Shouldn't let him go."

"OK, don't worry. I'll keep an eye on him."

"Thank you."

He went to the toilet and finished his unfinished business before washing his hands.

When he returned to the table, Ahmed began talking apologetically to Emin as if he were the one at fault:

"It doesn't happen much here. Mirza went to Turkey and came back; he started acting oddly. Our place is good. There are bad people everywhere. We have fewer, but they exist. I'm sorry."

"Ahmed, it's not your fault. You are right; there are good and bad people everywhere. It's just luck. I've been hit by it.

Anyway, it doesn't matter. I understand you. You're a good person. Don't worry about it."

Ahmed, whose relaxed facial features showed that he was relieved by these words, changed the subject:

"I think you got a phone call."

"Yes, she's in Belgrade."

"You spoke to your girlfriend?"

"Yeah, I spoke to her. She's coming over."

As soon as he said this, a wave of panic rose in him: "She will come, but what if my watch doesn't come back?"

"Ahmed, I need a watch. What if these guys don't come?"

"They'll come, don't worry."

"Still, let's find a watch. Whatever it costs."

"The shops are closed. We can't find any."

"I know. It's not like that. Wouldn't there be anyone here who sells his watch?"

"No one will sell it."

"Let's ask around."

At Emin's insistence, Ahmed reluctantly asked for the side tables.

Finally, a man offered to sell his watch but wanted 40 Marks.

Ahmed raised his concern:

"He's asking too much, but it's up to you."

"Yes, you're right; he wants too much."

Ahmed conveyed Emin's objection to the man. Then, the bargaining started.

"I think he's going to reduce the price. He says, 'How much will you pay?" Ahmed asked.

"Tell him I won't give him more than 25 Marks. Otherwise, I won't take it." Ahmed translated to the man.

"OK, he's agreed."

"Let's have a look at the watch first."

Emin opened the lid of the pocket watch with its chain and looked at it. He liked it. It is an old watch but ticking well.

"I'll take it."

As Emin took out the money and was about to hand it over, Ahmed interrupted the conversation with the man and turned to Emin.

"He wants thirty Marks. He says 'chain'."

"Twenty-five marks without a chain and thirty marks with a chain. Is it what he is saying?"

"Yes."

Emin took off the chain and gave it to Ahmed, along with twenty-five Marks, and Ahmed passed them to the man.

He opened the lid and looked at the clock again. It was twenty past eight. The time limit Jusuf had set was over.

"Ahmed, I don't want to trouble you, but could you go and tell Jusuf not to phone the police. There's no need. I found a watch anyway."

"OK."

While watching Ahmed from behind, he noticed Jusuf approaching. Ahmed paused, waiting for Jusuf to arrive. When they reached Emin, Ahmed delivered the news that Emin did not like.

"Jusuf has already phoned the police. 'Maybe not tonight, but the police will find him tomorrow,' he told me."

Emin was glad that the matter would be dealt with the next day. Rachel would have arrived by then anyway. Somehow, he could get out of this without a headache. He was no longer concerned about the police being informed.

"Thank you, Jusuf."

"Welcome!"

As Rachel's name crossed his mind, he had thanked Jusuf in English for some reason.

His comfort lasted for half an hour, only to be spoilt when the burly policemen, one a little shorter than the other but both tall and burly, came through the door. Jusuf showed Emin to the policemen he met halfway. When the taller of the policemen gestured to Emin, Emin called Ahmed to him.

Ahmed translated the words of the policeman showing the watch in his hand:

"Is this watch yours?"

"Yes."

"Here."

"Thank you."

"Welcome."

The policeman answered in English. Emin did not know what to say for a moment.

"Do I have to sign a report?"

"A report?"

Ahmed did not understand.

"I mean, do I have to sign a paper?"

First, the police answered Emin's question, upon Ahmed's translation of it into Serbian, in English, saying, "No problem, no problem." Then, they spoke to Ahmed in their own languages, and Ahmed spoke to Emin:

"No, no paper. Let's sit down."

As Emin followed Ahmed to the table, he noticed the policemen heading towards the kiosk, and he changed his mind. Emin followed them.

He interrupted the conversation between the policemen and Jusuf, who had gone to the other side of the counter, interlocking his four fingers and pointing to his mouth with his thumb, offering a drink.

"Beer?"

"No, thank you."

He made another suggestion, thinking that they might not be drinking because they were on duty.

"Coca-Cola?"

"No, thank you."

When Jusuf showed the food to the other policeman, he realised that they would buy something to eat, and he struggled to speak English, mangling the language."

"Me, money, pay!"

The policeman who gave the watch again objected, smiling and tapping Emin on the shoulder.

"No, no, no, no! Thank you. Go!"

He was muttering to himself as he went to his seat: "I think the Yugoslav policemen rob the foreigners as they enter the country, and the Bulgarians rob them after entering." He came to this conclusion when he combined his experiences with what his aunt had told him.

He returned to the table where he sat with Ahmed, but his eyes were still on the policemen. Emin waved to them as they left the restaurant with bags of food from the buffet. He saw them responding to his greeting similarly before leaving and sighed in relief.

"We've dodged a bullet!"

"What did you say?"

Ahmed's question made him realise that he was voicing his thoughts aloud.

"If such an incident happened in Turkey, a report would be made. I mean, they write down what happened on a piece of paper, then sign it, the complainant signs it and so on. Isn't there such a thing here?"

"Not always."

"So, this is over?"

"It won't end."

Ahmed's answer made Emin uneasy, but what he said afterwards somewhat relieved him.

"They will beat those guys all night long."

"Too bad."

"It can't be bad. These buggers are thieves."

"Then let them take it to court. Let the court punish them."

"Good for those guys. They don't want to go to jail. A bit of a beating. Then they're free."

"You mean these men would prefer to get beaten up than go to jail?"

"Prefer?"

"Prefer means they want which one or choosing."

"They want a beating!"

Emin couldn't help but chuckle at the straightforward statement, "They want a beating!" For the same reason or not, Ahmed joined him. Emin, with restored cheerfulness, raised his glass. Ahmed, too. When they finished their beers, Ahmed packed up. He had to leave. He would stop by his house and go to Belgrade with the last bus leaving at midnight.

"Don't pay the bill. I'll pay."

"I've already paid for it."

"When?"

"While you were sitting there."

Ahmed was pointing to the table where Emin was sitting with Mirza earlier. Emin only needed to pay for the last round of beers. Amin felt indebted.

"All right. Let's have another beer if you've got time."

"Thank you. I should go."

Emin held Ahmed's hand tightly with both hands while shaking hands. "Thank you very much. Thank you very, very much for your help."

"You're welcome. Have a good trip."

"Have a good trip, too. And I hope your brother keeps his spirit up. Say 'Hello' to him."

Emin ordered another beer and was alone at his table in the restaurant, which was slowly emptying. This time, he was not feeling the loneliness he had felt priorly in an unfamiliar country. He was not experiencing a profound sense of loneliness, whether because he knew it would end in a few hours or because he was clinging to a branch of hope. "Hope, I guess, becomes a cooling ointment on the searing wound of loneliness," said the voice inside him.

"This is one of the final nights. Tomorrow, I will say goodbye to this place, too. There is not even a single shred of emotion similar to what I experienced on my last night in Istanbul. That is to say, one experiences last night's sadness when leaving a place where one feels one belongs, even if it is a step to remove the 'thorn in one's foot'. A joy of liberation wrapped in the sadness of separation. Even if it is liberation from the absurdities I have experienced here, there is neither the joy of liberation nor the sadness of separation. This can be explained by a sense of belonging... but what is belonging?"

He found an answer to this question that would be confirmed once again by what he would experience in "The City, located on seven hills"[79], almost seven years later:

"Belonging is to be a part of the people of that land, not of a certain geography. The more you feel part of those people, the more you belong to that geography."

* * *

[Flashforward - 1995:

---

[79] Istanbul used to be called "The city on the Seven Hills".

From the autumn of 1972 until the winter of 1989, he had been away from Istanbul for more than a week five or six times. One of the longest had lasted six and a half months, the other seven months. If he added them all together, it would either be a year and a half or not. Each time when he saw the Tuzla signpost on the road, he would experience the feeling of "I've come to my home", and each time, Emin would take the ferry to take a breath of Bosphorus air. If he lived on the Anatolian side, he travelled from Kadıköy to Karaköy. If he lived on the Thracian side, he travelled from Karaköy to Kadıköy. Even if he had nothing to do, even if it was limited to going and coming back with the next one, these ferry journeys made him feel like he was breathing Istanbul. Emin did the same this time when he travelled to Turkey for the first time after so many years of separation.

In the minibus he got on in Kozyatağı, he sat behind the driver in the middle of the row. The window seat was full. They had gone a hundred or a hundred and fifty metres when the driver, who had overtaken the other minibus by speeding up in front of him, won the race and then stopped to pick up a slightly large man, who would sit down next to Emin. "Whoa!" Emin said inwardly, "This man is almost going to sit on my lap!" The man he glared at seemed to take no notice of it. Although Emin initially told himself, 'Be patient!' and tried to do just that, he couldn't bear it any longer. During one of the overtaking manoeuvres that the minibus driver attempted in the ongoing race with other vehicles, Emin turned slightly sideways and used his elbow to assert himself against the 'bear' sitting next to him as the minibus turned from Sahrayı Cedit towards

Göztepe. Afterwards, he felt more comfortable, but the initial experience of going out on the street during his visit to Istanbul after years had left a bitter taste in his mouth.

On the ferry's upper deck, the Bosphorus, which he had been watching from the back, had carried away what he had experienced in the minibus with its breeze. And the flavour he missed in the first bite of the fresh "simit" he bought at the pier, even though he was not hungry at all... The tea was not bad either; it was not carbonated like before. The beauties of Istanbul started to dominate its ugliness. The Bosphorus was flowing under the fluttering wings of seagulls. Orhan Veli's poem was caught in the waters flowing from the Black Sea to Marmara on the surface and from Marmara to the Black Sea at the bottom and waved this way and that, but it remained in the Bosphorus.

> *"In Istanbul, on the Bosphorus*
> *I am a strange Orhan Veli*
> *I'm Veli's son*
> *In unspeakable sorrow*
> *I'm sitting on Rumeli Fortress*
> *I'm sitting and crying out a folk song*
> *Istanbul's marble stones*
> *And they land on my head, they land on my head, seagulls..."*

Without knowing where he was going, he descended from the Karaköy pier, and his feet carried him to the absence of Istanbul, to the Galata Bridge, spontaneously.

He had felt a subtle ache when he heard that the Galata Bridge had burned in May 1992. "They burned my Istanbul!" The Galata Bridge hadn't burned; it had been set on fire! Like some others, Emin was of this opinion, too. When he read the news, he said, "They burned a whole history, together with my own little history. One day, if I go again, I will be going to an altered version of Istanbul" he had said.

This ugly new bridge, from which the ferries no longer departed, did not reach back to Emin's past. It was not the bridge that had been opened to prevent protest marches and that had been forced to go against them... and that they had shared with Nazli... this was not that bridge. He turned back when he was halfway across. His mood had been spoiled.

When he got on the ferry to return, he went up to the second floor, but this time, he didn't go out into the open. He wasn't going to smoke either, as his mouth was like poison from the back-to-back lit on the bridge. He settled in the window seat on the right side of the departure direction. A little later, at the other end of the opposite seat, a man of about the same age as him sat down with his tie, suit, clean shave and a briefcase in his hand. This man occasionally tilted his head to the right and glanced at those sitting in the open. Following him, a group of young men and women arrived and sat down in groups of three or five in the middle row, facing each other and making some noise. Jokes were following one another, and the young people, probably university students, were bursting into laughter from time to time. Even if he didn't hear their jokes, their carefree, joyful behaviour had made Emin smile. That is until the man around Emin's age, sitting opposite him, shook his head from side to side and made a disapproving sound of "tsk tsk" while looking at the two young people in the group who were getting cosy. The young people either didn't notice or didn't care about that man's reaction. Emin did, and he growled while staring at him:

"Grumpy old man!".

However, he had just realised that the words hissed through his teeth were directed at someone almost his age.

"Hey, you oaf! Most likely, around twenty years ago, you were also grinding away in those university benches. Who knows what kind of commotions you were causing back then? How quickly you've forgotten your own youth?!"

No one else had heard his words. He rose from his seat and walked to the open back deck, shooting the man a contemptuous, angry glare. His facial expression matched his gaze. He had craved fresh air, and he found it. He felt invigorated. He was among the last ones left on the ferry when it docked at the pier.

He had been invited to his mates for dinner. He was going to buy Sweet William flowers. He went around the Roma women who sold flowers. However, he couldn't find what he was looking for.

"Come, my handsome Abi, come and look at these. Your missus will love them."

Emin laughed.

"I don't have a missus. I'll buy some for my friends."

"Your friends love it too, my handsome Abi."

He knew there was no way out once he got into a conversation. He would buy flowers from this woman who had gathered her grey hair with a half-covering rosy headscarf like her dress, but he could not decide which flowers to buy.

The woman continued, determined to engage in conversation, perhaps out of fear that he might not like her flowers and would go to another vendor:

"My handsome Abi, why don't you have a wife? You're like a lion, mashallah."

"Oh, a handsome lion... even with his fur all fallen off."

Referring to his hair that had started to fall out, Emin's cheerfulness was restored, and he laughed.

"My handsome Abi is single?"

This time, a beautiful young woman florist from the next stand joined the conversation.

"What's the matter? Are you setting your sights on my handsome Abi?" the first woman replied.

"If my handsome brother wants it, he can have my eyes and heart!"

"Girl, you've started giving your eyes and heart; who knows what else you'll give!"

Emin, who even realised that he had a slight blush on his face, wanted to turn the flow of the conversation.

"I'm not handsome, but you are beautiful!"

"If she's beautiful, take her, my handsome Abi, but take the flowers from me," the first woman insisted.

"Yes, my handsome Abi, take the flowers from her, but take my eye, my heart, and me into your heart."

Emin laughed heartily.

"What are you laughing at, my handsome Abi; just take me. Or don't you like me?"

"I like, I like you; I said you're beautiful, but you're too young; a young man like you would suit you."

"My handsome Abi, you're beating around the bush."

"OK, OK; look what we'll do now... I'll buy a bunch of flowers from each of you, but you'll put them together, OK?"

"No problem at all. We'll put it together if you want."

The younger one finished the other's words:

"Just ask, my handsome Abi; we will even unite the two sides of the Bosphorus for you."

He handed them their money without thinking of bargaining and wished them "Good business."

"Thank you, and may you be blessed."

"Thank you, and may you be blessed, my handsome Abi. But think about the other good deed, you know. I'm here every day!"

He waved goodbye, chuckling at the younger woman's real intention of persuading him to buy flowers from her next time, and left. Still, his smile lingered on his face for a long time.

"These are the beautiful people of this land who exude joy. Those are the people who intricately embroider even the dance music with sorrow, who come out as a life sprouts like snowdrops in this geography. I began to feel myself in Istanbul with them. They made me forget the negativities I had seen all day long." This is what he recounted to his friends when listing these experiences in response to the question, "How did you find Istanbul after all this time?"]

* * *

The restaurant had emptied, and only Emin remained as a customer. Under the influence of the beers he had consumed, he was preoccupied with thoughts about belonging to the geography not because of the land itself but because of the people living in those lands, trying to pass the time with mental exercises. Finally, he headed to the counter to settle the bill.

"No, no. Alright!"

They didn't want him to pay for anything. Jusuf held his arm and seated Emin at the table they had prepared for themselves just in front of the counter, just like the previous evening. Jusuf was trying to explain by pointing at the watch on his wrist and the table where the incident occurred as the others joined him, nodding their heads and giving Emin the impression that they seemed to blame themselves for what had happened. They were repeatedly apologising:

"Sorry, OK. Sorry."

"Sorry."

After saying, "Nema problema, nema problema," he tried to explain that it wasn't their fault by saying, "You, no problem" in English, redirecting the conversation to another channel to avoid the apologies getting prolonged:

"Yugoslav police, OK, good. Finished quickly."

"Yeah. Yeah. It's good. Yugoslav police, Interpol one."

Emin looked puzzled as he didn't understand the last thing Jusuf said.

"Interpol tell, not German, English, French, but Yugoslav police top police."

Jusuf, with his limited English skills, was relaying that the Yugoslav police had been recognised as the best police organisation in Europe by Interpol. He thought, "If Interpol said so, there must be a reason! Didn't my experiment also confirm this in a way?"

"Yes, good, very good."

After the gesticulating staff invited Emin to eat and drink again, they continued the conversation at the table. He did not want to drink the "rakia" poured into his glass, fearing that he might pass out drunk.

In English, he responded, "No, no, thank you. No drink," to which the reply was that the beer bottle had replaced the "rakia" glass. Emin didn't object any further.

After the introductory round, where everyone listed their names, a moment of silence followed the clinking of glasses as the uncertainty of what they would discuss hung in the air. The common topic was eventually discovered by the person seated to Emin's left. A mixture of hand gestures, English, Serbian-Bosnian, and Turkish -which Emin had later jokingly referred to as 'Tarzanish'- was enough for them to create an imaginary football pitch on the table." When they realised that Emin was a fan of Fenerbahce, the goalkeeper Schumacher was mentioned for his "good saves," and coach Veselinovic for being "Yugoslavian." Fenerbahçe was "good"! Then Emin told the story of Sasu's goal:

"Corner. Shoot." He made a curve sign with his hand on the tablecloth and exclaimed, "Gooaal". But he got it wrong. Sasu was not Yugoslav.

"No, no Yugo. Rumunija."

They laughed. That's how much Emin knew about football!

Trying to say, "Rumunija, Yugoslavia, I got them confused; the names are similar", Emin used the English word meaning "same" instead of "similar". They objected in English. "No, not the same." Emin's minimal English skills shifted the conversation to another aspect.

The others pointed to Jusuf, "He is not the same", and "we are different". Emin was surprised. They tried to explain. Jusuf was a Christian; they were Muslims. Jusuf joined the conversation. Emin did not understand whether he was trying to explain that he was treated badly or differently. "We are all human beings", Emin said, trying to prevent the atmosphere from getting tense. The others insisted, "Jusuf should become a Muslim; he should also be circumcised!" They pointed to the small knife on the table, implying that it wasn't sufficient for the task of cutting Jusuf's foreskin. Then they gestured toward the large knife they used for cutting bread in the kitchen, trying to convey that they needed a giant cutter. It was all in jest. Emin put an end to it:

"Jusuf is a good man. Christian, Muslim, same. We are all brothers." While trying to express these words in English, he shook hands with each of them one by one to emphasise the sincerity of his message. The glasses were raised in a toast to brotherhood.

"You good man."

"You guys good."

In his three-word sentence, he tried to say that "they were also good" people, even though he did not know the word "also" in English. Nevertheless, the others all had understood!

When they placed their glasses back on the table, the question asked pointing to the ring fingers made Emin understand that the motel employees had not thoroughly checked his passport. The identity document in his passport listed him as "married."

'No. No, married. It's over."

While the three of them were speaking in their native languages and gesturing to Emin for confirmation, they learned he was married, separated, and had a child while they were all single. Emin realised from their jokes, especially those directed at Jusuf regarding his having a girlfriend, that he couldn't quite discern the reason for their laughter, which eventually turned into a hubbub. Emin noticed that Jusuf, who occasionally laughed at what was said, seemed somewhat uncomfortable, so he chose not to delve into it and preferred to remain on the periphery of the conversation. Although Emin did not fully understand, he picked up on a suggestion that he thought was probably related to the jokes between the others at the table.

"We'll find you a woman tonight!"

Emin was surprised.

"Tonight. Woman?"

"Yes."

The hand gestures made as expressions of male sexual acts were no different from those in Turkey. In their view, Mirza had dampened Emin's spirits, and this woman would fix it!

When he fully realised what was being proposed, Emin objected:

"No money, no sex."

He had misexpressed himself again. He didn't mean "No money, no sex", but rather "No sex for money".

What the person sitting on his left said was supported by the others.

"No money. Cigarettes. A packet of cigarettes."

Emin tried once more to explain what he meant.

"Money, no sex! Sex, yes; love, yes."

Jusuf, who showed he understood what Emin was trying to explain by putting his hand to his heart, clapped Emin on the back with his left hand:

"Romantic, romantic."

While Emin smiled at Jusuf's seemingly supportive gesture, he was turning over a suspicion in his mind: "Even if they didn't go through my passport... who knows, perhaps they did but didn't notice the details; maybe they went through my suitcase and saw the cigarettes in packs of ten.

It could have been the woman, the housekeeper. Perhaps she saw the cigarettes, and maybe the woman these guys suggested I have sex with was her. Most likely, it's her. Otherwise, with those flirtatious glances..."

He decided to put an end to the noisiness and nuisances at the table and get up.

"My girlfriend. Telephone. She... come tonight. OK."

Jusuf repeated what was said, showing his watch and adding his question: "When?"

Emin pointed to his watch as he answered, "Four-five. Door?"

Jusuf also wanted to end the insinuating giggles and chatter of the others, whatever he had said, then turned to Emin and continued while pretending to press the bell button in the air with his index finger.

"Nema problema. Girlfriend zrrrrrrrrr."

"No, no. I open the door!" Emin replied with sheer determination.

"OK, OK. Nema problema. Come, come."

Jusuf got up and walked to the door, signalling for Emin to follow. He turned the key in the door, opened it, and closed it.

"OK?"

He wanted to explain that the key would be left in the door, and Emin could open it.

"Thank you. I open the door."

"Yeah, yeah. OK."

"When they returned to the table, Emin did not sit down. He concluded his sentence that began with "Everything perfect' with a series of repeated "thank you". Jusuf's "welcome" response was echoed by the others.

When he went to his room, he started his shower with hot water, slowly cooled it down, and waited for about thirty seconds under ice-cold water. He felt invigorated. He drank two glasses of water even though he didn't feel the need. Thinking that the water, added to the beers he drank, would wake him up with the need to pee if he fell asleep, he went to bed after putting on his pyjamas.

"Since it's after 2:00 a.m., Rachel will be here in two hours. If she's late, three hours at the latest. The bus may travel slower at night. Especially when you get on those narrow roads. Why should it be late? What's the difference, an hour earlier or an hour later. The important thing is that she's coming. It's done. It's easy from now on. Easy, but... what if I fall asleep? She could ring the bell but must wait until the staff opens the door."

He became restless with this thought. He got up, placed his pillow on the window sill, and sat in bed. 'Even if I fall asleep momentarily, this position will keep me half awake.

He almost fell asleep, but the beers and water he drank fulfilled their functions as he thought they would after about an hour. He got up and went to the toilet. When he looked at his watch, the hour and minute hands were hidden in the darkness. He groped in the trousers he had thrown on the chair, took a match from his pocket, and struck it. It was ten past three. He went to the door and returned. He paced like that for a while.

It hadn't been ten minutes before he gave up on walking around the room to keep himself awake. He felt tired in his legs, even though his mind was wide awake. When he got up, he placed the pillow, which had fallen from the window, onto the bed, vertically on the back of the bed this time. He rested his back on the pillow, his arm on the window sill and his head against the glass. He had reduced the possibility of sleeping. A little later, when his right cheek turned cold with the coldness of the glass, he left his elbow on the sill and took his face in the palm of his hand. He was excited by the headlight lights suddenly falling on the road in front of the window. The passenger he was waiting for was coming. When he realised that the gradually intensifying light was coming from a pickup truck that he did not know which journey it was on, he passed his disappointment with the consolation of "She can't come at this hour anyway".

He was falling asleep again when he heard a familiar sound. The cuckoos, known for laying their eggs in the nests of other birds and having their young raised by these unsuspecting foster parents, were signalling that morning was approaching.

"They speak the same language here as Turkey."

He sat up a little from his bed, where he had been sitting half-lying because he was gradually sliding, and looked out the window. The two trees opposite, with branches swaying in the breeze under the cloudless sky's brightness, did not have what he was looking for. Although the day's first rays had not yet reached this point of the earth where the unknown action and longitude intersected, they were about to arrive. The singing cuckoos that greeted his arrival had enabled him to establish a relationship with nature, whose existence he had been reminded of by the murmur of the creek the day before without realising it, this time by feeling it. The news he had heard in Demirköy during his childhood days, in Marash when he was wobbling through the first steps of adolescence, in Kastamonu when he was burning with the fire of youth, was now being given by the cuckoos in Novi Pazar. And with the same notes.

"If they leave here and go there, or vice versa, they can still get on with each other. But is that how it is with human beings? As if languages were not enough, they have managed to dig an abyss within a square metre they share by bringing their religions between them. What will you take under the soil you cannot share, human being?"

His mind had connected the bird's song to the conversation he had, or more accurately, had tried to have, with the motel employees, to Jusuf's marginalisation, and then to the song composed by Onno Tunç, with lyrics by Aysel Gürel, performed by Sezen Aksu. The song had evolved into artists' advice by twittering its sadness - yet another layer of irony!

> *"This world would be left neither to you nor to me*
> *The world would not be left to you or me,*
> *It was not even left to Sultan Suleiman,*
> *It has been written in no book!"*

"No, it wouldn't, but why tear each other apart in the name of religion and nation? Wouldn't it be different if we could get to the root of the matter?"

* * *

[Flashforward - 2016:
"We can somehow overcome the language barrier, perhaps by learning each other's languages, and so on. There was once an effort to create a common language called 'Esperanto.' Why it didn't work is another matter. If that had succeeded, this problem would have largely been addressed. Yet, the chasm among people has deepened, multiplied, and diversified with religion, further exacerbating it with the fabrication of 'nationality'."

"Nationality is a social phenomenon."

"Everything is a social phenomenon if you look at it. Yes, it's right before our eyes, but how was it born? If we look at it carefully, we can solve it. According to these so-called 'heavenly' or 'Abrahamic' religions, everyone descended from Adam and Eve. Let's say we don't believe this, but according to Darwin's theory of evolution... Please attention! We used to say 'Evolution Theory' in Turkish. It is not called 'Evolution Theory' but 'Theory of Evolution' in English. The theory of evolution. Anyway... According to Darwin's theory, to put it simply, we evolved from monkeys in Africa. Then, they scattered all over the world. You can accept this or the other one. There were no nations in the beginning. So, what are these 'nations'? Actually, it is necessary to turn a presupposition upside down. I couldn't remember his name by then, but then I looked it up and found it. There was an Italian statesman: Massimo d'Azeglio. He said, "We have created Italy; now it is time to create Italians." This quote came to my mind at the time. As the old saying goes, 'mind gets functioning either while running away or shitting...' I thought of it while running away and waiting for Rachel at the window of the motel in Novi Pazar. I asked myself: 'Is this unique to Italians? Which state has not created its nation like this, France or Germany?... More than that, Turkey! Turkification is one of the most extreme examples. Moreover, it is imported from the Germans. They, too, have a policy of Germanisation, which started in the nineteenth century and culminated in the disaster of Nazism. Although similar policies are found everywhere, as far as I know, they are not expressed in the literature with terms such as 'Germanisation' and 'Turkification'. Interestingly, these two are the two most well-known examples of genocides. 'The student becomes the master.' Although Turkification was implemented after the Germanisation policies, it was the human tragedy that culminated in the 'Great Catastrophe' in 1915 that gave birth to the concept of "Genocide". Moreover, the Germans were complicit during the 'Great Catastrophe'. It was even a kind of rehearsal for them, which could serve as a basis for their later audacity. Hitler's bold statement, 'Who, after all, speaks today of the annihilation of the Armenians?' should not be underestimated."

"But it is alleged that Hitler did not say those words."

"There is confusion there, too. Most probably a distortion. I will tell you why, but let's look at the facts. Those who say 'Hitler didn't say' claim that during the Nuremberg Trials, 'the American journalist who announced the testimonies to the world made a mistake'. What mistake was that? Let me find my notes and quote them word by word."

Emin went through the web pages listed on his computer for a while.

"Oh, here it is. Look what was written: 'When it was realised that the AP reporter had mixed up the speeches, those sections were removed from the minutes. Nevertheless, this situation was leaked out of the court as if those words were actually said.' Should I, too, say the excuse is worse than the misdemeanour? No, actually, it is the annexe of the misdemeanour. Another photograph emerges when we scrutinise this mix-up and how it happened. This is one. I'll come to that. The second is that the words are first recorded in the minutes, then they are removed, but on the other hand, it is also debated that they have leaked outside.

Who leaked them? I won't say ask the genocide deniers this question. Don't we know what answer they would come up with? It is customary to attribute everything to the Armenian lobby! They will attribute this, too. Let's move on. According to this narration, those words were entered into the minutes, although they could be extracted later. In other words, the document obtained from the journalist was somehow presented to the court. Whether the document can be accepted as evidence in terms of legal technique is a matter of debate rather than its accuracy. And who is the American journalist who allegedly intercepted the calls? Louis Lochner. He's called Louis, but he's really Ludwig. Born on 22 February 1887 in Illinois, his father was a Lutheran clergyman. His mother was Maria Lochner née von Haugwitz. The family was of German origin, and German was spoken at home. He graduated from the Wisconsin Conservatory of Music in 1905 and the University of Wisconsin in 1909. In 1914, he headed the Emergency Peace Federation. The reason I am giving these details is simple. The man is not Armenian. German is spoken at home; he was born, raised and educated in America. So, his English is also excellent. How can the allegation that someone with a perfect command of both languages is mixed up in the speeches be taken seriously? Moreover, he stayed in Berlin, where he travelled in 1924, right after the First World War, for twenty-two years until 1946. During that time, he interviewed Hitler twice. In addition to his articles, interviews, and translations, he wrote books and pamphlets. However, for some reason, as far as I can see from my research on the internet, he did not write anything about the Armenian Genocide... In other words, he was not particularly concerned about the Armenian Genocide; he was a journalist who leaked the information he obtained at the time to the USA and the UK. According to another source, those words allegedly removed from the minutes of the Nuremberg Trials were 'not accepted as evidence.' Everyone should be aware of the fact that not being accepted as evidence doesn't necessarily mean that Hitler didn't say them. If there is any confusion, I think it is the Zionists and their lobby who tried to turn the Armenian Genocide into 'once upon a time'. Why? The Zionists justify the state of Israel they are establishing based on the Genocide. Mentioning another one might weaken their hand. It is impossible to meet the demands of the Armenians on the same grounds. This could alienate Turkey, with which the Allies tried to ally against the Soviets. Every inch of land to be given to the Armenians will also be given to the Soviets. If the Armenian Genocide is recognised, the justification for the State of Israel will be weakened. Therefore, ignoring the Armenian Genocide is in favour of the Zionists. My conclusion is that the exclusion of those words from the minutes or not accepting them as evidence is a conspiracy set up by the Zionists to lower the demands of the Armenians from the agenda. The source of the mix-up is not by the American journalist. Yes, there is a mix-up, but it is a Zionist mix-up! Let me make an additional point relevant to our time without further digression. Turkey's collaboration with the Zionist lobby on the international stage, and especially in the United States, is likely not a coincidence."

"You have almost digressed."

"What can I do? It's all connected! Let's go back to what I was saying. This state-nation relationship... Nations do not create states; states create or try to create nations. It is the same in Turkey. It is those state structures that fuelled nationalism. In our case, it is a complete disgrace. As a result of the First World War, Anatolia received immigrants from all over the Ottoman Empire. Especially from the Balkans, and more specifically from Greece, the immigrants from there have been champions of nationalism. Why? Based on their declarations, they were given fields, vineyards, and gardens, including my grandfather. Whose were these properties? Armenians, in the first place, and all the Christian peoples who were victims of the Genocide. Religion also comes into play here. Here is the Turkish-Islamic synthesis. What is the result? What I call 'deed nationalism'."

'What you're saying is interesting but a bit complicated. You should sit down and write it down without getting sidetracked."

"When I talk to you, I do a bit of brainstorming. It helps me clarify what I've been picking up here and there, what I've been debating in my mind."

Like this occasion, Zafer found himself held captive by Emin from time to time, enjoying conversations and provoking him to elaborate on his thoughts further.]

* * *

Noticing the taxi's headlights first and then Rachel getting out of it, Emin swiftly woke up from his thoughts on the disintegration of humanity and rushed downstairs to the door. With a small suitcase on the floor at her feet, Rachel was paying the driver while Emin turned the key in the lock. Despite the cold of the night, he went out in his pyjamas to prevent Rachel from having to carry the suitcase. Rachel hugged Emin as if they were two friends who had known each other for years, even though they had only seen each other once in Istanbul.

"Hello, how are you?"

He answered Rachel's understandable, albeit accented, Turkish in half English and half Turkish as they walked to the door of the motel.

"Thank you. I'm fine. How are you?"

"Thank you. I'm fine."

"Your Turkish has improved."

"I regularly practice every day!"

He let Rachel in, and before going upstairs, he turned the lock on the outer door, ensuring it was shut tight and locked.

Emin hadn't even switched on the light in his room as he hurried down, but he switched it on as soon as he entered.

"This is our room. This is your bed. But we can switch if you want."

"No, no, it's fine."

"Your Turkish is really good. We can communicate easily."

"Fine, but I don't know many words."

"No' don't worry. I have a dictionary."

"I'll practise my Turkish more with you. It'd be a surprise for Osman when I return."

"Yes, we will. When do we go to London?"

"We'll go on Monday. Tomorrow, we go to Belgrade."

"Yeah. Sorry, I forgot. Would you like to have a drink? Are you hungry?"

"Thank you. No, no, no. I'm too tired. It's better to sleep. We'll talk in the morning. OK?"

"Yeah, OK. No problem."

"Yeah?"

"I mean, yeah, we'll talk in the morning. I'll go out, you get changed."

"You're so kind."

Emin went out smiling. He closed the door behind him and waited.

"OK, you come!" Rachel called.

Rachel was already under the duvet when he returned.

"Shall I switch off the light?"

"That'd be good."

"What time do you want to get up?"

"I need to get some sleep. Five or six hours. No need to rush. Is that all right?"

"Yeah, all right. I couldn't sleep at all tonight. That's good."

"Good night, sweet dreams."

"Thanks. You too, Rachel."

Despite all the excitement and getting the energy of joy, Emin didn't need to toss and turn to fall asleep. The tiredness of the day and the comfort of having shed the stress he had experienced with Rachel's arrival made it easy for him to slip into the dream realm.

Yet, in the morning, he woke up before Rachel, haunted by a nightmare he had experienced repeatedly in earlier days. However, its grip on him didn't last long. He opened his eyes to a sparkling sky. He felt a serenity he hadn't experienced since the beginning of his journey. He lay in bed for a while, careful not to disturb Rachel. Eventually, unable to contain his eagerness to start the day, he rose and dressed slowly. As he was putting on his shoes, Rachel, still half-asleep, asked:

"You're awake? Let's get up."

"No, no, you go back to sleep. I'll go downstairs. A friend was coming. I'll look for him. Go to sleep."

"OK, thank you."

The breakfast table was set when he went downstairs, but he didn't want to eat. It would have been inappropriate to eat without waiting for Rachel.

"Dobro yutro."

"Dobro yutro. Your friend is here?" Jusuf inquired.

He smiled at the awkwardness of communicating in English with a Yugoslav Turk and in Turkish with an Englishwoman but mainly at the joy of Rachel's arrival.

"Yes, she's here. She's asleep."

He took the tea served upon his arrival and lit his cigarette. Pointing to the breakfast items on the table, he tried to convey to Jusuf that he could clear them away. Since it was uncertain when Rachel would get up, he didn't want to be in a demanding situation after the nighttime hospitality.

After three cups of tea, accompanied by two cigarettes, the call of his daily routine became unavoidable. This time, he had to set aside his habit of not using the toilet used by everyone. Since he intended not to disturb Rachel, he refrained from going upstairs. Upon returning from the toilet, he asked Jusuf, chatting with another waiter behind the kiosk, if they could leave their suitcase in the room until midnight when they would check out. The answer was simple: "No problem," and they wouldn't have to pay extra.

He had taken another cup of tea and was about to sit at the table to light his cigarette when İbrahim came in.

"Dobro yutro Ibrahim, come. Would you like some tea?"

"Dobro yutro. Yes."

He did not eat himself, but he should have asked Ibrahim if he wanted breakfast because of his invitation the night before.

"Bring him breakfast."

"No, no need. I ate."

"You always say that; did you really eat?"

"Yes, I swear I ate."

"OK."

"Your friend's here?"

"She's here."

"Then you don't need my uncle's son."

"No, I don't. Thank you very much, though. You've helped me a lot."

"You're welcome!"

Emin decided to act on the impulse that had just struck him. As much as he loved it, Emin knew he wouldn't need the pocket watch, so he decided to give it to İbrahim as a gesture of gratitude. With that in mind, he took the watch out of his pocket.

"Ibrahim, I want to give you this. I bought it here last night. My watch was stolen, so I got this one. But then, my watch was found, so I don't need it anymore. You helped me a lot, so I want to give it to you as a gift."

"No, I don't want to," Ibrahim replied sincerely.

Emin, fully aware of Ibrahim's honesty, continued to insist. Yet, Ibrahim didn't accept. Meanwhile, Jusuf, who had brought İbrahim's tea and placed it on the table, was about to leave, but Emin stopped him by grabbing his arm. It crossed Emin's mind that there might be another reason for Ibrahim's stern expression despite his poverty. He asked Ibrahim to translate his words to Jusuf while using hand gestures to underscore his point:

"You know this, I bought it last night. Now I'm giving it to Ibrahim. You're a witness. OK? You're a witness. I'm giving this watch to Ibrahim."

"OK, OK. Nema problema."

"Yes, nema problema. OK, Ibrahim?"

Finally, Ibrahim consented.

"Thank you."

"Good man, good man," Jusuf patted Emin on the back this time as he spoke.

Upon Ibrahim's question, he explained in detail what had happened the night before.

"I'm sorry," İbrahim said.

"Everyone said, 'I'm sorry. Now, you did, too. But it's not your fault. Anyway, the police caught those swindlers quickly."

"Well, you're a guest here."

"These things happen, never mind Ibrahim. I'll go and check on my friend now. Maybe she's awake. If you're not busy, can you wait? We can go around together."

"I'm not busy. I can wait. Where do you want to go?"

"I don't know. Let's show my friend around."

"Would your friend like to go to the monastery?"

"I don't know. We'll ask Rachel."

He went upstairs and knocked on the door. The answer was in English.

"Who is it?"

"It's me, Rachel."

"OK, Emin. Come on in."

Rachel, who had already dressed and was applying makeup, started speaking Turkish again. Ibrahim was already waiting when they came downstairs, and Emin introduced them.

"İbrahim helped me here."

"Me know. Osman told me."

"Shall we have breakfast?"

"No, not now. Is there a chemist here?"

"Chemist what? Here, let me get the dictionary," Emin asked.

"No, no, no. You buy medicine. Chemist."

"I see. Pharmacy. Is there a pharmacy open, İbrahim?"

"Yeah."

"Come on, let's go."

"Wait, can you hold on a minute? There's an English-Turkish dictionary. I'll get it before we go," Emin insisted.

"OK, hurry up."

He ran to the room, rummaged through his suitcase and found the dictionary.

When they set off under İbrahim's guidance, Emin could not overcome his curiosity and asked:

"Rachel, are you OK? Are you sick?"

Rachel whispered, leaning in Emin's ear:

"It's women's day. Not normal. It's early. Because of excitement, I think," Rachel said. She began with an English sentence, then continued in Turkish before switching back to English for the last sentence.

"OK, understand!"

When they reached the pharmacy, Rachel instructed them in simple Turkish:

"You wait here. I go and get it. I get it."

She came out a bit later, trying to fit a plastic bag into her bag.

"Let's go now. Breakfast. All right?"

"OK. İbrahim, where can we have breakfast? Let's go somewhere nice."

Emin wanted to treat Rachel to a good breakfast, thinking, "There's no shortage of money now, anyway."

"There's a big hotel. Is that OK?" İbrahim asked.

"Sure, let's go. But you eat too this time."

İbrahim remained silent. Rachel ordered a croissant with her coffee but settled for a freshly baked Bosnian bun. She briefly left and returned before her order arrived. Emin and İbrahim, who opted for tea over coffee, spread fresh clotted cream and jam on their buns, which Rachel hadn't touched.

"Are you dieting?" Emin asked.

"Yes."

"To maintain your weight?"

"You can ask such things in Turkey. It's considered impolite in England. Men don't ask women about this!"

Emin felt upset when he realised he had made a blunder while trying to build a closer connection.

"I'm sorry."

"OK, OK. It's OK. But you will learn. England is different, Turkey is different. Tradition... What is the word in Turkish?"

Emin checked his dictionary, which said, "Tradition, custom." He repeated it.

"Hah, the custom is different in England. You have to learn."

"Yes. You teach me the customs, and I will teach you Turkish."

"But promise me. You should be patient. You teach me Turkish."

The atmosphere had become more relaxed.

"OK, I promise. What should we do today? There is not much to see. There is a historical monastery. İbrahim says we should go there if you like."

"Let's go."

"It's quite a bit far."

"Is it too far? We can walk?"

"You can't walk. Take a taxi. Three or four hours, you go up and back," İbrahim intervened.

"Quite far."

"But we have time. The bus is at twelve at night. Midnight."

"We better go during the day; we don't go at night," Rachel stated.

"Right now?"

"At noon. In an hour or two."

"OK, it's up to you." Emin had recalled Osman's advice.

Emin had initially planned to set off at midnight, but he was happy with Rachel's suggestion. If the police attempted to take a statement regarding the previous night's incident, they wouldn't be able to locate them. After settling the bill and returning to the motel, Rachel took the key and headed to their room. At the door, Emin bid farewell to Ibrahim, once again expressing his gratitude.

"I'd like to come and say 'goodbye' to your mum. We don't have much time. Kiss her hands for me."

"Yeah. Have a good trip."

When he knocked on the door and entered the room with the call, "Come on in", he found Rachel sitting on her bed with her suitcase packed and zipped up.

"I'll pack my bags. Then, we'll go."

They checked out and asked for the bill. After Emin paid, while receiving his passport, Rachel inquired:

"How much money do you have?"

"Around eighty or ninety Marks, I think. I can give it to you?"

"No, no, I don't want. Keep it, just in case!"

Emin paused, trying to count the money in his wallet, and asked:

"Just in case, what does it mean?"

"Maybe you'll need it!"
"Why?"
"Just in case!"

Confused, Emin stopped counting the money, put the wallet in the inside pocket of his jacket and took out the dictionary from his side pocket. Rachel was saying, "Just in case... Maybe you'll need it!"

"Got it. OK! Shall we go or wait?"
"Let's go. It's better. We'll take the first bus."
"So, we'll get the first bus."
"Yes."

This time, Emin repeated the words he had just learnt.
"Just in case!"
"Yeah, just in case!"

Rachel chuckled at Emin's effort. Emin discreetly handed ten Marks to Jusuf while bidding farewell to the motel staff.

Although they had to wait for Jusuf to find a taxi, they still arrived at the bus station with ten minutes to spare before the noon bus departed. Taking their seats in the middle rows on the right side, Emin gave the window seat to Rachel, thinking, 'Let her enjoy the view; she had not been able to see much in the darkness of the night at first.

While Emin thought so, Rachel didn't seem interested in the surroundings. As soon as the bus departed, she pulled a map of Belgrade and a booklet from her bag.

"We need to find a hotel."
"OK."

She studied the booklet and the map on her lap for nearly an hour. Then, she pointed to a spot on the map she had marked with a pencil and said to Emin:

"See, this hotel. It's not expensive."

Emin glanced at the spot Rachel indicated, but he didn't particularly care where they would stay. Rachel continued:

"Close to the city centre."

"Fine, if you say so."

She neatly folded the map and placed it in her bag along with the booklet labelled "Belgrade." Rachel glanced around before resting her head against the window, and drowsiness quickly overcame her. The fatigue from the previous night still lingered. Emin suppressed his growing desire for a cigarette so as not to disturb Rachel, waiting until the bus made a stop. Upon reaching the rest area, he gently touched Rachel's arm, noticing she was still asleep.

"Shall we go and eat?"

"You go. You eat. I will sleep."

"Can I get you something?"

"No."

With half-opened eyes, she went back to sleep after her answer. Emin felt a sense of guilt as he entered the restaurant at the rest stop. He changed his mind as he was about to sit at the table. He decided to buy the buns he saw at the door entrance. Emin extended his cupped hand, in which he had collected the small change remaining in his pocket, to the woman who wrapped four pastries in paper and handed them to him, just as he had done at the post office earlier. The woman behind the counter counted the money. It wasn't enough. He felt frustrated by the "no" she uttered with a nod when he took ten Marks from his wallet, but there was nothing he could do. Emin made three signs with the fingers of his left hand and showed the change in his right palm. The woman left a few coins and took the money. She took one of the buns from the packet, and Emin left with the remaining ones. By the time he threw and extinguished his second cigarette, other passengers had started to arrive. As he boarded the bus and went to his seat, Emin sat down gently, mindful not to wake Rachel, who he noticed was still asleep. However, the noise of other passengers boarding woke Rachel, and she responded to Emin's smile similarly. Rachel didn't refuse the offering Emin handed her, taking one of the buns for himself, but she asked:

"Are these two for me?"

Emin took refuge in a lie, thinking, "After all, it's white" and confirmed:

"Yes. I ate one bun before."

He was unsure how to respond to Rachel's second question as she was about to finish the first bun.

"Drink?"

"Ehm, not enough money."

"You had eighty Marks."

"They didn't take Marks. Only Yugoslav Dinars. It wasn't enough."

"But I've had some!"

These words, uttered while the bus was in motion, implied that "you should have come and asked me."

"I didn't want to wake you."

"OK. No problem."

Rachel wrapped the package and put it in her bag without eating the second bun. It was Emin's turn to succumb to sleep, weighed down by the feeling of satiety from the bun he had eaten, even if it was only one. Although there were exceptions, Emin could not sleep on journeys unless highly exhausted. He closed his eyes. He started to think about the plane journey.

He would board an aeroplane for the first time in his life. It's not that his problem of looking up from the ground, let alone down from above, hadn't crossed his mind, given his enslavement to acrophobia, a fear of heights. Nevertheless, he was now flying inwardly, feeling lightened, and about to drift into sleep. Rachel's arrival dispelled the uncertainties and tension Emin had been experiencing, allowing him to sleep soundly until the bus entered the outskirts of Belgrade.

While the bus conductor, standing in the aisle, was looking at the point on the map, shown by Rachel over Emin without touching him, Emin woke up and saw the city lights. The bus conductor took the map entirely for a closer look. Sleepy, he could not understand what Rachel was trying to say, nor what the driver's 'OK, OK' was about. He asked Rachel, who was folding and putting the map back in her bag with the same neatness as before:"

"We arrived?"

"Yeah, yeah. A little more."

Before reaching the coach station, as the bus was slowing down to stop somewhere in the city, the driver called as he was gesturing towards them:

"Lady, lady."

Rachel realised she was being called and stood up from her seat, and Emin followed her. After handing Rachel's suitcase, which was the size of a large handbag, and Emin's suitcase, the bus driver jumped on the slowly moving bus. While they were signalling for passing taxis on a well-lit street in Belgrade, hoping to catch one, Rachel explained:

"The bus station is quite far. Our hotel is closer to here!"

Finally, a taxi stopped a few steps ahead of them. Five minutes later, they were at the hotel. On the side of the marble stairs curving upwards to the upper floors, just opposite the entrance door, the receptionist of the high-ceilinged hotel was talking to a man in an exquisite coat. Emin noticed a woman at the first step of the stairs whom he hadn't seen when he entered, her right hand resting on the handrail. When their eyes briefly met, she raised the fur collar of her coat with her left hand and half-turned as if attempting to conceal her face. Emin's intuition told him what the woman had come there for with the man at the reception desk. The man, taking his key and leaving the reception, started to grope the woman's buttocks over her coat as they climbed the stairs, which put an end to Emin's curiosity. His assumption had been proved right. Meanwhile, Rachel was trying to explain to the receptionist, who did not speak English, that she wanted a room with two beds in the cheap hotel she had chosen, unknowingly that it was used for such things.

As Rachel put her suitcase on the floor next to one of the beds, Emin tried to find English words to express what he wanted to say.

"Dinner. Out."

"Yeah, go out now. To eat. I'm going to the loo first."

When she came out of the loo, Rachel was again flipping through the map of Belgrade she had spread out on the bed.

"Rachel, I'm going downstairs. I'm going for a smoke; I'll wait for you there."

"OK, I'll be right there."

In the insufficient light of the dimly lit street, he, as he sometimes did, flicked the nearly smoked-up cigarette, trapped between his index and middle fingers, onto the smooth asphalt. Rachel's arrival had taken longer than he expected.

"It must be the state of womanhood. What must that condition be like, one we do not understand by living it ourselves but only witness its existence?" This question reminded him of a shy request made by a female friend with whom he had developed a close friendship, both with her husband and with herself, during a meeting of the Party Central Committee sitting next to him. His friend, who had requested a break in the meeting about half an hour earlier, leaned over and whispered in his ear after giving his elbow a nudge, "Can you ask for a break? I requested one before. I've just started my period and need to use the toilet. I can't ask again now." Aslihan, another female friend of his, once summarised the closeness he had developed with some of her female friends: "We forget about our genders when we're in the same environment with you. Around you, we're neither women nor are you just a man." Recalling this incident from the past, which made him smile, Emin realised that he hadn't revisited his memories as often as he had throughout the earlier stage of his journey since Rachel's arrival.

"Focusing on tomorrow somehow makes us forget about yesterday today. However, it's crucial to remember that yesterday brought us to today when we contemplate tomorrow. The phrase 'fish memory' must have originated from here! When this is experienced on a social basis... Not when it is experienced, but when it is made to be experienced! For this purpose, the rulers rewrite history over and over again. The incoming ones erase the outgoing ones and start the history with themselves. They put themselves at the centre, and the 'fish' takes the bait!"

Rachel's question, whose arrival he had not realised, snapped Emin out of his thoughts:

"I was late because I phoned Osman at the hotel. He's not at home. I left a message. I will call again in the morning."

"OK!"

Emin had compressed his answer with one word while Rachel was trying to make sense of the stillness on Emin's face and dug deeper:

"You upset ... ... 'yüzgün'?" Rachel wanted to utter the Turkish equivalent of "upset", but instead of saying "üzgün" she had told yüzgün, which means hundred days in English.

"No, no, no. I've been thinking."

"Think? Think what?"

Emin squirmed, silently urging himself, "Come on, speak now if you can... If you can explain it..." Then, responded to Rachel:

"It doesn't matter. Friends... Past."

"I don't understand."

Were the words he used incomprehensible, or was it his contemplation of the past? He couldn't quite tell. Changing the subject, as they walked in the direction they had arrived by taxi, Emin pointed to the road ahead with his hand:

"Is there a restaurant in this direction?"

"The city centre is in this direction.

They peered through the restaurant window on the right side of the street, which became more illuminated as they distanced themselves from the hotel. All the tables were covered with white tablecloths, on which the spoons, knives, forks, and plates set, each featuring a long candle in the centre, were available except for one. A waiter in a black suit, noticing them peering through the window, fiddled with the middle of his bow tie, then opened the door. Upon realising that Rachel and Emin were speaking a different language, he invited them in English:

"Welcome, welcome."

They echoed each other's words as it was getting late: "We stop searching further." This was followed by the waiter's reiterated 'welcome,' and they went inside. Rachel took the chair the waiter pulled out for her while Emin sat opposite her.

After a while, as they perused the menus the waiter had brought, Rachel confirmed Emin's judgment.

"I think it's expensive," she said, glancing at the prices listed in English under each dish. Nevertheless, she declined Emin's suggestion to go somewhere else as he was anxious about being a burden. On the other hand, she added a glass of red wine for her to her order.

"Don't worry! I'll get a glass of red wine. And you?"

"OK, same."

Their food had not yet arrived when they clinked their wine glasses for the first time. Then, a trio of guitar, accordion, and violin players appeared by their side, carrying a song that seemed to rise from their instruments. The song "Two Strangers," originally sung by Frank Sinatra, enveloped the table where they sat. Emin had noticed them approaching and briefly had thought they were headed for what appeared to be a stage a little beyond their table.

"You'd wish Osman were here now, wouldn't you? It would be romantic."

"They think we were 'lovers'."

"Yes, they assumed we were two lovers."

"Assume or think?"

As they attempted to communicate in Turkish, Emin tried to explain the difference in the meaning and use of these two words. Seeing Rachel's puzzled expression, Emin took a dictionary from his pocket and listed the English equivalents of the words.

"There are many words. They are different. Give me the dictionary, please?" Rachel requested.

Rachel, while looking at the English equivalents of the Turkish words and then their Turkish counterparts, the small orchestra, realising they were not being attended to, continued their songs without interruption, walking towards the other occupied table in the hall. When Rachel noticed the musicians departing as the music grew faint, Emin interpreted her facial expression as a sign that she was pleased they were leaving.

"Turkish is difficult. Same word, many meanings."

"Yes. There are many English equivalents."

"They... wanted money, I think."

With a swift glance, she pointed to the trio continuing their song at the other table.

"I think so."

"I looked at the dictionary at length for the word 'masus', said Rachel, meant to say "on purpose."

"I noticed that, but the word is not 'masus' but 'mahsus'. Can you repeat after me?".

Rachel kindly warned Emin, "Say, 'Please.'"

"Please!"

"Yes, you must say 'Please.'"

Rachel realised that Emin was trying to correct her pronunciation by noting the omission of the letter "h" in the word "mahsus". She responded to his request by repeating it:

"I did it 'mahsus'. I don't want to give money to them."

The mutual language learning-teaching endeavours ended upon the waiter's arrival carrying a large tray laden with orders.

Emin, who had avoided the trouble of choosing food by saying 'the same' no matter what Rachel wanted, recognised the taste in his mouth as he dipped a piece of bread on the tip of his fork into the sauce of the dish and took the first bite. It was vegetable stew. He even ate the courgette, which he doesn't usually like. The salad was a familiar shepherd's salad, as people call it in Turkey, with extra pieces of feta cheese. After finishing his plate, he didn't feel he was full. 'Yugoslav butter is delicious,' he concluded while buttering and eating the pieces of bread he tore off, just as Rachel had done.

"Nefis!" Rachel said. It was the equivalent of the word yummy!

When Emin repeated the word "Nefis?" with a question mark, as if asking where she learnt it, Rachel replied:

"Osman told me."

"Osman taught you?"

"Osman taught me, he told me."

"Taught, you should say, not told."

"Osman told me when I cooked."

"I see. Osman said, 'Yummy' for the meal you cooked!

"Yeah. He always does."

* * *

[Flashforward - March 1989:

"The fish is ready. I am going to put it in the oven. Now, Emin can prepare his magic salad. But less salt, please!"

Rachel, who had prepared the fish and was about to put it in the oven, announced that she could leave the cramped kitchen to Emin to make the salad she called magical. The English woman, who ate even cucumbers half-boiled, had "learnt to eat salad like a salad" since she got into a relationship with Osman; however, she had loved the salad Emin had made for her when she visited Istanbul. While preparing the salad, for which she said, "Osman doesn't make it like this," Emin would rub the finely chopped onion with salt. After washing it a few times and removing the salt, he would mix salt, oil, and plenty of squeezed lemon on the finely chopped cucumbers, tomatoes, fresh peppers, and parsley. As he was making the final touch on the salad, Emin gave Osman a further hint about his secret:

"Garnishing with parsley is a made-up fairy tale. Parsley should also get its share of salt, oil, and lemon. When you chop the parsley, the aroma really comes out. There's your magic salad."

Rachel handed Osman the tray of fish, which she had taken out of the packet and placed in the oven earlier, without even adding salt, let alone any sauce. Osman was distributing the fish while simultaneously slurping and muttering to himself.

"Nefis! Nefis."

Emin was again being a "straight shooter"!

"Wait, you haven't even tasted the fish yet!"

"Obvious, it is nefis, nefis! Look how good it smells!"

Rachel looked at Emin with a questioning expression, even though she smiled, pleased that what she had done was appreciated by Osman. She didn't quite understand what Emin was saying. Emin was unaware she felt uncomfortable when neither she nor her work received praise. Osman hadn't lectured Emin on this matter yet.

Emin was trying to enrich the bland taste of the fish by putting plenty of salt on it and the salad while questioning Osman's remark inwardly, "How delicious it is!".

As the plates were being cleared away, Osman praised them again. "Nefis... It's marvellous. Thank you."

"Emin, the magic salad is nefis!" Rachel praised.

Realising that it was his turn to say something. Emin joined them:

"Nice fish. Thank you."

"Welcome!"

Pleased to be liked, when Rachel came into the kitchen with plates in her hand, Emin couldn't refrain himself:

"You're exaggerating, Osman. What is 'nefis?!"

"Never mind. This is how it is here. You give compliments. Make people feel good. And it wasn't bad."

"I didn't say it was bad, but it wasn't 'nefis' either."

"Learn it, learn it! You'll compliment women every chance you get. You haven't figured women out yet."

"When you tell people what they lack, they improve themselves and can do better. Otherwise, they will keep repeating themselves if you say, 'Oh, how well you are doing.'"

"Oh, never mind all that. It's just a meal. The English don't have a culinary culture anyway!"

"Yes, I had heard that, but when I came here, I realised it was almost true."

Emin got up and went to the kitchen.

"Rachel, you get out. I'll do the dishes."

Osman, who was coming behind them, stopped in the doorway.

"Come on, get out, both of you. I'll do the dishes. One of you made fish, and one of you made salad. Make it equal."

Osman repeated as he followed Emin out of the kitchen, intercepting Rachel at the door and planting a kiss on her lips:

"Nefis!"

"Which is it? Food or Rachel's lips?"

"Both!"

Rachel jokingly scolded them both in Turkish: "Ayıp! Ayıp![80]**"]**

*   *   *

Emin praised the food and the butter, which he could not get enough of because he was starving.

"Yes, it was delicious. Very similar to our food."

"A cigarette after a delicious meal would be a different pleasure," he thought; yet, he couldn't light his cigarette after Rachel's warning:

"I'm not done eating. Please wait."

"Are you going to smoke too?"

"No, I don't smoke. I never smoke!"

Rachel tried to explain Emin's question, "So, why then?" as if she captured it from his gaze.

"In England, everyone finishes the food. Then cigarettes."

"No one smokes until everyone's finished eating."

"Yes. Tradition, as in... Huh, custom. You should learn these things."

"OK, thank you."

"You're welcome. Did I say that right?"

"Yes, that's what we say in Turkish."

"Thank you, too."

Although Rachel made mistakes when she spoke Turkish, Emin let them go without correction as his mind focused on the dessert menu brought by the waiter. Even though he felt hungry, he preferred not to increase the bill amount. Consequently, Emin agreed to follow Rachel's request for the bill. They walked back the way they came after the meal, and Emin lit a cigarette. Still, he didn't derive

---

[80] "Shame! Shame!"

the same pleasure he usually did when smoking without getting up from his seat. Then he lit another one.

"You smoke too much. Not good!"

"It's a bit stressful, but I'll stop when I go to England."

Although he was thinking about it, he mentioned quitting to prevent getting any advice on this subject. For some reason, he was annoyed getting lectures on health from anyone.

"Yeah, that'd be good."

When they arrived in the room, one was in the bathroom while the other put on their pyjamas, each mindful of their privacy.

When the lights were switched off, he responded to Rachel's words, "Good night, sweet dreams," with the exact words. Emin, who was worried, "Who knows when I'll fall asleep on a full stomach, especially after sleeping so much on the bus?"

It didn't take long for Emin to fall asleep. Later, he explained, "I think it was the impact of the Balkan air, the effect of the weather change, or the feeling of being free from anxiety, or perhaps a combination of them all."

The sound of running water from the bathroom told Emin Rachel that she was taking a shower when he woke up from that recurring nightmare of the moment of failing in the attempt to run away. Emin turned towards the window. The bathroom door was out of sight. It was a precaution against the possibility of Western women coming out of the bathroom naked, which he had seen in films. Rachel came out wrapped in towels, and when she went to the window and opened the curtains, he wanted to announce that he was awake:

"Good morning."

"Good morning, Emin. Are you going to take a shower?"

"Yes, now."

"Without looking at the towelled Rachel, he pulled clean underwear from his suitcase, which he had hand-washed himself in Novi Pazar. After quickly grabbing his shirt and trousers, he entered the shower, making sure Rachel could dress comfortably while he was in the bathroom. To prevent his clothes from getting wet, he placed them under his pyjamas on the top shelf. He knew his habit: everything got soaked while he took a shower.

When he came out, Rachel was already dressed and busy applying her usual light makeup.

"Hope you feel refreshed and well."

"Thank you."

Seeing Emin had already dressed, she asked him to sit next to her:

"Now, let's talk briefly about what we will do. I'll tell you one by one. There's a plane leaving for London on Monday at nine. When the plane arrives in London, I get off first, and you leave after. You don't say at the customs in London that we travelled together. You will learn three sentences before we arrive and say them at passport control in London."

"OK. Let's write it down."

"Yeah, that can be good."

Rachel took out a small notebook from her handbag, tore off a piece of paper on which she wrote three sentences, and handed it to Emin.

"This passport is fake. I am applying for asylum. I want an interpreter."

Rachel explained the meaning of what she wrote on the paper, emphasised the importance of conjugating verbs correctly, as recommended by Osman, and reiterated what was written:

While Running Away

"This passport is fake. I am applying for asylum. I want an interpreter. Now you say these in English."

Emin tried, but Rachel didn't like it. She attempted to correct each of his mistakes and asked, "Repeat after me!" With one exception, everything was more or less going well. He couldn't say "this" the way Rachel wanted him to. They repeated it over and over, but it didn't work. They became tired.

"We'll practise again later. OK?"

"OK, fine. There's just one problem."

"Problem?"

"Yes. There is no Yugoslavia entry stamp in my passport."

"I don't understand!"

"I'll show my passport."

He sat down next to Rachel again after pulling out his passport from the inside pocket of his jacket, which he'd hung on the back of the chair. He flipped open the page with the Bulgarian customs entry and exit stamps.

"These are stamps from Bulgarian customs. No Yugoslavia."

After taking it from his hand, Rachel flipped through Emin's passport. She spotted the Turkish and Bulgarian customs stamps, but that was all.

"Why not?"

He summarised what happened.

"Too bad."

"Yes, it's bad. Here is the entry stamp for Bulgaria, and the exit stamp from Bulgaria to Yugoslavia is on the same page."

"I see. Still bad. Maybe it's a problem."

"Yeah, I know."

Rachel's facial expressions, which showed that she had been thinking for a moment, eventually relaxed with the relief of finding a solution.

"Osman advised me that if there was a problem, we should pretend to be a couple in Yugoslavia."

"Yeah, Osman and I had thought and discussed it before. That's what actually I said at the motel in Novi Pazar."

"Whenever there's a problem, I could say, 'This is my boyfriend.' You and I are going to meet my family in London. If we run into trouble at passport control, I'll bang my fist on the table and play the role of a snobbish English woman. 'I demand you to call the British consulate!' That's what I am going to say and do."

"What does 'snobbish' mean?" Emin asked.

Rachel was unsure of the Turkish equivalent of the word.

"Wait, let me look it up in the dictionary," Emin said as he searched for the word.

Rachel, eager to learn the Turkish equivalent herself, attempted to read and pronounce it.

"Your pronunciation is good."

"You got it all now, OK?" Rachel asked with a smile, wanting to double-check.

Yeah, if there's a problem..." Emin imitated Rachel's previous gesture of banging her fist on the table, "You'll bang your fist on the table, just like an English woman with a snobbish manner and say, 'Call the British consulate!' All right?"

"Yes. You should also call Osman. A bit later, at the reception, Osman will provide further instructions and let you know what you need to do. However, you must work hard, OK? And 'memorise' three sentences. Understand?"

Emin nodded, realising that the word "memorise" meant something like "remember", although he did not know the exact meaning.

"It's all right. Don't worry about it. Shall we go? Let's have breakfast." Emin suggested.

"First, we phone. Then breakfast. "

"Oh, yeah."

This time, someone else at the reception desk, even with limited English proficiency, understood what Rachel was saying, and after a while, the telephone connected. Rachel did not prolong the conversation after the greetings with Osman and handed the receiver to Emin.

"Hi."

"Hi. How are you? You met Rachel without any trouble."

"Yeah, yeah. No problem."

"Listen to me carefully. Tomorrow morning, you'll board a plane to come here. As I mentioned to Hasan earlier, you can't stay there for more than six days. Your time there will expire tomorrow, so please be mindful. You've got to catch that plane. I've got a kick-ass human rights lawyer lined up for you, one of the top dogs. We'll be hanging out at the airport, waiting for you. Rachel has to breeze through customs first. It's essential to keep her out of this. So, you should remain on the plane and leave as late as possible. The solicitor will be there during your interview. Wait for her to arrive before saying anything. Don't mention Rachel. Basically, state that you came alone. After the interview, they might detain you and send you to the camp for a while. Don't stress about it; we'll work on getting you out as early as possible. But remember, they might also release you. Be prepared for anything."

"Hasan mentioned that you already have my documents, including the officially stamped court judgment. Isn't everything clear? I have a conviction. Why would they detain me?"

"The documents have arrived. We can't hand over your whole martial law court file to the immigration office; it hasn't been translated yet, and it's quite a lengthy document. The court's summary judgment has already been translated, which should be sufficient. At the interview with the immigration officials, describe the tortures you endured. You can even exaggerate."

"Do I need to exaggerate? I even have a forensic report."

"I didn't receive the forensic report."

"I know. We don't have the report, but we can get it from the Bursa Courthouse."

"OK, mentioned that at the interview. Stop being a 'truth teller' and start exaggerating."

"Won't it be detrimental to me if it turns out to be untrue?"

"It won't, it won't. I know what everyone exaggerates, but it's up to you."

"I think it's the right not to. It's not good if the truth comes out later."

"OK, let's not debate this now. By the way, while I'm thinking about it, when you go to passport control, be relaxed and speak with a confident, upright stance. Don't give the impression of a frightened, timid person. After all, they are officers of the state. Sometimes, they may aggressively talk to you. Just ignore it. Is there anything you want to ask?

"No, there's one thing. I mentioned it to Rachel, but probably she didn't tell you."

"What is it?"

"They didn't stamp my entry into Yugoslavia at customs, but they did stamp me when leaving Bulgaria, which shows where I came from. So, Rachel and I will stick to our plan of posing as a couple."

"That's not ideal! Nevertheless, we have to minimise Rachel's involvement. Follow her advice."

"Alright, don't worry."

"OK, see you tomorrow, inshallah. Let's not prolong the call any further."

"I hope so. Do you have anything to tell Rachel?"

"Yes, do pass it to her."

"Alright. Thank you very much for everything."

He heard Osman say, "It's nothing," as he handed the phone's receiver to Rachel.

While Rachel talked, she glanced at her watch from time to time. She greeted Osman with a "Hello," followed by a few "OKs." However, Emin couldn't hear what Osman was saying. After giving the phone to the receptionist and settling the bill, Rachel briefed Emin about her conversation with Osman.

"Osman is worried about the stamp issue. But you'll follow in my footsteps. So, no problem."

Although Emin suppressed the laughter from within due to the change she made in the word's meaning, Rachel caught the smile on his face.

Emin had found the word's meaning change, caused by the dots above the 'I,' amusing. Rachel had said 'Cani sikildi' in Turkish instead of 'canı sıkıldı,' which doesn't mean 'He is worried' but rather "Murderer got fucked."

"What is it?"

Emin avoided getting into a discussion about the amusing pronunciation and briefly confirmed his cooperation:

"It's all right. OK, I'll do whatever you say. Aren't you hungry? Shall we have breakfast?"

"Fine. We'll go to the city centre. We'll have breakfast."

"Shall we have breakfast in the city centre?"

"Yeah, hang on. I have something to ask the receptionist."

Rachel retrieved a Belgrade map from her bag and laid it on the reception desk. The receptionist answered her questions, marking points on the map as Emin observed, trying to understand. When their conversation was done, Rachel, as she folded the map and stowed it in her bag, explained:

"The bus stop for the buses going to the airport is not far. In the morning, we will take a taxi, then the bus to the airport. We'll take the taxi now and go to the city centre. OK? You got it?"

"Yes, I understand."

They didn't have to wait long for the taxi the receptionist had called after talking to Rachel. In less than ten minutes, they reached Terazije Square. Emin was immediately drawn to the square's cleanliness, surrounded by old-style three or four-story buildings, much like their hotel.

"Clean city."

"Oh, yeah. London is filthy."

"Filthy?"

Rachel added more details to the answer to Emin's surprised question. "Some districts are clean. Many districts are dirty."

Emin, unfamiliar with the term "district," reached for his dictionary, assuming it meant "neighbourhood." Rachel objected, and he put the dictionary back in his pocket.

"Don't always look at the dictionary. Understand? Come, this cafe seems nice. Now, let's have breakfast there first."

The café facing the square wasn't crowded, despite being close to noon. Inside, Rachel and Emin glanced at the food displayed in the long buffet showcase, which stretched from one end to the other, with only one-meter entrance and exit spaces on both sides, creating a rectangular hall. Three young waiters, two women and one man, stood behind the kiosk, smiling at the two strangers. As they returned to the buffet's centre, the male waiter gestured toward the tables, signalling for them to sit down. Another young waitress, wandering around the hall, waited for them to sit down at the third table from the door, by the window overlooking the square, and handed them menus. Rachel ordered two croissants she couldn't find in Novi Pazar the day before. She was going to drink coffee again. Emin, unable to order eggs due to concerns about his gall bladder and not wanting any trouble, ordered two scones, like the day before, along with tea, butter, and honey. The coffee arrived in porcelain teapots, just like the tea, alongside the rest of their order. The service wasn't what Emin had heard about Soviet Union restaurants; everything they ordered came quickly. Emin also requested lemon, and the waiter promptly brought a half lemon cut into thin slices even before the tea was poured into his cup.

Although he tried to slow down, Emin finished his breakfast before Rachel and thought of the shop in Kadıköy Fishmongers Bazaar, which he had discovered when he lived in Söğütlüçeşme and started to buy strained yoghurt. "Sir, try our butter. It is fresh, daily from Beykoz. It's as good as Trabzon's one." He was comparing the butter he had just eaten with the one he had started buying from that shop. He began to tell Rachel where Beykoz was, where the bazaar and that shop were. Rachel remembered this bazaar, a ten-minute walk from Hasan and Aslihan's house in Moda, where she stayed as a guest. It was Emin's attempt to kill time by chatting. He was waiting for Rachel to finish her breakfast so he could light a cigarette. While telling these things, he consulted the dictionary, which reminded him of their conversation when they left the hotel. What was the word "district"? He looked it up. He had guessed correctly. He would remember this experience in London when he was learning the language. His teacher would advise him that he could deduce the meaning of a word not only with the help of a dictionary but also by looking at its place in the narrative, suggesting that it would be better to do so.

They ordered more tea and coffee. Emin went to the public toilet for his daily morning routine, although he doesn't prefer using it. When he returned, Rachel was looking for places to visit and ways to pass the time. She mentioned some museums, but Emin didn't mind. His thoughts were on the next day. After spending about two hours at the café, they left for a walk and later to the cinema, as Rachel had suggested. Although the sky was gathering clouds, the weather was warm, and the sun shone brightly on 12 February. Emin remembered that it was the "liberation" day of Marash. The city was claimed to have "Liberated itself", Marash, where his family had settled, a family initially stretching on one side to Birecik in Urfa and on the other to Kastoria.[81]

***

[Flashforward - 2015:
"MARASH... is described as 'The city that liberated itself.' "Before he wrote his note beginning with these lines, on the centenary of the 'Great Catastrophe' of the Armenian Genocide, he had made an interpretation of 'self-liberation' based on the history of his own family. Still, until that day, he had never searched the internet

---
[81] Kastoria is a city in northern Greece in the region of Western Macedonia.

on this subject, on the Armenians of Marash. When the clue provided by his family history coincided with some information from across the country, he was sure of his conclusion and the corresponding course of action. Nevertheless, reinforcing this with additional data could have enriched his conclusion. He shared the video titled *"Memories of Marash"*, which he came across on YouTube, on his Facebook page with a note of his own:

"MARAS... *It is described as 'the city that liberated itself'!* Is there any other untold history?

By 11 February, the Turks were not in the city but in the surrounding villages to which they had retreated. Still, the French troops suddenly evacuated the city that night, taking as many Armenians as possible with them.

Is there an under-emphasised connection between the return of some of the Armenians who survived the genocide in 1915, after the First World War and 'self-liberation'?

Let's look at the following from another source:

'On the night of 11 February 1920, the French and Armenians, knowing the situation of the people of Kahramanmaras, suddenly ceased the fire and made preparations to flee. (...) They started to flee at midnight. In the meantime, the people of Kahramanmaras switched off the lights ['had they switched off the lights' or had the Turks evacuated the city? -My note-], **thinking that a raid could happen at any moment.**

'As a matter of fact, the French and Armenians set fire to some houses at night and started to flee. Upon this, the people of Kahramanmaras grabbed their knives, axes, pistols, picks and shovels and did not give up their pursuit.'

Those who 'grabbed their knives, axes, pistols, picks and shovels' behind those who fled... And the name of the stream flowing in Marash is KANLIDERE, the BLODYSTREAM.

What does that tell you?

And also... Apart from the confectionery and ice cream businesses, the Armenians owned the businesses... And then... Whose hands did the property and assets of Armenians later fall into?

Did the return of some Armenians signal a different danger? Were the people of the 'self-saving city' actually saving these 'properties'?"

"Do you know, Zafer," he would later explain, "they poured nationalist poisons into all our brains. It wasn't only in primary school that our brains were dumbed down. Being attached to an idea with faith makes a person stupid. That is how the brain of the children of the Republican generation was dumbed down. Our families, whose brains were also dumbed down, were active participants in poisoning us. One side of my family is Kurdish, yet we were part of the 'Citizen Speak Turkish' campaigns during secondary school. Again, in those years, we shouted 'Cyprus is Turkish and will remain Turkish' against the 'whore Greek' during the marches in Marash. The tragicomic thing was in 1988, when my maternal aunt's daughter told me the news, 'Oh Abi, do you know, our maternal grandmother was originally Greek, but they hid it from us!'

One side of the family was a 'Byzantine bitch', and we, including myself, were swearing at them! But I have never ever sworn at Armenians in my life; I have never used the term 'Armenian' as a swear word. Do you know why? I'll tell you why... but let me admit, I didn't think about it before. But now I know."

His eyes began to fill with tears. He gulped. His voice, trembling as he tried to control it, became muffled as he continued speaking.

"In the first months of my schooling in Marash, I heard people boasting about why Kanlıdere was called 'bloody' in Marash: 'For days that stream flowed bloody, they cut up all the Armenians, children, women, girls, from the age of seven to seventy, and threw them into that stream'. When I heard this, I had visions of a child's throat being slit. It must have settled in my heart. Even in those days when I considered myself a socialist, I remember swearing at the Greeks with nationalist feelings and chants. Nevertheless, Armenian and Armenianness never came together with swearing in my language. I remained a child, with those beheaded children who always remained children inside me."

Tears welled up in his eyes as he talked about the children. Neither he nor Zafer made a sound for a while.

"Go wash your face," Zafer said as he sat down at the computer, "and in the meantime, I'll have a look at that video of the 'self-liberated' city you were talking about."]

* * *

On another 12 February, as they left the café in Belgrade, the clouds thickened, and the "dumbfounding" drops began to fall; they went to the cinema. Even the film's title in English with Serbian subtitles did not interest Emin. He, who tried to keep himself awake for a while by his effort to understand, gradually became detached from the film. His eyelids drooped. From time to time, he would open his eyes for a short while and wake up, but he would soon fall asleep again. At the film's end, he woke up with the audience's voices added to the lights.

"You slept too much."

"Yeah. I didn't understand. I didn't understand the dialogues; I fell asleep."

"You listen, you'll learn quickly. Understanding is not important."

"I think you're right."

He was sincere when he said this. He remembered a friend of his at the bank. Cemil had told him that after he started learning English, the English radio was always on at home, and he had never turned it off, even when sleeping.

There was no trace of rain when they left the cinema. It had sprinkled and passed. They were going to eat somewhere near the hotel, where they decided to return on foot. On the road Rachel found on the map, they did not come across a restaurant close to the hotel. They didn't want to pay a high bill like the night before, so they went in and out of side roads. Finally, they found a small, affordable restaurant but not very tasty for Emin. Still, according to Rachel, it was "nefis".

Rachel took her pyjamas from the suitcase when they returned to the hotel.

"I will take a shower."

"All right. I'll go downstairs and have a cigarette."

"You're smoking too much again."

"Yeah. I told you before, it's a bit stressful."

It was apparent Emin wanted to drop the subject. Rachel realised and changed the subject.

"When you come back, we'll do some practice."

Emin, whose hand involuntarily went to his jacket pocket, felt something missing as he found and took out the paper on which those three sentences were written. He checked his other side pocket. It was not there.

"No dictionary. I think I left it in the café."

"It's no good. You'll need it, maybe on the plane, maybe at Heathrow."

"Heathrow?"

"Airport, London."

"Oh, I see. Shall we go and have a look?"

"It will not be there. It's late."

"Anyway, it doesn't matter."

He reassured himself, "I have less than twenty-four hours to get to London. I managed mostly without a dictionary this far before Rachel arrived, and I'll get the rest, too", but what really gave him relief was the thought that he had less than twenty-four hours to get to London.

Turning his back to the light from the hotel window, he tried to memorise, smoking one cigarette after another. When convinced that he had memorised it, he tore up the paper. There was no need for it; besides, if it was found on him at passport control, he could get in trouble in Yugoslavia.

He had lingered long enough to give Rachel a chance to shower when he went upstairs and knocked on the door.

"Come on in."

Rachel was already in her pyjamas and half-sitting on her bed.

"You memorised?"

"Yes, I did."

"Good, say it!"

Emin repeated all three sentences one after the other. Rachel, who put down the book in her hand and focused her attention on Emin, was not pleased. She was stuck on the word "this" again. Emin couldn't pronounce the word correctly even though he tried to make her say it by showing the movements of his tongue between his lips and teeth. She finally surrendered!

"OK, OK. No problem. Everyone understands. We'll get up early in the morning. We were required to be at the airport an hour before. Two hours before is good. We'll buy you a ticket. Then we'll have breakfast."

"OK, it's up to you."

"I will read a book for a bit. Light a problem for you?"

"No, no problem. I don't mind."

After going to the bathroom and putting on his pyjamas, he went to bed. He dreamt about the next day.

He didn't see Rachel switch off the light or hear her say "Good night". Before he fell asleep, he dreamt of her calling his mother and friends from London to tell them the news.

It was not yet light when the phone rang in the room. The hotel receptionist had called at 5.30 am, as he had been instructed the day before. And, for the first time in several nights, Emin woke up before his nightmare visited him. It didn't take them long to get ready. When they paid the bill and left, they got into the taxi called by the hotel employee. It was almost six o'clock when Rachel showed the driver their destination, which the receptionist had marked on the map of Belgrade the day before. They travelled for about seven or eight minutes. When they reached the passenger stop, the airport bus was coming towards the taxi a few hundred metres behind. "We're just in time," they rejoiced, only to be in for an unpleasant surprise when the taxi driver pulled the lever on the lower right side of the steering wheel in front of him to open the boot. The handle, whose connecting wire was broken, was left in the driver's hand.

Nevertheless, he went to the back of the taxi and tried to open the boot lid. The bus, which had stopped on Rachel's hand signal, honked its horn and continued on its way when it saw that all the efforts of the taxi driver did not yield any results. One of the passing cars finally stopped and came to help, but to no avail. Gesticulating, the driver told Rachel that they had to find a garage. Willy-nilly, they got back into the taxi. They set out to find an open mechanic shop in a neighbourhood where repair shops were located. The driver pointed at the time on his wristwatch to indicate that it was too early for repair shops to be open while driving through the narrow streets where the repair shops were located. The driver hit the brakes in front of the first garage he saw lifting its shutters. As he got out of the car and explained his problem to the mechanic, Rachel and Emin looked at their watches simultaneously.

"Quarter to seven."

"Yeah, but don't worry. We were at the airport an hour earlier."

"It's enough, right?"

This question was an expression of concern, a search for reassurance. Rachel tried to comfort Emin.

"It is enough. We'll go to the airport by taxi."

The mechanic probed the gap in the wire to which the boot handle was attached, inserting his forefinger through the hole. After saying something to the driver, he walked toward the workshop. He used pliers to reach through the hole, grabbed the end of the wire, and pulled it towards him. Waiting at the back of the taxi, the driver opened the trunk and took their two suitcases. He placed one of the suitcases on the passenger seat next to the driver's seat and the other in the footwell. He made a fist and raised his thumb, signalling "OK" to Emin and Rachel. He said something to the mechanic, then got behind the wheel and drove off without paying anything.

"We want to go to the airport! How much is it?" Rachel inquired.

The driver, seeking confirmation that he had understood Rachel correctly, asked again if the inquiry was about the destination and the fare.

"Airport?"

"Yes!"

"Twenty Marks."

"OK. Please be quick!"

Whether he understood that Rachel wanted him to be quick or he thought he had to hurry, for whatever reason, he shifted gears rapidly. He managed to get his passengers to the airport in just twenty minutes.

They arrived almost half an hour later than initially planned but about the same amount of time, half an hour earlier than they should have. The attendant who said "No" to Rachel, who wanted to buy a ticket by giving her the passport she had taken from Emin, worried Emin. Still, he did not interrupt Rachel, who continued to talk. Finally, Emin sighed an "Oh" when Rachel paid for the ticket. After giving the suitcases and getting the boarding passes, Rachel answered Emin's question, "What happened?".

"No economy class for you. Last minute. First class only!"

Emin, who had never been on a plane, didn't fully comprehend but didn't ask further. "The ticket is bought; that's what matters," as the overwhelming sensation of hunger followed his relief.

"Shall we have breakfast now?"

"No, no, no, no. Passport control first. There might be an issue!"

He followed Rachel, who was obviously more worried than he was.

Initially, Rachel handed her passport to the officer. The officer first examined the photo on the passport, then glanced at Rachel's face, back to the picture on the passport, and stamped the exit mark before returning Rachel's passport to her without uttering a word. Rachel received her visa, stepped away from the control booth, and stood to the side, waiting.

The officer repeated the process he had followed with Rachel's passport, examining the photo and glancing between Emin and the picture. He picked up the stamp and started flipping through the pages, searching for the entry stamp, but couldn't find it. Again, he turned the pages of the passport, one after another. Not finding what he was looking for, he once more flipped through the passport pages, one after another. He said something in English to Emin. As he didn't understand what was being said, Emin looked at Rachel for guidance and asked, 'What?' Stepping forward and leaning towards the officer, Rachel inquired:

"Problem?"

"Yeah, there's a problem. Big, big problem."

He repeated the word "big" in English, stressing and elongating it.

"What is it?"

"Are you travelling together?"

"Yeah. Yeah. Emin is my boyfriend. What's the problem?"

"No entry stamp into Yugoslavia."

"I understand. Emin arrived by bus through Bulgaria. See, there's a stamp from Bulgaria. You can enter Yugoslavia through that, correct?"

"Yes, but no stamp."

"This is your problem. Your officers didn't do their job when he entered. It's not my boyfriend's fault."

Likely realising that the mistake originated from his colleagues, the customs officer changed the subject.

"Why are you heading to England?"

"I reside in England. I'm going to introduce my boyfriend to my parents. We plan to get engaged."

"Give me your passport."

Rachel's complexion turned pale, but she could do nothing except comply with the request. Still, she asked the officer as she handed him her passport:

"Why?"

"I'll make a note of your passport details."

After meticulously recording the details from Rachel's passport one by one, the officer returned the passport to Rachel, glanced at Emin's photograph and then at Emin, and once more shuffled the pages.

"What's your name?"

"Sunullah Devir."

"What is your date of birth?"

"1 January 1962"

Memorising this date had been easy. Emin would simply add a decade to his actual birth year. The day and month were the ones typically chosen by families who, for some reason, did not want to specify their child's exact birthdate. Emin somehow managed to stay calm during moments of danger, and once again, he answered the questions with great confidence. The officer didn't drag it out any longer. He stamped Emin's passport, which Emin took and placed in his pocket. Then, he went to the waiting room with Rachel, arm in arm. Rachel chose two vacant seats and guided Emin toward them.

"Let's get something for breakfast," Emin said, glancing around the lounge.

"No, we'll eat on the plane."

"Aren't you hungry?"

"No, we'll eat on the plane."

Shifting his eyes from the hall to Rachel, Emin noticed she had turned pale.

"Are you alright?"

"I'm fine, but it's too bad."

"I don't understand."

"I'm fine, but the guy wrote down my passport. That's too bad."

"Why?"

"You don't know. A passenger came in illegally to England. Fake passport. Yugoslav plane. British police found out and fined Yugoslav Airlines. A fine of one thousand pounds. The officer noted down everything that was on my passport! They'll find me."

Rachel was searching for a specific Turkish word. However, her limited Turkish vocabulary made it difficult for her to find it. Frustrated, she switched to English:

"They will pass the penalty to me!"

"I don't understand."

"I pay the fine, not Yugoslav Airlines. Now, two officers are looking at us."

As they left passport control, two customs officials were stationed in the gate doorway they had just passed through. At Rachel's alert, Emin noticed that they were observing their direction. İgnoring them, he held Rachel's hands with both hands, pretending they were engrossed in conversation. During this time, he devised a plan in his mind to ease Rachel's:

"If you're fined. I mean, a thousand pound fine. I will pay for it. I'll get it from Turkey. I have national insurance from my bank work. I'll get it."

Even though Emin couldn't clearly explain it to Rachel, he tried to convey that he would withdraw the insurance he had been paying the Bank Retirement Fund for seven years. He was unaware that it was not enough to cover the amount that may be required. He later discovered it was only two hundred pounds when he needed to withdraw the money in the future, all to avoid burdening her family.

"It's too bad."

Half English, half Turkish, Emin tried again to calm her down:

"Don't worry. Calm down now. We have to act normal. You normal, me normal. With those two uniformed officers looking on. OK?"

Emin removed his hands from Rachel's grasp and calmly lit the cigarette he had taken from the pack. The first-morning puff, taken on an empty stomach, left a bitter, rusty taste on his tongue. He didn't have time to finish his cigarette because of Rachel's alert in response to the announcement that passenger boarding was beginning.

"You first class. I'm not. You go first. I will be in the back."

"OK."

Rachel gave him these instructions as he extinguished his cigarette in the ashtray two seats away and walked towards the flight attendants who were checking the entry to the aircraft.

"You take out the passport. Take out the boarding pass. Show it to flight attendants, OK?"

"The ticket?"

What Emin referred to as a ticket was actually a boarding pass.

"Yes, a ticket. That's it, the boarding pass for the aeroplane."

While Running Away

Rachel stayed behind while Emin headed towards the flight attendants, observing their actions. The person in front of Emin handed his passport and card to the stewardess, who then took them and disappeared down the corridor. Emin handed his passport and boarding card together. The stewardess, who first examined the picture on the passport and then gazed at Emin, suspected that things might get complicated when she asked for his name, something she hadn't done with the other passenger.

"Sunullah Devir."

He had just provided his response when Rachel rushed to intervene.

"Is there a problem? He is my friend. He speaks limited English. Can I help you? I can translate into Turkish."

"No, no, there's no problem. I just checked the gentleman's name."

While responding to Rachel, the stewardess wished Emin, to whom she had returned his card and passport, a "Good flight."

The comfort of "Ah, finally, it's over" was short-lived for Emin, replaced by the anxiety of boarding an aeroplane for the first time as he walked down the corridor leading to the plane. The stewardess who welcomed him at the aircraft door examined his boarding pass and directed him to his seat. Another stewardess stood with her arms crossed in front of another curtain separating the flight deck from the passenger area. Emin reached his seat, labelled 3C on his ticket, and took off his coat. He attempted to position his folded coat on the upper shelf using only his right hand, avoiding using both hands. Refraining from raising his left hand, he aimed to conceal the tear in over half of the lining under the armpit from the stewardess and the man occupying the window seat in the same row. He had refrained from retrieving his own suits from his home, where he hadn't returned since August, to evade any potential police surveillance. Due to financial difficulties, he couldn't afford to buy a new one. Aydın, whose measurements were similar to his own, had a suit that was still wearable, although a bit outdated, and he was currently wearing it. As he settled into his seat, he nodded in acknowledgement to the man sitting by the window, discreetly observing how the man had fastened his seatbelt. The man reciprocated the greeting with a slight nod of his own.

His hands, loosely holding the seats when the aircraft started taxiing, stuck to the seat like ticks with the take-off. His eyes remained closed until the plane completed its ascent and started to move forward as if suspended in the air. The peanuts in the palm-sized package the stewardess handed with a napkin were unsalted and not roasted. When she asked, "What would you like to drink, tea or coffee?" the question made him smile, reminding him of a well-known joke. So, he opted for tea, smiling, and snacked on the peanuts he actually preferred to be salty and roasted to satisfy his hunger. And, a cigarette. What caught his attention was that the passenger beside him had requested whisky so early in the morning. It reminded him of something he had observed while breakfasting at the Kosova Motel's restaurant.

"It appears to be a common practice in this country to begin drinking early, regardless of nationality or religion...

A sudden headache struck him like a knife above his eyebrows, hindering further thought as the plane began to descend.

"We couldn't have arrived in London yet. It's only been about forty-five minutes since we left Belgrade. But where are we landing? If the customs officers there had handed over their information to the secret police and decided to intervene before the plane left Yugoslavia, things could go wrong. Even though it's somewhat open now, this is still an 'Iron Curtain' country." His concern that "The secret police probably restrict freedoms here, too," pushed the headache aside as the wheels touched the ground.

The passenger seated by the window in Emin's row in the first-class section, where there was no one else but themselves, collected his belongings and disembarked as soon as the doors were opened. Emin tried to figure out their location. Through the tiny plane window on his side, he could see the windows of the airport terminal. On the other side, there was a vast open space at the end of the runways, where the earth met the sky on the distant horizon. He remained in an uncomfortable silence, refraining from asking questions, as he knew that explaining his problem might arouse suspicion. Rachel had previously discussed flying from Belgrade to London in their conversation. "So where is this place? Why did we stop here?" The concern behind the question was further exacerbated when one of the pilots emerged from the cockpit, parting the curtain to look around.

"If they remove me from the plane, my only option is to seek asylum in Yugoslavia, despite Eşref Abi's advice. I believe they won't reject my application. I don't believe they would reject my application. In Tito's country, where Kivilcimli was hosted, and the hospital was ordered to provide him with the same level of care as Tito himself, I wouldn't face the same humiliation as in other socialist countries. Besides, unlike what the Bulgarians might do, they would unlikely ask me to engage in espionage activities."

At that moment, he remembered that the piece of paper containing the address given to him by the Bulgarians when he left Bulgaria was still in his wallet. When the pilot returned to his cabin, he retrieved the paper from his wallet. His initial intent was to discard it in the toilet. Still, the red light of the occupied toilet sign dissuaded him. He glanced around and found no stewardesses nearby. Therefore, he discreetly tore the paper into several pieces, placing a few between his seat and the adjacent one and a few more between the middle seat in the front row and the window seat. When he turned to place a few pieces between the seats in the rear, he noticed one of the stewardesses approaching, so he put the remaining pieces in his mouth and began chewing.

"Paranoia is the highest stage of awareness!" This expression, which he didn't know where he recalled from, came to the tip of his tongue. "If the Yugoslavs apprehend me, they will undoubtedly subject me to a thorough search, unlike anything I've experienced before." His attempt to dispose of the address, motivated by the fear of being caught with it, culminated in the pieces of paper landing in his stomach, leaving a bitter taste in his mouth.

He muttered to himself, "This was your breakfast! If we proceed without encountering any problem, I'll sit by the window and watch the take-off despite all my fears of heights."

His stubbornness had resurfaced, and once again, he recalled the writings of Uğur Mumcu, which had come to mind as he was setting off:

"Only the brave has the right to live!"

As the wheels started to turn, he moved to the window seat to fulfil his promise and noticed the large letters on the platform from which the plane was departing: "Zagreb Airport."

He didn't know whether to feel angry or laugh at himself.

"Only the brave has the right to live," he has been reminding himself, yet as he watched the take-off, he couldn't help the palms of his hands from sweating, once again gripping the seat edges.

After all, the human being was a ball of emotional contradictions.

Soon, the stewardess would come to the rescue and offer Emin a glass of wine. He thought it would help him relax. This time, he ate a sandwich before drinking the hostess's offering of red wine. He lit a cigarette and then made a toast to himself:

"To freedom!"

This word retook Emin to his memories, from which he had been away recently.

* * *

"Yes, Aydin, you are right. This is our paradox. We are trying to obtain our freedom by taking refuge in the Western countries we despise and reject as 'bourgeois democracy'."

There was no reason for Emin to object to Aydın's emphasised paradox. So be it, but with the question he was about to ask Aydın, he aimed to remind him that there was no alternative path:

"If you were in my shoes, wouldn't you do the same? Is there anywhere else you could go?"

"Maybe I would have chosen socialist countries."

"The TKP would be waiting for you with open arms, wouldn't they?"

"Actually, it's the downside of it!"

"Would you collaborate with the TKP?"

Emin, seeing Aydın's silence, pressed further.

"Never mind the TKP, is it easier to digest living in those countries that have emasculated both socialism and freedoms compared to bourgeois democracies?"

"Maybe life is easier in the socialist countries."

"Yes, life may be easier, especially if you adapt to them and submit to their wishes, but that's not what I'm asking."

"I don't understand."

"I think I used the wrong word when I said, 'Is it easy?' Let's say, 'Would you stomach it?'"

"After all, it's socialism and better than bourgeois democracy."

"Don't force me to talk like Panait Istrati."

"You are no better than him in saying whatever comes to your tongue without thinking about where it will end up! Go ahead, say it, and feel the relief anyway.

"OK, OK, OK. Let's not get sidetracked."

"You started it! Anyway, go on."

"That socialism lagged far behind the bourgeois democracy that we despise and look down upon regarding freedoms. Did the bourgeoisie embrace human rights and freedoms, which are looked down upon as 'bourgeois concepts floating in the air', because the bourgeoisie was so liberal? We can question this. However, there is a fundamental reality that we have overlooked. Those freedoms were obtained due to the many painful struggles of the masses. To sneer at those freedoms is to sneer at those struggles... Aren't I right? Do you remember what was debated at the Kuruçeşme Meetings?[82] Our left first discovered that allowing other socialist parties was

---

[82] The series of special meetings organised in Istanbul by specific socialist movements aimed to establish a unified political party.

necessary for 'socialist democracy' and then started to discuss whether there was room for bourgeois parties. At that time, I pointed out the absurdity of the concept of 'socialist democracy', and don't forget to put it in quotation marks here, too. It is a tautology like democratic democracy. If we consider how the freedoms provided by bourgeois democracy were acquired and who earned those rights through their own struggles, the conclusion becomes evident. I'm uncertain about the accuracy of labelling it 'socialism' and persisting in using that concept, but that's another matter.

Nevertheless, since we cannot replace it, let us continue to use it so that everyone can understand it. Socialism is not socialism if it falls an inch behind the freedoms offered by bourgeois democracy. On the contrary, it has to offer more than those freedoms and provide the material possibilities necessary to realise the freedoms it offers. Then those freedoms will no longer remain on paper; they will be realised."

"Including the freedom of private property?"

"In a way, yes. There will be this freedom, but naturally, it will not be of any value."

"You ignore the relationship between private property and exploitation. Where there is exploitation, the freedoms on paper do not materialise. There is confusion here."

"No, there's no confusion. Furthermore, private ownership of the means of production must also be free. The objective is establishing a society where this freedom naturally fades away, remaining only on paper, without resorting to coercive means. When I talk about 'being left on paper in contemporary socialist countries', I reference the problem of destroying it by force power. Becoming unnecessary and invalid in the face of the possibilities offered by life, which is an utterly different matter. When Kivilcimli said, I don't remember the exact words, that in a socialist order, even the bourgeoisie could turn to socialism, I think he meant how private ownership of the means of production would become unnecessary and useless. In such a system, the freedom of private ownership of the means of production, even if it exists on paper, would be naturally irrelevant. Will anyone be left to want it?" Who would want it?"

"Wow, you're the one who's saying this! The one who proposed to send a telegram of condemnation to the Spanish Communist Party for rejecting the dictatorship of the proletariat... The conference had accepted that proposal unanimously, right?"

"Who could have objected?!"

"From which point to which point have you traversed? Reaching the point of freedom for private ownership of the means of production!"

"For God's sake... Don't shift it to a demagogic ground. What I'm trying to convey is the absence of impositions and prohibitions in front of humanity. Moreover, the attractiveness of a system that emerges from the womb of a class society becomes a centre of attraction with what it offers to humanity, leading people to embrace it joyfully. Not because it is imposed. In that case, instead of stepping back from the freedoms existing in bourgeois democracy, it might even be possible to uphold and advance them."

"Well, since you have been travelling to the cradle of capitalism, there you will lay the seeds of the new order in the womb."

"Supposedly, you made a joke, ha; let me try to laugh! Ha... Ha... Ha!"

* * *

"Emin quickly said "thank you" in response to the flight attendant who had taken him from the memories of his argument with Aydın. On the way to London, he shouldn't get drunk, even if only on the verge of being tipsy. He asked for coffee instead of wine."

After thanking the stewardess for the coffee, Emin resumed digging into his memories.

"The point that Aydın objected to is essential. Without clarifying that point, it is impossible to explain the issue of not compromising on the freedoms brought by bourgeois democracy, even if you are right. The problem is of greater importance beyond which country you sought refuge in. How can it be possible to explain this to our leftist, who thinks having learned socialism from a shallow and scholastic "theoretician," Georges Politzer, or I should say, a lesser understanding of it since it was a process of surface learning? Especially when the shallowness of the conception of socialism is evident even within the Doctorist movement, which should have had a different perspective than the others provided by Kivilcimli."

When he finished his coffee and put out his cigarette, he went to the small toilet of the plane. "This is what a coffin must be like." The fact that he had not been able to completely get rid of the tension created by the danger of being arrested at any moment since he had set off from Istanbul had brought to his mind the cells of Sansaryan[83] Han, about which many stories had been told, even on the plane he had travelled to eliminate this risk. "It's OK now.

---

[83] The Sansaryan Han (Inn): Donated to the Armenian Patriarchate in 1881 by Miğırdiç Sansaryan, a Russian Armenian, was confiscated by the Turkish government in 1935. It is a building with a very dark history. Although, on the surface, the building appears to be like any other, Sansaryan Han had predominantly served as an interrogation and torture chamber.

You are leaving all this behind," the thought comforted Emin. Although he washed his hands and face by repeatedly stepping on the tap, whose water was constantly cut off when he returned to his seat, a heaviness had settled not only on his body but also reached his eyelids. He reclined his seat and surrendered to the drowsiness that had been suppressed due to an early wake-up, and it was about to deepen...

"Excuse me, Sir!"

The stewardess was handing him a card.

"Thank you," he said, and when he turned his eyes to the card he had received from the hostess, Emin realised that he had to fill in the blank spaces with dot-dot digits. Rachel hadn't mentioned that. "I guess she didn't think I needed to fill it in." He decided not to fill it in. "The information I will put on the landing card is invalid. It doesn't matter if I put my name and number on the passport. I will declare that they are fake at the passport control anyway." With these thoughts racing through his mind in a flash, he took his passport from his pocket to put it between the first page and the cover. When he noticed the stewardess was looking at him, he changed his mind. He had to fill it in to avoid arousing suspicion. The stewardess responded to his gesture by handing Emin the pen she took out of her apron. As he opened the tray on the back of the seat in front of him and meticulously transcribed the information from the passport to the card he had placed on it, the headache that had troubled him during the landing in Zagreb resurfaced. He felt the need to pee and thought washing his face would also be good. On his way to the toilet, he thanked the stewardess vaguely and handed the pen back.

When he returned to his seat, the pressure he felt in his ears was added to the sharpness of his headache, like a stabbing pain. The headache he tried to alleviate by rubbing his forehead clung to him with all its stubbornness. When the aeroplane landed at the airport, Emin deliberately continued to rub his forehead, even though the pain was almost gone. He had decided to hide behind this unexpected excuse to linger on the plane and disembark late.

"Sir, are you OK?"

He gestured with his hand to the flight attendant, who was asking if he was OK, and then continued to rub his head from where he had left off.

"When a lie is hidden behind a truth or a truth is emphasised to tell a lie, it becomes more convincing. The flight attendant must have seen me rubbing my head since the start of descending. At least, she must have noticed it as I came out of the toilet and passed by her. Now, I can continue as much as I want, which gives me the time I need."

It had been at least ten minutes since he started to hear the noise of the passengers in the economy class, which he could not see, talking about the rush to get off. He did not see the need to prolong his game. He got up slowly, put on his coat with the same slowness, picked up his suitcase and headed towards the exit door.

While he couldn't fully grasp the stewardess's words as she expressed her gratitude for flying with Yugoslav Airlines and her hope to see him again, he smiled and responded with a "Thank you!" So did the passenger in front of him! As if taking a leisurely stroll in a park, he began strolling down the corridor connecting the aircraft to the lounge at Heathrow Airport. He was in no rush. Meanwhile, he muttered to himself:

"Gosh, I've sought refuge in lies many times since I left Istanbul! Since no one is branded a liar unless their lies are exposed, I'm not considered a liar by others. This, too, is ironic. They label the one who gets caught as a 'liar,' when, in fact, that person is only exposed because they're unable to tell a convincing lie. The skilled liar, on the other hand, escapes such a stigma. On the other hand, the liar knows they are lying, and at this point, irony turns into a paradox. I know this from my own experiences. You will tell a lie, but you will tell it in such a way that others cannot see the lie hidden behind the truth. Especially if the truth is so strong, there is no room for denial... If that truth's glare is so dazzling, it prevents the lie or deceit hiding behind it from being seen. It is the sort of starting point of a lying witness: 'The truth, the whole truth, and nothing but the truth.'"

* * *

Emin stopped at the end of the exit corridor, where he had been walking while contemplating the lies he had sought refuge in since he had set out from Istanbul. He waited for the crowd, consisting of individuals with shorter stature and distinctive eye features, emerging from another corridor in a hurry. Looking at their cameras, most of which were either hanging around their necks or in their hands, Emin came to the conclusion that if he mingled with these people, as he was not taller than them, whom Emin thought were Japanese, he could give Rachel the time she needed to get out before him. When he joined them, he took it slow again to stay at the end of this wave.

When he entered the hall where the passport control was conducted, the passport control officers at the opposite end were lined up side by side at their desks at the height of the dais, busy interrogating those arriving in their countries. A tall, thicker pencil moustache, just to Emin's left, one step away from the leftmost table, was scanning the passengers entering the hall with his gaze. Emin couldn't help but look a bit bewildered at the man's posture and the air he projected.

"This guy must be a security guard, a cop or something. Do cops all over the world look alike?"

He was right in his thoughts; the man was a policeman, and even though he was not a policeman, he was trying to see Emin in the hall, scanned by his gaze according to the description he received. After watching the man's behaviour for a while, Emin started to observe the passengers in the queue going round and round.

"You can see any and every type of people. Individuals of various ethnicities, those with slender frames, others with more robust builds. Next to those with blonde hair cascading over their shoulders are those with black, curly hair. People of every hue, those with diverse eye colours".

His thoughts had turned to an inquiry once again. "When we refer to 'people with colourful eyes,' it typically encompasses those with green, blue, or hazel eyes, but often overlooks individuals with black or brown eyes. It raises the question: Aren't black and brown also considered colours?"

He came back to the same subject:

"We look at events and phenomena from where we are. In the words of our Haci Dal, 'Everyone sees the world with his own eyes!' I wonder if we call others 'colourful eyes' only because of the abundance of brown and black eyes, or is there something more to it; is there othering? Among the Balkan immigrants in Turkey, from whom many people who are more nationalistic than anyone else come out, are there not more people with green or blue eyes than anyone else, and average? Have these distinctive eye colours become a criterion leading to unfair labels or prejudice, as they were subjected to the slur 'giaour seed' by others? Haven't I witnessed this many times? Isn't it ironic?

"When Balkan immigrants spoke among themselves in other languages, such as Bulgarian, Bosnian, or Greek, depending on where they came from, rather than Turkish on the streets, did they not feel themselves under the icy cold shower? This became particularly pronounced during the intensification of assimilation policies, notably with the 'Citizen, speak Turkish' campaign as a part of the psychological warfare against the Kurds, especially during the escalation of such policies following the 27 May 1960 junta. Sadly, it seems that these immigrants sometimes harbour more hostility toward Kurds, a situation that is both poignant and ironic. When a racist attack is directed against a people, all the other peoples living on that land also get their share, sooner or later, no matter how they define themselves.

"Institutional racism, which gets shuddered, lashes out with 'Separatists!' when it hears the cry of 'All peoples are brothers and sisters!' Through its own courts, it condemns many people to spend years behind bars due to these accusations. Even though it is essentially an attack against the Kurdish people, don't other peoples also get their share from this by forgetting the languages they brought with them, or more accurately, by being forced to forget it? Their kids, the next generation, cannot speak these languages at all. Since Rachel told me 'You'll ask for an interpreter', I won't be told 'Citizen speak English!' here. On the other hand, I'm not a citizen!"

The circling in the queue had come to an end. The queue where Emin was positioned at the back would now move forward vertically towards the passport control. His eyes travelled from the big-built, blond, green-eyed officer with a dark blue, red and white striped tie adorning his suit, directing people in the queue to the desks at the front of the line, all the way to the leftmost row. When he entered the hall, the man Emin had suspected to be a policeman was nowhere to be seen.

When it was his turn, he straightened his shoulders and walked confidently toward the table to the left of the one in front of him. He remembered Osman's warning. As he handed his passport to the young woman with shoulder-length blonde hair, green eyes, a smiling face, petite shoulders, and a scarf tied around her neck matching the colour of her eyes, Emin rapidly delivered his sentences like a machine gun:

"This passport is fake. I am applying for asylum. I want an interpreter."

The smile on the young woman's face froze. She looked at the photograph in the passport and then at Emin.

"What?"

Emin, who understood the meaning of "what?" this time, listed one by one what he had said in his broken English:

"This passport is fake... I am applying for asylum... I want an interpreter..."

"Hold on a minute, please!"

Understanding that he was asked to wait, Emin watched the young woman as she approached a glass-enclosed booth a bit further beyond the desk; curious about what would transpire with her slim arm extending gracefully like her slender body, the young woman approached the booth while holding her passport as if she were displaying it to someone in her right hand, her short-heeled shoes producing authoritative clinks with each step. Sensing something unusual as he observed the female officer approaching with a passport, a man stepped out from the glass-enclosed booth above waist level. They engaged in a brief conversation, followed by a phone call made by the man who returned to the booth. When he reappeared, Emin deduced from his accompanying head movement that he had instructed the young woman to return to her seat. Then, he gestured to Emin by raising her index finger and said:

"Wait a minute, please. OK?"

"OK!"

Whether it was one minute or a thousand, Emin would "wait". "Do I have another alternative?" he thought but didn't put this thought into words in English. Even if he wanted to, he couldn't express it with his extremely poor English.

A few minutes may or may not have passed when Emin looked up at a man whose arrival he hadn't noticed. The man had started the conversation without any greetings. This was the same man who had made Emin wonder, 'Do police officers worldwide look alike?' when he had entered the passport control hall earlier. Now, the man stood before him and was speaking in Istanbul Turkish:

"Tell me what you want?"

Emin ignored the commanding tone of this sentence and answered in Turkish too:

"My passport is fake. I'm seeking asylum. Are you an interpreter?"

Emin had deliberately used the informal singular form of "you" in Turkish, emphasising that the other person was not superior to him.

"Yes, I'm the interpreter."

"Well then, translate what I say."

While Running Away

The man who said he was an interpreter gave Emin a glare and translated the words to the officer, who asked, "What is he saying?"

"The young woman, seemingly convinced by what she had heard, requested Emin's real name and surname. The interpreter spelt each detail one by one, and she noted Emin's full name, date of birth, and place of birth on a piece of paper, which she then handed to him. Subsequently, the interpreter conveyed her question:

"She wants to know if this information is correct.'"

"Yes, correct!"

"Questions and answers flowed with the interpreter's assistance.

"Where do you come from? Which plane did you take?"

"Turkey, but I flew in from Yugoslavia on Yugoslav Airlines."

"When did your plane depart?"

"Nine o'clock there."

"When did your plane arrive?"

"A short while ago."

"Did you travel alone, or was someone with you?"

"I travelled alone."

"Indicating the three rows of four chairs on each side, enclosed by cordoned-off sections, the interpreter, whom Emin suspected to be a Turkish police officer, repeated what it was said in a commanding tone once again:

"Go sit over there.'"

"OK," Emin said with a "Fuck you" intonation and a grimace.

When he took his seat, he attempted to calm his frayed nerves. Yet, as he compared the Englishwoman's politeness ending in 'please', which the interpreter omitted as he translated, and the Turkish interpreter's impertinence, his anger grew even more. "An asshole. He's gotten under the English police's skin, throwing his weight around like that."

He hadn't had a cigarette for nearly two hours, not since he smoked one with his coffee on the aeroplane. "I think this is making me even more nervous!" He glanced around to see if anyone was smoking but couldn't spot anyone doing so. He was the only person in the section where he was sitting, and there wasn't an ashtray in sight. While it was understandable that people queuing in the rush for their turn didn't smoke, none of the officers were smoking either. His wristwatch showed 13:40. As he adjusted it by setting it back an hour, he remarked, "It's been over two hours since I smoked."

"Think of something else!" he advised himself. He had tilted his head back slightly and closed his eyes, trying to follow his own advice, when he heard the voice of the interpreter:

"Do you have a suitcase?".

"Yes."

"Give me your receipt, and we'll get your suitcase."

From the inside pocket of his jacket, he retrieved the boarding pass with the baggage receipt attached and handed it to the interpreter with a disdainful gaze. He didn't know if the man who had purchased the boarding pass and receipt and gone to collect his suitcase had noticed this expression, but he knew how he looked at him. Memories of a similar experience from years ago flooded his mind.

* * *

Nejat had touched Nurten's elbow as they walked side by side.

"Look at Emin, how he's looking at the girls across the street."

At that time, Nurten, who had no make-up on her face except for the cream she applied, asked as she turned her gaze to Emin, who was walking to the right of Nejat:

"Why are you looking at them like that?"

"What do you mean?"

Nejat interjected:

"You're looking at the girls with a disdainful gaze."

"Is that so?"

"Aren't you aware of it?"

"No, no. I just looked. With these people's clothing and make-up, they resemble coquettes."

Where had he heard the term 'coquette' that slipped from his tongue that day? He couldn't recall. He also remembered that using this description later, when comparing a woman he saw on a bus during a journey to Bursa to Nazli's mother and referring to her make-up, had angered Nazli. It was too late when he realised he had offended Nazli, whom he had never seen wearing make-up. That's why Nazli confronted Emin, who only recognised the extent of his "ass-like behaviour" during their silent treatment for a week, but months later."

"It's normal; they are petty bourgeois girls," Nejat said, and Nurten tried to hit the nail on the head.

"Your Ceyda wears make-up too."

Ceyda was one of the few female students who had chosen the Department of Mathematics at the Bursa Institute of Education. In the literature class, she was Emin's classmate who tried to establish intimacy with him after he had read his 'surrealist' story, as the lecturer called it. She was beautiful, often dressed in a miniskirt just above the knee, skilfully applying make-up to accentuate her features.

Emin, however, wasn't particularly interested in her." Emin hadn't shared the information about his private life regarding Gülnihal with his friends, a high school senior in Kastamonu. The same year, Gülnihal's father, an army officer like Emin's father, was transferred to Bursa. Although it seemed that Gülnihal had responded to Emin's interest in her when they were in Kastamonu, she acted distant when Emin and his father paid a visit to her family house during his enrolment at Bursa Education Institute. Emin attributed this change in demeanour to the presence of their fathers. Gülnihal held a special place in his heart for the very same reason! Unlike others who had just started wearing make-up outside school, she never applied cosmetics. "They don't know that the one I have in mind never wears make-up, unlike Ceyda and others." He didn't want to share all this and attempted to brush it off:

"She's just a classmate. She wants to come and chat between classes."

"And yet you're her favourite!"

Nejat teased, but Emin took it seriously.

"I don't associate with people who wear that much make-up, and she's not interested in politics either."

The journey through his memories jumped to another momentum.

"When Nükhet expressed her interest in a crumpled piece of paper that was left on my desk... What interest? Never mind, don't dig into it any further.... On the Island ferries that call at Kadıköy, I went to the bottom deck where smoking was forbidden... We nicknamed it the 'basement' of the ferries... Did not Nazli's makeup-free face, in contrast to Nükhet, play a decisive role in my decision to stop going down to the 'basement' of the ferry, where Nükhet and her closest friend were seated, and start going upstairs, knowing that I would find Nazli? And the sadness in her eyes... How strange the games the human mind plays. It starts from a gaze, runs into an inescapability... And even while escaping! Nazli, whom I thought I was running away from, was the one, as Yunus put, 'I have an 'I' within me, deeper than myself.' The one I carried in me even when I was running away from her.

"As I run away from Turkey now, I wonder how much distance will come between me and the land where I was born and raised and how much it will tear me away from it? After this age, will you be able to say, 'Homeland is not where you were born, but where your stomach is filled? What is 'Homeland'?"

He was about to dive into aphorisms on "homeland" once again... He heard the dominant language of the lands he had left.

* * *

"Take your suitcase. Come with us."

The interpreter arrived with another staff member, who had a turban wrapped around their head—Emin would later learn that this was a headgear worn by Indian Sikhs. The second immigration staff member had neatly trimmed facial hair, with a full beard and Mustache, and was dressed in a suit with a fairly dark complexion. Emin followed the two, engaged in conversation, one step behind. They entered a large room to the right of their original location, where ten plastic chairs were lined up side by side against the walls on either side of the door. Six chairs were leaning against the wall directly opposite the door. He would count them when left alone in the room, more out of curiosity than as part of a game to pass the time. At the end of the left wall, at the end of the chairs, was a coin-operated cupboard with layers upon layers of drinks, and opposite it was a door with a toilet sign. The interpreter translated what the Indian immigration officer said.

"We'll interrogate you. Until then, you'll wait here. There's a toilet on the right. You can use it if you need to. We'll give you three tokens. You can use them to buy any drink you want from the machine. Tea, coffee, soup, cocoa. The shapes on the machine guide you on how to operate it. If you encounter any difficulties, please let us know, and we'll be happy to assist you."

When the immigration officer was sure the translation was finished, he handed Emin the three coins he held.

"Thank you."

Emin was surprised when the Indian officer said "No problem!" to Emin's English 'thank you' while taking the tokens because it was the first time he heard it as a response to a "thank you."

"You are not to leave this room until we come and get you. Is that clear? Do you have any questions?"

"I see. Can I smoke here?"

The interpreter answered without even asking the officer.

"No, smoking is not allowed in this room."

Then, he told the officer what the discussion was about.

Emin began his loneliness, which seemed endless and could not be ended by counting minutes, by going to the restroom. While attending to his need, he also attempted to decipher the note hung over the flush tank.

"Please flush the toilet after use. You can dispose of your used paper hand towels here. The British sewerage system can handle it."

When he saw it again in another toilet on a subsequent visit, he could not fully understand what was written, which he would decipher by looking at the dictionary. The words British and system gave him the feeling that there was something strange about what was written.

While waiting in the passport control queue, he had sweated a little. He took off his jacket and shirt and washed his face, arms and neck to get rid of the sticky feeling. When he came out of the toilet, he went to the drinks cabinet opposite and examined it. Following the instructions on the cabinet item by item, he first put the coin into the machine he would use for the first time and dialled the number; he realised from the signs that it was vegetable soup.

"If I had the biscuits I left at the Bulgarian customs, I would have bought tea now, and how nice it would go with it", Emin said when he tasted the first sip from the glass he took. He liked the choice he made. The warmth from his throat to his stomach brought his hunger to the surface and suppressed it. He immediately sat on the chair beside him to enjoy the vegetable soup.

"Sometimes the existence of an absence that we do not realise the importance of in our lives unless it imposes itself bleedingly makes itself felt when we find a remedy for that absence. Until that moment comes, we helplessly endure it."

Upon finishing his soup, his train of thought was interrupted when he went to throw the plastic cup in his hand into the bin next to the drinks cabinet. It had been almost half an hour, and still, no one was coming or going. He walked to the door to see who was around.

"It is likely that the young blonde woman has returned to her desk to continue her work. It is impossible to see her from here, but neither the Indian immigration officer nor the interpreter is in sight."

He walked to the opposite window. They were not there either. He walked back and forth on the same route for a while as if he was pacing. He changed his path. He wandered around the room randomly with slow steps until he felt tired. With the boredom of "Where are they? How long do I have to wait?" his endeavour to understand whether any movement outside through the glasses on all three sides prevented him from concentrating on any thought. Only once, as he sat down, did he succumb to sleep for a short time. It didn't take him long to wake up. He got up and took a cup of coffee from the machine, with no sugar and no milk, and it would be as tasteless as it was unpleasant. Despite the awful taste, he drank it to the end, anxious to keep his mind clear.

From time to time, he tried to think of what might be asked in the interrogation. Still, each time, he was stuck on the question, "What could be more than the story I told the Bulgarians, two oral and one written?". He could not think of more.

It was ten minutes to four when the interpreter arrived with another immigration officer.

"Take your suitcase, come with us. We'll go to the interrogation room. Your solicitor is there."

The other attendant stayed behind this time, and Emin and the interpreter walked in front. When he entered the room, a blonde, taller woman with a slight build and glasses stood up from her seat and held out her hand.

"Hello Mr Soganci."

Though momentarily struck by the unusual pronunciation of the letter 'g,' devoid of the umlaut that imparts softness, Emin tried to grasp every word emanating from the woman he now recognised as his lawyer.

"My name is Louise Christian. Nice to meet you."

"This woman is your lawyer. She says, 'Nice to meet you.'"

The interpreter also said "Hello" to the woman he had shaken hands with while translating. They all sat down. The interpreter was next to Emin's solicitor on the narrow side of the rectangular table; to his right were Emin and his lawyer, and opposite them were two blond men almost the same age as Emin. They introduced themselves through the interpreter. They were officials of the Immigration Department who were to conduct the interrogation.

When the solicitor indicated that she was ready to start, the officer in front of him asked Emin, through an interpreter:

"If you're feeling well, we can start the interview. Shall we?"

"I'm fine. We can start."

"Tell me when you don't feel well or are tired, and we'll take a break."

"OK."

"If you do not understand something during the interview, do not hesitate to ask again. Try to answer our questions most truthfully. If you say something untrue, it will work against you."

"OK."

"At 12.20, you arrived at passport control and declared that your passport was fake, claimed asylum and asked for an interpreter. Are all these correct?"

"I didn't look at the time, but I think it was about what you said. Yeah, that's what I said."

Next to the officer posing the questions, the officer across from the solicitor was making notes, and the solicitor was also taking notes.

The officer was reading the questions and Emin's answers from the passport control one by one, glancing at the paper in his hand, then asking Emin, "Is that correct?" Emin responded consistently, "Yes, that's right," to each query. Until... After reading the question, "Did you come alone?" along with Emin's answer, "Yes," at the passport control, the officer paused momentarily and replaced his routine question, "Is that correct?" with a different one:

"Now, I'll ask you again. Did you arrive alone?"

The interpreter interpreted when the solicitor intervened and stated:

"You know Mr Soganci was not alone. We notified you of this when we were informed of his arrival. Following the advice he had received, Mr. Soganci complied during the check and said, 'I am alone. He is not at fault in this matter."

Emin was trying to recover from his surprise at the lawyer's word while questioning it himself. "Why was I told 'say, you are alone,' but they stated the opposite when they informed the British officials of my arrival? Didn't they realise this would put me in a difficult situation?"

He was not in a position to dwell further on this nagging question. The officer turned to Emin and repeated the question, "Did you come alone?" despite the lawyer's explanation. He tried to save the situation with his answer.

"I travelled alone from Turkey to Yugoslavia. I waited for Rachel in Yugoslavia. We boarded the plane together, but I sat alone and went to passport control alone."

"Why did you say, 'I'm alone!' at passport control?"

The solicitor intervened again:

"We explained that to you. We also told you Mr Soganci was not alone when we informed you of his arrival."

"I want to hear it from him. Why did you say, 'I'm alone'?"

Emin had noticed from the beginning of the interview that the interpreter was being polite, unlike before. At first, he attributed this to the presence of the British officials and the lawyer. From the way he translated the last sentences, 'You said' in a formal and polite form, rather than casually and carelessly, and with a sly, faint smile on his face, Emin concluded that the interpreter was in the mood to imply, 'Aren't you cornered now, you lucky beggar.' Realising that he had to answer without pausing, without giving the impression that he was "trying to make something up", he pushed aside his thoughts about the interpreter and responded:

"I took the advice that was given to me. I didn't want another person to get into trouble because of me, so I took it as good advice."

The interpreter had the same sarcastic smile. According to Emin, it was a "sly smile!" As the interpreter translated what was said, Emin questioned this attitude: "Who was this interpreter? Could they be using Turkish police as interpreters for the British?"

"We warned you at the beginning of the interview to answer honestly, to tell the truth. I want to remind you of that warning."

"OK, I'm telling everything honestly during this interview. When I entered, I followed the advice and made a statement accordingly because I found it sensible. Upon entering, I gave my real name and didn't hide the fact that the passport was fake."

The officer began the sentence with, "Now, I will repeat your identity information." As he repeated Emin's name, surname, date of birth, and place of birth by reading the notes from passport control, Emin responded with," That's correct" to each one individually.

While Emin was answering questions about his marital status and his daughter's identity details, he could not remember the dates of birth of his ex-wives. He had utterly forgotten these details, even though he remembered the years. However, he was remembering some other things more, even though they took place much earlier than that, in his Uni years.

* * *

[Flashforward - 1999:
Despite the sweltering heat of July, Emin and his maternal aunt's daughter rushed to the Kadıköy ferry departing from Karaköy.
"Let's go upper deck, to the top, into the open."
"Nah. Come on, Abi, let's go around this side and sit at the stern."
That corner of the ferry means Nazli for Emin, which held memories of his shared moments with Nazli. He had tried to put those memories aside and didn't want to revisit them. However, he finally gave in to his persistent cousin's insistence. As they took three or four steps forward, asking for permission from fellow passengers, some of whom had their feet on the side railings of the ferry, a woman standing up waved and called out:
"Emin... Emin..."
Emin stretched his head over the shoulder of the cousin in front of him to see this familiar voice better. He recognised the voice correctly. It was Nazli. The last time he had seen her, sixteen years ago, again in July, in those days when they had such an unexpected encounter, Nazli, who had cut her hair to a length just below her ears and had given it a different shape, had this time returned to the hairstyle of her university years.
Unlike Nazli, Emin shook hands in an extremely distant, cold manner.

"Emin, you sure haven't changed a bit," said Nazli, smiling.

"Come on, how come? Look, the hair has fallen out, for example. Face and eyes wrinkled."

Even though he thought, he didn't say: "You haven't changed much either, but the lines of old age are very evident. Especially above your lips."

Nazli continued:

"No, not much. I would recognise you wherever I saw you. On the other hand, I met some friends I didn't recognise. Do you remember Fikri?"

Again, he didn't say, "How come I wouldn't!"

"Yes, I remember."

"They work at the same place as my brother. We bumped into each other by chance. You should have seen him. The nape of his neck, his belly, he's a completely different person."

Emin would not say it once again, even if he thought about it: "You have stayed as the Nazli from our university years in me, and the Emin from those years has stayed in you. Perhaps, now, we are finding in each other whatever resembles what we could remember from those days."

Finally, Emin felt he had to say something and said:

"You haven't changed much either."

Nazli introduced the young woman, who was watching them closely while she was returning her seat next to her:

"This is my daughter Aygül. She's grown up, hasn't she?"

"Yeah, she's grown up. Hello."

Emin's hello clashed with Aygül's one:

"Hello."

Emin pointed to his cousin sitting next to Nazli, who left a space between herself and Nazli for Emin, who had shown no interest in sitting there but had kept standing facing Nazli.

"Bilge. My aunt's daughter."

And they exchanged "hellos".

"Long time no see, eh? Over ten years."

Emin, who remembered both the month and the year, corrected her:

"Sixteen years."

"Has it been that long?"

"We met in the summer of 1983."

They were both silent for a moment. Emin broke the silence.

"Don't you come and go in England?"

"I came from time to time. When was the last time we went to Aygül? I think it was last Christmas."

Nazli's daughter nodded.

"If I'd known, we'd have met. You don't have my number, though. How were you going to let me know? The number I wrote in the letter has changed."

Nazli skipped Emin's reference to the letter.

"Have you been to France?"

"I was going to come the first year of my arrival in the UK, but it didn't work out. There was a visa problem. At that time, I only had a refugee travel document. I needed a visa for that, too. I came last year, and I only stayed for three days. I phoned you too, hoping to see you, but no one answered."

"When?"

"Early April."

"I was in Paris. Possibly we weren't at home. It would have been nice."

The cold fog Emin had put between them began to dissipate.

"Actually, your ears must have been burning the day before yesterday. I met up with Nevin and Serap. They mentioned that you might be here at this time. 'It would be nice if we could all meet,' they said."

"Oh, sure, that'd be nice. If you call our home on the Island..."

Emin jumped in before Nazli could finish her sentence, a hint of nostalgia in his voice:

"Still 351 8... Is that your number?"

A quarter of a century after he had noted that number, Emin listed it without hesitation. He noticed a hint of surprise in Nazli's daughter's eyes. Back in 1983, during their initial meeting, Emin had said, 'Don't let me call, so there would be no inconvenience. It'd be better if you called.' Despite providing his number, he didn't ask for hers. Nazli might have observed this and realised that Emin still remembered her house phone number... Now she seemed unsurprised when Emin uttered the same numbers again...

"Yeah, it's the same, but you need to dial 0216 first, considering the changes in Istanbul."

"I know, just like on the Kadiköy side."

"Phone and come to the Island. Yakup is here; we'll all meet together."

Did she want to emphasise "I'm still with Yakup", especially in front of his daughter? Emin didn't mind. He encrypted his message himself. He put the sentence that would remind her of his attitude towards Yakup at the beginning and asked the question he had been wondering for years:

"When I first went to England, I wrote you a letter and telephoned you in 1989, too. I couldn't tell from your voice whether it was you or not. Did you answer that phone call?"

"Me, I suppose?"

Emin grew angry at this response, which didn't shed enough light on the mystery he wanted to clarify. Deciding to set aside any cryptic references, he repeated his question as if they were alone and talking like they were talking years ago. Although he controlled his tone of voice, he expressed his anger through his gaze.

"How, 'probably'! Was it you? The voice and the way of speaking were different. I couldn't recognise you then?"

"It was me. I was probably the one answering the phone."

They remained silent for a while. In the first moment they encountered each other after years, the cold fog that had briefly existed came back and settled between them again.

Nazli broke the awkward silence by asking about Emin's brother, steering the conversation toward a typical discussion between old friends reuniting after many years. She inquired about Emin's mother, whom she had only met and spoken to twice. She lost her own mother.

As the ferry crossed Haydarpaşa and travelled towards Kadıköy, Nazli decrypted the message she had given earlier with her words:

"We'll meet Yakup at the pier. He went to his father in the hospital. His father is very sick. He will pick us up on the way out."

For Emin, this person was in his book of the living dead. His answer had to be appropriate. There was distance in his voice when they met:

"OK, I'm going to Aslihan's, to Moda. Bilge, what are you going to do?"

In addition to not saying a word about Yakup or Yakup's father, with the question he asked his cousin, Emin wanted to say that he was uninterested in what Nazli would do and had entirely ignored everything about Yakup.

Advancing with the advantage of standing as the ferry approached the pier, he said, "Good day." His cousin followed him. Unable to wait any longer, Bilge asked when they got off the ferry:

"What happened, Abi? Why did you treat her that way?"

"What did I do?"

"You didn't even shake hands when you left. And at one point, you looked at Nazli... as if you were furious with her."

"Are you talking about when I questioned who answered my call?"

"Yeah. It's a pity. When Nazli saw you, she jumped up and called you excitedly. She was so warm in her behaviour towards you!"

"Never mind! It was necessary to be like that!"

"What do you mean?"

"She is my friend from my university years. It was a platonic relationship. Actually, you know, I have never raised my voice to her. Sometimes, I have conveyed my anger and resentment with my chosen words and sometimes with my glances. This time, it's one of these... Those moments... In one of those moments..."

While Emin hesitated on whether to share or not, Bilge persisted:

"In one of those moments ..."

"In one instance, I hastily tried to write a missing article for our association's newspaper, isolating myself in a small room to focus on my writing. Suddenly... I was startled by Nazli's unusual, almost hysterical laughter, a sound I had never heard from her before. Our eyes met as soon as I jumped out and opened the door. I must have stared intensely; I had looked, but whatever it was in my gaze... She later described it as *'I went and slumped in the corner of the hallway due to the impact of your gaze...'* That was what she said. In another one, we had become estranged, not seeing each other for a long time. I wasn't going to school during those days. I needed a student certificate from the school administration for the newspaper editor post. I was waiting at the Student Affairs office. I hadn't seen her coming. Suddenly, I heard her voice: *'If you have time, can we talk?'*. I replied, *'Yes, we can talk. The officer is preparing a document for me. If you wait a bit,'* and so on. But the way I said it, however I said it... She later told me, *'You were talking and looking at me in such a way that it would have been better if you had slapped me.'* There was also an incident that marked the beginning of her interest in me. It all began when I unknowingly occupied her desk during our first year at Uni. I had no particular reason to choose that seat. Our bloody Constitution lecturer habitually spoke softly and based exam questions on his lectures rather than books. I had unknowingly taken Nazli's usual seat, all to ensure I could listen to the lecturer comfortably. At the time, I was still unaware of her presence in the class.

Finding an empty seat, I settled down. She had just stood by the desk where I was sitting, but upon noticing her, I calmly asked, *'Was this your seat?'* and promptly stood up. Yet, however, she had interpreted my actions and the look in my eyes... After the class had concluded, as she said, she had ventured to the student cafeteria during the break, a place she had never visited before. She had etched *'A slap from me to Belmondo'* onto one of the tables. Although I don't think I look like Belmondo, Nazli had thought so. She later recounted all of this to me.

"As you can understand, this is a dialogue between her and me that goes beyond words. It's a long story. One day, perhaps, I could tell you how we lived on the things we left unlived."

"Interesting, but how do you remember the phone number after all these years?"

"Somehow, the number has been etched in my memory! I told you, it's a long story!"]

* * *

He told the immigration officer who interviewed him that he could find the dates of birth of his two divorced spouses, which he could not remember. He promised when the officer asked him to bring them to the following interview, hoping his parents could look at the divorce papers and provide him with these details.

Transitioning from questions about his family circle to inquiries about his political activities, reiterating what he had previously stated in Bulgaria. The difference lay in the details of his arrests and the subject of torture, topics the Bulgarians hadn't inquired about. He refrained from exaggeration, contrary to Osman's advice, and mentioned that he could provide a certified copy of the torture report issued by Forensic Medicine that had carried out the medical examination on the orders of then President Fahri Korutürk. However, he couldn't commit to a precise time.

After more than two hours of ongoing interrogation, the situation took a dramatic turn when he mentioned that he had been convicted under Article 141 of the Turkish Penal Code. The Immigration Officer asked, "Which offences does TCK 141 cover?"

"This is an article imported from Mussolini's Italy Criminal Code, applied against socialists and communists on the grounds of their membership in and management of organisations to impose one class's dominance over other classes."

Instead of translating Emin's words, the interpreter argued with him.

"It wasn't just applied to socialists and communists; it was also used against Menderes and his colleagues following the 27 May 1960 coup."

"It was an exception. While the law introduced by the overthrown government was applied to them, its primary intent remained directed towards the socialists."

Despite Emin's explanation, the interpreter persisted:

"It wasn't exclusively applied to communists, even though that was its intended purpose."

"Emin, unwavering in his interpretation of the situation, continued to assert his opinion:

"The fact that those who overthrew the Democratic Party applied these articles exceptionally against those who introduced them into the Penal Code does not alter the primary purpose of introducing these articles, which was to be used against socialists. As history has shown, with this exception aside, these articles have consistently been employed against socialists. This reinforces my argument about the intended purpose behind introducing these articles."

The solicitor had initially assumed that the conversation between the interpreter and her client was aimed at achieving clarity on her client's explanation, yet when she realised that it had actually turned into an argument as Emin's tone of voice grew louder and harsher. Then, she thought she had to intervene:

"Why is the interpreter arguing with my client? Why doesn't he translate?"

The duty officer stepped in upon warning.

"Why don't you translate? Are you two arguing?"

"Mr Soğancı said that this article was used against socialists. I reminded him that this article was also used against the overthrown government after the 1960 revolution."

"You just translate. Don't get into any arguments."

"OK," said the interpreter in a low voice and translated Emin's initial remarks.

After completing his note-taking, the official suggested a short break in the interview to diffuse the tense atmosphere. Following the ten-minute intermission, Emin continued narrating his story. He described how he had waited until the last moment, hoping for a reversal of the military court verdict. After the Court of Cassation upheld his conviction, he had decided to run away. Emin shared the details of his escape, which included obtaining a false passport, his journey to Yugoslavia, and the pivotal moments of meeting Rachel and how their paths had crossed. His account of his experiences until his arrival in Bulgaria mirrored what he had previously conveyed to the Bulgarians.

The British officers did not inquire further about Emin's explanation regarding being detained for a day in Bulgaria: "The Bulgarians suspected me, questioned me, and let me go because they were convinced that I was a socialist who had been convicted and escaped." What interested the British officials was determining whether the person they were dealing with was genuinely an asylum seeker who had fled for political reasons. His account of what happened after Bulgaria briefly summarised his experiences.

At the end of the interview, they had the interpreter read out the notes they had taken one by one. After obtaining Emin's approval, the British officer asked him to sign the minutes. Decision time had finally arrived. The immigration officials left the interview room to deliberate among themselves during the break. The solicitor, gently patting Emin's arm, said, 'Well done, Mr. Soganci, well done!' as she tried to offer him a bit of hope and morale. They exchanged smiles. Emin had grown accustomed to the variation in the pronunciation of his name.

When the officers returned, the interpreter, who had waited outside instead of remaining in the interview room during his brief absence, also entered the room.

"We are granting Mr. Sogancı temporary residence permits until the next interview. On 12 April, when he comes for the next interview, we ask him to bring the birth dates of his ex-wives, the torture report (if he can provide it), and any other documents related to his asylum request. During this period, he is not allowed to work, but he can receive social assistance and attend a free public school to learn English."

The officer handed photocopies of the statement report and a copy of their signed decisions to both Emin and his solicitor and asked the final question:

"Do you have any questions?"

Neither Emin nor the solicitor had anything to ask. After shaking hands, Emin and his solicitor left the room with smiles of joy on their faces. They passed through customs control without being subjected to any questions or searches. Osman, who was waiting for them in the arrival hall of international flights, welcomed Emin with an enthusiastic embrace.

"We did it!" he exclaimed.

He turned to the solicitor right after him.

"Thank you very much, Louise. You are fantastic."

"Mr Soganci did very well."

As they walked to the airport parking lot, where the solicitor had left her car, she conveyed to Emin the details of her intervention during the interrogation regarding the argument with the interview interpreter, with the assistance of Osman's translation:

"At first, I thought you were making a statement. However, my concern heightened when you started talking agitatedly. Fortunately, it turned out to be advantageous that the interpreter engaged in a dispute with you. There was a possibility that immigration officials might not have allowed your entry into the UK, leading to potential detention until the subsequent interview. Nevertheless, such a dispute served our purpose to some extent. Your responses during the interview were commendable. Additionally, your overall statement was undoubtedly strong. While the documents might have been sufficient, I believe they also anticipated our potential claim that the interpreter they provided was not impartial due to the disagreement. Consequently, they decided to let you go. This was a significant advantage in our favour. As Osman had previously told me, you demonstrated intellectual and intelligent qualities."

"Thank you very much, Louise. You did an excellent job," praised Osman, turning to Emin this time:

"I had briefed the Immigration Office m about you. When we informed them of your arrival, I specified your role in the Party Central Committee's Cultural Commission. I told them that if our party came to power, you could have served as the Secretary of National Education and Culture."

They had almost forgotten the lawyer's presence and shifted back to speaking in Turkish.

"You kind of exaggerated again," Emin remarked.

"Well, wouldn't it likely to be something along those lines?"

Emin chuckled, replying, "We never really thought or discussed who would become a minister or anything. Even though it's stated in our constitution, seizing power wasn't on our minds."

"Well, what do they know? They bought into it."

Once they got into the solicitor's car, Osman translated the conversation between him and Emin for Louise, who was curious about their cheerful talk, aligning it with what was shared at the immigration office. The solicitor shouldn't know more than what was disclosed to Immigration!

Due to the solicitor missing a road turn while responding to the thanks and compliments extended to her, the journey took nearly two hours, and they arrived at Osman's house well past ten o'clock at night.

The next day, as Emin and Osman talked extensively about the past, they delved into how the party documents ended up in the hands of the police. The conversation then shifted to Emin's relationship with Nazli and Yakup's role in the police's confiscation of the Party documents.

"Even if Nazli wasn't initially aware of it, it's highly improbable that she remained unaware of what happened within their circle, given the many years they've spent together. This is the point I resent. The person who says to me, 'You are different from the others' and attributes this to my honesty, is blessing this characteristic because she herself must possess the same virtue. A person embraces a value that they glorify. Or, to put it the other way round, she values a person because she sees in the other person a virtue that she also possesses. Actually, she was glorifying that virtue, not a person, not me. Then what? Look at what happened! It means that that virtue no longer has any value for her. This is what I can't digest."

Emin's hesitation about whether to write to Nazli or not ended when Osman said, "Write, you will learn from firsthand."

Dated 16 February, he sat down at the beginning of the letter he had written to Nazli in a relatively dry language, different from the previous ones, after tearing the first one up and throwing it away. He tore it because...

In the summer of 1983, during their telephone conversation before Nazli left Istanbul, Emin said, "I would like to write to you. I would like to write as I feel like writing, not just dry scribbled lines or writing for the sake of writing. Seems this is not possible under the conditions you are in", to which Nazli replied, "Write as you feel, no problem".

Emin wasn't aware that there was an Elsa hidden in Nazli then... The Elsa, Aragon's Elsa!

And while writing from London, he was still not aware of that. Not because of this nor because of Nazli's "circumstances," but by saying, "How much can my broken heartstrings vibrate after everything that has happened. Moreover, a letter far from my old style can convey my resentment to her with its style," to himself, Emin started writing a "completely "dry" letter!

"Hello!

"Being able to say 'hello' again after many years, in unexpected circumstances.

"Let's use the phrase the British often use: 'Oh my God!'

"I'm in London. I arrived on 13.02.89, having left my homeland on 05.02.89. So many incidents, so many disgraces.

"This is my second letter. I gave up sending the first one after three pages.

"I'd like to meet up. I'll include my telephone number. I'm usually at home after 20:50 UK time. However, it would be better if you could come over, even for a day or two on the weekend, or make some other arrangement. I'll also provide my address. If you won't write or meet me, let me know so I can, at least, be aware of it.

"I don't know if there's something left between the two of us. However, I especially want to hear from you about the facts behind the VP court case and the events you became indirectly involved in, even if you didn't want to be a part of it. Let's not discuss this matter over the phone, though. I ask this from you because, despite everything, I can trust you more than the others. I don't want to meet with Yakup and the other related parties, at least not initially.

"To write a completely dry letter! It's not like me. I wish I could write down my resentment to you. But after leaving that first letter incomplete, I made a promise to myself. I will write this letter like this.

"Let me just say this at least: I won't be able to end my letter with 'With love.' What love? Where is it? Has it drowned in the mire of betrayal, perhaps?

"Regards."

He didn't write his name, only put his signature. Underneath, he had added his telephone number and then his address.

When he finished re-reading it, he felt the need to add something that he thought was unclear.

"PS: When you receive my letter, could you, at the very least, write a note to let me know whether you received it or not. You can decide whether to respond later. Once you make your decision, also inform me of your choice regarding a response."

There was no word from Nazli... Almost three weeks had passed. Although Emin filled most of his day with books he read and notes he took, in the mornings, after waking up from the recurring nightmare of the moment of failing in the attempt to run away, he would check the mail, asking, "Has a response arrived?"

One night, when he knew Osman and Rachel would come home late, he took his pen and paper and went to the nearby pub. He started writing to Nazli again. Alcohol had erased the boundaries in his mind. Towards the end of the five pages, filled with lines spaced as tightly as possible, he would tell Nazli how he wrote.

"I'm writing again in haste, without a draft. No proofreading. I explained the reason years ago. Perhaps you don't remember. Let me reiterate. If I were, I could make corrections when I proofread. But I don't want to. I want to write as I feel in my heart, with all naturalness, to reach you as I am. If there are spelling and grammatical errors, forgive them."

The sentences he wrote in tightly spaced lines were relatively smooth, and so was his handwriting. The fact that he wrote as he felt in his heart brought Emin to the point of expressing what he had kept to himself until then. So much so that, in his letter dated 07.03.1989, he had started his conversation with Nazli directly without any introduction, just like he used to in the past.

"Today, I'm filled with a sense of disquiet... I can't shake it off.

"It's like in 1977 when I was in prison. I don't know if it's similar to the disquiet you felt in Paris that year, but I assume it's identical. Not knowing what to do... Even though it's temporary, it's such an uneasiness. Actually, it stems from not receiving any reply to the letter I wrote you..."

"I'm in a 'pub' right now. I've come here to get rid of a sense of disquiet.

"Due to this disquiet, again, it's you that I'm writing to.

"Coming back to the same point after all these years... AGAIN, THREE DOTS... This time from London!"

"Why am I here in London? It's quite obvious... But who or who is responsible for it? Even though I already know the answer, I wanted to hear it from you. I wished for everything to align in my mind... But still, not a word or even a breath from you! Did you not receive my letter? If not, why not? Shouldn't it have been returned if the address was incorrect or changed?"

"Or... This is a matter of great concern to me. Did it get into the hands of people who shouldn't have had it, and you were prevented from getting it? It's not unlikely at all. In September '80, I actually broke up with Hüsniye... When we met in late spring of '81 (although Yakup knew when Hüsniye and I broke up), you didn't know about it; you asked me how Hüsniye was doing... Although I understand the situation, I tell you, 'She is fine' or something like that... In June '81, I officially broke up with her. About two months later, about a year after we broke up, you asked me about Hüsniye again. I understood that although Yakup knew everything, he hid it from you again. (Believe me, I was going to say, 'She's fine' or something like that again.) Bakir jumps in and says, 'They broke up.' Then, do you remember we met once more? Two people who wanted to say a lot but couldn't. You say something like, 'Which marriage is going well?' It sounded a bit like consolation. I didn't want to delve into it. Now I understand and 'Ahh'. What's the point of being damned chivalrous? But again, my mind is no different in '83. Even though you said your marriage bond with Yakup was broken, I avoided mentioning Yakup's behaviour in '81."

Emin, writing non-stop until this point in his letter, set down his pen. In both meetings where Nazli inquired about Hüsniye, he deliberated internally, contemplating Yakup's silence.

"Let's say I let the first one slide. Nothing came out. In the second one, Bakir, the 'meathead' next to us, revealed the 'secret' that Yakup was hiding from Nazli. What happened between Nazli and Yakup after that? Later, when we met again, and Nazli asked me about the reason for our separation, there was no reference to her relationship in my response. I refrained from making any comments or inquiries about her relationship with Yakup. I explained it briefly: 'My marriage was not a relationship based on love. When the stone of politics is removed from the foundation of the union of two people who have come together because of being in the same political structure or because they were brought together by the environment, that union collapses. It is possible to summarise what happened in this way.

"Let's say I avoided digging into her words 'Which marriage is going well?' that day and blocked the way for her to open up. In '83, I didn't even have to dig into what Nazli said about her relationship that 'didn't work out,' especially her words, 'You were still in love with me. Why did you get engaged again after a failed marriage?' Why did I ignore that she had somehow received the news about me when she said, 'You broke up with her too'? Couldn't she have concluded, based on this behaviour of mine, that 'he has lost interest in me'? Moreover, could she not have taken the fact that I had not written to her, despite her saying, 'You can write to me as you feel like it,' as a presumption for this conclusion? If the letter I sent when I arrived played a role in reinforcing this thought both in terms of its style and content... Even if it's in her hands, she doesn't reply. That's one possibility... No... At the very least, to prevent me from writing again, she would say something like, 'I received your letter, but what's there to write about?' or something similar. No, it hasn't reached her. Yakup wouldn't have delivered it if he had seen it first."

Although Emin asked himself, "Let's assume that, then. How can you be sure that this letter won't meet the same fate? Why are you writing it?" he continued writing. What he wrote extended to five pages. Upon revisiting his words the following day, he abandoned the letter and did not send it. He had re-entered the dark tunnel of waiting.

It had been over two months since he wrote the first letter. During this time, Osman had managed to obtain Nazli's phone number. A payphone required ten pence coins to operate in the corridor leading to the hostel's outside door, where he had recently moved into a single room. Uncertain whether Nazli would pick up and, if she did, if Emin could have a substantial conversation, Emin planned to start with a brief chat using a series of ten pence coins. After ensuring he could speak to Nazli, he intended to visit the nearby tube station to make a more extended phone call. He needed to be cost-conscious.

However, it turned out that he didn't need to go to the station. After hanging up the phone, he immediately took pen to paper. He wanted to write down his feelings while they were still fresh, mainly to remind himself of what he had experienced when needed in the future.

He began his notes, dated "London, 13 April 1989," by jotting down what Nazli had said on the phone.

"'There's no need to call. I received your letter. That's why... You don't need to call.'"

He had represented Nazli's pause as well as his own during writing with ellipses. Then, he tried to describe himself slowly, adding one cigarette after another without striking a match.

"This is the answer given in sixteen words, ending with 'You don't need to call.' How strange the voice is. It's really not Nazli's voice in tone, colour, etc... It doesn't sound like Nazli at all. Is it possible? Can one's tone and colour of voice change that much? I'm not exaggerating at all. Or 'It doesn't just sound like that to me... This is a voice I really don't recognise at all. There were people I hadn't seen for years. And when I met those people years later, when I spoke to them (directly or over the phone), I recognised and remembered those voices. But this voice... The voice I always knew and was familiar with in 1974, 75, 77, 78, 80 and even 83... The voice of the person I spoke to about ten or twelve minutes ago is not this voice.

"It can't be anyone else. I said it was sixteen words. No... No... Not... Nineteen words. I forgot three more words: 'Yes, it's me.' I say, 'Hello, Nazligül?' She answered: "Yes, it's me."

No, it's not you. It can't be you. If you are you, you're not the one I know of. Everything changes, but does the shift in voice, too?"

* * *

Whenever Nazli came to his mind, Emin read his note, dated London, 13 April 1989. He firmly embedded his resentment in his heart, unaware that it was just resentment, thinking for years, "It's over! She's gone now..." While reading Chernyshevsky's "What Is to Be Done?" one more time to try to adapt it into a play in 1995, with the arrival of the gentle spring breezes, Nazli quietly and unobtrusively seeped through the gap opened by memories. Whatever was in those memories while living on, which cannot be escaped while running away, came back while writing on.

The falling curtain of the stage would actually be opening while closing!

Ω Ω Ω

Printed in Great Britain
by Amazon